Can we just be HAPPY NOW?

TISA MATTHEWS

Author's Note

Dear Reader,

Thank you, from the bottom of my heart, for picking up this book. Of the endless stories that exist, it means everything that you have chosen to read this one.

Sophie and Cooper's journey is about the struggles of young love, discovering what you want from a partner and exploring new territories in relationships. This includes on-page sex scenes. In the state of Oregon, anyone under the age of 18 cannot legally consent to sexual activity. While actual sex does not take place until both characters are of age, and both characters are consenting at all times, there are explicit scenes involving Sophie as a minor.

Please read with this awareness, and if this is a subject you are uncomfortable with, perhaps pick up one of my other books instead.

Other trigger warning includes: strained parental relationship.

Enjoy the ride.

With love,

Tisa

To all the girls who look back on
their early 20s and cringe a little.

1

COOPER

NOW

Cooper, 21; Sophie, 18

Remnants of cheap liquor seep into the air around me when I push through the cold glass door at the entrance of Jameson's bar, its burn promising to eradicate yesterday's memories.

Still in the same black joggers and old maroon high school football hoodie I've worn for two days in a row, the denial that Sophie is dating clearly isn't working for me. It's consumed me. I haven't slept. Or eaten. Fuck. I probably should have stopped by Hawaiian Time for dinner before I drank away my problems. It's too late now.

Running my fingers through my hair, I scan the room for an empty table, but the dingy red spotlight over the bar draws my eyes to the one thing I want to forget. Every part of my body freezes except my wildly beating heart. *You have got to be kidding me.*

I've already been mentally preparing myself for what it will be like seeing Sophie on Thanksgiving in a few days–two months after our breakup. Our families always celebrate together, so as much as I'd love to forget everything that's happened between us, there's no escaping her–not really. Still, I'm not fucking ready to see her leaning into some guy standing next to the bar.

His blue jeans are dark, his fitted white T-shirt sleeves are rolled a couple of times and aviators are hanging from the collar. He has a barbed wire tattoo around his bicep–*Seriously?*–and his hair is slicked back. Putting a face to the douchebag responsible for my need to get drunk tonight is not helping the situation.

He has one arm draped casually over her shoulder like he's comfortable with her, his other hand resting on the wooden bar top as he grips his shot glass. She holds her shot in front of her, her flowered, green sundress making her look equal parts adorable and fuckable. God, the way I would slide those straps off her shoulder as I kiss my way down her body if we were alone. If we were together.

It's so much different than the first dress I remember her wearing. It was the same color green, but with ruffle sleeves and a giant bow in the front. She was four and sitting on my porch when I got home from my first day of first grade. Before I even closed the door of my mom's van, she was twirling in front of me. I think she wore that dress nearly every day for a year. Once she finally gave in to wearing different colors, she never stopped collecting them. The look is so signature Sophie, she crosses my mind anytime I see a sundress. *She's always on my mind.*

There's a shy smile on her face, but her new relationship nerves are evident–something she hasn't felt around me in years. She glances at him before shooting back the liquor, choking immediately–because she never drinks. My hands twitch at my sides, fighting the urge to see if she's okay, especially because *he* is too busy checking out the girl who temporarily blocks my view as she walks by. *Again, seriously?*

If Sophie's brother, Dean, knew the details of our relationship, he wouldn't have told me she has a boyfriend. I can't be mad at my lifelong neighbor, ex-teammate and *barely* friend for being the messenger. It's not his fault he and Sophie aren't close enough to swap dating stories. She rarely lets anyone in. I feel bad for bolting out of the University of Oregon football game after he introduced me to the girl he was with, but I'm not mad at him. I just couldn't stay there anymore, knowing that on the other side of the stadium, Sophie had a different guy sitting in the seat that's always been mine. I was upset hearing about it, but seeing him with my own eyes is what elicits a level of rage inside me I didn't know existed.

Sophie's curls are pulled into a loose ponytail, a few strands of dirty blonde framing her face–the same unruly strands she's been trying to tame since middle school. She hates the flyaways, but they're one of the many things that make her . . . well, *her*. My heart thumps more erratically than the pinball flying through the maze in the machine next to me at the thought that she might change. She already is changing. Maybe her hair is the same, but the girl that I knew inside and out because she was completely mine is fading into someone hard to recognize. She was perfect before. I thought she loved who she was. I don't understand the shift. It's like instead of checking items off her college bucket list, she's crossing off the parts of her personality I fell in love with.

Is she doing it to make me jealous? Or to make it clear she's over me, that she's changed her mind? The thought makes me sick. This wasn't how I interpreted the agreement. Maybe it was in her fine print. Or maybe it's *me* that made her want to change. I hate every possibility.

My fists ball to prevent me from grabbing her hand. From begging her to leave with me. From taking her away from him and back to where we used to be. I know she won't let me.

Fuck, this is infuriating.

She hasn't spotted me, so I turn to where Jace, the bouncer, is checking IDs outside the door. I could get him to kick her out, considering she's eighteen and a freshman. But if I do that, chances are she'll leave with that douchebag. I want that even less than I want to watch the scene in front of me unfold. I'd rather her be where I can keep an eye on her.

Jesus Christ, I've got it bad. The way she's fucking with my head makes me lose my mind. My body needs to get on board with the promise I made about giving her time, but this doesn't seem like the same Sophie I pleaded with for forgiveness two months ago.

I need to find *that* Sophie before it's too late. This isn't how it's supposed to be for us.

"Hey. I thought you were going to get us a table?" Troy's confusion breaks me out of my trance as someone pushes past where I'm blocking the entrance of the bar.

Shoving my hands into the center pocket of my hoodie so my best friend doesn't notice my clenched fists, I step out of the way. "Yeah, sorry. I just got here." I turn toward him. He's much more put together than I am right now in jeans and a navy sweater pushed up his forearms. His summer breakup trip to California is still evident in his tan and perfectly styled hair that's a little more blond than normal. Maybe I need to get out of here.

Veering to the right of the front door, I scan the booths lining the front wall. A few girls are sliding out of one, and I take a breath to avoid any residue of anger in my tone. "Hey, are you ladies leaving?" I ask the brunette holding her short skirt down as she stands.

"Yeah. You can have this booth."

"Thanks." I step back to give the four girls room to vacate their seats as Troy's hand slaps against my shoulder repeatedly. I follow his gaze–despite it being unnecessary.

"Look." He hits me once more. "Is that Sophie?"

"Yup." I pop the P then grind my teeth.

"Who the fuck is that guy? He looks like a tool."

He really does. Taking another shot, the guy slams the glass upside down onto the bar top, surely leaving sticky liquor for the bartender to clean up. Dick. This guy is nothing like me, and I don't know if that makes this worse or better.

Shaking my head in an attempt to clear my thoughts, I take a hard seat in the booth, the fabric of my sweats sliding across the black leather as I kick my feet up on the bench. I lean into the wall behind me as if it could physically hold up my life. "Someone she shouldn't be with, that's who," I mumble.

Troy mirrors my position as the bartender, Jess, sets a beer in front of him and a vodka Red Bull in front of me. She slips away without more than a friendly greeting. It's crowded enough that Sophie still hasn't seen me.

Pinching the black straw against the side of the glass so I can tip it back, I down half of it in one gulp.

"You okay?" Even though I can't take my eyes off Sophie, I feel Troy's on me.

"Not really."

Troy is the only one who knows the ins and outs of my relationship with Sophie. He sighs, his head falling against the wall too.

"Do I really deserve this? I know I fucked up, but . . ." I'm not sure how to finish my thought. But what? I should get a second chance like I gave her one? I should control Sophie's timeline for getting over it and how she handles it? I know that's not fair even if I hate it. If Sophie thinks she deserves better than me, I want her to have it. But there's no fucking way this dude is better, and this punishment doesn't match my crime.

"You made a mistake, but you had good intentions."

Swirling the ice in my glass with my straw, I force my eyes away to glance at Troy. "We were supposed to be endgame."

"I know. I thought so too."

"So, what? Is this just the end, instead?"

"Maybe it's just a game right now." He offers more hope than I currently have.

Shifting back to my previous view, my eyes narrow on Sophie's boyfriend's movements as he whispers in her ear. She nods, and he slaps her ass, abandoning her for the bathroom and leaving her to slide onto the barstool, alone. Her gaze avoids the rest of the room but flickers to her pink crossbody bag. I know there's a book past its zipper, but she refrains from pulling it out.

I chug the second half of my drink before setting it on the table and slipping out of the booth.

"Where are you going?" Troy shoots off in a warning tone.

"Just checking him out. I'll be right back." Before he has the chance to stop me, I make my way down the dark hallway to the men's room. A handful of guys stand along the graffiti-covered wall, waiting in line for the one stall bathroom. I scan the row, finding the one I'm looking for at the end. Perfect. Why that's perfect, I have no fucking clue. But here I am, knowing I'm doing everything I shouldn't be, fully aware no one will be able to stop me until I get answers.

He leans casually against the dried red spray paint, his legs crossed at the ankles as he scrolls through his phone . . . to the side, rather than down. Jesus fucking Christ. He's on a dating app, and he's not even trying to hide it. My adrenaline spikes–far more than the Red Bull would be capable of influencing–but he's oblivious to my heating rage as I watch over his shoulder. He swipes on a girl he's matched with and immediately types out a one-word message. *DTF?*

The typing bubbles appear instantly, my eyes glued to them like a terrible reality show you can't look away from. *JT, can't wait to see if we really match. Let me know when and where.* Of fucking course this fuckhead has the same name as Sophie's favorite character in our show.

JT the jerk finally catches me staring and looks over his shoulder. "You got a problem?"

"Yeah, I have a problem," I spit, my fists clenching again in my hoodie. Dammit. I can't punch him. That won't convince Sophie it's time for us to work things out. "I just really have to take a piss," I grumble before turning on my heel and walking away so calmly I'm almost proud.

I say *almost* because I know myself better than that–I know there's no avoiding ultimately fucking things up more when it comes to the girl I'm storming toward. My toe stubs against the leg of her stool, the only thing stopping me from hurtling forward. Searing pain stabs through my foot like a slap against a sunburn, but I ignore it. My abrupt appearance sends her hand flying to her chest.

"Cooper," she whispers when she regains her breath, her pretty brown eyes wide at the sight of me. The vanilla and jasmine on her skin overpower the grungy bar, reigning in a sliver of my anger. "What are you doing here?"

"What am *I* doing here?" I whisper-yell, caging her in with one hand on the bar and one on the back of her stool. She shrinks away from me, but I don't back off. "Since when do you drink, Sophie?"

"I'm not an innocent child," she says shyly like she's unsure of her words, twisting a curl of her ponytail through her fingers. The hot pink highlights from summer have faded, and I miss them. I miss her.

"Oh, I know. I was there." I pin my gaze to hers, knowing she's recalling the night I took her virginity. I thought it was the beginning–not the beginning of the end. What I would give to go back to that night, to make sure I never made her feel anything less than I did in that moment.

"Well, you're not the one here anymore," she says frankly, straightening in her seat. "Plus, it's on the list."

Christ, this stupid college bucket list is going to kill me. "Neither is that piece of shit. He's making plans to fuck another girl tonight. Did you know that?" A pang of guilt thuds in my chest knowing my words are mean, but it's hard not to want her to feel the pain she's causing me–even if it is my fault. I don't even know why I'm mad. If he's fucking someone else it means Sophie won't be in his bed.

"How would *you* know that?" Her face remains stoic like this isn't more than a conversation about the weather.

"Not the point, Sophie."

"What is your point?" she snips. "He's here with me right now. You're not the only guy who wants to spend time with me, Cooper." The red glow from the lights above the bar make her narrowed eyes seem even more harsh.

"Dean says he's your boyfriend," I growl, my fingers white from how hard I'm gripping the back of her stool. "You're not supposed to have a boyfriend." I want to pull her to me, protect her from this douchebag and all the others. Her boyfriend should be me.

"My brother doesn't know shit about my life. JT is *not* my boyfriend–not that it's any of your business."

"That's not what it looks like." Sophie wouldn't let just anyone bring her this far out of her comfort zone, even for the list. She wouldn't be illegally drinking in a bar if she wasn't trying to impress someone. She doesn't even like being around this many people. "He's bad news."

"You don't know him. You're just mad at yourself, and you need to stop taking your mistakes out on me."

"Jesus Christ, Sophie. You're gonna believe this jerk you've known for five minutes over someone you've known your whole life? I'm telling you, he doesn't give a shit past getting under your sundress."

"Like you wouldn't say anything to get under it," she snaps with an uncharacteristic snark.

I scoff. "Really, Soph?" She and I both know that's not true. "We wouldn't be in this fucking situation if that's all I wanted from you."

She opens her mouth like she's going to retort but then closes it. I stare back into eyes that are no longer familiar. There's nothing left to say because even though I'd do anything to get *my* Sophie back, the girl in front of me is not her.

Without another word, I twist my tennis shoes on this fucking ugly green and brown carpet and walk away from this stranger, praying this time I'll be strong enough not to come back.

2

SOPHIE

NOW

"Hey, Squirrel." I cringe at the nickname JT addresses me with when he returns to where I've been waiting for him at the bar. The weight of his arm suffocates me as he flings it around my shoulder.

"Hey." Running the end of a curl repeatedly between my thumbs and forefingers, I try to ignore the emotion coursing through me from my argument with Cooper a few minutes ago. I knew there was a possibility I'd run into him, but I wasn't prepared for the way it shook me–and not just from the way he practically launched himself at me. His closeness reminded me how hard these two months without him have been. But the way his rage possessed him also made it clear he's not taking what I said to heart.

"You ready to get out of here?" JT tugs me toward the door with his grip around my neck.

"Yeah." As I slide off the barstool and my feet hit the floor, the last shot we took infiltrates my thoughts, blurring them like leaves swirling in a gust of wind. I've never had even a sip of alcohol–I've never had the urge. But when JT asked me to hang out tonight and showed up with a fake ID for me, I felt like I couldn't say no.

We met by chance two months ago, and I assumed he'd eventually lose interest when I didn't put out. He hasn't, though. He's continued to do nice things for me, and I'm starting to think he might really like me. The day we met was a total coincidence. I thought I hit something while I was driving–possibly a squirrel, hence the ridiculous nickname–and he pulled over to help me. He convinced me to take my car to his mechanic shop so he could check it out for free. I had been a little hesitant but felt it was better than following my instinct to call Cooper and hoping he'd be there for me after I had so recently told him I needed time apart. Ever since, JT and I have been sporadic friends. I'll meet him during his lunch break between my classes sometimes. He always pays and never tries to cross the boundaries I've set in terms of a physical relationship.

I try to sit again to brace myself from the slight spinning of the room, but JT keeps pulling me toward the door. Am I drunk? Is three shots all it takes? Is that what made me so on edge with Cooper? No. *He* makes me on edge, acting like such a know-it-all and trying to control me. It's the way he thinks life is simple and we can just be together and it'll all work out even though I don't trust him. He treats me like I'm the naive one when in reality it's him.

"You alright?" JT laughs, and I can't tell if it's a genuine concern or if he's making fun of me.

"Yeah. Can you take me home?" I pause in the doorway when the cold November Oregon air hits my skin with a wave of sobriety that breaks as fast as it came to make way for another hit of drunkenness. For the first time, I regret not taking Mom and Dad up on their offer to let me move into the dorms even though we only live ten minutes from campus. "Actually, can I stay over?" I don't want my parents to know I've been drinking. They've always been comfortable with Dean and me drinking before we were twenty-one as long as we're safe, but JT made such a good impression on them at the football game yesterday. I don't want them to think I'm making bad choices with who I hang out with. I'm not.

I hadn't even planned on inviting him to the game, but at the last minute, Dean said he wasn't coming with us. My parents told me to bring a friend like I had an entire roster full of them. Besides Cooper, I only spend time with my best friend Chastity. She already had plans, and I couldn't stand to seem like a loser to Dad–especially since he's constantly driving home how important it is for me to make the most of college. JT was the only person I could think might want to spend the afternoon with me, and he did. Or at the very least, he was down for a free football game. Either way, we had a good time.

"No," he says coolly, unlocking the passenger side door of his lifted '50s style convertible and opening it for me. This car had so much potential, but then he had to ruin a classic. The body sits well above the tires, and it looks ridiculous. If it wasn't for that, I would love it. It reminds me of the one painted outside of my favorite diner in town. A flood of memories rushes through me of one of my and Cooper's favorite spots, but I fight the urge to think about how much I miss him and redirect my attention. Why did JT even bother locking his car if he left the top off?

"Oh, okay," I whisper, keeping my eyes focused on my hands in my lap once I'm seated on the white leather. Maybe I can sneak into the house without waking my parents. I should have just stayed home and read instead of letting my book call to me from my purse all night. Of course Chastity had to call right when JT's text came through. It's a curse and a blessing that her assertiveness rubs off on me when she pep talks me long enough.

JT walks to the driver's side of the car, hopping over the door instead of opening it. "Don't look so sad, Squirrel. You made it clear we're just friends. I'm trying to respect that." He turns the key in the ignition, and the car roars to life. He glances at me, his wrist resting on the steering wheel as he leans against the seat. The street lamp casts a glow across his face. He's not Cooper, but he's appealing in the "bad boy" sort of way, and even though he's never crossed a physical line, he's made it clear that he's attracted to me. I didn't plan on sleeping with him, but I'm *supposed* to take advantage of everything college life has to offer. Right now it's offering me a hunky man, and I shouldn't waste an opportunity to end the night feeling better than the way Cooper left me. Plus, Cooper has experienced other people, so I should too.

"Sometimes friends stay over, don't they?" I lock my gaze on him when he takes his eyes off the road for a moment, hoping he catches my drift. Cooper needs to get it through his head that he can't control my life and that he doesn't always know what I want.

"Sometimes," he says with hesitation, forcing his attention back to the street. A smirk tugs on his lips. "Alright." He pulls out his phone and sends a message before sliding it back into his pocket and turns down the next street.

Twisting my ponytail around my hand, I attempt to keep it from tangling as the cold night air whips around me on the dark backroad drive to JT's house. Goosebumps cover every inch of my skin, and I will myself to not visibly shake. JT doesn't appear cold at all, and I don't want to come off like a baby. It would probably be different if I was his girlfriend, but I'm not, and I don't want to be. That's not part of the plan. But still, even when we aren't together, Cooper always checks if I'm comfortable when we drive anywhere. I can't compare my friendships to him, though. That's unfair, especially since most men didn't have a mom like Melissa raising them to have perfect manners–although she clearly never taught him how to handle a breakup. Managing his temper has always fallen on my shoulders.

As if he's reading my mind, JT's hand lands on my thigh, the warmth of his body spreading through mine as his hand slowly slides up my skin. By the time we pull into his driveway, the cool air has nearly sobered me up, nerves replacing my buzz. I can't decide if I enjoy the feeling of being drunk yet, but I already know my mind feels chaotic as the alcohol wears off. He leads me inside his house through a door in the garage, flicking on the kitchen light.

Scanning the room connected to the kitchen, I take in his place for the first time. There's not a lot to it–a worn black leather couch in front of a big screen TV that's longer than the stand it sets on. His gaming console is on the carpet in front of it, surrounded by a couple of controllers. A giant neon Budweiser sign is lit up on the wall by the window. It's so tacky, but he can afford to live on his own, and I can't say the same, so who am I to judge?

The suction of the freezer door opening draws my attention back to JT. "Drink?" he offers as he pulls out a bottle of tequila.

The jury is still out on whether or not I like being drunk, but right now I need to feel anything besides my longing for Cooper. "Yeah, I'll have one." Or three.

3
COOPER

THEN

Cooper, 18; Sophie's 16th birthday

The passenger door of my black 4Runner opens as I turn my key in the ignition, my car humming to life for the last time in my high school's parking lot. Sophie slides into her usual seat, her last day of school smile as bright as her yellow sundress covered in little white flowers. Her big brown eyes find mine as she clutches her yearbook to her chest.

"What?" She chews on the bottom corner of her lip.

"What?"

"Why are you smiling like that?"

My hand instinctively drags across my mouth. I didn't realize I was. "How was your day, birthday girl?"

"Perfect." She grins. "Everyone was so busy celebrating the end of the school year, they forgot it was my birthday."

"Only you would get excited about that." I chuckle, ignoring the way my stomach twists at the idea of anyone forgetting Sophie. She's unforgettable.

Her shoulders lift into a shrug before falling. "Sixteen isn't a big deal anyway. Especially since Dad still won't teach me how to drive." She releases her yearbook so it falls flat against her thighs and runs her hands over the cover. "But enough about me. How are *you*? You're officially done with high school!" Her smile is infectious when she looks back at me. "How do you feel?"

"Immediately more mature." I tug on one of the dirty blonde curls hanging over her shoulders and smirk before putting my car in reverse.

"I didn't know you were capable," she teases and tucks her hair behind her ear. "I wish I didn't have two more years until I graduated." She sighs.

"It'll be here before you know it."

"You don't sound excited. You're just happy to be away from me, aren't you?" she jokes.

"No." I've been trying to suppress my hesitation. "Just a little nervous."

"How come?" If anyone besides Sophie was asking, I'd brush off this conversation. Then again, anyone besides her probably wouldn't have picked up on an issue.

"You know I suck at math."

"You don't suck at math, Coop. It's a hard subject."

"I know, but there's a bunch of classes I'll have to take for my business degree." Leaning back against my seat, I adjust to just one hand resting on the top of the steering wheel as I pull to a stop at the light.

"You'll do great. I can try to help if you need it."

I flash her an appreciative smile. Sophie is great at math, at anything with numbers, really. She's also a killer artist. She's really got both sides of her brain working for her. "I don't want Dad to think I won't take real estate seriously because my grades make it seem like I'm not taking school seriously." I put my biggest fear on display with a sigh.

Sophie reaches over, her fingers brushing reassuringly over my arm as the light turns green. The innocent touch sends a spark of comfort through me even before she adds, "You can do this, Cooper. You just have to work hard like you do with football, with your friendships, with skating. All of those took time and effort to perfect. And oh, remember that time you built a bookshelf for me?"

I roll my eyes. "That took me six months." She showed me a picture from Pinterest of a non-traditional bookshelf she wanted. It was a bunch of cubes that looked like a flower when you assembled them correctly. "I couldn't figure it out. I broke it like eight times."

"But now it's perfect."

"I would have given up if it wasn't for you."

"And you won't give up on this because it's important to you too." Her smile fixes everything.

"Yeah, you're right. Thanks."

"Anyway, you don't need to worry about this right now. You're done with high school, and that's something to celebrate. Are you going out with Troy and the guys tonight?"

Flicking on my blinker to take a left at the stop sign to turn onto our street, I glance flatly at her. "And miss out on birthday cupcakes? I don't think so," I tell her as if it's the dumbest question she's ever asked.

She shoves my shoulder playfully. "You know I'll save you one. Come on, Coop. I'm not doing anything different than any other year. Making cupcakes with Mom then reading whatever book you got me."

"Hey, how do you know that's what I got you?" I arch a brow.

She humors me with a fake laugh. "You better have!"

I bite my lip to hold back my grin. It's been a tradition for the past three years since she turned thirteen. It's so fucking hard finding presents for a girl friend who isn't your girlfriend–not that I have experience with that. Somehow I ended up with her Amazon book wish list, and I pick one out for her each year. I usually read the description before choosing one, so I know they are love stories. She went into a rant one time about how she's too embarrassed to ask anyone else to buy them for her, so I'm assuming there's sex in them. I'm not sure why I'm the exception or how we got to this point in the first place since we've never had an actual conversation about relationships or sex–real or fictional. I wanted to pry because I'm sure I could help her feel more confident about it, but I selfishly want to remain the only one she's this comfortable with.

"I guess you'll have to wait and see."

She rolls her eyes in response as I pull into my driveway. "Bring me my book before you go out, please. I'm withholding your cupcake until you do."

"You wouldn't." I shift my car into park and turn it off, shooting her a playful glare before we get out.

"Try me." With a grin, she shrugs, then skips over the stepping stones toward her midnight blue house, the edges of her sundress fluttering around her. Once she's inside, my glance falls back to the stepping stones. There are four of them, two with our childhood handprints pressed in them, and the other two with slightly bigger prints belonging to our older brothers. They've been here so long, I don't remember making them. It's weird to think I'll be moving out of the only place I've ever lived in a couple of weeks.

The hum of Troy's white Honda Civic pulling into the driveway flips my attention back toward our sage green home. He steps out of his car, and I meet him outside the front door, greeting him with the ridiculous "secret" handshake we created when we were like twelve. I have an older brother, Carter, but Troy might as well be my brother too. He's lived with us since I was nine. He's a year older, though, and in his first year of college at the University of Oregon. Since we only live ten minutes from campus, he's still here all the time.

"Congrats, bro. You're done. How are we celebrating?" he asks as we head inside.

"I was thinking about hanging with Sophie for her birthday."

"Let's all do something. I'll call Emily." He digs his phone out from his front pocket to call his girlfriend.

I reach my hand to cover his screen. "Nahhh. That sounds double date-y."

"And remind me again why you two aren't dating?"

My eyes roll at the question I've been asked far too many times. "We're just friends." I groan. It's not that I've never thought about what it would be like if Sophie was my girlfriend. She's beautiful. We have a blast together and never argue about anything. We have the set up of a good relationship. But I have this idea in the back of my mind that it's all because we've grown up together–like the comfort and consistency of it is the reason I love her, not anything more. Everything appears better when it's familiar. Something about the thought of our friendship being *more* feels foreign. I look across the living room through the window facing the house next door and wonder if she feels the same.

"The way you look at her says otherwise," he states over his shoulder as we walk into the kitchen. My mom is standing at the gray slate counter sprinkling Ritz cracker crumbles on top of homemade mac and cheese. "Mom," Troy continues, "Help me out. Coop totally looks at Sophie like he wants to see under her sundress, huh?"

"Troy Bolton. Do not talk about that sweet girl that way." She pauses before looking at me and chuckling.

"But sorry, sweetie. You follow that girl around like you're a puppy."

Mom bites off half of a Ritz cracker as Troy adds, "A cute one, though!"

My head tips back, my hands dramatically dragging down my face. "No ganging up on me." I groan. I know we are lucky to be raised in a home where conversations like this aren't uncomfortable. Mom has taught us everything we need to know about relationships, and I appreciate that. But I'm also annoyed. Maybe there's been curiosity around Sophie, especially as we've gotten older, but I'm a guy, and she's cute as hell. Friend or not, I'm human.

Choosing denial and planning my escape route, I walk to the rack by the front door for the keys to our motorcycles. "How long until dinner?" I yell back at Mom.

"Not until seven when your dad gets home from work," Mom says.

I turn to Troy. "You want to go for a ride?"

"Let's do it."

Saying goodbye to Mom on our way out the door, I toss Troy his keys and we push our bikes past our cars from their place in the garage.

After buckling our helmets, Troy pulls out onto the street first.

I follow him out of our neighborhood to the backroad that winds through the trees toward a few of the nearby wineries. An hour later, we're back in town and flip out our kickstands in a parking space at Skinner Butte. No one else is in our vicinity as we make our way to the edge of the overlook.

"Is whatever you're pondering as serious as it looks?" Troy asks, our feet dangling over the side of the brick wall. This park in Eugene is where we end most of our rides before heading home. The winding road brings us high enough to have a birdseye view of the entire downtown enclosed by trees that are currently a perfect shade of spring green. I love Oregon.

I kick the heels of my black Nikes against the brick. "Nah, probably not. I'm overthinking it."

"Just tell me," he presses, leaning back on his hands.

Letting out a long breath, I ask, "You're teasing me about Sophie, right? You don't actually think I should date her, do you?"

He chuckles. "The only thing that's funny is how ridiculous it is that the two of you *aren't* together yet."

I roll my eyes.

"You've really never considered it?"

"Maybe I have, but more in fleeting thoughts. Sure, I'm attracted to her, and I've had the urge to kiss her a few times–"

"You have the urge to kiss a lot of people," Troy interjects. He's not wrong. I've kissed a lot of girls, but it's never gone past that.

I laugh. "Making out is fun. It's weird you don't think so."

He shrugs. "Other stuff is just *more* fun." Grinning, he adds, "So, why don't you kiss Sophie?"

"What if it ruins our friendship?" I tug on the strings of my hoodie hard enough to scrunch the hood around my neck.

"What if it makes it better?" he counters. "I've seen the way she is around you. I know probably better than anyone. She's different around you–more open, happy, confident . . . more herself. You could have easily had sex with anyone you want by now. You don't think you're holding out for her?"

"Uhhh." The thought hadn't crossed my mind, but that's not to say it isn't my subconscious intention. "I've been busy with football and finishing high school."

"Uh-huh. I've lived your life, dude. I'm living your future life right now. I can tell you with certainty, if you want to have sex, you'll find time for it."

"How did we get from kissing to sex?" I shake my head at the ridiculousness of this conversation.

"I'm just throwing out thoughts you're afraid to say aloud." He shrugs, tossing a broken fragment of brick to the hill below.

"So, you think I should make a move?"

"What's the worst that can happen? She rejects you? At least you start college soon. You don't have to see her as much if things go south."

"I've seen her almost every day since I was like three years old. I can't imagine not having that."

"Exactly my point." The look on his face is playfully condescending as he slaps me on the back.

4

SOPHIE

THEN

My phone skips lightly across the white marble kitchen counter when it vibrates, and my heartbeat falls in sync. Dropping the frosting-covered knife into the KitchenAid bowl, I pick it up.

Cooper: *Meet me at our spot?*

When I look up, a cupcake is frozen in Mom's hand as she stares at me. It's our tradition every year to make homemade red velvet with cream cheese frosting.

"What?"

"I could ask you the same thing. What is making you smile like that?" She raises an eyebrow.

"Nothing," I say, wiping the look from my face. "Just something Chastity said," I lie. Seeing Cooper is always a bright part of my day, but I'd never admit that to anyone. Mom and Dad have made it clear they think I'm too young to date, so I'm sure they'd hate the idea of me having a crush on someone over two years older than me. I don't think they'd stop me if I did want a boyfriend. They might even be supportive because they love Cooper, but I haven't brought it up. It's not worth the effort since it's one-sided.

Mom gives me a questioning look as I pick up a frost-ed cupcake. I survey our progress. The first batch is almost completely decorated, and the second still has ten more minutes in the oven. I already put away all the baking ingredients while Mom did the dishes. "I'm going to bring Cooper a cupcake. He asked for one when he dropped me off."

"Okay, honey." She smiles, picking up another cupcake to frost.

"I'll be right back," I say, slipping out the sliding glass door leading to our backyard. I make my way, barefoot through the grass, until I reach the edge of the trees that run behind all the houses on our street. *Our spot* is two layers into the woods. You can barely make out our houses from there. It's quiet and secluded, the ground covered in dirt and dead leaves from last fall. We've been hanging out here since we were four and six, making mud pies and hiding from our brothers.

As I approach Cooper, his back is turned to me, giving me the perfect view of his short brown hair. The urge to run my fingers through it is as strong as it usually is, despite knowing that will never happen. The crunch of the leaves beneath my feet causes him to turn, revealing the bag of bird seed he's using to fill the little red birdhouse his dad helped us build in middle school. He sets the bag on the ground by the tree the house is attached to, brushing the seed off his hands.

Taking a step toward me, he reaches for the cupcake. "Uh-uh." I move it behind my back, a grin on my face.

My eyes follow his redirected reach to the pink plastic tubing lawn chair, its back facing the tree that separates us from our houses. It sits next to a matching blue one, both cracked and worn from years of use. He picks up my new book. "Is this what you want?" He smirks, holding it out for me, a stream of light from the setting sun fighting its way through the trees to glimmer in the space between us.

I nod in admittance as we make the swap.

"Thanks, Coop." My eyes run over the sketched purple palm trees on the cover excitedly. This book is at the top of my list.

"You look especially excited about this one," he notes.

Biting into my lip nervously, I debate what to tell him. These discreet covers make it so easy to mislead people. "Yeah . . . it's my first one that has actual spicy scenes in it."

His eyebrows scrunch in confusion.

"Sex scenes," I clarify, my skin heating from saying the word aloud.

He chuckles. "Oh, I assumed all the ones I got you did."

"How do you decide which book to get me anyway?" I look up for his answer right as he takes a typical teenage boy sized bite of his cupcake.

He chews and swallows, licking the cream cheese frosting off his lips before answering. "Usually it's random. But the guy in this one is named Cooper, so it won."

"Great, how am I supposed to not think about you during the sex scenes then?" The thought slips out of me, followed by my heart lodging itself in my throat. I did not mean to say that aloud. I go to take it back, but he's quicker in his response.

"You say that like it's a bad thing." He shrugs and nonchalantly shoves the other half of his cupcake in his mouth.

I stare, his gaze caught in mine, and my stomach flips, awakening an eclipse of moths. Is he serious? Did he mean that as a joke? Which way am I hoping for? I know seeing Cooper as more than my friend has crossed my mind, but it's an idea I don't let invade my thoughts when I can help it. He's more than two years older, first-string on the football team, one of the most popular guys in school and about to leave for college. Not to mention I'm sure he's far more experienced than I am. I'm the quiet girl who reads at lunch and has two friends. I'm happy enough with my book boyfriends anyway. And again, one-sided feelings wouldn't make for a good relationship.

"Don't get shy on me, Soph." He laughs, watching me lost and awkward in thought.

"I am shy," I whisper, my eyes darting to the dirt.

"Not with me, you're not. I'm the person who buys you sex books."

"They aren't sex books," I defend, folding my arms across my chest.

"There's sex in this one." He nods to the book tucked under my arm.

"Well, yes, but–"

"Nope, no buts. If there's sex in them, they are sex books."

I look at my fingers where they tug on the ends of my dirty blonde curls. He's always been a straightforward kind of person, and we've always been open with each other but never forward about this kind of thing.

"Is it weird to you, talking about sex with me?" He wraps his fingers around my wrist, tugging me to our plastic chairs. "Sophie?" he says when I don't reply.

"Yeah. Umm. I don't know. It's kind of weird."

"Why?" He leans back in his chair, digging his heels into the ground to keep from falling over as he tips the chair and himself backward.

"I feel like only people in relationships talk about it."

"Pretty sure friends talk about it too."

"Yeah, but it's you. And I'm me."

"What does that mean?" He chuckles.

I drop my book to my lap, my hands covering my face in embarrassment, my skin flush underneath. My best friend Chastity told me the sex scenes in this book are really good. I've never had sex before, but now I'm imagining what it would be like with Cooper, and I'm worried my body's reaction will spill my secret. "I don't know. Maybe you don't want to hear about that kind of stuff from me. I wouldn't even know what I'm talking about." I'm not even sure he can hear my voice muffled through my hands.

He pries my fingers away from my face, forcing me to look at him, and not letting go of my hand. "I want to know what you think about anything and everything, dork. It's weird we've never had this conversation," he states like it's an indisputable fact.

"Why?"

"We've been friends for sixteen years. You'd think every subject would have come up by now."

"You know I don't open up to a lot of people."

Releasing my hands, he tugs on the strings of his maroon football hoodie, amused as his bright blue eyes taunt me. "I'm not *a lot* of people."

"I know." I can't believe he wants to talk about sex with me. It's not that I don't want to be as comfortable with Cooper about this as I am with Chastity. I just never expected it to be a thing for us.

"I'm attractive. You're attractive. We're friends. Good friends. It's bound to happen eventually."

My eyes widen, my mouth falling open. *What did he just say?*

He laughs. "*Talk* about sex." With a pause, he rolls his tongue against his teeth like he's debating whether to free his next thought.

When he doesn't add anything, I stare blankly back at him. "I thought we were talking about my books," I whisper.

His brows scrunch together. "I think this is all coming out wrong."

"Umm. Yeah."

"Let me try again. You're my best friend."

"Troy is your best friend," I reply without a second thought. Cooper is one of my best friends, but I've never thought I was his.

"Yeah." He shakes his head, contradicting himself. "But it's different. You're my person. The one I want to ask about their day after school. The one I want to share cupcakes with. Argue about TV characters with. Do homework with. Do nothing with. And all of that is about to change."

"You're only going to be ten minutes away."

"You know, Troy asked about *us* today." He chuckles like this new information won't freak me out. *What is happening right now?* "And it got me thinking . . ."

His playfulness falters.

"What?" I whisper, curiosity overcoming my struggle to comprehend what he's saying.

He takes a breath. "Actually, maybe I shouldn't say anything."

I'm nervous, but now that he's brought it up, I want to know. I reach over to his arm resting on the edge of the chair. He glances at where we connect. "Tell me." I bite into my lip, anxiously awaiting his response.

"Only if you promise not to hold it against me."

I nod, hoping he can't sense how much my heart rate has picked up.

His eyes flicker across mine as he decides on his words. "I don't know, Soph. I just wonder . . . what it would be like if we were more than *just* friends."

He must sense my panic. The plastic of the chair squeaks as he shifts to face me more. He reaches out for me but withdraws his hand before it makes contact, grabbing onto his hoodie strings instead. "If I keep talking, are you going to run away?" he says, unsure of himself all of a sudden.

I shake my head slowly, as if the speed could counteract my heart rate.

He takes a deep breath, and it reminds me to take one. "Everything is easy with us. I guess I think if we hooked up, things would either get better or ruin our friendship. I figured bringing this up wasn't worth the risk."

"Why are you bringing it up now then?" My gaze falls back to where I'm twisting my curls in my fingers.

"If it freaks you out, promise me you'll forget I said anything."

"I promise," I say after a small hesitation. Whatever he's about to confess doesn't feel like it's something I'll easily forget.

His hoodie strings drop against his sweatshirt when he releases them to cautiously rest his hand on the nape of my neck. His touch feels both unfamiliar and comforting at the same time, my skin heating as chills take over. Like when you have a fever and are simultaneously too hot and freezing.

On occasion, when we are watching movies, I'll rest my head on his shoulder. We hug regularly. Sometimes he drapes his arm around my shoulder as we walk into school. Nothing that's a big deal. Nothing as intimate as this. I hold a bated breath, waiting for whatever happens next.

"Lately, I don't know." Nerves etch into his features as his eyes shift across my face. Lack of confidence is rare for him. He takes another deep breath then the words come out rushed. "Sometimes I get an urge to kiss you, and it takes a lot not to just do it."

He's so close his scent overwhelms me, the spiced apple cider comforting me like a blanket and a good book at Christmas. I'm tempted to see if he tastes as good as he smells, knowing he just ate the cupcake I brought him. His eyes continue to flicker back and forth across my face, waiting for my reaction.

My heart rate would surely set off an alarm if I was attached to a machine. My hands sweat against the fabric of my sundress. I don't know what I want. I don't know what to do. I've never kissed anyone before. And Cooper isn't just anyone. He's my person too. My only good friend besides Chastity. I can't risk that for a kiss. What if I suck? How could we pretend it never happened?

"I'm sorry, I have to go back inside. My mom is waiting for me," I say quietly and watch him deflate before I pull away from his hold, standing to leave.

"Fuck." He mumbles the curse as I walk away, and I picture him running his hands through his light brown hair, the way he does when he's stressed. I debate turning around, but I don't look back.

5

COOPER

NOW

Cooper, 21; Sophie, 18

Pulling the casserole dish filled with sweet potatoes from the oven, my mouth waters at the layer of bubbling marshmallows on top. I walk it to the living room, setting the dish on the only uncovered hot pad on the round poker table–also known as the "kids table" even though we're all adults now. It's covered by Mom's fancy white linen and an excessive amount of traditional Thanksgiving food.

Our nearest extended family lives four hours away, and Sophie's family doesn't have any on the West Coast, so ever since our parents moved next door to each other and became best friends, we celebrate everything together. It's always made a holiday that could be underwhelming something to look forward to. But today, I'm not looking forward to my favorite day of the year. I don't care about the football pool we drew up this morning. Or the annual spiked apple cider Mom made. I'm hardly excited to see my brother, Carter, for the first time this year. My brain is stuck on one track–one that loops around the memory of my interaction with Sophie at the bar three days ago. Part of me doesn't want to see her. The other part can't wait until she's near me again. *Fuck, I miss her.*

"Cooper!" Dad calls from across the living room.

Grabbing my drink off the table, I approach where he's standing with Sophie's dad, Jack, each with a beer in their hand. Jack has been here since 9 a.m. drinking beer and watching the football pregame show. Sophie's mom showed up even earlier, helping Mom prepare dinner like they do every year. Her brother, Dean, came over early too. He played basketball in the driveway all morning with Carter, Troy and me. But it's almost time to eat–we are *dinner at noon on Thanksgiving* people–and I still haven't seen Sophie.

"What's up?"

"Tell Jack everything we went over last week," Dad insists. "About outsourcing."

"Yeah, we hired someone from the Philippines as a virtual assistant." Dad takes a sip of his beer, tuning out. I shift toward Jack, proud of this change that I convinced Dad we needed to make for productivity and higher profits in his real estate business. "Outsourcing our graphic design and marketing work to her will save us a ton in payroll expenses. Not to mention, it'll free up our agents to sell more homes."

"Reasonable given the market. Especially from the financial perspective. You researched that and made it happen on your own?" *Don't act surprised.*

"Yup." I take a swig of my beer. I've felt so much pressure to convince Dad I'll be a good fit for the family business. I've done way more research than I normally would for something. "Just wait until I'm an agent."

I catch the dismissive look from Jack before he gets Dad's attention again. "Looks like next year will be a big year for you, Mike."

"Prepared for it to be the best yet. Cooper has done a ton in terms of streamlining our processes. He's already an invaluable asset to our team."

A knock rattles against the front door, my body immediately tensing. Mom passes us on her way to answer it. "Stop talking shop," she says over her shoulder as she reaches for the knob. "Time to eat, everyone!" she yells to no one in particular as she welcomes the final guest.

Sophie's sweet voice greets Mom from the other side of the door. I take a breath, thankful for the out of this conversation. I feel Jack's eyes on me as I walk away but ignore both him and his daughter's arrival as I scan the table.

Carter has already taken his seat next to Troy. Dean slides into his place next to Carter, leaving two empty spots next to each other between him and Troy. My only option is to sit next to Sophie. Of fucking course, I internally curse, even though this has been my seat at Thanksgiving dinner every year since Troy moved in. The thought of being so close to her in an intimate setting feels almost paralyzing today. If things hadn't ended between us, I'd be able to keep my hand locked on her thigh while we ate, rubbing my thumb across the skin below the hem of her dress, letting her know how thankful I am for her. I'd be able to sneak a few kisses between dinner and dessert, pinning her to the wall in the hallway. And she'd curl up to me on the couch to watch the game after we ate.

But as we simultaneously and hesitantly slip into our seats, my closeness to Sophie in her perfectly fitting maroon dress has me conflicted. I'm equally broken *by* her and attracted *to* her. I don't want to let go, but it doesn't seem like she wants me to hold on.

I'm so lost in the battle in my head that I don't notice the usual upbeat chatter is nowhere to be found until Carter breaks the silence. "What the hell is going on around here? Y'all are sad sacks." He raises his eyebrows in confused acknowledgment of the mood. "Troy, it's been like three months since you and Emily broke up. It's time to let it go, man." Troy shoots him a death glare, and my brother rolls his eyes before directing his attention to Dean. "And what's up with you? Word on the street is you finally got yourself a girlfriend. You should be happier than all of us right now."

"Yeah, she seems nice," I add in an attempt to keep Carter's interrogation away from Sophie and me.

"You have a girlfriend?" Sophie's curiosity gets the best of her, and she breaks her silent treatment to me when she turns and adds, "You met her?" She's confused like this is the first time she's heard about Maci. Then again, she was preoccupied with JT the jerk when Dean introduced me at the football game a few days ago.

"She's not my girlfriend," Dean mumbles then chugs his whole beer like it's a lifeline distraction for whatever turmoil is rolling around in his head. He could have fooled me with the way he was looking at her like she single-handedly makes his world spin. I could see that despite being in a rage over learning about Sophie's boyfriend.

Her boyfriend. It sinks in all over again that it's not that she didn't want to be in a relationship. It's that she didn't want to be in one with me. My fists clench under the table. "Sophie's got a boyfriend too," I stir the pot.

Apparently, I woke up today choosing violence.

"No." She hesitates, pushing her green beans around her plate. "I don't." Her cheeks turn pink and her eyes flash to mine for only a split second before they shift back to her plate.

"Why aren't you in a better mood, Soph?" I taunt, channeling all my misery into antagonizing so I don't unsuccessfully beg her to take me back again. "Honeymoon phase shouldn't be over yet." The fire in her eyes reignites our ongoing battle.

"He's not my boyfriend," she snaps, mirroring her brother's words but fueled with anger.

"Oh, so what? You're just sleeping with him?"

Dean coughs, choking on his food.

Troy slaps me upside my head, but it's not enough to snap me out of it.

My eyes are locked on Sophie's as I watch tears well in them. She bites into her lip and blinks away the moisture. "No." The lie comes out soft, but it hits me like a car running a red light and slamming into me. I blink, and it feels like I can see her clearly for the first time tonight. She slept with him. When the accusation flew out of my mouth, I didn't think she actually *had*, but the way her eyes glossed over with guilt gave her away.

She slept with him. My stomach bottoms out. For no justifiable reason, I'm crushed like she cheated on me. I pull my gaze from hers to glare at my plate. I can hardly look at her. I can hardly think about touching her now that I know he has. It makes me sick to think every precious inch of her, the parts of her that she had always saved for me, are no longer mine.

"Whoa, whoa, whoa," Carter cuts me off before I can find a response. "I don't know what is going on between you two," he wiggles his finger between us as he holds his beer bottle, "but you're best friends. And we are all family. And it's Thanksgiving. No more hostility, no more moods, definitely no more talking about our precious little angel doing the deed. Everyone say what they are thankful for." A collective groan leaves the four of us, and I try to wash the vision of Sophie and JT from my mind. "I'll start. I'm thankful for my new job." Carter had no desire to join the family business and wanted to "leave the nest," so he took off for Nevada a couple of years ago and recently got his Master's degree in Kinesiology. He was immediately offered a PT position for the athletic program at the college, so he's not moving home. It's part of why I feel so much pressure to follow in Dad's footsteps. "I'm thankful all my hard work is paying off, and that I was still able to come home and visit you morons. Troy."

We all glance at my best friend, expectantly and dreading our turn.

"I'm thankful to be part of this family," Troy says the same thing he says every year, with a sincerity and level of gratitude that puts everything into perspective.

"Me too." I squeeze his shoulder. "I'm also thankful for my *friend*," I emphasize the incorrect term for the girl sitting next to me as I look at her, "making me cupcakes since I don't like pie." Even though I've lost my appetite completely.

She stares back, and the joke I made all of a sudden seems life or death—like if she didn't do this it means it's really the end of us. Once she was old enough to help her mom bake, cupcakes became their *thing*. For Christmas one year they made a batch of red velvet that was so good, I begged for them at Easter. Sophie has made them for every holiday since.

My forced grin fades. "You did, right?" I ask, hoping the concern making my stomach flip isn't evident as I touch her shoulder. I pull back after my fingers barely brush her bare skin, instantly regretting the contact.

It feels like forever before she nods and a sigh of relief leaves me for more reasons than one. Confusion covers her face like she doesn't understand its significance. "I'm thankful that Mom and Dad are taking us on vacation tomorrow and I get to leave here. I'm excited to explore Honduras with my brother." She directs half a smile toward Dean.

"Me too," Dean agrees. When it's clear he doesn't have anything else to add, Carter holds out his beer, and we all do the same, our drinks meeting in the middle of the table.

"To the people who will always be around no matter what shit life throws at us."

Our glasses clink, and my eyes find Sophie's. I wonder if she's one of them.

6

SOPHIE

NOW

Pulling the crystal glass filled with spiked apple cider away from the cheers, I realize this is the first time I've had alcohol around my family. But I need it. Regret is probably too strong of a word. Even though I had already crossed *have sex* off my college bucket list, it feels like Cooper didn't count, especially since I'm on a new passive aggressive mission to complete this list "right." Chastity's entire reasoning for the list in the first place was to get me out of my comfort zone, and everything with Cooper is comfortable–even when the tension between us is thick enough we would need the carving knife to cut through it.

Sleeping with JT a couple of nights ago was fun–not that I have more than the one other time to compare it to. I still wasn't completely sure when I got to his house, but one drink led to another and then he kissed me and the night ended in sex. It was nothing compared to any intimate experience I've ever had with Cooper, and I felt guilty for thinking about him the entire time. JT seems interested in doing it again based on the texts he sent the next day, but I'm torn. I know he doesn't want me to be his girlfriend, but I'm not sure I'll be able to sleep with someone consistently and not see them as my boyfriend. I also don't think I could date anyone and not compare everything they do to Cooper–not expect from them everything I got while I was with Cooper. That's part of why not dating until I'm ready to forgive him is part of the plan.

I eat my dinner in silence, successfully avoiding being roped into any conversation between the boys. The second my plate is clear, I leave the table, noting Cooper doesn't even acknowledge me abandoning the seat next to him.

Entering the kitchen, I make my way to the small pile of dishes from the dinner prep. I managed to stay away all morning, claiming I needed to pack for our trip, but I can't exactly eat and run on Thanksgiving. The dishes will have to suffice as a cover for me avoiding everyone for now.

The stream of hot water cascades off the plate in my hand into the stainless steel sink. Not bothering to turn the faucet off once the bubbles are gone, I turn to the dining room where the boys are still messing around at the table. My eyes lock on Cooper. His light brown hair is messy styled and the glow from the chandelier reflects off his bright blue eyes as a goofy grin lights his face. The light facial hair he's had since he started college makes him look older than the picture of Cooper I have saved in my head, but I love it. It hits me how time keeps ticking by and the two of us are stuck in this forever moving wave that brings us back together and pushes us apart. I wonder if it'll be like this forever, and I pray we'll be on the right side when all is said and done.

Cooper glances my way like the pressure of my stare finally reminds him that I exist. Confusion furrows his brows, but it only lasts a second before his attention falls back to our brothers.

A new stack of plates clinks against the counter tile next to me.

"Thank you, sweetie," Melissa says, reaching past me to turn off the water.

"You're welcome." I put on my best smile for Cooper's mom.

"Do you think your mom will trade you for one of the boys? They never do my dishes."

"Boys are useless." I laugh.

"But we love them anyway, don't we?"

"Yeah, we do." Tears float on my eyes, betraying my attempt to hide my chaos of emotions out of nowhere. I don't know how much she knows about Cooper and me, and I'm not sure what this conversation is actually about, but I don't think we are talking about dishes.

She runs her thumb across my cheek. "You know I love you like a daughter, right, Sophie?"

I nod, afraid if I speak, I'll cry.

"I hate seeing you two this way."

"Me too," I admit. Part of me feels like I am partially responsible for how things are right now, but I don't want him to think he can get off that easily when he messes up. Still, "It sucks," I add in a whisper, the tears finally draining from my eyes.

Leaning her hip against the gray slate counter, she reaches to tuck a curl behind my ear. "Did your mom ever tell you about the time we almost stopped being friends?"

My eyes widen as I swipe away the emotion from under them. "What? No. I don't remember that."

"I think you were five or six. Cooper was in third grade. Mike and I almost got divorced."

"You did? But you two are perfect together."

"Nothing is perfect, Sophie."

"Well, you make relationships look easier than every-one else–like you're the exception."

She gives me a soft smile then confides, "When Mike lost his job, he struggled a lot–to the point where it negatively affected me and the boys. He was depressed and didn't look for a job. He stopped taking care of himself. He felt so much pressure to take care of us that he was crippled by the anxiety of it."

I can't picture Mike that way. He's owned a success-ful business for as long as I can remember. He works harder than anyone I know. "What happened?"

"I was going to take the kids and leave him." My stom-ach knots just at the thought of what life would have been like if Cooper and I hadn't been neighbors our whole lives.

"But you didn't."

"No, I didn't. I decided to choose *us* over choosing *me*. I recommitted to what I knew in my heart–that Mike was the person I wanted to love for the rest of my life, no matter what. Best decision I ever made next to marrying him in the first place."

"How did you know he was *the one*?"

"Besides my uncontrollable urge to stalk him at col-lege?" She laughs. "Sophie, *the one* doesn't just magical-ly exist. Yes, there's chemistry and commonality and all that. But you *choose* who *the one* is. Once you choose them, you have to continue to choose them every day, every season–no matter how hard it is. It's not just a one-time thing where you decide then hope things stay easy and hold a grudge when it's not–not only with whoever you date, but friends too.

"The true test of any relationship isn't an outside situation putting strain on you. The true test is your ability to decide that when things inevitably happen 'to your relationship' it's not a sign you aren't meant to be together. It's to show you how strong you can be together."

Am I being too petty and turning my breakup with Cooper into a way bigger deal than it should be? Should I have at least tried to work through things *with* him instead of apart? Denial pushes the thought aside. "Wait, what does this have to do with my mom?"

"She's the one who talked me out of leaving."

"And you were mad at her for that?"

"Pride is a funny thing, sweetie. I thought I knew what was best for me. I thought my way was the only right way, and I was mad at Diane for telling me otherwise."

I can't imagine my mom and Melissa not being friends. They've been as close as sisters since they ended up neighbors the month before Dean was born.

"But all your mom wanted was the best for me. After everything she's been through, she knew that what Mike and I were going through was there to remind us how meant to be we are–that this wasn't something critical enough to break us. It wasn't like both of your parents' first marriages. It also made me realize I felt the same about your mom. We're stronger together because we have each other's back even when the other person can't see clearly. The intention was for her to help me through this, but in turn, it was a test of our friendship. It showed me that we can disagree on things and still be friends. Sometimes I'm right and sometimes she's right, but it doesn't matter who's right. It matters if you have someone who loves you enough they are willing to stand up to you when it's in your best interest."

"It's hard to stand up when the other person keeps fighting you on being wrong," I say under my breath.

"Then maybe it's time to ask yourself if you *are* wrong."

Am I wrong? We just had one fight. The only time Cooper ever made me question him.

"Whatever is going on between you and Cooper, ask yourself if it's more important to save your pride or your friendship." She pauses like she's hesitant about it, but adds, "Or relationship."

But if he can break my trust once, how can I believe he won't do it again? "What if I actually am doing what I should?"

She sighs. "All you can do is commit to a side and be willing to accept the consequences of that either way."

"Thanks, Mrs. Montgomery." I wipe my hands on the kitchen towel and hug her.

"Anytime, sweetie." She pulls back. "Here." She reaches toward the windowsill. "Cooper!" she yells loud enough for him to hear.

A moment later he appears in the kitchen, his eyes drifting to me before they focus on his mom. "What's up?"

She holds last year's dried wishbone toward her son. Every year since we were old enough to grasp the concept, Cooper and I break the previous year's wishbone. Melissa says letting it dry that long versus waiting a few days for the current year one makes the wish granting power stronger. I think she's crazy, but I love a good tradition. "Make a wish."

He hesitates then steps forward to take the bone from his mom. I take a breath and invade his space, close enough I can feel the tension between us again, his spiced apple cider cologne overpowering the other smells of Thanksgiving. Melissa makes a quiet exit from the room, leaving us alone.

Cooper nods to the end of the wishbone he holds out in front of us, and I pinch it between my fingers. Disappointment is clear in his stare, nearly bringing my tears back. "I wish for a relationship less fucked up than ours." With an angry energy, he pulls his side away from me before I have time to object.

Before it snaps, I silently wish that I'll be able to convince him that we can heal from this.

We both examine our pieces, broken evenly in half. With only a humorless laugh and a small shake of his head, Cooper turns on his heel, chucking his half of the bone in the sink as he leaves me again.

The only thing preventing me from running back to my house and crying in my bed is the fact that I don't want to be away from Cooper–even if he doesn't want to be near me right now.

I wish my family wasn't leaving for Honduras. We never go on vacation this time of year, but my brother begged us to take this trip with him. It's not that I don't want to travel somewhere incredible–any other time I would be excited. But I'm not sure we'll have service. Even though Cooper and I haven't talked much lately, our pending relationship revival seems like it needs immediate attention, especially now that I've made my decision.

Melissa's words run through my head. *You choose who the one is. Is it more important to save your pride or your relationship?* If I'm going to forgive him eventually, what am I waiting for? Why am I waiting? I can't even answer those questions, and that tells me everything I need to know. It's time to forgive him. It's time for us to be *us* again. I keep trying to have all these experiences on my own, but all I want is for him to be with me. If I'm being honest with myself, being with JT is all it really took to know that Cooper is the one I want. I need to come up with a plan to force him to sit down and talk this through with me and make him believe me when I tell him that.

7

COOPER

Now

Carter flips one of the smoldering logs in the stone pit, and the fire roars to life with a loud crackle. Satisfied, he leans back in his camping chair, mirroring Troy and me. "So, what's up with you and Sophie, bro?" It's been three days since Thanksgiving. I'm surprised it took him this long to ask. "Crush gone wrong?" He laughs.

I tug on my hoodie strings aggressively enough to bunch my hood around my neck. "It's not a crush." Being four years apart, Carter and I have never been that close, so he's never been attuned to my business. Plus, by the time we started dating, he had just finished his undergrad and was leaving for Reno.

Regardless, I've only ever said the words directly to one other person. At this point, though, figuring out how I feel about Sophie is not brain surgery. I look next to me, finding my best friend's eyes full of sympathy between the flickers of firelight.

"Oh, shit. You're actually in love with her?" My brother picks up the cues like I expected him to. There's no point in hiding it. "You two dated?"

"Yeah. I'll get over it, though. Maybe when Troy gets over Emily." I shoot Troy a knowing look.

"Not funny," Troy says, shaking his head in amusement and taking a sip of his beer. "At least I'm *trying* to get back out there," he throws back.

"Do you think I should already?" I don't bother filling in my clueless brother. "She just said she needed time to get over what happened."

"Wait, what happened?" Carter interjects.

Troy ignores him. "Actions speak louder than words. We saw her with that guy the other night. He definitely didn't look like just a friend. Not to bring it up again, but it does sound like they are doing more than friendly things."

"Ooohh, drama," my brother commentates.

I groan. "Fine." Getting back out there is the last thing I want to do. I can't drop the idea that Sophie is the one for me, but it's been over two months. If she can't forgive me, I can't keep holding on. It's too fucking hard.

"Alright, I don't know what's going on, but it sounds like we are going out?"

Conceding, I nod. "We're going out."

Carter gets the hose, putting the fire out as Troy and I exchange smoky sweats for nice jeans and T-shirts. Reaching into my sock drawer for a clean pair, my fingers skate over the small cardboard jewelry box. I pull it from where it's tucked in the corner and lift the lid. There's a fine gold chain with a single charm. It's a sun–the rays also made of gold and the inside is filled with little pink gems. A client Dad and I found a house for owns a jewelry making business. I saw this necklace a few weeks after Sophie and I broke up, but I couldn't resist getting it. I planned to give it to her at Christmas, thinking we'd move past all of this by now. I guess not. I sigh, resigning to my fate as I push the box to the back of the drawer.

By the time we are ready, Carter already has my 4Runner warmed up. I slide into the passenger seat, Troy sitting in the middle back, leaning over the center console. "Jameson's?"

"No way," Carter says, turning the headlights on.

"Why not?" I challenge my brother. It's the only bar Troy and I go to. His pseudo uncle owns it. Plus, it's comfortable there. If I'm being forced into moving on, at least I can be in my zone.

Carter looks over his shoulder to back out of the driveway. "If you're going to find new girls, you need a new scene."

I know he's right, but I let out a groan anyway.

"Do you need a slice of cheese to go with that whine?" My brother asks and Troy chuckles. I roll my eyes. I should have stayed home.

Ten minutes later, we miraculously find a parking spot along the curb up the street from the place my brother chose. Waiting in line to get our IDs checked, Carter squeezes my neck in a headlock before I can react. "First time out with my little bro," he says, his knuckles pulling at my hair as he digs them into my head for a noogie. I squirm out of his grip, shoving him off and noting his navy blue shirt with "Nevada" and a picture of a wolf head printed across the front in white. He abandoned his green and yellow UO wardrobe the second he left. Traitor. I can't believe I'm going to be seen in Duck territory with him.

"Not so little anymore."

We take a step closer to the bar entrance. "Guess not. I can't believe you're old enough to legally drink."

With my birthday being at the beginning of September, I barely missed the cut-off date for school, making me almost a year older than most of the people in my grade. I'm not complaining, though. It feels like I get an extra year going out with Troy and my fraternity brothers.

The bouncer hands back my ID, and I step into a packed bar. Neon blue light streams from the ceiling over the sleek black bar and surrounding high top tables. They're dimmer over the empty space in the back for dancing.

"Hey." My card isn't even in my wallet when Carter's hand slaps my chest before he points toward the bar. "What about her? She's cute."

I follow his line of sight. The girl leaning against the bar *is* cute. I sigh in defeat, knowing I should rip off the bandaid. "Yeah, alright." I make my way to her, taking a breath and inhaling any good energy available around me. I feel like I've forgotten how to flirt with anyone who isn't Sophie. I have no idea what to say, so I lead with my default setting.

"Hey. Can I ask you something?"

"Sure," the pretty brunette says, slightly distracted attempting to get the bartender to notice her. Once she glances at me, she pauses, giving me her full attention.

"Are you a magician?"

"Huh? No . . ."

I don't have to force a smile. "Because when I look at you, everyone else disappears."

She bites back a laugh. "Does that work for you?"

I hold my hand out to wave down the bartender. "I've actually been waiting months to use it. You're the lucky recipient. So, you tell me."

"It'd work better if you could make a drink magically *appear*."

"Your wish is my command." I wink, and not even her eye roll can hide the way she leans in closer.

The bartender stops in front of us, and I let my new friend order before asking for a vodka Red Bull.

Thirty minutes later, Troy closes in on where I'm standing alone at the bar, the club music thumping through my body. "What happened? It looked like things were going well," he yells.

"Yeah, her friends wanted to leave."

"Did you at least get her number?"

"She gave it to me."

"But . . ."

"But I'm not going to use it."

"Why not?" There's annoyance in his voice.

"How does she do this? Being around anyone else doesn't feel right. Maybe I could talk myself into it the first time, but that was when we were still kids. These aren't teenage feelings anymore," I admit with a frustrated groan.

He sighs. "It gets easier. Give it time." He flags down the bartender for another round of drinks. I hope that's all it takes. "Until then, focus on the fun of first dates. Someday you won't have any more."

I would have been fine if my very first one had been my last.

8

COOPER

THEN

Cooper, 18; Sophie, 16

Stuck in my blue plastic chair, I scrub my hands up my face and through my hair. I didn't turn around to watch her walk away. I know she didn't run. I could tell by the way the leaves crunched slowly under her feet until she got to the grass of her backyard. But she still walked away. Fuck. I don't know what came over me. Maybe I should go after her. After talking to Troy, I panicked thinking about how I'll be moving out in a few weeks. I know I'll only be ten minutes away, but change is inevitable. I kept wondering if I would ever get a chance again if I didn't take it now. Apparently, I don't have a chance anyway.

I know Sophie, not enough to have predicted her reaction to this, but well enough to know the longer she sits with whatever she's thinking, the more she'll panic or pull away. I dig my phone out of the front pocket of my jeans.

Me: *I'll see you tomorrow, right? For B & B?*

Sophie forced me to watch this show–*Beauty & the Beast*—with her when it came out almost two years ago. I thought it would be some chick flick I'd hate, but there's a ton of action, and I'm kind of hooked–not that I'd tell any of my friends. Now it's our tradition on Thursday nights to watch new episodes.

Sophie: *I don't know . . .*

Me: *I'm sorry, I shouldn't have said anything. It was stupid.*

Sophie: *It's not stupid. I like that we can tell each other stuff. I just panicked.*

Me: *Understandable. I crossed a line. Please don't let things get weird. We can talk about it if you want, or I promise I'll never bring it up again.*

A full minute passes without so much as typing bubbles appearing in our thread.

Me: *You have no reason to say no since you promised to forget whatever I said.*

Sophie: *It's kind of hard to forget.*

Me: *Come on, Soph. You know you're my excuse to watch without anyone razzing me. Don't leave me hanging. I promise I'll be totally normal.*

Sophie: *Okay.*

Sophie: *I'll see you tomorrow.*

I let out a rough breath. Thank god she didn't reject me again. I was not prepared to go down that path. I got ahead of myself, envisioning what life down a different road could have been like.

The Goldfinch that frequently visits our birdhouse chirps in a way that feels like a lecture. "Yeah, I know I'm an idiot, Sunshine," I mutter to the bird.

9

COOPER

THEN

Fresh out of the shower, I pull a pair of black athletic shorts from my dresser and tug my maroon hoodie over my head. I probably didn't need a shower, but I'm stalling. This trip next door feels different than the others. Every walk before had Sophie looking forward to seeing me at the other end. Tonight I'm walking into a house not knowing how she feels about me after my confession yesterday.

On my way out the back sliding glass door, I slip on my house slippers before taking the twenty-ish steps to get next door, our back porch lights and muscle memory guiding my way. There used to be a fence between our two yards, but when it got worn enough to need replacing, our parents left the dividing one down.

It would have made more sense if I was better friends with Sophie's brother, Dean. He's only one grade above me and we played football together all through high school, but he has his own group of friends. Carter and I never went through any phases of life together. At first, I'm sure Sophie and I spending so much time together was a way for our parents to keep us occupied. But it evolved into a conscious choice. At school, I'm usually with my other friends, but I make time for Sophie every day. We skate to the park. She studies next to me while

I play video games on my couch. She'll read while I do homework at her kitchen table, helping me if I need it. She'll make us cheese and crackers for a snack break at *our spot*.

We've been pretty inseparable just like our parents have been since they met. They have weekly poker nights, attend mine and Dean's football games together and have been going on an adult-only cruise every year since we were old enough to stay home alone. We spend holidays together and host a dozen barbeques each summer, alternating between backyards.

Despite feeling at home at Sophie's house, I knock on the sliding back door. Diane glances up from where she's fixing herself a cup of tea in the kitchen, and her smile welcomes me inside.

"Hey, Mrs. Porter," I say as I slide the door open. "How are you?"

"Hi, honey. I'm lovely. Just heading to bed." She knows why I'm here at 9 p.m. on a Thursday–not like she ever has a problem with me showing up. "I think Sophie is in her room. There are still a few cupcakes left in the fridge too."

Guilt washes over me thinking about things I've recently fantasized about doing with her daughter, but I hide it with a grin. "You know I can't resist your baking."

"Please, eat them all. And you'll set the alarm when you leave?"

"Yup."

With my confirmation, she thanks me and heads up the stairs, passing her daughter on her way to her room. When Sophie sees me standing here, she hesitates on the step, her fingers immediately picking at a thread on the hem of her pink flowered pajama shorts. She's wearing an oversized white T-shirt and her dirty blonde hair is piled on top of her head in a messy bun. God, she's cute. It's like once I admittedly saw the potential with her as more than a friend, I can't unsee it. Now that I know she doesn't feel the same, I need to figure out how to stop obsessing.

When she realizes her hesitation, she makes her way toward the fridge, pulling out two cans of Squirt–regular for me, and Ruby Red for her. I reach to the cupboard next to me, grabbing two glasses. As I make my way to the fridge to fill them with ice, Sophie's eyes follow me.

"Hi, Soph." I chuckle at how nervous she is. I've never been responsible for creating that feeling for her, so it's amusing. She stares back. I set our glasses on the kitchen island counter. "Come here. You need a love hug." A couple of years ago, Sophie learned in one of her science classes that when people hug for at least twenty seconds, oxytocin is released–the same hormone released during sex. It decreases stress. Ever since she learned that she forces long hugs on me, or love hugs as she likes to call them. It's not all the time–mostly when I've had a bad game. Really, it's more when she needs one for whatever reason, oftentimes ones I don't quite understand. Girls. Either way, they seem to make her happy, and they always pull me out of whatever mood I'm in.

She doesn't make a move. I grab the soda cans from her hands and set them next to the glasses. I take the step that closes the distance between us, wrapping my arms around her neck, crossing them and pulling her to my chest. She's stiff for a moment, but then relaxes into me, her head nuzzling into my neck and her arms wrapping around my waist. Her flowery body spray is hardly noticeable now that it's faded from the day, but it's comforting. *She* is comforting–like when I get into clean sheets after a tough practice and a shower.

I listen for the numbers. She usually counts to twenty out loud so I can't pull away early, but I don't feel her soft words against my neck. "Soph?" I start to pull back.

She doesn't let me go. Her grip on my sweatshirt tightens in her fists. I give her another moment, but I think this stupid oxytocin hug is making me feel way more about it than I should. I need to get out before I do something stupid again. I pull away. This time she lets me, stepping back and looking at me with her beautiful brown eyes. "You good?" I ask, reaching for our glasses again to avoid brushing a stray curl from her face.

She nods. "Yeah."

"Alright, let's do this." She keeps her attention on the glasses as I pour our sodas, the fizz of the Squirt flowing through the ice the only sound in the room. She follows me to the living room. Taking her place on the left side of the couch, as always, she curls her feet underneath her and reaches for the remote. I sit on the right and kick my feet up on the ottoman then tug the fuzzy blue blanket off the back of the couch, draping it over my legs and leaning back into the cushion.

She flips to the CW as the black and green logo appears on the screen. We watch the first half in silence, sipping on our sodas. When the next commercial comes on, Sophie fidgeting with her fingers distracts me. I'm so damn irritated with myself for making this awkward. Our friendship being easy is one of the best parts, and I fucked it up. I should apologize again. I go to speak only to be cut off by Sophie's whisper.

"Can I have some of your blanket?"

"You can have whatever you want." I chuckle, and lift the side of the soft navy throw, waiting for her to join my side of the couch. Her gaze catches mine as she scoots closer. She curls her feet under her again, her thighs an inch from mine. I drop the blanket over her and direct my attention back to the TV in an attempt to ignore the warmth coming from her body.

I'm sucked into the scene on TV when her voice pulls me away. "Coop?"

"Mhmm?" I hesitate before glancing over at her.

"Whatever I want?" she whispers.

"What?"

"You said I can have whatever I want."

"I did . . ." Not sure where she's going with this.

Her gaze shifts away from my eyes and falls to the blanket. She pulls her hand out from under it. Before I can react, she reaches for my hand, threading our fingers together. I know it's not possible for your heart to actually skip a beat, but mine definitely did some weird flutter thing.

When I look back at her, her eyes are still on our hands, but a moment later she looks up to me as if she's waiting for reassurance. God, she's so fucking cute right now—so innocent and nervous. Am I nervous too? My palms are clammy all of a sudden. I debate pulling away from her to wipe them on the blanket but think better of it. Instead, I squeeze her hand lightly and smile at her. She smiles back nervously, then leans her head on my shoulder.

I can't take my eyes off her. I continue to stare, watching her watch the TV, and I don't realize I've missed an entire section of the show until the elevated volume level of the next commercial segment startles me.

She's either finally realized I'm staring or is just now choosing to acknowledge it. "Stop looking at me." I can tell by her tone she doesn't mean it. "Is this weird?" she asks, her eyes flicking to our conjoined hands.

"Do you think it's weird?" I challenge.

She shakes her head, her messy bun flopping about as she does.

"Do you want to tell me what you're thinking?"

She studies me for a second as if she's unsure her secrets are safe with me. I rub my thumb along hers in reassurance, my body automatically reacting to her needs without thought.

"It feels normal. Besides your sweaty hands." She unlinks our fingers and dramatically drags her hand down the sleeve of my sweatshirt, giggling as she does.

"Hey!" I grab the wrist of her hand running over me and playfully push her backward, pinning her to the couch before I relentlessly tickle her. She squirms under me, fighting to get away–the unbridled playfulness stroking my previously depleted ego. I ease up when she starts giggling so hard she can hardly breathe. I pause, my face hovering over hers, and her laugh ceases.

God, I want to kiss her so badly, but I know she's not ready. Instead, I let our gazes stay locked for another moment before pulling away from her and sitting. She stays on her back and flings her legs over my lap dramatically with a sigh. "Cooper?"

"Yes, my little cupcake?" I look at her with a smirk, squeezing her calves. Fuck, her legs are soft. I focus on her face to avoid running my hands up toward the ruffles on the edge of her sleep shorts. The only light in here is the glow from the TV. I can see her scrunch up her nose at the pet name I've never used, but she doesn't complain.

"I like you."

I can't help but chuckle. "I would hope so, Soph. It would be weird if you were just pretending to be my friend for sixteen years."

She slaps at my arm but misses based on her position. "You know that's not how I meant it."

Her nerves have dissipated a bit. I note tickling as a tactic to use in the future. Maybe next time I'll kiss her after. Fuck, I want to kiss her. "I know." I grab her wrists and tug until she's sitting up. "Of course we like each other. Relationships are simply friendships with extra benefits." I wink at her before adding, "We're great at the friendship part. We better be after this long. Are you trying to tell me that maybe you're interested in the extra benefits part?" Any mild curiosity I had before has transformed into a full-blown desire to know what she tastes like in the past twenty-four hours. I'm praying she's starting to crave the same.

She chews on her bottom lip. "I want to tell you something, but you can't make fun of me."

"Promise." I reach out and run my thumb along her cheek. A shiver runs through her at my touch, and I remind myself it's too soon to pull her lips to mine. I let my hand fall to hers in her lap. "Tell me."

She takes a deep breath. "I don't have much experience with that part. Not as much as you."

My brows furrow. "What kind of experience do you think I have, Sophie?"

"I don't know. We've never talked about stuff like this." She shrugs. "I've seen you making out with girls after football games."

I never realized she'd seen me. For some reason, I wish she hadn't. "It's just kissing." I laugh, but her face remains serious. "Wait. Have you never kissed anyone?"

"You promised you wouldn't make fun of me," she pouts. I've wondered recently if she's been kissed before, but I wasn't sure either way. All of a sudden this feels like a lot of pressure. I don't want to fuck it up for her.

"I'm not, I'm sorry. Come here." I wrap my arm around her shoulder and tug her into me. "Yes, I've kissed girls, but let me set the record straight. That's all I've done."

She pulls back enough I can see her eyes go wide in the glow of the TV as the credits roll.

"Don't act so surprised." I chuckle.

"But, Cooper, you're you." That's the second time she's said something like that.

"What is that supposed to mean?"

"You're good-looking, you're popular, you're a football star and all the girls drool over you."

"You think I'm good-looking?" I tease. She's not wrong about what she said, although I'm not sure there's actual drool involved. I know I'm one of the more popular kids in school, but I've never cared about that.

"Shut up. You know you are."

"I mean, yeah, but I've never heard you say it."

"Apparently we've never said a lot of things before," she sasses.

"And that changes now?"

She nods. "Yes, please. I hate the miscommunication trope."

"The what?" I have no idea what she's talking about.

A grin covers her face. "In my books, the main love interests always keep their thoughts hidden, and it blows up in their face at some point when the situation could have easily been avoided."

"Ahhh. I see. Okay, so from now on, all thoughts are on the table, all the time, no matter what?"

"Yes, even if you change your mind. Promise you'll tell me."

"Same goes for you."

"Sooooo, you've really never had sex before?" she asks in a whisper.

"Nope." I pop the P.

"What about . . . all the other stuff?" she asks, a little more confidently this time.

"None of that either. Don't doubt how well you know me, Soph. All I've done for the past four years is eat, sleep and breathe football. I didn't have time for a relationship." According to Troy, I just didn't make the time, but I wasn't willing to sacrifice my time with Sophie. If I had a girlfriend, I'm sure that would have had to be the first thing to go.

She smiles at that. "One more thing."

"You can have as many things as you want."

"If I'm a terrible kisser on the first try, you have to give me a second chance before you change your mind about me." She's dead serious.

"So, you want to kiss me?"

Her teeth tug at the edge of her lip as she nods, and I almost kiss her right then.

"You're not going to be terrible, but deal," I assure her. She stares back at me, waiting. "Sophie?"

"Yes?"

"I'm not going to kiss you right now."

"Oh." She deflates.

I rest my hand softly on the nape of her neck. "I want to. So fucking bad." My face is close enough to hers that if she wasn't holding her breath I'd be able to feel it on my lips. "But I think this has been a lot for you tonight, a lot for us. I want to make sure you're ready." When she doesn't argue, I know she agrees. "Walk me out?"

She nods, standing with me.

When we get to the sliding back door, I pull her into a hug. She doesn't count to twenty, and I know it's been far longer than that by the time I reluctantly pull away from her. I kiss her forehead. It's something I've never done before, but it feels surprisingly normal. She smiles at me. "I'll text you later, okay?"

She nods, and I move to set the security system. "Oh, wait!" She runs to the fridge and comes back with a Tupperware for me. "Take these with you."

"I'm not taking the rest of your birthday cupcakes."

"They were never for me," she says, then turns on her heel and skips across the kitchen before heading up the stairs, leaving me standing there and questioning everything I know about this girl.

10
SOPHIE

THEN

Sundresses are pretty much the only thing I own even though I live in Oregon and they aren't weather appropriate more often than not. So why I'm staring at my closet stressing over my outfit is beyond me. I've never been too selective about my clothes. I basically own twenty of the same dress in different colors. But today is different from every other day, so I think I want to look different too.

I'm not sure why I care. Cooper saw me in no makeup and pajamas last night like he does every week, like he has my entire life. This is ridiculous. I could probably wear pajamas again considering once I'm in his car tonight I don't have to get out of it until we get back home. Regardless, I yank my pastel pink sundress off its hanger. It's a little nicer than the ones I typically wear and cut into a deep v compared to the usual sweetheart tops I like.

I slip it over my head, loving the way I fill it out compared to the last time I wore it. Running my hand over the strip of intricate lace detail around my waist, I feel a little more sexy than usual, knowing you can see my skin through it.

Cooper invited me to the drive-in movies. I'm still not completely sure this is a date. It's something we've done so many times before, but everything feels different since yesterday. I hardly got any sleep last night after he left, running the evening over in my head, wondering what was going to happen next and if he was overthinking things as much as I was. There's no doubt in my mind that I want to try being more than friends with him, but that doesn't mean I'm not nervous. He confessed to not being as experienced as I assumed. That puts me a little more at ease, but there are so many things that can go wrong to ruin our friendship or make it awkward. I'm wondering if he couldn't sleep either because his text came through at 6:30 this morning asking if I'd block off the night for him.

Mid twirl of a curl, I hear a knock on the front door. I glance at the time on my phone. 5:30. We have to leave by six. It's almost an hour and a half drive to the theater. It's far, but it's one of our favorite things to do in the summer. When we were younger, our parents would take us every week. Me, Cooper and our brothers would bring all our blankets and pillows and make the bed of my dad's–well now my brother, Dean's–truck all cozy.

The last soft ringlet bounces as I tug it free from the clip of my curling iron. I click it off, ready to head down the stairs to meet Cooper. I stop in my tracks when I hear him talking to Mom. I'm not sure what makes me hesitate to interrupt them, but I lean against the wall at the top of the stairs, listening to the voices in the entryway.

"Hey, Mrs. Porter." If I'm not mistaken, he sounds a little nervous.

"Hi, honey. What are you and Sophie getting into tonight?" I'm only sixteen, but my parents have never had a tight leash on Dean and me. We have never given them a reason not to trust us, and I don't go out often anyway. I prefer to get lost in imaginary worlds.

"Ummm, we are going to the drive-in." I imagine him tugging on the strings of his hoodie, the way he does when he's nervous on game day.

"Is everything okay?" My mom picks up on his uneasiness too. Of course she does, she's known him longer than I have.

"Yeah. I just . . . I wanted to tell you . . ." My heart thumps in my chest. What's he about to say?

Mom must give him a questioning look because she doesn't speak again before he continues.

"Sophie and I are going on a date. If that's okay." He's talking softer than his usual loud and playful voice, so I'm surprised I can hear him. I'm glad I can. This is something I'd totally swoon over if I read it in one of my books. Leaning against the wall as my heart flutters in my chest, I hold my breath–like the sound of it might prevent me from hearing my mom's response. I didn't think we'd keep it from our parents, but I didn't consider we'd say anything tonight before we even knew what might be happening between us.

"Oh, wow. I had no idea you two felt that way about each other."

"It's new."

"Well, I didn't see that coming." She chuckles in a way that makes me unsure of where she stands on the topic. "Thank you for telling me. I trust you'll take care of my daughter?"

His sigh of relief makes me smile.

"I will, I promise."

I run back to my room, through the first door on the right, when I realize Cooper is walking toward the stairs.

Taking a seat at my vanity, I swipe another layer of mascara across my lashes—the only makeup I'm wearing. I feel him standing there before I see him. After screwing the wand back into its tube, I look at Cooper leaning against my door frame watching me. He looks good in his black joggers and green Oregon hoodie. I knew that's what he'd be wearing.

"You almost ready, Soph?"

I can't help the smile that comes over my face. I'm excited about this, so much more than I expected. I leap from my chair and take the five steps that separate us before throwing my arms around his neck. He laughs as he steadies himself, one hand bracing him to the doorway and the other wrapped around my waist.

"What's this for?" he says into my hair and squeezes my hip.

"Just being you," I whisper back.

He releases me. I smile at him before moving to my closet to grab my jean jacket. When I turn back around, he's staring at me, his hands stuffed in the pockets of his sweats.

"What? Do I look okay?" I glance down at my dress, running one of my hands down the fabric.

"Okay? More than okay. You're beautiful, Sophie. I'm the one wearing sweats on our date." He looks like he's just internally face palmed, and I can't help but chuckle.

"You're the more sensible one. That's what we've worn every time we've gone to the drive-in."

"This time is different, though." He grins, reaching his hand out for mine before I can respond. "Let's go."

The feel of our fingers linked together sends a wave of giddiness through my body, energizing me in a way I haven't experienced before. Last night on the couch, it felt surreal being with him, like a temporary glitch in the matrix. For some reason, this feels more real.

When we get to the car, he opens the passenger door for me. He hesitates for a moment, his tongue slipping out to wet his lips while I buckle my seatbelt. I smile at the thought that *I think* he wants to kiss me. He won't, though. Not yet.

"Let's go." I grin, my words forcing him out of the moment.

As he walks around the front of the car, I connect my phone to his speakers. Opening my Spotify app, I scroll until I get to the playlist labeled *Summertime*–we were obsessed with Kenny Chesney the year we created it, the summer we spent almost every day having picnics and swimming at the creek. There are 719 songs on this list, ones we've added over the years that we both love, for our car rides to school or the diner or anywhere else we go. I push play, worrying that navigating this uncharted territory between us will be weird. Do we talk about the same things we always have? Or are there different topics reserved for people in relationships?

"So," Cooper says over the soothing tone of Darius Rucker's voice, and I reach to turn down the music. "I was thinking about asking Dad if I can start working for his company while I'm in school. What do you think?"

"Will you have time?"

He chuckles. "I've heard enough financial responsibility talks from both our dads to know I can't afford to not make the time." He's not wrong. Dad's a financial advisor, and he's always going on about investments and savings and all that.

"I think you should definitely ask him."

"You don't think I'm too young to deserve a shot before people who have worked in the industry for a while? I don't want a job just because I'm the owner's son."

"Your dad didn't build a successful company by handing out favors, Coop. He's not going to give you a job unless he believes you can help. Which you can. He'd be lucky to have you."

"How do you know I'm capable? It's not like I have experience."

It's not like Cooper to be missing confidence, but when he is, he tends to confide in me. I love being his person, and I try my best to keep that job. "That's not true. You've been around the business practically your entire life. I'd bet you know way more than just the basics."

"Yeah, maybe."

"And you know he'd love for you to join him and make it a family business. Your last name is on the building already. You being part of it is inevitable, so you might as well start sooner rather than later, you know?"

"Yeah. Okay. You're right. Thanks, Soph." He shoots a genuine smile my way, and I add another tally to my column in the "Sophie vs. Cooper's doubt" chart I've saved in my head.

The next hour of the drive flies by, a cool breeze from the cracked window swirling around us, the voices of Keith Urban and Thomas Rhett filling the car more than mine and Cooper's. My seat is slightly reclined, and I'm relaxed against the black leather. Every once in a while, I feel his eyes on me and spare a glance his way. Whenever he's caught, he grins. It says more than words ever could, and I soak up being here with him and this moment I never expected.

It's not until we pull up to the ticket booth that I'm hit with a storm of equal parts anxiety and excitement. Because I'm actually going on a date with Cooper Montgomery. Regardless of how things go tonight, it will change everything. As much as we say nothing will alter our friendship, I know this will. Even if things feel completely normal right now, I know nothing will be the same after tonight.

11
SOPHIE

NOW

Cooper, 21; Sophie, 18

Even though my phone is face down on the night-stand, the glow from a notification seeps into the dark room and wakes me from my uneasy sleep. Expecting the text to be Chastity, drunk at a party, I flip over my phone. The skip in my heart shoots an alertness through me, and I sit in bed, rubbing the exhaustion from my eyes.

Cooper: *I just want my heart back.*

The time in the upper left corner of my phone screen reads 3:07, which means it's 2:07 in Oregon. We've been in Honduras for three days now, and Cooper is all I've thought about. I tried my best to have fun exploring the ruins, white water rafting and snorkeling, but my constant restlessness since seeing him on Thanksgiving has prevented me from relaxing.

I miss him so much. I hate that he's hurting. I hate that *we* are hurting. I want to fix this. I took Melissa's advice to heart, and I'm ready to choose Cooper and for things to go back to how they were before. I want to be near him, hold him, let him hold me. I miss the way it feels when I'm in his arms and nothing else matters.

I tried getting his attention before the end of that night, but he kept brushing me off, ignoring me like I was a ghost he could see right through. It feels like he's slipping away, and that can't happen. I know if we are going to fix our relationship, it's not something that can be done from 3,000 miles away in the middle of the night, but I hope it's not too late by the time we get home.

Staring at his text, I debate my response.

"Sophie, turn off the light." My brother groans from the other twin bed in our room at the house we rented.

"Sorry," I mutter, sliding from under the fluffy white comforter, and making my way out of the room. Barefoot, in nothing but my sleep shorts and an oversized Duck shirt I stole from Cooper, I quietly open the sliding glass door in the living room that leads to the patio. The 60° night sends a chill through me, but I lay on one of the lounge chairs anyway. It's too dark to see much, the stars the only thing lighting the space. In the daylight, our view is beautiful. This porch overlooks a jungle of green, with the ocean in the nearby distance.

Turning to lie on my side, I hit Cooper's contact and press *Video*. The FaceTime call doesn't even ring a second time before he declines.

I try again.

Then one more time.

Me: *Coop, please pick up.*

I wait until he's had time to read my text, and then try again.

This time he answers, my screen blurry as his video loads. When it does, a shadowed version of Cooper comes into grainy view. He's in a hoodie, sunk into his couch. "What do you want, Sophie?" The devastation in his voice breaks me. I don't want to wait until I get home. I can't stand to see him this way anymore.

"I want to make sure you're okay," I whisper.

He pulls a glass to his lips, chuckling before taking a swig of his drink.

"Are you drunk?" It crossed my mind that it was a possibility when he texted me so late.

He shakes his drink in front of his front facing phone camera, ice rattling against the glass. "This shit doesn't fuck me up nearly as much as you do." He must toss his phone on the couch because my view jerks around before it settles on the ceiling.

Okay . . . he's really drunk.

"Cooper," I say loud enough he should still be able to hear me.

"What?" His voice is distant.

Needing to bring him back, I say, "I want to be with you."

There's silence for a moment. Then his laugh fades into a scoff.

"Cooper, pick up your phone."

He snatches it from the couch, giving me a quick jarring tour of the room again before his camera brings his face into focus. "You know what makes me mad?"

I'm afraid to know. "What?"

"You. Everything about you. How you always make me feel better. And make me confident enough to do shit I'm afraid to even though I can't even call and tell you about it. The way you're so fucking pretty all the time. Like you probably are right now if I could see you better. With your stupid curls that I want to mess up with my fingers. And the little gold specks in your eyes that only come out with the right lighting. And your oversized shirts you don't let anyone see you–hey." He pulls his phone closer to his face. "Is that mine? I've been looking for that shirt."

"I wanted to feel close to you."

"You want to know what else I hate?" He takes a sip of what I'm assuming is vodka–hopefully without the Red Bull or he'll never get to sleep. "That I've been with other girls. A lot of them." My stomach drops, hating that it's true. "And none of them kiss me like you do. Or make me happy like you could. Or get rid of this anger inside me that just seems to build every day. It's not fucking fair, Sophie. Because you don't care, and I hate you for it."

A tear slips down my face, and a light breeze sends another chill through me. "Coop," I whisper. "Let's talk about this when I get home." I know he's not in the right mindset to have this conversation. "When you're not drunk."

"Seeing you with him hurt me. Hearing you've *been* with him . . ." He shakes his head. "I'm constantly scared of losing you, and you're not even mine."

"I know. I'm sorry, Coop."

"Whatever, Sophie. We both know that when you come back, you're not coming back to me."

"I am." My voice cracks on the promise.

He stares at me, the glow from the soundless TV in front of him the only thing lighting his face. Then the call ends.

I call back immediately, but he doesn't pick up.

I try two more times, and send three more texts, reassuring him we're going to be okay. Then I wait twenty minutes for a reply before giving up and going back to bed.

12
COOPER

THEN

Cooper, 18; Sophie, 16

"You don't seem nervous at all," I say to Sophie, the glow of the sunset framing the massive white screen ahead as we pull past the ticket booth of the drive-in. We've done this a hundred times, some of them just the two of us, but never like *this*.

"Oh, I am. I didn't sleep like at all last night." She giggles, and it's fucking adorable.

"Well, you don't seem like you are."

"Oh, sorry, should I call your mom and stumble over my words? Would that make you feel better?" she teases.

"You were eavesdropping, weren't you, you little sneak?" I raise my eyebrow at her as I continue my one mile per hour pace turning down an empty dirt row.

"I sure was. You're romance novel main character worthy, Cooper Montgomery."

"Is that so?" I grin at her as I put my car in park and set it to accessory mode. "Just trying to avoid that miscommunication thing you were talking about." I was nervous as shit to talk to Diane, and I probably should have talked to Sophie about it first, but as much as it was a risk she wouldn't want me to be alone with her daughter anymore, I figured it was more of a risk to hide it and have her find out later.

"Are you nervous?" She combs through the tip of a dirty blonde curl with her fingers repeatedly while she waits for me to answer.

"To talk to your mom, yeah. But not about you." I twist in my seat so I'm facing her now.

"It's kind of weird this doesn't feel weird. At least not yet."

"Not going to get weird. We've been friends our whole lives." I pause. "I was thinking, you know, if for some reason this doesn't work, we'll just go back to being friends. Right?" I don't want her to feel any pressure, and I think I need that confirmation for myself. I've only known what it's like to have Sophie in my life, and I don't want to even imagine it any other way. Though, I can't imagine this not working. I've already spent sixteen years with her, and we haven't had a single issue yet.

"Right." She smiles brightly at me and happiness pumps through my veins. How did I not see before that *this* is how we are supposed to be? *Together.*

"Okay, wait here for a second." When she nods, I pop my trunk and hop out of my car. I already set up the back before I picked up Sophie. I folded down all my seats and covered them with the five huge blankets I pulled from our linen closet and all the pillows off my bed. I arrange all the pillows that have shifted on the drive over and pull the Squirts and candy I got at the store earlier out of the plastic bag.

Sticking my head through the opening between the two front seats, I see Sophie reading her book–the one I got her–using the light on the rearview mirror to read. She hesitantly pulls her eyes away from the words when she hears my laugh. "You brought your book on our date?"

"I bring a book everywhere." She shrugs. "Plus, his name is Cooper, remember? So, it's totally okay." Her smile lights my fucking world.

"I forgot to turn to the radio station," I tell her to distract myself from obsessing.

"I got it," she says, already turning to the dials on the dashboard. She clicks it to the correct channel, and I glance back at the screen, noting the Coke commercial lining up with the sound.

"Okay, now get back here." Instead of getting out of the car and walking around to the back, she crawls between the two seats, almost flashing me as she haphazardly attempts to hold her dress down. That fucking dress. She always wears them, but there's something different about this one. She looks . . . older, maybe, like she's no longer the little girl I grew up with.

She settles herself in the back, next to me, with her feet curled under her and her dress safely hitting right above her knees. Damn, Cooper, one step at a time. Just because I've never had sex doesn't mean I haven't thought about it. It's not that I haven't had the opportunity either. Being a football player definitely has its perks if you want them. I also happen to have a mother who is very open about sex and has somehow convinced me it's special and not worth doing with just anyone. Sophie isn't just anyone, but even if I decide I'm ready, I know damn well she won't be anytime soon. I can wait for her, though.

"What did you get for us?" she asks, already reaching for her Ruby Red Squirt. She unscrews the top of the bottle and takes a sip.

"What do you want first, Nerds Rope or Fun Dip?"

I watch her eyes light up in the glow of the drive-in movie screen. This girl is so easy to please. All I have to do is get her books and candy you can play with and she's happy. "Mmmm Fun Dip, please."

I hand her the red packet–her favorite–before I rip off the top of my blue one. The drive-in screen goes dark, making it nearly impossible to see her for a second before the movie projector rolls. She licks one side of her white stick and dips it into her paper packet. Pulling it out carefully, she licks the other side and then grins before reaching over and pressing the newly wet side into the blue sugar. As she licks her sugar off, I dip my own, biting the end of it as soon as it's in my mouth.

"Cooper, that's not how you eat it." She rolls her eyes as she dips her stick back into her cherry flavored sugar.

I shrug. She moves to lick the sugar off her stick, but I reach out, pulling her hand toward me and sucking it off instead. The roughness of the sugar scratching against my tongue explodes into a sweet cherry flavor. "Hey! Rude!" She laughs, not actually bothered, and dips her candy again.

I dip my own, intending to suck the sugar off this time, but before I make it to my tongue, Sophie's hand wraps around mine, tugging it to her until it's close enough to lick. After she's positive she's gotten all my sugar, she releases my hand, but her eyes meet mine. Her smile fades into something more serious. I'm sure we're only looking at each other for a second, but the time that passes before she speaks is like waiting for a pot of water to boil.

"Cooper?" My stomach flips–not from the sugar but from the softness she uses in saying my name.

"Sophie," I echo, shoving what's left of my sugar stick in the packet and setting it down next to me on the blanket to give her my full attention. She does the same.

She swallows. "I don't want to wait any longer."

Immediately knowing what she's talking about, I search her eyes for confidence in her decision. I wet my lips, tasting residual sugar on my tongue and reach up and rub my thumb across her cheek. "Me either," I whisper in case she has any doubt. Her breath hitches, but her eyes stay on mine as I settle my hand at the nape of her neck.

A small panic rushes through me. Whether it's for me or her, I'm not sure. I lean in close enough to feel her warm breath on my lips. Before I can capture it with a kiss, she pulls away, sliding out of my grasp.

There's hardly enough time for me to process before she has her knees pulled tightly to her chest, her eyes trained on the fabric of her dress.

"Soph?"

Silence.

Hooking my finger under her chin, I raise her gaze to meet mine. The tip causes one of the tears floating in her eyes to fall. "Hey," I say softly, pulling her to me. She resists, then concedes, twisting how she sits and letting me hold her. "What's wrong?"

In her silence, my eyes flicker to the movement on the drive-in screen but quickly settle back on my view of her cuddled into my chest. I smooth my hand over her hair, slowly and consistently until the slight shake of her body stops.

"I'm scared," she whispers.

"Of what?"

Silence again.

Pressing her away from me, I encourage her to look at me again with my hand locked on her neck. "To kiss me?"

She nods. "What if . . ."

I give her space to continue.

"What if I mess it up? What if I suck? What if you don't like me anymore?"

Taking a deep breath, I stroke my thumb across her cheek, and I don't miss the way she leans into my touch. I'm nervous too, but I know I'm the one who needs to reassure her. "You're not going to suck. It's mostly natural instinct. You'll know what to do without even thinking about it."

Her eyes search mine for sincerity. "I heard you and Troy talking once. About this girl you kissed. You said it sucked. And you've kissed a lot of girls."

She's not wrong. I could probably count if I thought hard about it, but I don't even have a guess off the top of my head. "Soph," I hold back a chuckle, "It sucked because I wasn't into her. And it doesn't matter how many girls I've kissed. None of them are you."

"How can you say that when you don't know if I'm any good?" Her voice is still weak.

As worried as she is, I'm not concerned in the least. "I have enough confidence for both of us, but let's wait until you feel it too. It's okay," I reassure her. I've waited this long. I can wait longer.

"I'm sorry," she mumbles, another tear slipping down her pretty face. I brush it away, the wetness rolling down my thumb.

"No reason to be. Come here." I lay back, tugging her with me until we are on our sides, facing each other.

I tuck a stray curl behind her ear, leaving my hand to rest on her neck. Her hand lands softly on my hip, and she twists the fabric of my shirt between her fingers. "Thank you."

"You don't have to thank me. You should never do anything you're uncomfortable with. I just want you to feel the confidence I think you're worthy of." She nods, a little more accepting of the situation. I kiss her forehead and relax into my previous position, fingers woven into her hair, eyes locked on her. "I'm happy we're here, together, regardless of what we do or don't do."

My shirt stops twisting against my skin, and her hand flattens against my side. Then, she presses her lips against mine.

Her lips are soft, and the smell of her flowery body spray invades the space around us. It's perfect. A little surprised, I pull back slightly to gauge her reaction but don't loosen my hold on her. Her brown eyes reflect the movie I forgot was playing, and before I have a chance to check in, her fingers gravitate to the strings of my hoodie, pulling me back to her by the tug on my neck. She kisses me again once, softly. Then, as if she's done this a hundred times before, she presses against my mouth, her lips parting just enough to give me better access to her. Our tongues tangle, and it's sweet. In how she tastes. In how she moves in sync with me. It's like everything around us fades away, and it's just me and her, like this is how it's supposed to be.

We keep kissing, for who knows how long–neither one of us wanting to break the kiss. We only get the first one once, and I don't want it to end. I'm so damn hooked on this girl already. Maybe I always have been.

She pulls back first, but only enough that our lips could still brush if I leaned in at all. It's so dark I can hardly see her, but I feel her smile before she speaks. "That was easier than I thought it would be."

I chuckle, brushing my thumb across her cheek. "Everything is easy with you."

"So, it wasn't bad for you? Remember, you promised to give me a second chance if it was." She's dead serious as if she doesn't know she just ruined me for any other girl with that one kiss.

"Sophie, I'm going to kiss you, a lot more than one more time, but it's not because you need another chance. You're perfect." I whisper the last words against her lips before I kiss her again, just once.

When I pull back, she looks so relaxed, happy and comfortable being here with me. I wish I could bottle up the way I'm making her feel at this moment so she could always feel that way.

"Hey, Coop?" she asks, pulling me from my thoughts.

"What's up?"

"I have no idea what movie we are watching."

I laugh again, searching my brain in an attempt to recall something besides that kiss. "*Neighbors 2.*"

"Oh, I wanted to see this movie." Her words don't match the lack of sincerity in her tone.

"Well, we can watch it now," I say, having no idea how far into it we are.

"Maybe just a little bit." She leans against the pillows and holds out her hand. "Nerds Rope, please!"

I chuckle as I make sure our still half full packs of Fun Dip sugar are out of the way before grabbing her a rope and lying down next to her. She pulls the candy from my hand, but before unwrapping it, she looks at me, then scoots over until there's no space between us. I maneuver my arm until it's around her, and she falls onto my chest as if that place was made for her. I don't watch a single minute of the movie. I watch *her* as she eats her candy, as she snuggles into me, as she falls asleep–already counting down the days until I move into my own place, and we can do this all the time.

13

COOPER

THEN

"Today is such a good day," Sophie tells me as I help her into the passenger seat of my car. I reach across her with the strap and click the buckle in place. "You don't have to do that, you know." She giggles.

"I'm not that chivalrous. It's just another excuse to get close enough to kiss you." One hand on the center console, I slide the other against her face, brushing my thumb over her cheek before pressing my lips to hers. She smiles into the kiss, not bothering to respond any other way. I fucking love that I can kiss her now. I know it's only been a week, but being in a relationship with Sophie is like taking all the best parts of our friendship and making it better with stolen kisses during all the other things we'd usually do. It's the best case scenario for sure. "I could do this every day."

"Me too," she sighs, her smile as bright as the midday sun shining through my moonroof. Each day of this first week of summer break has been equally similar as they are perfect. We've been skateboarding in the mornings. Sophie makes us a charcuterie board for lunch. We've gone to our favorite diner a few times too. This afternoon she was reading her book while I played my video game. The weight of her head on my lap instead of on the other side of the couch was the piece to our relationship I didn't realize I was missing. My talking to the TV and aggressive touch on the controller above her head didn't bother her. Every so often she'd glance up at me, and I'd miss a Madden play staring right back. But after an hour she asked if we could take a drive. "Where should we go?"

"Hmm." I consider where today's drive could take us as I walk to the driver's side and slide in. "We can go toward all the wineries?"

"Okay," she agrees as I back out of the driveway.

Fifteen minutes later, we're on the outskirts of town, where stoplights don't exist and there's nothing but trees and farm land on either side of the road. I glance over, Sophie staring at the blurred green out the window. Today's sundress is plain and the same light blue as the sky behind her. Zac Brown Band gives her a soundtrack as her hand surfs the wind waves bringing a cool breeze through the car. "What's up, Soph?" It seems like something is on her mind.

She pulls her hand inside the car, turning toward me. "Thanks for always driving us everywhere. I feel bad that I can't."

"It's not a big deal." I reach over, my hand landing on the soft skin above her knee, and she gives me a reluctant half smile.

"I know. But I still wish I could drive."

"Did you ask your mom about taking you this week?"

"Yeah. She told me to ask Dad again. That he wants to be the one to teach me."

"I haven't seen him around much lately."

"He's been working a lot. But even if he wasn't I feel like he would come up with another excuse. I think he just doesn't want me to have my license. He keeps asking me what my rush is."

"Maybe he isn't ready for his little girl to grow up?"

"Yeah, maybe. It feels like more than that, though. Like he doesn't think I could handle it. Or I don't know."

"Do you think you could handle it?"

"Yes."

"Let's see then." I slow to nearly a stop then turn down the dirt road dividing two pieces of farmland and throw my hazard lights on.

"Wait what?" Sophie's eyes widen as she looks at me.

"I'm going to teach you how to drive."

"What? No. You can't do that. I don't know how to drive."

I chuckle. "Exactly the point. You have to learn somehow."

"I don't know, Coop."

"Don't you trust me?" The magic words that get her every time.

She sighs, knowing their power too.

"Come over here," I wave her over as I step out of my car. She hesitantly makes her way to me, kicking up dust as she drags her not-so-white-anymore Chuck Taylor's through the dirt. I can't help but chuckle as she reaches me. I pat the leather seat, and she climbs onto it. "We'll go slow. Don't worry." The road in front of us is two car lengths wide and straight as far as I can see. I also don't spot any other cars. I'm not concerned.

She nods but bites into her lower lip as she takes in everything on the dash.

"You don't have to stress about all of those lights. Right now just focus on the steering wheel, and the gas and brake." I point. "That pedal on the right is the gas. The one on the left is the brake. But you'll use your right foot for both."

"Why don't you use your left foot to brake?" This girl questions everything.

Chuckling, I adjust the seat forward a little. "I have no idea." Jogging around to the passenger side, I get in and turn off the music. "Okay, so when you're ready to go, press down on the brake. Then you'll move this." I lightly toggle the shifter. "Into drive. That little 'D.' We might move a tiny bit when your foot comes off the brake even before you press the gas." I try to proactively think of anything that might freak her out. "It also doesn't take too much pressure to go forward, especially since we aren't going fast."

She nods.

"Are you ready?"

She stares at me, eyes wide, then they soften as she smiles. "I need a kiss first."

Wetting my lips, I grin, leaning over the console to give her what she wants. "Okay, are you ready now?"

She nods. Looking at her feet, she makes sure her foot is perfectly positioned over the brake before she presses down. Once she's satisfied we won't move, she adjusts the shifter into drive. She hesitates, and I don't rush her. A moment later, I watch her foot slide toward the gas. Before she even presses on it, my car moves ever so slightly. Her foot flies back to the brake, the urgency in her movement rattling us more than anything. I bite back a laugh, not wanting her to think I'm making fun of her.

She looks over at me, the contrast stark between my black steering wheel and how white her fingers are from gripping it so hard. "You got this, Soph. Try again."

Eyes back on her feet, she moves from the brake to the gas, this time completing the task. We jerk forward when she presses too hard, her body tensing with panic as she slams on the brakes again. This time the whole car shakes.

"I'm sorry," she whispers, her hands shaking.

"It's okay. Hey. Look at me." She looks at her foot again first to make sure it's on the brake. I push the shifter into park and she relaxes a bit before letting her gaze meet mine. "Come here." I hook my finger and curl it toward me, motioning her closer until she twists in her seat. When she's close enough, I kiss her, holding my lips on hers until I can feel her body relax. This past week, I realized love kisses seem to work even more quickly than love hugs.

"Okay. I'm ready," she says confidently as she returns to the correct position. Shifting back to drive, this time when she presses on the gas we crawl forward without jerking at all.

"See!" I try to contain my enthusiasm so it doesn't distract her. She smiles, biting into her lip, not taking her eyes off the dirt road.

"I'm doing it! I'm driving!" she squeals, her grips still tight on the wheel and her focus locked on the road.

"Told you you could. Proud of you."

She continues down the road, consistently between ten and fifteen miles per hour. After about a mile, we come up to a house, and she stops. "Okay, you turn us around. And then I want to know what all these lights are for."

"Okay." I grin.

"Thanks for this, Cooper."

Experiencing life with this girl just became my favorite thing. "Anything for you."

14

SOPHIE

Now

Cooper, 21; Sophie, 18

Leaning against the back of the couch in the front room, I try to manifest Cooper pulling into the driveway next door. Our flight didn't land in Eugene until late last night, and I've been debating how to contact him all day.

As if the Universe is on my side for once, a black 4Runner pulls into the Montgomery's driveway. A flash of the memory of Cooper teaching me how to drive two and a half years ago pops into my head. A smile at the recollection and a surge of panic war with themselves. I'm nervous, but I don't want to miss this opportunity. He can't hang up when he's in front of me, like he did on our FaceTime call four days ago. I pull my phone from the coffee table.

Me: *Meet me at our spot?*

Me: *Please.*

I stare at our text thread full of one-sided blue bubbles from when I tried to convince him to call me back while I was in Honduras. The typing dots appear almost immediately and continue long enough for me to flip through all the different scenarios in my head.

Cooper: *Ok.*

I try to run through my speech, but the only thought in my head is wondering how hummingbirds can even breathe when their heart beats this fast. Somehow I make it to the woods behind our houses, reaching our chairs before Cooper. A little yellow bird chirps from where she's perched on the feeder, unbothered by my presence. "Hey, Sunshine," I say softly, and she chirps again.

"Hey." Cooper's voice comes from behind me, and I spin in the dirt to face him. My heart goes from a hundred miles an hour to flatline when I see him in front of me.

"Coop. Hey."

"What's up?" His hands are shoved into his hoodie pocket, and he remains a few feet away.

"Umm, I was hoping we could talk."

"Okay. About what?"

"About us."

He hesitates. "You meant what you said? That you were coming back to me?" There's a war in his eyes between hopefulness and skepticism.

"Yes, of course I did. I'm done playing games with us. I want to be with you."

He takes a step toward me, and my heart flutters. "I–"

"Sophie! JT is here!" My stomach lurches, knocking the flutter from my chest, as my dad yells from the back porch. *What the hell is JT doing here?* Feeling the blood drain from my face, my eyes shoot to his voice out of instinct, but I quickly look back at Cooper.

"Of fucking course," he mutters under his breath and starts to walk away from me.

"Cooper, wait," I beg. Sunshine's chirp pierces the air as if she's on my side, wanting him to stay too. My eyes flash to where she's perched on the edge of the red feeder before they're back on Cooper.

"What, Sophie?" His anger sends a shot of pain that I feel *everywhere* in my weakening body.

"I had no idea he was coming over."

He scoffs. "Sure you didn't. When are you going to stop lying and just admit that when you said you didn't want a boyfriend right now, what you really meant is that you didn't want me?"

"No–"

He inhales deeply, his eyes closing for the moment. "Look, I understand you're not ready to let go of what I did, and you have every right to be upset. But I didn't expect the process of forgiving me to involve you hooking up with other guys. I was willing to give you time, but I can't watch you be with someone else."

"But Cooper," I beg again, wanting to explain the situation, wanting him to know I'm not choosing JT over him. Anyone else would always just be a placeholder.

"I'm not your boyfriend, Sophie, so this," he flails his hand in chaotic circles in front of me, "is not my problem. *You* are not my problem anymore. Seriously, Sophie. Go." The growl in his voice implies he actually means *fuck off*.

Watching him slip away from me jams up my thoughts. "No . . . he's just . . . Dad must have invited him over," I stumble over my words.

He holds my gaze for a moment. I'm frozen, not knowing what to say or how to make this better. He shakes his head and walks away, leaving me standing there calling out after him.

Arranging the charcuterie board mindlessly, I observe my dad and JT sitting on the couch, deep in conversation about the football game on TV. Mom ran to the store, so I'm standing here awkwardly, unsure how to act. I invited JT to a football game with us before Thanksgiving–as friends. He and Dad hit it off so well that I guess Dad invited him over to watch the away game today. Since my family has been in Central America for the past week, this is the first time I've seen JT since we slept together. I don't want to see him. I definitely don't want Dad forming some kind of bond with him, but he seems set on it considering he somehow got ahold of him without even asking me.

JT glances over his shoulder like he can sense me thinking about him, and when he catches me staring he shoots a wink my way before turning back to my dad. It feels like I've been inserted into a movie scene that I don't belong in, and I wonder for the hundredth time how I ended up here.

When my dad abandons his spot on the couch–probably to get beer from the cooler in the garage–JT makes his way to me in the kitchen. "Hey, Squirrel," he says, reaching for an apple chunk from my board on the kitchen island next to me and plopping it in his mouth. He's been so occupied by my dad, I've hardly been near him since he arrived.

"Hey," I whisper. I don't like that he's invaded this aspect of my life, a place that only feels right for Cooper.

Bracing one hand against the island, and shoving the other through my curls, he pulls my lips to his. I lose my breath from the way his kiss catches me off guard. It's different from the way it's hard to breathe when Cooper's lips touch mine. I push the thought of my ex away, feeling my blood pump through my veins thinking about how he didn't even give me the chance to talk to him. He's been waiting for me to forgive him, and now that I'm ready, he doesn't want to hear it. Annoyed by Cooper's hot and cold, and not having the energy to argue more right now, I lean into JT's kiss, my hands pressing into his chest–it's a good kiss.

He pulls back slightly before kissing me softly once more then brings his lips to my ear. "Mmm, I can't wait for the things I'm going to do to you later." Yeah, that's not going to happen, but I'll make that clear on his way out the door. His hand trails down my back until he squeezes my ass. Giving it a light tap, he turns back to my cheese board as if the past few minutes didn't happen.

"This looks good, Squirrel. Thank you. Are you coming to watch the game with us?"

"Yeah." I give him my best smile, hoping he can't tell I'm faking it.

15

COOPER

NOW

As soon as Sophie retreats to her house, sliding the glass door behind her, I turn back to the woods. I'm not ready to go inside and get the third degree from my mom. For some reason, she's been asking how things between Sophie and me are a lot more than usual.

My phone buzzes in my pocket, and I pull it out, assuming it's Troy telling me he's on his way over to watch the game. A picture of Sophie skateboarding when she was sixteen lights the screen. She's wearing my favorite pink sundress, looking over her shoulder, smiling at me, reaching out her hand which was holding mine as we glided down the street by our houses. How did we get from *that* to *this*?

I decline the call. A few seconds later her text comes through.

Sophie: *Please, can we talk after the game? You're misunderstanding things.*

I toss my phone onto Sophie's pink chair and sink into my blue one, the hinge held together with duct tape. Why does everything have to be ten times harder than it should be with us? It used to be so easy. I stare mindlessly into the trees, only distracted by the flicker of movement from Sunshine abandoning her perch on the birdhouse and leaving me alone.

I stay outside–hoping the fresh air will clear my head–until Troy gets here. Making my way back inside, I glance at the Porter's house. Through the kitchen window, I can see Sophie standing next to the island doing something–probably making a cheese board for the game. She loves those things. I should go talk to her. I don't see JT, so maybe she was being honest. Maybe he is there to see her dad.

With my first step toward her house, JT comes into my line of sight. I freeze. They are just talking. Maybe she did tell the truth.

Then I watch him take a step closer to her.

I watch his hand grip her neck and pull her to him.

I watch them kiss.

And I watch Sophie lean into it.

Me: *I'm not misunderstanding anything.*

Searching for the nearest thing I can break, I pick up my blue chair. A loud crack echoes through the trees as it snaps against the wood, the duct tape I had used on its previous break no longer holding it together.

Leaving my chair in shambles, I walk away from it and the small thread of hope I had for our relationship. Even though we didn't define it, I thought we were on a break. Clearly I've been in denial. If she's not serious about us, I refuse to be serious about her. With a new determination, I plan my focus for anything besides the image of Sophie kissing someone else and catching her in a lie. I'll ask Dad for more responsibility at work. I'll spend more time with my little brother in the fraternity and pick up extra volunteer hours. What I need to do is go fuck another girl. Eventually, I'll forget about everything Sophie and I could have been if she had meant what she said.

16

SOPHIE

THEN

Cooper, 18; Sophie, 16

"Morning, Mom!" Skipping the bottom two steps, I jump onto the kitchen floor and skip toward her. The front door clicks open in the entryway behind me, and I assume it's Cooper without looking to check. Excitement bubbles inside me like a book release day for my favorite author, anxious to immerse myself in a new story. "Where's Dad?"

"He's getting ready for work. You're up early too and in a good mood," she notes.

I can't help my bright smile as Cooper walks into the kitchen, leaning against the island next to me. "Good morning, ladies."

"It's moving day!" I tell my mom. "Coop and Troy got the keys to their new house. I'm going to help them." I already checked to see if it was okay a few days ago, but I remind her anyway.

"It's so strange with all the boys gone now." Cooper is the last of the four to move out. Troy lived in the fraternity house his freshman year, but now that Cooper is starting college, they are moving into one of Mr. Montgomery's investment properties. The college kids that were living in it just graduated, so now they get the whole summer to adjust to their new place. "Sounds fun. Let me know if you need help with anything," she says to Cooper but then turns to me. "Be home by 10:30, please."

My excitement shifts to confusion. "I've never had a curfew before."

"You've never had a boyfriend before." She shoots me a pointed stare, and Cooper chuckles as I roll my eyes.

"Boyfriend?" Dad enters the kitchen through the hallway, briefcase in hand. His glare pins on Cooper before shifting to me. Both of us freeze. We never said anything to him, not the way Cooper talked to Mom. I thought she'd say something for us.

My mom takes the lead. "We talked about this the other day, Jack."

He grumbles. "Right. Be home by ten."

"But Mom just said 10:30," I whine.

"She'll be back by then, Mr. Porter," he assures him, grabbing my hand and tugging me toward the front door. "Come on, *girlfriend*." He grins, unfazed by my dad's remarks. I let it go too.

Girlfriend. I've never been called that before, but hearing Cooper say it is so dreamy. God, he's cute. I can't believe he's mine.

I snap my seatbelt into place, but before I can face forward again, Cooper's lips are on mine. It's been two weeks since we first kissed, and we've kissed a million more times since then. I always wondered if the characters in my books got tired of kissing so much. I don't think they do, at least not if it's anything like kissing Cooper. Kissing him is satisfying in a way I didn't know was possible. It gives me that feeling I've always turned to reading for, an exciting escape from the mundane.

"Cooper." I swat at him playfully as I pull back from our kiss. "We have places to be and things to do!"

"I'd rather do you." He smirks, turning on his car and moving his hand to the back of my seat as he checks to make sure we're clear to back out of the driveway. We haven't had sex. We haven't done anything except kiss. I don't know if I'm nervous because I'm not ready or just because I have no idea what I'm doing. Luckily, Cooper hasn't pushed me.

"I don't think Troy would appreciate that," I tease.

"Hey, don't speak for him," he jokes. "He probably wants an excuse to be alone with Emily now that he's out of the fraternity house."

"Is she going to be there today?" I try to hide the disdain in my voice.

"Tell me how you really feel about her." Cooper laughs.

"She's fine. I just think Troy can do better."

"Is that so?" He doesn't disagree but doesn't add his opinion either. I think he's trying to refrain from saying anything bad about his best friend's serious girlfriend. She's fine, she's just not someone I enjoy spending time with if I have the choice, and I think she takes Troy for granted.

"Don't get any ideas, though. *You* can absolutely not do any better." I stick my tongue out at him.

"I know." His voice is much more serious than mine was as he slides his hand against my thigh, stroking my soft skin with his thumb. He's completely kept his hands from wandering below my waist since we decided to be more than friends. I love that he's being respectful and following my lead, but having that control feels like a lot of pressure.

As his thumb rubs against my thigh, a new sensation washes over me, an ache for him to move higher. A trickle of heat to my core reflexively makes it tighten. *Whoa.*

"What's that look on your face for?" His voice startles me.

"Nothing," I manage to mumble, crossing my legs and forcing his hand still.

"Are you okay?"

"Mhmm. Oh look, we are here!" He puts his car in park in the driveway and raises an eyebrow at me.

I swing my door open and hop out, nearly crashing into Cooper's dad with my redirected excitement. "Whoooa, Sophie. Don't start too strong. Your energy needs to last us all day." He laughs.

"Sorry, Mr. Montgomery."

Cooper meets me where I'm at, and as soon as his dad walks out of our line of sight with a box of things from his G-Wagon, I'm pinned against the car. Cooper presses his lips against mine, one of his hands on the nape of my neck and the other gripping the fabric of my dress at my hip. His kiss is more intense than usual, my body heating as his tongue swipes across my lip until I give him the access he requests.

When he breaks our kiss, I'm nearly out of breath. Pulling back from my lips, he leans to whisper in my ear, "Just wanted to make it clear that you have the same effect on me that I seem to have on you."

Damn him for being able to read me so well. "I have no idea what you're talking about, Cooper Allen Montgomery." I flutter my eyelashes and spin out of his grip before skipping into the house.

Cooper's mom, Melissa, and I spent most of the day helping the boys make their house how they wanted it–plain and colorless, with only the necessities. To them, that means beds, dressers, TVs, video games and all thirteen of Cooper's signs with funny sayings he insisted we hang around the kitchen. The one I got him today as a house warming present hangs on the wall in between the kitchen and the living room. It's black and white and says, "Education is important, but football is importanter." He was so excited, going on about how well I know him. I'm not sure I'm anything special. He's not that hard to please, but I'm happy to be the one to do it.

By the time the signs are hung, furniture is assembled, boxes are unpacked, we've gone to Target twice–after convincing the boys they needed to own a set of dishware instead of a Costco sized pack of paper plates–and ate dinner, it's 7 p.m. Cooper's parents left a few minutes ago, and Troy and Emily disappeared into Troy's room. I'm finishing loading the dishwasher when Cooper calls me from his room.

"Sophiiieeee."

I dry my hands on one of the new black kitchen towels before making my way to Cooper's new space. I've been in his room at his parents' house a few times, but it's never been a place we hang out. This feels different. The only things in here right now are his bed frame and bed with new navy blue bedding and his dresser that doubles as a TV stand.

As soon as I walk through the door, Cooper pulls me into his arms and steps us backward a few paces before reaching out and shoving the door hard enough for it to click closed. "Finally, I have you all to myself."

I smile against his lips. I can't believe two weeks ago I had never kissed anyone, and now it's one of my favorite things. Though, it might have something to do specifically with Cooper. It's insane it took us so long to take this step in our relationship. It feels so natural being together. "We have our own space now. I'm excited."

"Oh yeah? What do you want to do with our new freedom?" He grins, pulling away to flick on the TV and turn off the lights. "Our show isn't on for another two hours. Oh. I saw *That Awkward Moment* got added to Netflix. I know how much you like Zac Efron," he teases.

"I had that poster when I was twelve. Are you ever going to let me live it down?" I roll my eyes.

"Nope," he pops the P. "Never." He grins before backing me up to his bed. My body sinks into the mattress as he lowers me onto it. He hovers over me, framing my face as he leans on his forearms–his hot football player forearms.

"Well, I have a new crush now," I flirt, looking up at him. "And I'm hoping he wants to do more than watch a movie." I don't know why it's so easy for me to be more bold around Cooper. All the glances he's been sneaking at me all day and flashes of his fingers running over my thigh this morning are probably fueling my desire too. How much he wants me makes me want him that much more.

"I love how you are around me," he whispers against my lips before he kisses me.

"Me too. Hey, Coop?" I run my fingers over the hem of his T-shirt, my heart racing.

"Hmm?" The sound vibrates against my lips in another kiss.

"Ummm . . ."

He rolls onto the bed, propping himself up on his arm as I turn slightly toward him. He reaches to tuck a fallen curl behind my ear then rubs his thumb across my cheek. I feel so safe with him, so comfortable. He doesn't push me to say whatever's on my mind. He just waits patiently now that he's realized I have something serious to say.

"This morning . . . in the car . . . you had your hand on my leg."

"Was that okay?" he worries. "I've done it a few times, I think."

"Yeah . . . it's just, this time felt different."

"Different how?"

"I think I'm ready." I pause. "For more." I hope he catches my drift. "Are you?"

"If you're sure you are," he answers without hesitation. "What do you want?"

"Umm. I don't know." My voice is hardly audible above the banter on the TV. "Maybe for you to touch me." Nerves ricochet around my stomach, the moving light on the screen flickering across his face. "Can we start there?"

"Have you done that before? You know, with yourself?"

I shake my head and feel my cheeks heat.

"Don't you ever get turned on by your books?" He speaks like this conversation doesn't make him uncomfortable at all. It makes me feel more brave about it.

"Yeah, a little . . . but . . ."

"But what?"

"I don't know. I've never experienced it, so maybe I can't relate enough yet."

"You weren't curious enough to try on your own?"

I focus on where my fingers still play with the hem of his T-shirt.

"You can tell me, Soph," he whispers as he uses his thumb under my chin to draw my focus back to his piercing blue eyes.

"I just imagine what it'll be like if you're touching me." He bites into his lip at my words. "I feel like it'll be so much better than if I tried it myself," I add, shifting my gaze to the mattress.

He groans into the kiss he presses to my lips. "God, Sophie, I want you so badly."

He kisses me softly once before he deepens it, his tongue urgently tangling with mine. He's still propped up on one arm, partially hovering over me, his fingers whispering along the strap of my sundress as we makeout, leaving a trail of goosebumps in their wake. He squeezes my breast lightly, a deeper ache for him flowing through me. His hand continues down my body, stopping to squeeze my hip as he scrunches a handful of my dress, pulling it up my leg slightly. When I bite into his lip, he groans again and pushes my dress up. His hand falls to my thigh, running up my skin until it catches on the edge of my pink cotton underwear. I'm glad I finally convinced my mom to buy me cute ones–pastel colored with a thin strip of lace around the edge. He hooks his finger in it, then pauses, breaking our kiss.

When I open my eyes, he's staring at me. "Are you sure about this?" he rasps, his breath ragged from the intensity of our kissing.

I nod slowly, looking into his perfect blue eyes. "I trust you, Cooper. More than anyone." My own words come out on uneven breaths.

Those words do him in more than any of my previous ones. He tugs on the end of my panties, and I help him kick them off, my heart rate climbing even more. His hand runs up my thigh again, this time his thumb grazing my skin further up than he ever has before. His touch is so soft. It doesn't tickle, but I don't know how else to describe it. All I want is for him to move his hand higher, but every time he does, my heart stutters in my chest.

"Promise you'll tell me if you want me to stop," he whispers, and I can sense a little nerves in his voice.

"I promise."

"And if I'm hurting you."

"You'll never hurt me, but I promise."

With that assurance, his lips meet mine again, and in the next instant, his thumb swipes over me. My breath catches in our kiss. His finger rubs small circles against me, a tingling sensation I've never felt before shooting through my body, heightened from the one this morning. My hand reaches along the side of his face until my fingers are threaded through his hair, pulling him deeper into our kiss.

He's gentle as he presses his middle finger against my entrance. I roll my hips into him on instinct, and the tip of his finger slips barely inside me. My breath catches enough that it breaks our kiss.

"You okay?" His voice is soft and soothing but laced with concern. He withdraws his finger but doesn't break contact.

I nod. "Keep going." As soon as the words leave my lips, he slides back inside me, a little further than the last time. I'm surprised by how wet I am. It's such a strange feeling. Cooper's finger pulls back again before he pushes all the way inside me this time. I moan into our kiss. He goes slow at first, pulling out and pushing back into me. Holy sensations. Tingles spark through me from the inside out. He speeds up a little and pressure builds in my stomach. He slows down again, curling his finger inside of me like he's getting more comfortable with what he's doing. Whatever spot he hits sends a rush of pleasure through me. "This feels so good, Cooper," I whisper.

He kisses me harder but stays steady with whatever magic he's doing. I feel his finger working inside of me and the palm of his hand rubbing against me. Suddenly, my body is on fire, an all consuming rush of heat flowing through me without warning. I break our kiss, biting into my lip, overwhelmed with this feeling. It's so good, so strong. I can feel myself tightening around Cooper's finger, and I wonder if he can feel it too. He groans against my skin, kissing my neck, his finger pumping in and out of me slowly.

What I'm assuming is an orgasm seems to last both forever and only a few seconds. I miss the feeling as soon as it's gone, but crave finding another way to get closer to Cooper. Still breathless, I press my lips to his, willing to deprive myself of the oxygen I need. His finger slides out of me and the second it does, I run my hands under his shirt and up his back as I press my body into his.

Cooper snakes his arm under me, breaking our kiss but pulling me into a hug, squeezing me tight to his chest. "How do you feel?" His eyes search mine as if he'll find the answer in them.

"Not let down by the hype," I say with a content sigh.

He laughs, and it vibrates through me. "Happy to hear it." He pauses before whispering into my hair, "Thank you for trusting me, Sophie," and holds me for longer than twenty seconds. I don't have to count anymore, and that might be my favorite part.

17

COOPER

THEN

When I pull in my parent's driveway, both theirs and the Porter's garage doors are open. Perfect. I grab my skateboard where it rests in the wall mount my dad made. I've been living at my new house for about a month now, but it's still strange not being able to walk next door to see Sophie. Making my way across the stepping stones between the houses, I spot Sophie's board in plain sight, leaning against the wall in the corner. I pick it up and carry both to the front door and knock.

A few seconds later, Sophie answers, a book in her hand, the page she's on marked with her finger pinched between the sheets. A smile lights her face the moment she registers it's me. "Hi. Did we have plans today?" Her face scrunches, searching her memory for something she forgot.

"No, but I wanted to see my girlfriend." The past few years, we usually spent an hour together each day outside of driving to and from school. It usually involved one of us studying because I was always busy with my other friends and football. But it was enough to keep our friendship strong. Now an hour isn't nearly enough. And if I go a day without seeing her, I can't stand it. I've seen her almost every day for the past six weeks since her birthday. Funny how you can find more time for someone when you want to. "Do you want to skate?"

"Yes, please." She retreats a few steps to the couch, picking up her bookmark which is a photo strip of the two of us making funny faces. It's from Troy's cousin's wedding last summer. I took Sophie as my date because Troy brought Emily. I didn't want to be a third wheel, but I didn't want another girl to read anything into it. I knew I'd have fun with Sophie, and once I convinced her to dance with me, we had a blast. I think that was the first time I ever thought about kissing her. At the time I chalked it up to love being in the air.

She slides the makeshift bookmark between the pages and sets her book on the arm of the couch before coming back to the door and sitting on the floor to lace up her white Chuck Taylors. Her dress rides up a bit as she bends her knee to slip the shoe on, and my dick practically jumps to life.

I promised myself I'd be as patient as I needed to be with her. We might have started our relationship at the same level sexually, but she's still over two years younger than I am, and I don't want to push her to do something she isn't ready for. It's been fun getting to know her body slowly over the past month since the first time I fingered her. She hasn't returned the favor yet, but I don't mind. She gains confidence each time I touch her, and I love that we get to do this together.

She finishes tying her shoes–lucky for me, without catching my ogling. "Ready!" She hops up, taking her skateboard from me. The bottom of her board flashes in my direction before she tips it upright and sets it on the ground. It's covered in stickers–most of them from Sunriver from every summer we've gone to Troy's uncle's cabin. My whole family started going with Troy every year since he moved in with us, and the past few summers Sophie has tagged along when Troy brought whoever he was dating at the time. It's just now occurring to me why people have been so confused about it taking us so long to date. Everyone would probably say Troy is my best friend, but we are more like brothers. Sophie has always been my go-to person and probably knows more about me than anyone. I just think I wasn't actively aware of that.

I set my board on the driveway next to hers, our feet pushing off the ground simultaneously as we glide toward the street. We make a left without discussing it, habit taking us to the park a mile away. When we were younger, the four of us had scooters, and Sophie and I got stuck with ours–even when Dean and Carter switched to skateboards–until Troy moved in and talked Mom into getting us ones too. We've been skating ever since, mixing and matching who we go to the park with, but more often than not it ended up being Troy, Sophie and me.

Sophie pushes hard off the ground, sending her and her board catapulting down the street, the wheels scraping against the cement, and leaving me in the dust. I laugh as I half-ass try to catch up, enjoying watching her with this new appreciation I have. She looks back, and noticing I'm so far behind, she skids her shoe against the concrete, bringing her to a stop. When I reach her, she's standing with her hand reached out for mine, a huge grin plastered on her face. "You're so slow," she fake whines.

"Just admiring my view," I say, taking her hand in mine and jerking forward slightly when she kicks off the ground intensely again. I stand both feet on my board, letting her pull me as I reach for my phone in the pocket of my shorts. By the time she realizes she's doing the work for both of us, I have my photo app open. She looks over her shoulder, and I catch a picture in the split second she's smiling at me–her pink sundress fluttering in the breeze–before she rolls her eyes and drops my hand. *God, I'm obsessed with this girl.*

We skate the next half mile to the park, stopping when we get to the path in front of the pond and the playground. She watches a family of ducks float by while standing on her board. I step off mine and walk in front of her, cutting off her view. Wrapping my arms around her waist, I pick her up as I kiss her. Her board flies out from under her, and I place her feet back on the ground but refuse to break our kiss.

When she finally pulls back, I tuck her wind-blown hair behind her ear, biting into my lip and tasting her cotton candy flavored lip gloss.

"What's that look for?" she asks, taking a few steps to retrieve her board.

"I like that I can kiss you now."

"We are pretty good at it." She reaches for my hand, and I let her lead me to the swings where she commands I sit. When I do, she straddles me, not concerned at all if there's a weight limit on this thing. The metal chains hold up, the smell of them overpowering the fir trees surrounding us. I wrap my arms around her waist, rubbing my thumbs across her lower back and gently rocking us back and forth with my heels on the wood chips. "I love us together," she says with a soft smile before she kisses me.

"Me too." *So fucking much*, I add in my head. "It's going to suck not being at the same school anymore."

"It'll be okay." Her words reassure me, but her tone removes some of the believability. "It's not like we ever had classes together before or anything, you know?" I nod. "Are you sad to be done with football?"

"Not the football part. It's a lot of work, and it's not as much fun as it used to be. Plus, I'll have the fraternity events to replace it. Mostly just hoping for the same brotherhood, and a little worried it won't be."

"How come? Isn't that the point of a fraternity? To be around people who always have your back?"

"Yeah . . . they're just established already, you know? And Troy has been there a year already so he has new friends."

"I know it'll be a change, but you're the best, Coop. Confident, fearless, outgoing. There's a reason you're so popular–in a good way. Everyone genuinely loves you. Those guys would be silly not to immediately welcome you to their family."

I give her a hesitant smile. "Thanks, Soph. I hope you're right. Either way, I'll have you. Plus, I'm going to start helping at Dad's company."

"You asked him?!" Her pride immediately elevates my confidence. This transition to the "real world" and the decisions that come along with it are way out of my comfort and confidence zone. I'm not naive to the fact that I had it easy in high school. My parents didn't make me work so I could focus on football. But it's time to step up. Mom and Dad didn't get the life they've made handed to them, and I don't want it for free either. Last week Sophie role played a conversation with my dad so I could present him with the idea. It was enough to talk me into actual follow-through.

"Yup. Thanks for helping me."

"Anytime." Her smile widens as she presses her hands against my chest. "Tell me about it."

"I said everything we practiced. How I don't want a handout. I'm willing to do whatever odd jobs he needs and learn as much as possible until I can take my real estate test and become a licensed agent. I already planned on paying the fraternity fees–if I get in–and rent, of course, but I reiterated that. I don't want him to think I just want money to fuck around, you know? I'm going to get a job either way, but I really want it to be this." I tend to joke around a lot, so I want him to know how serious I am about this opportunity he's willing to give me. "He still wants me to get my degree in case I don't love real estate for some reason, but I already know I will."

"I know you will too. We should go to the diner for dinner to celebrate. I'll even let you get a chocolate shake." She presses a soft kiss to my lips, her pride transferring from her to me through the contact.

"Also." I kiss her again, not able to resist. "He said whenever my credit and finances are ready, I can buy mine and Troy's house from him as my first investment property. Cool, huh?"

"So cool! I'm excited for you. You're going to be so great, and I knew your dad would agree. Plus, you can talk anyone into anything."

"*Anyone* into *anything*?" I raise an eyebrow. The way she's straddling me on this swing forced her dress to bunch around her waist. Thank god no one else is around. I run my hands up her thighs and rest them on her hips.

She giggles as my lips brush the skin on her neck. "Okay, maybe not *anything*." She moves her hands from the swing chain to my nape, playing with the hair at my neck as she kisses me, making me forget anything else but her exists. When she pulls back, she's more serious.

"It's okay that we haven't had sex yet, right?" The stress emanating from her body is enough to make me dig my heels into the ground, stopping our slow swing.

"Of course it's okay, Soph. I'd be lying if I said I don't think about it. My girlfriend is banging and is constantly turning me on. But there's no rush. It'll happen when you're ready, and then we can make up for all the time we waited." I smirk.

"Okay." She's still hesitant.

"Do you not believe me?"

"No, I do. It's just . . . I overheard some of Troy's friends talking at our Fourth of July party a couple of weeks ago."

This can't be good.

"One of them was talking about having sex in the bathroom at a party with some girl he didn't know. Another said he got a blow job from two different girls on the same night."

I've hung out with Troy's new friends a few times during his first year of college. They are fun, but their idea of a good time doesn't always align with mine. It's part of what has me concerned for the fraternity. "So . . . what are you saying?"

"I don't know, I'm not like that."

"Neither am I. I don't want to just fuck in a bathroom, Sophie." I pause. "Okay, maybe that's something we can do someday." *Wait.* "Is that why we ended up sneaking away before the fireworks?" I only fingered her, something I'd already done a few days earlier when I moved into my house, but my stomach drops at the thought of her feeling she *had* to do something.

She refocuses her gaze on where we connect on the swing. "Kind of."

The air feels like it's sucked from my lungs. "Sophie." I grip her face between my hands. "I would never want you to do something you don't want."

"I know. I still wanted to do it on my own. I'm comfortable with the step we took. I'm just worried the things I'm ready for won't be enough when you could have so much more."

I force her chin up with my thumbs so she's looking at me. "There is nothing I want more than you."

Her head falls to my chest and she nods against it. "Thanks, Coop," is all she says as I wrap my arms around her, resuming a slow swinging motion. A knot forms in the pit of my stomach, and knowing we have a party coming up with those same guys, I have a feeling it isn't going to untangle anytime soon.

18

COOPER

THEN

T-minus five minutes until the first party at mine and Troy's house, and I'm almost done getting ready. The slip 'n slide unrolls a few times when I kick it, but it's more folded up than rolled so it gets caught in our uneven backyard grass. I reach down to unroll it myself, looking up when the opposite side is tugged along with mine.

A smile instantly hits my face. "Hey, Soph." I drop the tarp and cross the four feet of grass between us. I can't get enough of her and want to soak up every moment I can before school gets in the way.

"Hey, Coop," she manages to get out right before my kiss cuts her off.

I pull back to look at her. I'm already in nothing but my maroon boardshorts hanging on my hips. Sophie shamelessly takes me in in a way she's never blatantly done. She looks equally as stunning. Her bare stomach does something different to me as I take in her white jean shorts and yellow bikini top. A stream of sunlight sparkles across her body as she twists all of her hair around her hand, pulling it to one side.

"Coop, helloooooo." She waves her hand in front of my face with a giggle.

It's not until her voice breaks me out of thought that I realize I'm biting into my fist. I pull my hand away from my face and reach for her hips, thumbs smoothing over the bare skin along the hem of her shorts. "Jesus Christ, Sophie. What are you trying to do to me?"

She grins and loops her arms around my neck. "You're the one throwing a slip 'n slide party. Did you expect me to show up in something else?"

"I don't know what I thought. I can't think at all."

"You've seen me in a swimsuit before," she says, closing the remaining distance between us. The skin of our stomachs touch for the first time ever, our bodies sticking together slightly with the heat, and I internally praise the extra hot temperature for August.

"Not since I've been able to touch you." I groan.

The way she fills out her bikini top.

The way her shorts hang on her hips when they are usually covered by a dress.

My hands skim up her back, getting caught on the ties of her suit. I wish I could tug them off. The thought of seeing her completely naked for the first time is more than I can handle.

A stream of cold water from the hose hits me straight in the head, soaking me and saving me from the wet dream worthy vision in front of me. Brushing the water from my eyes, I glance up to see Troy with his thumb across the end of the hose and glare at him. "You're a dick," I yell across the yard.

"Am I, though?" He's got a shit-eating grin on his face like he knows he's my personal superhero right now. Sophie giggles as she wipes water off her face, bringing my attention back to her.

"You're going to get me into trouble, missy."

"I didn't do anything!" She laughs as she unbuttons her shorts and slips them onto the grass while keeping eye contact.

"What the hell did you do with my sweet and innocent Sophie?"

She shrugs. "You're the one who gets me the books."

"I'll buy you all the damn books you want," I tell her even though I know her newfound confidence and initiative will only take things so far for now. I'm okay with that. Well, rational Cooper is okay with that, and I need to step the fuck back from my girlfriend to prevent irrational Cooper from entering the scene.

Superheroes to my rescue once again, a car full of Troy's fraternity brothers pull up to the house. From where I'm standing on the side of the yard, I see all four doors of the beat-up white van slam shut. The hub caps are painted yellow and a bold black font on the side reads: Van-imal. Shaking my head, I realize how wild college might actually be as my new friends bound toward us in their suits.

One guy, Ethan, crashes into me like he's already drunk, his arm looping around my shoulder. "Cooper, my man." His eyes drift to Sophie. "Who do we have here?"

"No one you need to concern yourself with," I growl, shrugging him off of me.

Sophie rolls her eyes. "Sophie," she says, laughing and reaching her hand for Ethan's.

"Nice to meet you, Sophie." He shakes her hand before dropping it and pointing his thumb at me. "Don't mind this guy here. He's not a brother yet and doesn't understand we take the dicks over chicks thing seriously. But still, you're going to need to save that suit for our car wash fundraiser in a few months."

"He doesn't have anything to worry about," Sophie's words come out sweet, but it's not enough to overpower my possessiveness. Noticing, she twists more into my arms. "Coop."

"What?" I ask, eyes still on Ethan.

"Hey." This time her voice pulls my gaze hesitantly toward her. "You don't have to fight for me when I'll always be yours." She glances up at me with adoration, and my arm wraps around her waist when her head lands on my chest, her words expelling the hostility from me like an exorcism.

A girl I've yet to meet strides up to Ethan, planting a kiss on his cheek. He grins, his eyes roaming her red bikini covered body shamelessly. Turning back to us, he points his words at Sophie. "See, you'll fit right in with all our girls."

I slap him in the chest.

Ethan chuckles before yelling to no one in particular, "Alright, let's get this party started!" Danny, another of my new brothers, tosses him a beer that he immediately stabs with a car key before cracking the top and shotgunning it.

"I'm going inside really quick," Sophie whispers against the spot right below my ear before she kisses it.

"Don't forget to come back." I squeeze her hip before releasing her.

Twenty minutes go by and Sophie still hasn't returned. Walking past the open sliding glass patio door, I wonder where she is. Troy passes me, stopping me in my tracks. "Hey. Have you had anything to drink yet?"

"Not yet, why?"

"Can you run to the store and get us some ice?"

"Yeah." I hesitate, debating if I should find Sophie first or make the quick trip to the store. "I got you." I grab my keys off the counter and shoot Sophie a text letting her know I'll be back in ten minutes.

Pulling up to the house with three bags of ice, I get out of my 4Runner in time to watch a car park against the sidewalk in front of our yard. Six people pile out of the compact, and I only recognize one of them. Fuck Greg. The dude is one of Troy's best friends, but I've always thought he was a tool. When we played football together, he would always grab shoulder pads to prevent a tackle. With all the holds called, he cost us so many yards in a championship game, I lost my shit and got benched for shoving him.

I chuckle at the memory as I sling a bag of ice over my shoulder. I was so mad, Troy whistled Sophie to the field from the bleachers because my cursing and kicking the astroturf wasn't helping anyone. She forced my focus to her, giving me a pep talk and making me accept a love hug until I let it ground me. That girl has always been the one to cool me off quicker than this ice currently piled in my arms.

Where is Sophie?

Dropping the bags on the back patio, I rip open the clear plastic and dump the ice into the cooler recently restocked with beer. I haven't had anything to drink, mostly because I don't want Sophie to feel left out or uncomfortable around so many new people. I've been worried she wouldn't have fun since she's never spent time with any of these people before. Whereas I can have fun in almost any situation, she typically prefers keeping to herself. Seriously, where is she?

With his hand on one knee as he leans over the cooler, Ethan rummages for the beer he wants.

"Hey, have you seen Sophie?" I ask.

"Nope. I'm sure she's somewhere around here," he says, unbothered as he cracks the can and walks away.

Bunching the empty bags into a pile behind the cooler, I scan the backyard. No Sophie. I check the bathroom and the kitchen, both empty. Twisting the knob on my bedroom door, I open it, my stomach dropping at the sight of Sophie leaning against my headboard reading her book.

Her eyes jump from the page to me, and she chews on her lip like she's nervous about getting caught. "Hi," she whispers as I shut my door and cross the room.

I sit on the edge of the bed, confused as my hand lands on her shoulder, my thumb running across the strap of her tank top. "What's up?"

"Nothing. Just reading."

"Did you try out the slip 'n slide?"

She shakes her head.

"You were so excited about it."

"I know. But . . ."

"But what?"

"All those girls out there look so good in their swimsuits." She sighs.

"Not as good as you."

"I'm your girlfriend. You have to say that."

"No, I don't. Sophie, you're gorgeous."

"I can't help but compare myself to them. They're so confident. I'm not like that."

"You practically stripped in front of me earlier." I deadpan.

"When it was just you. I'm comfortable around you." I love that she feels that way about me, but I hate that it doesn't translate to a constant state of mind.

I pull her book from her hand, slipping her bookmark in place before resting it on the nightstand. "Come on, Soph. One run on the slide. I think once you let yourself have fun, you won't be in your head so much."

"Okay," she says, like she believes any words I say are the truth.

Pulling her to her feet, I lead her to the door. I stop in front of it, tugging at her shirt. She hesitates, then strips it over her head. When the pink fabric is in a pile on the floor, I run my thumbs over the bare skin on her sides, leaving goosebumps in their wake. Kissing her forehead, I pull back, giving her a smile that she gives right back as I take her hand in mine.

As soon as we're out the back door, Ethan's arm is around my neck. "Dude, where have you been? I need a beer pong partner."

"I'm going to slip 'n slide with Sophie."

The same girl from earlier slides into the circle. "I'll go with her," she says sweetly, taking Sophie's hand from mine.

I start to interject, but Sophie cuts me off. "Go play."

"Are you sure?"

"Positive."

Before I can respond, she's pulled away from me, and I follow Ethan toward the folding table and red Solo cups set up on the other side of the lawn.

"You have to go once with me," Sophie begs, tugging on my arm. The setting sun casts an orange glow across her body that's covered in grass and has the start of tarp burn all over her stomach and legs. Her yellow bikini is a little dirty, and her blonde hair looks almost brown, wet and matted to her head. I can't help but smile.

"Okay," I concede. I'm tired from making sure our first party won't be our last. Somehow, at least thirty people ended up here. Everyone went home a few minutes ago, exhausted from the sun and day drinking, but Sophie stopped me when I tried to turn off the hose. It's the first time I've been with her since Ethan recruited me for a game of beer pong. One game turned into three, which turned into a cornhole competition, and then I grilled hot dogs for everyone. Every chance I got, I scanned the yard for Sophie. It seems she and the red bikini girl became friends. They've been slip 'n sliding all day between sitting in the lawn chairs drinking lemonade. I almost checked on her, but every time our eyes locked, she'd smile and wave. Today was a blast, but it would have been more fun if I got to spend time with her. I turn the hose back to full blast. "Ready?"

She nods, a huge grin lighting her face. "One, two, three, GO," she screams all in the same breath before taking off in a run and diving head first into the stream of water sliding across the tarp. I take off after her, my stomach feeling every rock under the grass as the polyester rubs against my skin. I come to a stop at the end of the slide where Sophie is already sitting and waiting for me.

"I think that was one too many." She laughs, looking down and directing my gaze to her stomach that's now slightly scratched and bleeding.

"You're addicted. There was no stopping you. Are you okay?" I sit before reaching out and softly run my thumb along the skin next to her scratch. She flinches.

"Yeah, I'm good. You were right. I ended up having a lot of fun today. Thanks for letting me crash your party."

"You're never crashing," I smile at her and mean it, "because you're always invited."

I expect a smile back, but instead, this girl reaches to her bikini top to get the water out of it by squeezing her boobs. Kill me now. I douse my dick with cold water in my head.

"Can I take a shower before you take me home?" She picks a few blades of grass off her arm.

"Of course. Let's go." I stand, reaching for her hands and tugging her to her feet. I turn off the hose, leaving the rest of the cleanup for later, and lead Sophie inside. Pulling two towels from the shelf in the hall closet, I walk to set one on the bathroom counter. Bringing the other to my head, I rub it across my hair before wiping it down my chest. Sophie slips into the bathroom behind me. "Do you need to borrow clothes?"

"No, but I need you to help me with this." I glance up from where I'm drying my swimsuit to see Sophie's back toward me with her hand behind her twirling the string of her bikini between her fingers.

Groaning, the tension from missing her all day and the appeal of her tease draw me closer to her. I wrap both her hand and bikini string in my hand and lean to whisper in her ear. "You're such a tease. Do you hate me?" I'm clearly joking, but the way *hate* in regards to me and Sophie sounds rolling off my tongue makes me cringe internally. I can't imagine a world where either of us would feel that way.

She spins quickly into my arms, pulling away her hand–and effectively mine–without letting go of the string. The bow falls apart, and her top loosens. Her smile is innocent like she doesn't have any clue what she's doing. "No, I love you." My heart beats faster. She doesn't say the phrase in an "I'm in love with you" way, but rather playfully, like it doesn't even occur to her that *is* how I feel.

"You're taking advantage of the fact that I'll never tell you *no*." I allow my hands to slide up her sides but stop when I reach where the fabric is pulling away from her breasts. I haven't crossed this line yet.

"So, just say yes then," she says like it's the obvious answer as she presses her body into mine, her hands looping around my neck.

"What do you want me to say yes to?" I need to know where her line is.

"Mmm. Taking a shower with me?"

I contemplate my options: see my girlfriend naked for the first time and struggle with my restraint or not see my girlfriend naked. "And what is going to happen in said shower?" I ask as I rub my thumbs against her skin.

"Shower things." She grins. "You know, soap, hands, bodies. Come on." She takes a step backward and tugs me with her before sliding the shower curtain open. Turning around, she slips her bikini over her head and drops it on the bathroom rug by my feet. When the hell did this girl get so sexy?

She steps in and closes the curtain behind her, leaving me standing there. I run my hands down my face, digging my fingers into my eyes. When I open them, Sophie has her head barely peeking out from the curtain as she stares at me. "Do you not want to?"

"Of fucking course I want to, Sophie." I step in behind her. The steam immediately surrounds me, but it's not thick enough to prevent my view. I glance from where her bikini bottoms hang at the base of the shower valve to her naked body. My eyes roam up her legs, lean from the skating we've been doing . . . to the place I've touched but haven't really *seen*. Holy fuck. I take in her toned stomach I saw earlier in her bikini, but the way the shower water streams over it is a new level of sexy.

I can feel her eyes on me but can't bring myself to meet her gaze because mine is stuck on her boobs. I know they'll fit perfectly in my hands, but I can't bring myself to grab them. I can't stop staring at her pretty pink nipples I suddenly want between my teeth. I bite into my fist to keep from . . . I'm not sure . . . attacking her with my hands, my mouth.

"Umm. Cooper?"

I clear my throat. Why the fuck am I nervous? "Yeah?" When I finally look at her face, it's flush–whether from the heat of the shower or my gaze, I'm not sure.

She reaches for me, tugging the string of my board shorts. Once the loops fall apart she continues to pull until I close the distance between us. "I missed you today," she says as my hands fall to her hips.

Sophie's lips are close enough to kiss when I return the sentiment. Once the words are out of my mouth, I seal them with a kiss as if our simple confessions are a promise. *I always want you near me.*

Her lips leave mine to kiss the skin below my ear instead. Fuck, I love when she does that. With her hands still holding the string of my shorts, she whispers, "Touch me, Cooper. I like when you do."

Jesus. I blow out a shaky breath as her eyes lock on me before fluttering closed as she presses her lips to mine again. I groan into the kiss as her tongue sweeps across mine. Her fingers link behind my neck to pull me closer. Mine dig into the skin at the side of her thighs as hot water splashes over her shoulder between us, finally washing away some nerves. Sliding my grip to her lower back with one hand, my other wanders into its favorite territory. My fingers part her, and I toy with her entrance, teasing her. Her gasp at the contact shoots straight to my dick, immediately more restricted in my shorts. She's just as wet inside, and I slip in easily. She hasn't been insecure around me since our first kiss, but her confidence these past few weeks . . . her willingness to be vulnerable with me . . . I'm obsessed with her. With us.

I plunge my finger inside her, and she immediately grinds her hips into me, fucking my hand. The rate she's becoming comfortable is making it a challenge to not hope for the real deal soon. But for now, I'll take what I can get, and I love every fucking second of it. I add a second finger, knowing the added thickness will tip her over the edge quickly. She stops her movement, letting me take over, and she falls apart, clenching around my fingers and releasing a whimpering breath. I pull out slightly then push as deep as I can inside her. I love how she feels as I stroke her with my fingers while I put pressure on her clit with my thumb. Sophie isn't the only one getting the hang of things. It hasn't taken me long to try new things until I find what works–at least what works for her.

Her head falls to my shoulder, and I feel the added weight as she loses the strength to hold herself up after her orgasm. The shower stream hits her hair, soaking every strand that wasn't already wet as she leans into me. If the water wouldn't run cold, I could stay this way forever, my girl satisfied by my touch and wanting to be close to me.

I slide my fingers out and hold her, my hands slowly brushing up and down her back. Only a few moments go by, and I feel a tug on my shorts. It doesn't take much effort to get them off my hips even though they catch on the tent I'm pitching. I'm so turned on from seeing Sophie completely naked, from having access to every inch of her.

I don't know what is going through her head, but I need relief before I lose my mind. Her name is on the tip of my tongue as mine rolls off hers. "Cooper." She pulls back from my chest, but instead of continuing her thought, her eyes go wide as they fall to my nearly completely hard dick.

Chuckling, I tip her chin up with a hooked finger. This is the first time she's ever seen me, and depending on what happens next, it'll be the first time she's ever touched me this way. "Soph."

"Mhmm?" she asks, nerves etched into her brows.

"You don't have to do anything you don't want to."

"No. I want to," she says quickly.

"Because *you* want to, right? Not because you feel like you have to?"

"I want to." She nods. "I just . . . Can you help me? Tell me what to do. You do this all the time, right?"

"More recently," I admit as I run my fingers along her jaw and tangle them into her wet hair. "Are you sure?"

"Yes." The word sounds confident on its own, but without warning she also takes me in her hand, her delicate fingers wrapping around my length. Holy shit. My head falls forward until it's pressed against hers. She's hardly applying any pressure yet, and I can tell this is going to be way quicker than any time I've ever taken care of myself–even the times since Sophie has been the only one on my mind. "Okay, what now?" she whispers as she slowly moves her hand.

I press my free hand against the back wall of the shower to stabilize myself. "You're doing great," I praise, strengthening my grip on the back of her neck and bringing my lips to her ear. "Use more pressure. You won't hurt me."

She responds by tightening her grip the perfect amount like she knows what she's doing. I'd give her more direction, but she doesn't need it. She swipes her thumb over the tip, pre-cum helping the friction as she increases the speed of her hand.

"Jesus Christ, Sophie," I choke out.

She stops immediately, pulling her hand away from me. The loss nearly has me falling over trying to keep contact with her. "What did I do wrong?" she asks in a panic.

Grinning, I grab her hand and place it back in its previous position. "Nothing. You're perfect. Better than me."

"Oh." She smiles shyly, and I can't help but kiss her as she resumes her job. God, I love kissing her. I love everything about her–especially how she's touching me in a way no one else has. Both her speed and pressure increase, and the edge of my orgasm sneaks up on me.

"Fuck. I'm going to come," I manage. If she's anxious about this next part, she doesn't show it. A rush of pleasure shoots back into my body at an equal intensity of my cum pouring out, warm against our legs only to be washed away by the now lukewarm water. The tingly sensation that floods me is better than anything I've ever made myself feel. I can only imagine how much better sex will be.

When I start to come down, I reach for Sophie, gripping her neck on either side and crushing my mouth to hers. She smiles into the kiss. I pull back just enough to ask, "Are you sure you haven't done that before?"

She shakes her head. "All my firsts are for you, Cooper Montgomery."

19

SOPHIE

THEN

"Where do you think they are taking us tonight?" Emily asks as we slide into the black leather pedicure chairs at the salon. "I hope it's that new steakhouse."

"That place is probably so expensive," I say, reaching for the remote to turn on the massage feature of my chair.

"So? We aren't the ones paying for it." Sometimes the things she says are an automatic turn-off. She's not someone I *want* to be friends with. I only agreed to this salon appointment because we are double dating tonight, and I know it would make Cooper happy for us to get along. But I can hardly stand her. We have nothing in common. I'm not even sure she and Troy have much in common. He's way too good for her.

"I'm just excited for a real date," I respond as I click the button that makes the balls under the leather knead my back. This is easily the best part of getting pedicures. "This is my first one." Technically, Cooper and I have done things that could be considered a date, but tonight I get to dress up and go out to a restaurant where there are other people on dates too. We've mostly spent time at his house–him playing video games and me reading. We almost always take a break by skating to the nearby park or going to the diner. And kissing of course. My mind flashes back to our shower after his slip 'n slide party a couple of weeks ago when I gave him a hand job. My cheeks heat, and I turn away to hide the embarrassment of my thoughts, pretending to fidget with my chair. Being intimate with Cooper is what *should* make me feel grown-up, but going on a real date for some reason seems so adult, and I'm giddy at the idea. I try to restrain my excitement, but Emily is hardly paying attention to me as she flips through the rows of polish colors. "Do you and Troy go on a lot of dates? What's college like?"

She perks up at the questions, holding the plastic color swatches out to the lady taking a seat on the swivel stool in front of her, her finger pinched against the shade of blue she wants. I politely ask my nail lady for light pink, and she nods, knowing I'm not picky. I come here often, but usually with Mom and Chastity.

"Oh my gosh. College is so much fun, Sophie." She exhales dreamily. "You'll see when you get there."

"I still have two more years." I sigh, sinking into my chair.

"Yeah, but you'll be dating a fraternity brother soon." Cooper hasn't rushed yet, but he and Troy are both confident about his chances of getting accepted. "You can go to all the parties at the frat house and everything. It'll basically be like you're in college too."

"What are the parties like?" Besides the slip 'n slide party, I've only been to ones my family or the Montgomerys host in our joint backyard.

"They're the best. There's almost always a theme, so you get to dress up. Like a few months ago, there was an ABC party–anything but clothes. So, you make an outfit out of . . . whatever you want. I cut up my old Twister mat and turned it into a dress." She raises her eyebrows suggestively. "And if there isn't a theme, anything goes. There's no one there to make sure your skirt goes past your fingertips or your tank top straps are three fingers wide." The three-finger rule at school is annoying. I rarely get away with wearing my sundresses without my jean jacket or a sweater in class. But the idea of themed parties is intimidating. "OH." She leans toward my chair like what she's about to tell me is classified. "There's also an endless number of hot boys. They are everywhere, Sophie. Ev-er-y-where." She sounds out each syllable.

My eyes go wide at her words as I try to process what she's saying and what that means for me.

A wicked laugh escapes her. "It's just window shopping, Sophie. You don't have to buy anything." Shrugging in reaction to my body language, she adds, "Or you can try things on in the dressing room and put them back." She pairs her words with a wink, and my stomach flips. Is she serious? "Don't be a prude, Sophie. It's not like the boys don't check out girls. Sororities can't host parties at their houses so there's always a ton of girls over too. That's how college works."

"So, Troy checks out other girls?" The answer to this question is as close as I'll get to how things will be with Cooper. Those two boys are as loyal as they come, at least that's always been my perception. I've heard how Troy talks about Emily when she's not around–he practically worships the ground she walks on.

"I mean, I've never seen him do it, but I'm sure he does. You can't help who you think is attractive, and you can't help who walks into the room. It's not a big deal."

I change the subject, overwhelmed by the thoughts swirling in my brain. Will I like these parties? I only have two friends, and that's more than enough for me. I have no desire to be around strangers, and it's not like I have the freedom to show up to every party, but will I be able to handle thinking about what could be happening at them if I'm not there?

An hour later, Emily is knocking on the boys' front door. Troy answers, an instant grin lighting his face. "Hey, girls," he says, leaning through the doorframe to kiss his girlfriend. The way he looks at her tells me he's oblivious to the person she really is. I hope I'm never blinded by love like that. If I am, I sure hope someone tells me. I want to say something to Cooper. Maybe he can talk to Troy, but there might be other things I need to talk to Cooper about first.

I can't stop thinking about how much he might be missing by being with me, not just when we're physically together. At his slip 'n slide party, he turned down drinks at least three different times that I saw. I think he's worried about what I'll think because I don't drink, or maybe he was concerned with making sure I'm comfortable. I love him for it, but I can't help but worry about all the opportunities he might enjoy that he'll pass up.

Troy is slipping on his white Adidas as Cooper's 4Runner pulls into the driveway. Coop steps out of his car dressed in jeans and a navy polo. He only wears that outfit if he's working on real estate stuff with his dad–which he just started a few weeks ago–so that must be where he was. He's so handsome in professional mode with his light brown hair perfectly in place and his biceps straining against the sleeves of his shirt. Gosh, he's dreamy. I walk to greet him before he reaches the front door.

"Hey, Soph." He looks me up and down, taking in my curls and favorite pink sundress to match my new nails. "You look beautiful."

"You don't look bad yourself." I grin.

"Thanks," he says, kissing my temple as he looks behind me to where Troy and Emily are walking toward us. He slides around me, reaching for his best friend. Their palms slap against each other then the backside of their hands hit on the return. They do some weird jazz hands, sparkle finger thing with their fingertips touching, then Cooper wraps his hand fully around Troy's head until it locks across his mouth. He kisses him through his hand dramatically. Troy grabs Cooper's hand, lifting it above his head so Cooper can twirl like a princess. It's a whole thing.

I'd say I'm weirded out by what's happening, but this "secret" handshake was created years ago and occurs regularly. I've accepted their ridiculousness, but Emily and I both roll our eyes anyway. "Do you even need us for this date?" I tease.

Cooper glances sideways at me then turns his back on his best friend. Linking his arm around my shoulder, he kisses my temple. "You're the most important part."

While Cooper runs inside to change, the rest of us get into his car. Not even two minutes later, he slides into the driver's seat next to me, looking as handsome as ever in the same jeans he had on, his blue polo swapped for the same color button up. Using the entire five minute drive where he's focused on the road to my advantage, I take him in, thinking about how there's no way everyone else can't see what I do.

My parents have taken Dean and me to nice restaurants a few times. We even went once with the Montgomerys to celebrate Dad when he got promoted to lead financial advisor at his company. But even though Mom and Dad can afford it, we tend to go to small, hole in the wall places more often. Regardless, this fancy restaurant on a date is a totally different experience.

"Thank you," I tell Cooper as he pulls my black leather chair out, and I slide into my seat at the white linen lined table. There's way more silverware on the table than seems necessary, and the cups for water look like wine glasses.

"You're welcome." He kisses the side of my head before taking the seat next to me as Emily and Troy sit across from us.

"It's so nice here, Coop," I whisper, insecurity seeping in. Low yellow lights glow over a dozen well-spaced tables. Each holds a woman much older than I am sharing intimate moments with her man. As excited as I was for my first real date, I'm not sure I deserve all the stops to be pulled like this. I feel like I've been dropped inside a random page of a book–completely out of place.

"I'm glad you think so. I want to give you all the nice things, Soph," he says effortlessly, like he wouldn't hesitate to give me the world if he could. I should be swooning, overcome with a rush of emotion–but all I feel is guilt. He grins and presses a soft kiss to my lips before reaching for his menu. I hesitantly reach for mine, Emily's words running through my head for the hundredth time since she said them earlier today.

College sounds . . . wild. Wild isn't me, but it sounds perfect for Cooper. He loves big crowds, he loves people in real life. I've heard him and Troy brag about how good they are at beer pong and flip cup and whatever other games they played when Cooper visited Troy his first year of college.

This entire time I've been thinking about how Troy and Emily aren't anything alike, but maybe it's actually Cooper and I who don't have enough in common. What if I stay the girl hiding in her bedroom to get lost in a fake world instead of the real one? The girl who would rather skate down the street to the park than show up to a party. The one who would rather play cornhole in my backyard with my family than beer pong in a fraternity house. How can that be enough for him?

Setting our drinks in front of us, the waiter addresses me first. "Are you ready to order?"

"Yes. I'll have the fettuccine alfredo, please." Cooper's hand squeezes my thigh as I hand the waiter my menu. His thumb rubs across my skin, sending chills through me. I force a smile, wishing we were alone so maybe I could talk to him about how I'm feeling.

"Is everything okay?" Cooper whispers, leaning toward me so only I can hear him. How does he know? This is exactly what I'm talking about, though. Somehow, he's so in tune with me. He's spent his entire life around me, learning me better than anyone and now that we are together, it's only going to become more of a distraction. How is he going to keep up with everything in college on top of me?

"How would you like your steak cooked?" The waiter talking to Emily draws my attention, maybe because I'm subconsciously trying to avoid Cooper's question.

"Medium rare, like it's supposed to be cooked, obviously," she snips. Wow, that was rude. With wide eyes, I turn back to Cooper, curious if he's on the same page, but he's already got an eyebrow raised at Troy. Cooper's mouth opens like he's going to ruin the mood with our shared opinion, so I lightly squeeze his hand on my thigh–a silent signal to take a breath. Troy shrugs off his best friend's suggestive reaction, giving his order politely. Cooper sighs, his hand squeezing my leg tighter. Letting it go, he takes his turn.

As soon as the waiter walks away, the conversation jumps to a discussion about the fraternity, my spiraling thoughts finding their way right back into my mind, and Cooper's concern for me all but forgotten. I love that he's thinking about me more often than not and always concerned for my happiness, but he looks so happy right now. His face is lit up as he and Troy joke about some of the guys and Troy tells him what to expect during rush week. Emily chimes in a few times as I sit there wondering what it would be like to be a part of that world and how much I'd have to force myself into it.

20
SOPHIE

THEN

Darius Rucker's twang flows through the small speaker on my kitchen counter when I enter, but his usually soothing voice did nothing to ease the anxious thoughts ricocheting around my head and heart. Every day since the slip 'n slide party, since the Fourth of July, since I talked to Emily, more and more doubt seeps in. It's nothing Cooper has done. He's perfect. I think I might even love him. I'm not sure if it's too soon or if I'm too young to feel that way, but it's the reason I feel pulled toward my decision. If I love him, I should do what's best for him, right?

"Sophie?" my dad calls from the dining room.

"Yeah?" I answer with a heavy sigh, peeking my head around the corner.

He scans my face. "Oh, pumpkin. What's wrong?" He sets down the newspaper he's reading and taps the cushion on the dining chair next to him.

Dad and I are as close as any other father and daughter I know. We haven't talked much about Cooper because I get the impression he thinks I'm too young to date-even though he hasn't stood in the way of us. Mom is just so easy to talk to. Plus, she asks-she's invested. But Mom isn't here right now, and I need to know I'm making the right choice. I sit on the chair, curling my legs under me and flatting my dress against my thighs before leaning into my palm on the table. After a long sigh, I confess. "I think I'm going to break up with Cooper."

He sits straighter, immediately on defense with a deep, angry tone. "What did he do to you?"

"He didn't do anything. Yet." Why did I add the *yet*? It's not like I think Cooper would cheat on me or do something at college I'd be uncomfortable with.

"What do you mean yet?"

"I just . . . he's going to college, you know? And I'm only sixteen. Even if we're on the same page now, it doesn't seem likely for us to stay that way, not when we're in completely different phases of life–different environments. It won't be the same."

"That's very mature of you. You're way more advanced than I was at your age."

"I am?" I shift my gaze from where it's focused on the mahogany table to Dad.

"Absolutely. I didn't listen to my gut when I was younger, and it came back to bite me. I'm glad you don't have to learn that lesson."

"I thought you liked Cooper?"

He hesitates, but his words contradict it. "I do. The Montgomerys are family."

"But . . ."

"I got married when I shouldn't have. I was so blinded by young love that I confused it with forever love."

He never talks about his first marriage. Anything I've ever heard has only been from Mom. "Your first wife?"

"Yes." His word is sharp and bitter.

"Not that I know much about it, but I don't think this is the same."

"The situations may not be the same but the under-lying issues might be."

"What do you mean?"

"When you're young, it's easy to get caught up in the romance of a first serious relationship. Everything is new, exciting–so much so that it can mask any issues."

"Cooper and I don't really have any issues." The statement causes me to re-question my decision yet again. "Maybe it's the wrong choice."

"You're going with your gut. Your gut usually knows best. Sometimes it knows the things you haven't realized or accepted yet."

"Like what?"

"Well." He takes a breath. "Take Mary for example." I sit up straight, my fingers moving to tug on the end of a curl. I can't believe I'm going to hear about my dad's ex-wife first hand. "I met her in high school. Her mom was my history teacher. She encouraged our relationship from the beginning–she made everything easy on us. She even–"

I hardly notice I'm literally on the edge of my seat until he cuts himself off. "She what?"

"Maybe you're too young to hear this."

"Tell me, please. I want to know."

He shifts, like he's uncomfortable, but continues anyway. "She enabled our relationship physically and emotionally. Her and Mary were planning our wedding before we even graduated. It was so easy, I was certain it had to be right."

"But it wasn't?"

He makes one quick shake of his head. "We rushed. But all good things take time, pumpkin. There's no hurry, especially when you're young. Time is the best gift because it allows you to see things clearly, from every angle–to make sure you have all the information."

"Like a hidden gambling addiction?" I ask quietly.

"Amongst other things, yes."

"I don't think Cooper has that."

"No. Neither do I. But while he's older than you, he still hasn't had time to grow into himself, to discover all the things he needs and wants and craves in life. No one or nothing but time can reveal that. And even with time, there's no guarantee you'd see it if the person is your whole world, if you haven't given yourself the time and space to find yourself outside of them too."

I can't think of anything Cooper does now that would be considered a red flag, but maybe it's like Dad is saying–we can't see things in the moment, through the love. "So, you think this is the right choice?"

"I do. There's no need to be in a rush to grow up. Just spend these next two years enjoying high school and college once you get there. Make the most of it because you can't get this time back. You have the rest of your life for the settling down part."

"Okay, I can do that. Thanks, Dad." I want Cooper to make the most of college, so it only makes sense that I should do the same with my time.

"You're welcome, pumpkin." He pulls me from my chair and into a hug. "Everything is going to be okay. You'll see."

I hope he's right.

21

COOPER

THEN

Sliding into the booth on the same side as Sophie, I fling my arm around her shoulder, singing the nonsense words from "We Go Together" far louder than I should in a restaurant even if it is '50s themed. This diner has been a go-to for us since I could drive–another one of my and Sophie's "spots." We haven't been on a dinner date since we went out with Troy and Emily a few weeks ago, but we come here for lunch at least once a week. Before we got together, we celebrated big and small accomplishments for either of us with cinnamon roll french toast, but now we don't wait for a reason. Maybe it looked that way before, but anyone looking in on us now must see how fucking cute we look as a couple.

I turn to my girlfriend with a grin on my face and lean in to kiss her. She pulls back right as my mouth is about to land on hers.

I freeze.

She doesn't look happy to see me.

"I'm sorry, baby. Did my singing embarrass you?" I chuckle. "How can I make it up to you? Strawberry milkshake?" I prefer chocolate, and Sophie is a strawberry girl, but somehow we compromised with vanilla. I glance at the black tablecloth covered in cherries completely clear of anything. It's actually odd that she hasn't ordered one yet since I'm a few minutes late and she likes to drink our shake first.

She doesn't respond. Instead, she looks to where her fingers are picking at the fabric of her sundress in her lap.

"What's wrong?" I reign in my good mood. When her gaze meets mine, her eyes are full of tears. "Soph, hey, are you okay?" I twist slightly on the red booth bench so I'm facing her. I rub my thumb across her bare shoulder. She flinches. What the hell is going on?

"I think we should break up." Her voice is barely above a whisper.

"Excuse me, what?" I laugh. "That's not a funny joke, Sophie." I relax, knowing she's playing around and turn to look for the waitress. Sophie's hand lands on my forearm, drawing my attention back to her.

"I'm not joking."

My eyes search hers, my eyebrow furrowing. "What is happening right now?"

"We're breaking up . . ." she says again in an unsure whisper.

She's unsure. Of course she is because this is a joke. "Our relationship is perfect. Why would we break up?"

"You're about to start college, Cooper. It's time we stop ignoring that."

"Uhhhh. I didn't think we were. We talk about it all the time. It's not like I'm going out of state. I'm literally ten minutes from you."

"I know, but–"

"But what, Sophie?" I'm vaguely aware we are in public and attempt to remain calm.

"It's going to be hard. You're going to be busy with school and your fraternity. I want you to have fun and not be worried about your high school girlfriend."

"Why would I be worried? I have fun with you." She's brought up a few concerns before but nothing *I* was worried about.

"It's not the same and you know it." Her foot stomps under the table.

I feel like I'm attempting long division in my head with how confused I am. "The same as what?"

"I want you to get the full experience of college, whatever that means. I know you, Coop. You'll come over on Thursday nights even if there's something going on on campus. You'll lose sleep making sure you have time for me on top of other responsibilities. You'll hold back at parties to make sure I feel comfortable with you being surrounded by college girls. I don't want that for you."

"So, you're breaking up with me because I'm a good boyfriend?" I can't believe this shit.

"No, I'm breaking up with you because I'm trying to be a good friend. I just want what's best for you, Cooper." The way her voice cracks on my name is what finally sets reality in like an ambulance showing up to a car crash. "I don't want you to feel like you missed out. I don't want you to resent me down the road."

"I could never resent you. Sophie, you're my favorite person." I can hear the panic in my voice as my brain scrambles to process. "How could you think I'll be missing out with you when all I'd be doing without you is missing you?"

"I know you don't understand now, but I think this is the best thing for you—for us."

"You're right, I don't understand. What the fuck, Sophie?" I run my hands down my face, stabbing my fingers in my eyes in frustration.

"I'm sorry."

"You're sorry?" I scoff. "Why wouldn't we at least *try* and see how it goes?"

"I know it'll be too hard. Plus," she lowers her voice, "everyone around you will be having sex, and I'm not ready for that."

My fingernails dig into my palms almost hard enough to break through my skin. "I don't give a shit about that, Sophie. Do you know me at all?"

"Well, it'll happen eventually and when it does it will make it harder when we inevitably break up. I think it's best we call it before we get in too deep, you know?" I can't tell if she is lying to me or if she truly feels this way.

"Is that what you think about this, about us?" Her words make me sick, the sudden whiff of french fry grease heightening my nausea. Is this how she's felt the entire time? Like this is just something to pass the time between school years?

22
COOPER

NOW

Cooper, 21; Sophie, 18

"Are you *sure* Sophie won't be here?" Troy asks for the third time as we slam his car doors and make our way through the darkness toward Dean and Marcus' backyard. She tried coming over after JT left her house the other day, but I brushed her off. If whatever she had to say was really that important, she would have made JT wait, *not me.* She wouldn't have had him over in the first place. She definitely wouldn't have kissed him. I was still tempted to talk to her after, but I was too torn between wanting to call her out and hoping she'd clear up a misunderstanding. In the end, I decided if she wasn't putting in more effort to prove me wrong, the answer I'd get isn't one I'd be happy with, so I've been trying to distract myself the past couple of weeks.

"I doubt she'd show up. Dean has a sweet and inno-cent view of his sister, and she likes it that way, so she won't party around him." I give him a more elaborate answer so maybe he'll believe me this time. I slide my hands into the pocket of my black hoodie, hoping to reduce some of the bite from the freezing December air, the gravel driveway crunching under my Nikes until we reach the grass.

"Well, that works out for us. Maybe you'll actually have a good time tonight without worrying about her. Hell, maybe you'll meet someone new–and actually use her number this time." I know he's throwing the same advice I gave him back in my face, but it feels way easier to dish it out than to hear it directed at you.

"Doubt it. It's always the same people." I groan. We veer around the side of the house, following the sound of crackling flames toward a bonfire so big it lights our path from a couple hundred feet away.

Before Troy has a chance to toss more words of wisdom my way, Marcus stops in front of us, a full, red Solo cup in his hand. "Hey, Troy. Coop." Even from this distance, the fire lights him from the side, his well-built frame and man bun casting a shadow on the grass.

"Hey, man," Troy and I say in unison. Marcus has been best friends with Dean since we were kids. They got this house near campus together and outside of the fraternity house, most of the parties we attend are here. They have a big, secluded backyard and a killer bonfire pit.

"Big turnout tonight," Troy says. I'm surprised I don't recognize many people.

"Yeah, it seems no one left for winter break this year, and I think Dean's girl brought friends again."

Troy smacks the back of his hand against my arm. My eye roll ends with a death glare. We've had the same friends forever. Chances are I've had access to all these people before, and if I didn't hit it off with them in the past, I doubt I will now.

"Oh yeah, I heard he's with someone," Troy comments. "Weird as shit. I've never known him to have a girlfriend."

Marcus chuckles. "Yeah, it's strange. But they're great together. We'll see what happens." His words trail off with the same distress I recall Dean having on Thanksgiving. There's definitely something happening inside that circle we don't know about.

"Well, good to see you, man. We're gonna get some drinks."

"Sounds good. I'll catch up with you in a bit." Marcus waves, taking off down the grassy hill.

"I'll grab you a beer. Go talk to a girl or something," Troy harasses me.

"Yes, Dad." I shake my head with irritation before breaking into a grin. Marcus did say there are new girls at the party tonight. Maybe I *will* meet someone to get my mind off Sophie. I keep my hopes up as I walk across the grass toward the bonfire.

I spend the next few minutes chatting with guys I played football with in high school. Troy slipped a beer in my hand at some point then walked off.

When my friends escape to get a drink, they are quickly replaced by Dean, who has a girl tucked into his side. "Cooper, hey," Dean says, pulling away from his girl long enough to bro hug me. "You remember Maci?" He guides her into my field of vision without his hand leaving her lower back. I was a little distracted when I met her at the football game–the one where I found out Sophie was seeing JT–so I take a better look at her now. She's cute. Her brown hair falls over her shoulders covered in Dean's high school football sweatshirt, and she's looking at him like he's her entire world. Damn. I've never seen him attached to a girl. Not his girlfriend, my ass. I chuckle to myself at his denial, wondering what the missing piece to this puzzle is that will make his claim make sense.

"Yeah, I do. Hey. It's good to see you."

"You too," Maci says before she gives Dean a look. He kisses her and whispers something against her lips before she waves goodbye. He watches her walk away then turns his attention back to me.

"How's it going?" my ex's brother asks. Jesus Christ, I can't go five fucking seconds without thinking about her. I miss the days when I saw him as my childhood neighbor, practically family. Now he seems like someone I should be estranged with after a breakup.

"You okay?" Dean chuckles.

Why do I feel like I'm about to tell a dad I'm obsessed with his daughter? I honestly don't know how we haven't had this conversation before. It's never come up. As far as I'm aware, he doesn't know the details of Sophie and me dating. He was already out of the house the first summer we were together and we've never been close enough to share dating stories. Still, I should have said something years ago. I bite the bullet. "I'd be better if I wasn't in love with your sister."

Beer mists out of his mouth as he chokes on his sip. He coughs a few times until his throat clears. "Sorry, I was not expecting that."

"Are you pissed?" I ask hesitantly, tugging on the back of my neck.

"Hell no. I'm a little confused why it's a bad thing. Carter and I have been taking bets for years. We knew you had a 'thing,' but I didn't realize it was ever serious between you two."

"Yeaaaah. We aren't on the same page." I try my best not to look guilty of seeing his sister naked. I thought Sophie was *the one*, but it doesn't seem like that's in the cards for us anymore. "I have to get over her, though. I'm trying to anyway." I'm not sure if that's the right thing to say to the brother of the one who got away, but it's what comes out.

"Making a little more sense why Thanksgiving was weird. I'm sorry it didn't work out with you two."

"Thanks. Me too. If only things were more black and white."

"Yeah, if only." He hesitates on his words like they are more loaded than they look at face value, but it sweeps away as he changes the subject. "Well, I was actually told to ask if you were open to being set up. Maci has a friend."

"Oh, really?" I wasn't expecting him to ask me that, especially after what I confessed. I am a little intrigued, but I feel guilty at the same time because I'm obviously not over Sophie.

"Yeah, I don't know much about her, but she seems cool. How do you feel about it? No pressure. Just have to ask. You know how it is when girls get ideas." He chuckles like it's an annoying trait, but I can see in his eyes he'd do anything Maci asked him.

"Do you think it's fucked up to date if I'm not over her? I'm going to get over her, right?" I chuckle, the second question more rhetorical and to myself than Dean.

"I hope so." He looks dejected like he's speaking from experience which makes no sense based on the way he was looking at Maci a minute ago.

"Me too." I sigh, bringing my beer to my lips.

His hand lands on my shoulder. "Look. It's not my business what went down between you and Sophie. But if she's moved on, maybe you should too."

Dean's probably right, and maybe this is the push I need. Clearly she isn't invested in our relationship. So, fuck it. "You know what? Let's do it. Sophie and I have been over for a while now. I have to move on at some point."

His energy lightens when he shifts his gaze to something behind me. Chuckling, he nods slightly, and I know when I turn around Maci and her friend will be behind us. It feels like we're in high school, but it's kind of amusing.

"Hi." Maci rejoins us, leaning into Dean immediately. "Cooper, this is my friend, Kylie. Kylie, Cooper." She grins. "Alright, we'll see you two later. Bye." The words come out rushed as she tugs on Dean's arm, pulling him away before we'd even have a chance to stop them.

I chuckle. "That was smooth."

Kylie is just as amused. "That's Maci for you–not awkward at all. Gotta love her."

The flames from the fire next to us flicker in Kylie's light green eyes. Her blonde hair barely hits her shoulders and directs my attention to the V-neck of her olive green sweater. Her black leggings hug her thighs and her short black boots make her barely under my height. The sparkle of the red gloss on her lips catch in the firelight as she takes a sip from her Solo cup. She looks hot. She actually seems familiar. "Have we met before?"

"Hmm. I don't think so." She leans in slightly, not shy at all about this setup.

"Have you been to a fraternity party recently?" If I have seen her, I imagine that's where.

"Yeah. Maci and I went to one a few weeks ago. A blackout party."

"That's my fraternity."

"Oh, random. Do you live there?"

"No, my buddy and I have our own house off campus. You're not seeing anyone from the party are you?" There's a strict dicks before chicks policy among my brothers, and even if I'm not super close with all of them, I will always respect that.

"Nope. Free agent over here. But for the sake of not wasting either of our time, I am looking to be off the market. I'm over the new party, new guy life. I'm over the drama."

I laugh at how much I relate. I spent my entire first two years of college with different girls in my bed trying to get Sophie out of my head, trying to convince myself I hadn't already found *the one*. "I feel that."

"Dating is exhausting."

"Yeah, it's easier to lower your standards," I joke.

"Oh, yeah. What's your bare minimum requirement?" she asks.

"You aren't one of those people who clap when the plane lands, are you?"

Kylie laughs. "Definitely not."

"What about string cheese? Do you string it or bite it?"

"There's people who *bite* it?" She covers her mouth, lurching slightly forward like she's going to throw up.

I laugh, happy with her reaction. "Good enough for me." I glance into her nearly empty cup. "Do you want another drink?"

"Yeah, I do." Her green eyes shimmer when they connect with mine, and I fight my brain on wishing it was Sophie looking back at me. "Oh, and by the way, if I don't bore you out of your mind tonight, I promised Maci a double date. Sorry." She shrugs, not looking sorry at all.

Chuckling, I pull her cup from her hand. "As long as I get one to myself first." I'm not confident in my ability to commit to someone else, but I'll *try*. A double date, though . . . with my ex's brother? That doesn't sound like a recipe for success.

23
SOPHIE

Now

Curled up on a pillowy black recliner reading on Christmas afternoon should feel perfect. The crackling logs in the fireplace have provided a consistent quiet soundtrack as they transition from wood to charcoal. The flames warm the left side of my body and my cheeks burn with the color they've brought to them. It doesn't always snow in December here, but light flurries flutter through the air on the other side of the Montgomery's living room window.

It *should* be perfect.

But as I stare into the mesmerizing flickers of orange and yellow, all I can think about is how nothing is perfect without Cooper in my life.

I'm not sure where he is, but it's probably for the best. Seeing him only makes my heart ache more than it already does. Part of me wishes I had been more open with my family about our relationship. Maybe then they wouldn't have made me spend the holiday here–even though we do every year. It's not that I ever tried to hide it, but I think because Dad isn't the easiest person to talk to about this kind of thing, I never went out of my way to bring it up with anyone. Mom knows the most, but even then, she doesn't know everything. She thinks I'm fine because JT was around for a while.

My fingers run over the page I'm on. I like being alone, but that's different than feeling lonely. That emptiness is consuming me as I sit here on the outside of the party. Our moms are drinking wine on the couch. Our dads are at the poker table set up on the side of the living room opposite me, playing with Troy and Carter. Everyone else is happy.

With a sigh, I close my book, retreating to the kitchen for a soda.

Reaching for a glass for my Squirt, I freeze. On the other side of the wall I hear Cooper, where he must be sitting at the dining room table. It's been so weird hearing his voice again. I didn't realize how much I've missed it in the past month since the JT debacle, since I tried to explain I want him back. I haven't figured out how to make this right if he won't talk to me, so I've done nothing.

"So, Costa Rica. Should be fun. Are you excited?" Dean graduated two quarters early, and he's moving to Costa Rica for the next year. He was originally planning on Honduras, but after we went there for Thanksgiving vacation and talked to a few locals, he ended up changing his mind. Either way, it'll be cool I bet—not that I'd be brave enough to go on my own. My brother and I both love adventure, but outside of what I've forced myself to do because of the list, I tend to read about it in books instead of living it.

"Yeah." Dean's word hold emmotions opposite to the excitement he had sharing about his plans around the parents earlier.

"Are you sure about that?" Cooper senses his shift. "Sad to leave Maci? What are you two going to do? Long distance?" Oh yeah, I forgot Dean has a girlfriend. He never talks about her, at least not to me. Though, I can't be mad. It's not like I've told him the details of Cooper or JT. I crack the top of my Squirt, pouring it quickly into my glass so I don't miss out on eavesdropping over the soda cracking the ice.

There's a long pause before Dean speaks. "No."

"Really? You guys seem great together."

"Yeah, we are . . ." Dean sighs. I've never heard him vulnerable like this before.

"I'm confused," the guy I feel the same about says. "She doesn't want to stay together?"

"I'm not giving her the choice."

"Is that fair?" The accusation in his tone is all too familiar.

"Maybe not. But I can't ask her to wait for me while I figure out my shit."

"Would she?"

"I think so. Which is why I'm not asking her. She deserves more than putting her life on hold for me. There's so much she wants to do." Hearing my brother talk about breaking up with his girlfriend with the same logic I had when I broke up with Cooper is so validating.

"Yeah, I've heard that bullshit before," Cooper chuckles. "I got that same speech from your sister once." Wait, do Dean and Cooper talk about me? "Hell, even knowing how it felt, I used it on her too. Do yourself a favor–If you're really not going to let her weigh in on your breakup, at least try to avoid making her feel like her opinion doesn't matter. She'll only hate you for it." Does Cooper hate me? From the first time we broke up or from the past few months? Is it too late? The thought ricochets around my mind, tearing up my heart in the process.

"Yeah, maybe it's better that way. Maybe it'll be easier for her," Dean mumbles like he's talking to himself. I almost didn't hear him. Abandoning my soda, I press myself against the dividing wall between the kitchen and dining room.

"You want her to hate you?"

"No. I want her to love me as much as I love her."

Cooper doesn't respond. I wish I could see him right now. I wish I knew what he was thinking.

"God, this shit sucks." Dean laughs under his breath.

"Tell me about it."

"To the girls we can't live without," my brother says, and their glasses clink together.

"And hoping it doesn't kill us."

The chair scraping against the floor startles me away from where I'm eavesdropping. I turn back to the kitchen counter, picking at the last few remnants of my charcuterie board even though I'm not hungry.

Cooper silently slides in next to me, setting his dessert plate in the sink.

"Do you hate me?" I whisper, afraid of his answer.

His eyebrows scrunch, and he opens his mouth to say something, but nothing comes out.

"You do hate me, don't you? I knew it. You got tired of waiting for me and all the resentment finally built up and now you can't even text me back and we're not even friends anymore and–"

"Sophie," he cuts me off. "Take a breath." His words are comforting, but his body language isn't. He hasn't taken a step toward me or wrapped me in a hug like he usually would.

"Time for presents! Get your asses in here!" Carter yells from the living room.

My attention redirects only for a moment but then it's back on Cooper. He's already pulling away from me to join everyone else.

My heart races as I follow a few paces behind him. I'm even more worried about presents than about the fact that I just spit a bunch of chaos at Cooper. Every year since I started high school, we do Secret Santa instead of gifts for everyone. Of course I drew Cooper's name this year.

How do you decide on the perfect gift for the love of your life who has made it clear he wants nothing to do with you? I've been trying to talk to him. I need to tell him I told JT I don't want to see him anymore. I want to make it clear I've forgiven him, that I want us to be together, but every text has gone unanswered and every call has gone straight to voicemail. Maybe I waited too long and he's really done with me.

Everyone finds a spot in the living room amongst the couches, recliners and floor. As the youngest, I do my job of passing out each present to the person whose name is on the wrapping. I hesitate as I reach Cooper's blue and white snowflake paper wrapped gift toward him, hoping for a *moment* between us. He glances up and takes it from me like he's not interested at all, immediately setting it on the carpet next to him and avoiding my gaze at all costs. My heart sinks, but I continue my tasks, trying to mask the way my heart sinks with a cheery smile. Once all the gifts have homes, I spin in a circle, looking for a place to sit. Of course the only available space between the nine of us is on the floor next to Cooper.

Carter is on the other side of Cooper. He opens his gift first, and everyone takes their turn from there. I wasn't worried about what I'd receive–everyone puts time and effort into their gifts. I'm genuinely excited by the architecture sketchbook someone got me, full of blueprint drafting paper and a new set of pens. I'm flipping through the pages and rolling the pens through my fingers and almost forget Cooper still needs to open his gift. Since I'm his Secret Santa, no one else seems interested in watching him, preoccupied with their own gifts and talking amongst each other.

I wonder if Cooper will know it's from me as he tears the wrapping from the thin metal sheets. His eyes flicker across the sign on top, the corner of his lips twisting up in amusement. It's a royal blue square with white writing: *I doubt vodka is the answer, but it's worth a shot.* He keeps his focus on his gift, moving the top sign to the side. The second is the one I'm nervous about. Not that anyone else will think twice about it–if they were paying attention–but there's no way it won't recall a memory for Cooper. At least that's what I'm counting on. This sign is white with black. There's an image of two stick people standing under a showerhead. Below them it says: *Save water, shower together.*

The first time Cooper and I showered together after his slip 'n slide party is a core memory for me when it comes to our relationship. Despite the pressure I felt to speed up our relationship, it was one of the first days I felt like we were perfect together.

Cooper sits with his forearms resting on his bent knees, holding a sign in each hand, eyes shifting between the two of them. I stare at him as his teeth sink into his bottom lip that he drags back and forth under them. Slowly he turns to meet my gaze, eyes narrowing as he studies me. My fingers tug my curls, nerves racing through me, not aware if anyone else is watching us. He opens his mouth to say something then clamps it shut. When he opens it again, all that comes out is a soft "Thank you."

24
COOPER

NOW

I've never joined in on the hype surrounding a new year, but I'm obsessively clinging to this whole "New Year, New Me" shit. I've crammed my time full of everything productive–anything to distract me from the memory of Sophie kissing JT that's *still* replaying in my head. I've been spending a lot of time with Kylie, although we never ended up going on a double date since Dean left. I'm grateful for that.

This first quarter of the year my focus is especially heavy on proving my worth to my Dad as far as securing my place within his company. It's my junior year of college, which means I have less than two years to guarantee myself an agent position when I graduate.

"Mr. Smith," I say, reaching for a firm handshake with the dad of one of my fraternity brothers–Ethan.

"Cooper, it's great to see you again."

"Yeah, you too. Thank you for meeting." We both sit on either side of a small circular table in the low-lit, upscale bar and restaurant. I first met Ethan's dad during my fraternity community service hours when we were volunteering with Habitat for Humanity freshman year. Initially, I didn't think anything of his paying job as a builder, but now that I've been spending more time with

Dad's company and trying to step into a leadership role, I don't know how this idea didn't occur to me before.

"Of course. Your timing couldn't be better. We're halfway done with building the houses in our new development and getting ready to sell."

"This is the third development you've been in charge of, right?" I did my research.

"Correct. The first one we partnered with a brokerage, but there were some issues we didn't anticipate with them. For the second, we tried selling without a partner, but it wasn't as efficient, so we're willing to give a partnership another shot if we can find the right person–preferably with an independent brokerage this time."

"You have thirty homes in this set right? Listing for around half a mil?"

"Yes. And finishing contracts to start working on two others around the same."

"Great. Well, all our agents sell above average. Between twelve and twenty-four homes a year. So, selling thirty quickly shouldn't be a problem."

"Impressive. Ethan tells me your father's business is well established."

"Yes, sir. He started his company twelve years ago. Each year has been more profitable than the last despite any dips in the market. He's a Eugene native, so he's built a lot of strong relationships with local business owners as well." It feels weird to sit here and brag about Dad and his company, but his success should speak volumes. "He's won the Good Neighbor Award, as have two of his agents. Five years in, he won State Realtor of the Year, and last year he received the Distinguished Service Award."

"Quite the list of accolades. I've met Mike a few times. Good man, it seems." Contrary to his words, he doesn't seem that impressed.

"Yes, sir. He works hard–we both do. I've learned everything I know from him." Sophie's voice echoes in the back of my head as I consider my next words. *Don't reference your dad for everything, Coop. You deserve recognition for your effort. Don't downplay it by acting like he's doing all the work. Show them what makes you special.* "But I bring uniqueness to the table."

"Oh yeah?"

Smirking, I say, "Me with the 21st century on my team. I started this TikTok series . . . You know what that is, right?" I joke.

"That's the app Ethan uses to send me all those damn monkey videos?"

I shake my head, amused. "That's the one." Monkeys taking baths. Monkeys wearing clothes. Monkeys hugging their humans. At the rate at which Ethan sends videos to literally everyone he knows, I wouldn't be surprised if monkey TikTok is single handedly fueled by him. "You have to admit the one of the monkeys eating spaghetti Lady and the Tramp style was cute as hell, though."

"Don't tell my son, but I watched it four times."

"Your secret is safe with me." I chuckle. "Anyway, this series I'm doing. I realized traditional marketing isn't as effective as it used to be–park benches, billboards, the side of a bus. We need to capitalize on any free resources available–TikTok being a major one that twenty percent of Americans use daily. It's a quick, easy way to get the word out."

"How do you plan to stand out amongst any other companies using the same tactic?"

I grin. This part of my job that I basically created is easily my favorite. "Funny and relatable content is where it's at because it's what people share on platforms that instantly have hundreds or thousands of viewers a day—thus creating a much stronger butterfly effect style of marketing. I have two series currently. One is parody videos about the struggles of homeownership. The other is going into houses we list and doing ridiculous activities. The caption will be something like, 'This windowsill is the perfect place for your ant farm. It's in the perfect neighborhood for riding your unicycle!'" A laugh bursts out of him at my words, and it fuels my confidence. "Did you know there's a sport called 'Extreme Ironing?' People iron clothes in random places. So, I took a video of me ironing a shirt against the exterior wall and captioned it, 'The perfect place to practice your EI.'"

He laughs, relaxing against the back of his seat. "That works?"

"Yup. That last one went viral, and we sold two homes from clients who found us that way. I was skeptical. I honestly started it as a joke to see what would happen. But then people started commenting with all these crazy details about their lives, tidbits that helped us pair them with the right agent and home. Figuring out unique ways to connect with people makes them feel more at ease during a stressful process, and it's more enjoyable and successful for everyone."

"Well, that certainly is . . . something." He chuckles. "It sounds like you know what you're doing."

"Whenever I don't, I figure it out."

An hour passes, mostly full of bullshit and a few more drinks.

Mr. Smith clinks his glass to mine before taking the final sip. "Cooper. It's been a great lunch, if I have anything to say about it."

"I couldn't agree more. I can have the contract drawn up this week if you'd like to proceed."

"Sounds great. Reach out to my assistant when you're ready, and we'll set up a time to meet with your father."

"I will. Thank you for your time." I reach my hand for his again, concluding our meeting.

The fifteen minute drive back to my dad's office has me antsy, my knee bouncing, my thumb tapping against the steering wheel. My dad is going to be so fucking proud of me. *Sophie would be proud of me.* The thought sneaks in, and I wish I could call her. I might be mad right now, but she knows how much this means to me–more than anyone. Somehow it's been easy for me to take initiative in every aspect of my life until it was time to step into my dad's shoes. He's *untouchable* in his field. It's a lot to live up to. I'm proud of myself, but this win doesn't feel as good without her.

Pushing the thought aside, I pull into the empty parking space in front of the red brick building with a black back-lit sign that reads *Montgomery Realty*.

Walking through the front door, I head straight to my dad's office. Leaning against the door frame in my khakis and navy polo with my hands in my pockets, I wait for him to finish the call he's on.

He glances toward me as he hangs up the phone. "Cooper. Good news?"

I grin, taking the seat on the side of the desk opposite him. "Can I help write the contract?"

"Yes." He leans forward, pride smeared on his face as he clicks his pen. "We'll do it now. And then we can meet with our attorney tomorrow."

"Okay, cool. And . . ." *Ask for what you're worth, Coop. You're worth a lot.* Sophie's words flash through my thoughts again. I have big goals with this company, and I can't start checking them off if I don't take what I want. It's terrifying because it involves asking my dad, but the worst he can say is no. "I'd like to talk about my compensation for bringing in this business."

Dad's lips turn up in a slight smirk. "Let's negotiate."

I know there are two options. Since I'm not a licensed realtor, I technically can't take a percentage of the commissions–at least not on the books. I could ask for an upfront bonus for making this deal, but I've read enough Dave Ramsey and Grant Cardone books to know the long game is always the better game.

"I want two percent of commission for each sale as a bonus." For a half of a million dollar home, two percent of the two and a half percent commission would be $250 a house, $7500 after we've sold all 30 homes we'll have a monopoly on selling.

His eyes narrow, but more in consideration than surprise at my boldness. "One and a half."

I reach my hand to lock in the deal. I would have settled for one.

We write the contract, and an hour later I'm on my way home, deciding how to celebrate. Pulling into my driveway, I scroll to my text thread with Sophie. The last text is from the day I watched her kiss JT. I wish I never saw that. With a sigh, I swipe out of the conversation and shoot a text to Kylie. We've messed around a little, but haven't gone all the way yet. While I've fucked a few girls the past couple of years since I started college, my body count isn't nearly as high as most of the fraternity guys. I've learned the whole experience is better when you've had the chance to learn the other person's body, and I think it might be time to lean into the distraction of exploring someone else.

Me: *Do you need plans for tonight? I have a bottle of vodka and a bed that could have your name on them.*

By the time I get inside and shower, she's responded.

Kylie: *That's a better offer than the one I had. What are we celebrating?*

I hate that it feels weird talking about my accomplishments with someone who isn't Sophie and ignore pushing through the discomfort.

Me: *Do we need a reason?*

Kylie: *You asking is enough for me. I'll see you in 20.*

True to her word, Kylie is standing inside my kitchen twenty minutes later with a shot glass in her hand. As the clear liquor burns down my throat, it hits me that even though it's been three months, I'm not sure I'm ready for Sophie to no longer be the last girl I had sex with. Pushing off the decision, I take another shot straight from the bottle then pour one for Kylie and me.

The slit of sunlight through my curtains wakes me. I rub the sleep from my eyes then pinch them shut again in an attempt to blink away the pounding headache of my hangover. Taking in the scene, I see Kylie's naked body tangled in my sheets, my blue comforter in a pile on the floor. I ended up caving last night, knocking the memory of Sophie exploring every inch of my body out of its place as my most recent sex memory. It needed to be done. Especially since she didn't keep that space for me. I wish it had felt like its own experience. I wish I could have given my full attention to Kylie. I don't think she noticed–likely thanks to the seven shots of vodka–but every time I closed my eyes, it was Sophie in my vision. Her hands running up my body. Her lips pressing into mine. It was her I imagined, but everything felt different. Wrong.

Reaching for my phone on the nightstand, I check the text notification. It's from my dad letting me know what time our meeting with the attorney is later today. Noting Kylie still sleeping, I open my emails.

My stomach lurches at the subject heading of the top one from Ethan's dad: *Change of plans*. I close my eyes, taking a deep breath before opening the message.

Cooper,

I regret to inform you that we've decided to take another route with the new builds. To my surprise, my sister has recently gotten her real estate license with the intent of partnering with me. I hope you can understand that family comes first. I will keep Montgomery Realty in mind should we need a partner in the future. Thank you for your time and meeting with me yesterday. Send my regards to your father.

Jason Smith

Fuck. I groan, slamming my phone against my mattress harder than I intended. Kylie stirs, opening her eyes slowly, letting her surroundings filter in.

"Hey," I acknowledge her. "Sorry."

"Morning," she says sleepily, keeping the sheet wrapped over her chest as she sits. "Is everything okay?"

"Yeah. It's fine."

"Umm. Are you sure? Do you regret last night? I can leave." My poker face is clearly non-existent when it comes to work disappointment.

I sit, moving a little closer to her in the process. It's not her fault I'm mad. "No regrets." I force a smile. "Sorry, just work stuff."

"Do you want to talk about it?" she asks, relaxing a little.

Do I? Yeah. I've never talked about this with anyone besides Sophie, but I can't exactly call her up right now. And if I don't talk it through, I might not be able to approach the situation with the right mindset. Sighing, I take her up on her offer. "I've been working for my dad."

She nods. She knows that much already.

"I worked hard the past couple weeks to secure a really good deal for him, something to prove he made the right choice hiring me before I graduate. Well, it just fell through, and now I have to tell him I failed to deliver."

Kylie reaches for me, and I will myself not to pull away. The pity in her eyes takes away from any comfort that could possibly come from her touch. "It's okay. He's your dad. He'll understand."

That's the thing, though. I don't want to be off the hook because I'm his son. I want reassurance that I can do this. That I can fix this. That I can earn my place without relying on a safety net. Ethan's dad might believe family always comes first, and maybe I believe that when it comes to being given an opportunity. But I think you have to prove you deserve it going forward. I feel like Kylie doesn't understand that about me, and without giving her a chance, I immediately shut down. "Yeah, you're right. It'll be fine."

She smiles in a way that makes me think my poker face is believable this time.

Racking my brain, I shuffle through my options for what to do at this moment. I need to call my dad, cancel our meeting and break the news to him. Instead, I pull Kylie into a kiss and ignore reality for the next twenty minutes.

168 TISA MATTHEWS

our meeting and break the news to him. Instead, I pull Kylie into a kiss and ignore reality for the next twenty minutes.

25
SOPHIE

THEN

Cooper, 18; Sophie, 16

"Well, it'll happen eventually and when it does it will make it harder when we inevitably break up. I think it's best we call it before we get in too deep, you know?" I say the words as if I'm not in love with him.

"Is that what you think about this, about us?" He scoffs.

I'm flooded with guilt as I look anywhere but at Cooper. The antique jukebox. The waitress in a poodle skirt walking by with two chocolate milkshakes piled high with whipped cream and red heart sprinkles. The black and white checkered floor. Of course our breakup isn't just about him being ready for sex when I'm not. But I'm trying every angle to make him understand that this is what's best for us. Maybe we are right for each other, but not right now, not like this. We're too young for a relationship with this much distance. Yes, we'll be ten minutes apart physically. But mentally, we aren't even close to being in the same place. I've heard the aftermath of what happens when you try to force timing from both of my parent's first marriage. I don't want Cooper and I to become just a sour memory down the road.

"Tell me, Sophie," he spits my name like it's poison, and I almost take this all back. I almost tell him it's a joke. Watching him break in front of me is nearly unbearable. It's breaking me watching his love manifest as anger.

I take a breath, finally meeting his gaze and preparing to finish my speech. "It's going to be too hard. It will be easier to just call it off now–you know, before we fall in love or whatever."

He takes a deep breath through his nose, closing his eyes for a moment. They shoot open and pin on me with his outbreath. "You think we aren't there yet? You think I don't love you, Sophie?"

I ignore my heart shattering in a million pieces, begging me not to let him go. I look away, not knowing what to say.

"Is this seriously happening?"

Standing my ground, I nod slowly, and he moves to get out of the booth like he can't sit here with me for another second.

"Cooper, wait." He turns back right as he was pushing off the table. "Can't we go back to how things were before?"

With one palm pressed into the table and the other against the back of the booth, he locks eyes with me. "No. We can't."

"But . . . we promised we could tell each other if we changed our mind." How can I get him to understand that this is what's best for us? That our friendship is more important than the inevitable downfall of our relationship?

An unamused laugh escapes him. "We didn't change our minds. We're supposed to be together."

It doesn't slip past me that "We Go Together" fades into a new song at this exact moment. "I made my decision, Cooper, and it was hard enough as it is. Can you please just accept it?" I beg.

Without waiting for me to respond, he turns on his heel and walks out the door.

The flood gates open as the door to the diner closes behind Cooper, the slipknot around my heart tightening with each step he takes further away from me. I'm choking on my tears when the waitress, Shirley, approaches. "Sophie, sweetpea, what's wrong?" the typically peppy older woman asks. Without permission, she slides into the spot Cooper just occupied, wrapping her arms around me. "What did he do? I know people who can take care of him if you want," she teases.

A chuckle slips out between sobs. "You might need to use them on me."

"How about I get you a strawberry milkshake instead?"

"Yes, please." I nod, taking a deep breath and wiping the tears from my eyes as she leaves. I didn't have a choice, I remind myself. Cooper deserves to have the full experience of everything college has to offer. I don't want us to go through the same thing my parents did, getting stuck in a relationship and not having anything outside of that. They both fell apart when their first relationship broke and they didn't have anything to fall back on. It's not that I think Cooper and I would fall apart, but we're so young. He's not like me. He needs friends to be happy and social activities. He needs to prepare to help his dad run a company. All of that on top of having a high school girlfriend will be too much for him.

Or maybe that's just my excuse and it'll be too much for me.

Emily's words about the weekly fraternity parties repeat in my head and insecurity sweeps through my body. I'm not a college girl. I'm not mature. I don't have the freedom to do whatever and be wherever. He should be with someone who won't hold him back.

Shirley appears with a strawberry shake so fast I think she must have stolen someone else's for me. Sliding it onto the table, she leaves me to my thoughts. Lips pinching around the thick red straw as I stare into the red heart sprinkles, I take a long sip of my shake. A shadow falls over the table, and I glance up.

"Cooper?" My eyes continue to widen as he leans down, kissing the top of my head. "Wh-what are you doing?"

He nudges me until I slide over, letting him back in the booth. "Okay."

"Okay, what?" I go to wipe a new tear from under my eye, but he reaches out and does it for me.

"I'd like to talk about your concerns. But if you still feel they are valid, we can go back to being friends."

"Really?" My voice cracks.

"I think we might need to take a little time apart first. But yes. I'd rather have you in my life than not at all, Soph. I can't lose you."

My relief comes in a massive wave that results in me falling to Cooper's chest. He wraps his arms around me as a sob racks through my body.

"Shhhh," he soothes, his hand running over my hair, holding me to him until my ice cream has melted and my tears have run dry.

26

COOPER

NOW

Cooper, 21; Sophie, 18

A grin lights my face when I open my front door. "Hey, baby," I greet Kylie, taking in her outfit before leaning in for a kiss. The theme for tonight's party to celebrate making it through the first few weeks of the new year is 80s, and Kylie nailed it. She's wearing a black, off-the-shoulder sweater with giant pink lips on the front, a hot pink tutu and leg warmers and teal heels. Her crimped blonde hair completes the look perfectly and that lipstick isn't going to last long tonight if I have any say in it. We've only been seeing each other for a month, and I've successfully avoided the conversation of a title, but it's been easy and fun.

"Does my outfit look okay?"

She looks as epic as I do in my dad's old matching geometric pattern windbreaker jacket and pants. "I can show you how much I love it if we go inside right now."

She slaps at me playfully but then loops her arms around my neck, bringing her lips to my ear. "You can show me later." I can't help but grin. She pulls back. "I have to complete this scavenger hunt, though, so we have to at least make an appearance."

She pulls up a list on her phone and flips the screen to face me. "Alexis, Taylor and I are having a competition to see who can check everything off first. Losers have to do all the dishes and laundry in February."

I laugh, taking a better look at the list.

Dance on a bar or table

Buy a stranger a donut

Kiss someone besides the person you came with

Switch sweatbands with someone

Save someone from a conversation they clearly don't want to be a part of

Get someone to give you a condom

Take shots with a new friend

"I guess we better get going then." I tug on her hand, leading her down the street toward the fraternity house. "We'll stop by Voodoo Doughnut on the way."

She rambles about which donuts are her favorite, easily convincing me we need some for ourselves too. Twenty minutes later, we're licking frosting off our fingers and pushing our way into the fraternity house. The silence of the cold night air is immediately replaced with bright kitchen lights and a hundred voices talking over each other.

"Will you be good with your list for a few minutes while I go make tonight's cocktail?" I yell over the group of already drunk girls by the fridge screaming the lyrics to "Jessie's Girl" playing from the speaker.

She's already scoping out the scene to see what she can check off. There hasn't been a dull moment with her yet–in the best way. "Yes! I refuse to get stuck with laundry."

"Hey, it doesn't hurt me when you run out of underwear."

"I'm sure it doesn't." She shakes her head in amusement and gives me a chaste kiss before wandering off, her heels clicking against the hardwood floor and her long legs on full display under her way-too-short tutu. I cannot wait to have those wrapped around me later. I stare shamelessly until she walks out the sliding glass door to the backyard then turn toward the kitchen.

I pull the clear plastic tub we typically use for jungle juice out from the bottom cupboard and coax the drunk girls away from the fridge long enough to get out what I need. Dumping in an entire handle of Smirnoff, I add three containers of white cranberry juice–just enough to make the concoction a milky white color. Perfect. I chuckle to myself. I stir the mixture with a ladle and pull the stack of Solo cups from the corner.

A girl I don't recognize invades the space where I lean against the counter. "Hey."

"Hey! Would you like a Cup of Cooper?" I ask, ladling the white drink into a cup.

"Come again?" she asks as if she didn't hear me correctly. She did.

I wink. "Exactly."

The girl stands there dumbfounded for a second, but my words register then she rolls her eyes as she reaches for the cup in my hand. I laugh as she walks away, and I fill a handful of cups to disperse, determined to have that joke land at least five more times tonight.

After passing out a few more drinks, I search for Kylie. Her tutu makes her easy to spot even from the back. The moment I see her on the other side of the living room I know she's crossing the *kiss someone besides the person you came with* item off the list. My eyes widen, unable to pull my gaze away. What I didn't know was a girl would be on the other side of that kiss. She asked me if I wanted her to skip that one, but I wasn't worried about it. I know all the guys here, and they know we've been seeing each other. It didn't occur to me she'd kiss a girl, but I'm even more on board with that.

I take a step toward her, a threesome joke already on the tip of my tongue, right as she pulls back.

What.

The.

Fuck.

She didn't just kiss a girl.

She kissed Sophie.

The moment they break apart, I get a better view of her. Jesus Christ, she's hot. She's wearing teal leggings with a high-cut hot pink leotard and matching leg warmers and sweatbands. Her dirty blonde hair is tied up in a high ponytail that swings slightly when she laughs at something Kylie says. How the hell is she even here? It's rare for freshman girls who aren't in a sorority to get invited. And as far as I know, none of my brothers know Sophie outside of her connection to me.

When Sophie tugs her sweatbands off to give to the girl I came with, she catches my stare. She freezes, clearly ignoring whatever else Kylie says to her. Turning on her heel to walk away, Kylie's eyes also find mine, and she bounds toward me happily.

"Two-for-one! I'm so going to win this." She smiles as she leans in to kiss me, and I taste remnants of familiar cotton candy lip gloss. My eyes don't close. They stay locked on the girl still staring at me from across the living room.

When Kylie pulls back, I force my attention to her. "Did you kiss that girl?" I cough out a laugh to cover up the bile rising in my throat. I thought seeing Sophie kiss another guy was bad, but seeing her kiss the girl I've been hooking up with was another level. You'd think I'd be less mad about that, but it feels like the Universe is fucking with me, seeing how close it can get before I crack.

"Yeah . . . are you mad?" She fidgets her fingers, twisting them together in front of her.

"No, not at all," I reassure her, pulling her into a side hug and kissing her head. "As long as you're kissing me the rest of the night." I force a smile, and her features soften.

"I don't know . . . she is a pretty good kisser," Kylie teases.

Don't I know it. "Doubt she'll kiss you all the places you like to be kissed, though," I murmur against her lips before wrapping my arms around her waist and pulling her into a kiss that would be way too much PDA if we were anywhere but a fraternity party. I know Sophie is watching us, but I need *their* kiss to not be the most recent thing on my mind. Maybe part of me wants Sophie to know what it feels like to see the person you love kiss someone else. Why the fuck is she even here?

Kylie giggles when I finally release her. "Okay, you win."

I grin. "You're just saying that so you win later," I tell her with a wink. Although guilt rushes through me at the thought that it'll be impossible not to think about Sophie in that outfit the rest of the night.

"Exactly. After I win this." She pulls her phone out of her bra, checking off the two items Sophie helped her complete. "I'm like halfway done. I need to take shots with a new friend, dance on a table, score us a condom for all the promises you made me tonight and . . ." She scans the room. "Oh, perfect. That girl *definitely* looks like she needs saving from Ethan."

"Save away. I'm going to get another drink."

"Okay, get me a Cup of Cooper, please."

"You get as many as you want," I say, smacking her ass as she walks away. I need to get out of here.

Making my way back to the front door to get some fresh air, a hand locks onto my wrist.

"What do you want, Sophie?" I ask before I even turn to confirm it's her. I'm mad and confused, along with a few other feelings about her being here.

When I do, I can see the effect of alcohol in her eyes, matching the tequila on her breath. "You have a girl-friend? And she just kissed me?"

"Yup." My voice is flat, and I don't bother correcting her. I need to find out why she's here first. And why she's drunk enough to be kissing someone she doesn't know.

27

SOPHIE

NOW

My stomach twists like a tangled necklace chain. He has a girlfriend? How? When? "Oh," I whisper, dropping his wrist and looking to where I pick at my pink fingernail polish instead. Cooper turns away from me. "Wait." I don't know what else to say, but I don't want to leave him yet.

"Shouldn't you be with your boyfriend?" The remark is a punch in the gut because I wish Cooper was my boyfriend.

"I told you, he's not my boyfriend. Can we talk for a minute?" I don't give him a chance to answer. I reclaim my lock on his wrist and tug him toward the hallway. He reluctantly follows, and my heart sinks. I once assumed Cooper would always follow me everywhere, and I took that for granted. I pull him inside the downstairs bathroom, closing and locking the door behind us. Now that we're alone, the booziness of his spiced apple cider cologne intoxicates me more than I already am, making it hard to respect his space.

Leaning against the counter, he folds his arms across his chest, putting more physical space between an even bigger emotional divide. "What are you doing here?"

"Chastity got invited. She brought me with her." Living off campus, still with my parents, has made it a little difficult to make friends. But Chastity is fitting into college life so well and always invites me. I've done more socializing than I need.

"So, you party now?"

"I'm in college, Coop. It's what you do."

He brushes off the remark like he can see right through me. He knows I don't drink. Well, I didn't. Chastity finally got her own fake ID and has been convincing me to go out more.

"You know this is my fraternity."

"Yeah." I chew on the edge of my lip, feeling guilty. I *did* know I'd see him–or at least I hoped I would. I didn't expect him to be here with a girl, though. "I miss you, Cooper. You haven't given me the time of day lately. I needed to see you."

"I haven't given you time because the last time I did, you let me down."

"Because *my dad* invited JT over?" That was almost two months ago. Why can't he let that go?

"It doesn't matter who invited him over if he's *your* boyfriend."

"For the last time, he's not my boyfriend!"

"So, you've made a new habit of kissing people who aren't your boyfriend?" What is he talking about?

"I haven't kissed JT in months. I can't even remember the last time." I scan through the few memories I've pushed away, placing the most recent one in my kitchen during the football game.

"I fucking saw you, Sophie."

What? How? There's no way he saw *that* kiss.

He rolls his eyes at my confusion. "In your kitchen. Don't even try to deny it."

God, that was so stupid.

He sees the recollection on my face. "Yeah, that's what I thought."

"That wasn't what it looked like."

"You didn't kiss him?"

"I mean, I did. But that was the last time. I swear. I haven't even seen him since."

"Uh-huh. So, what have you been doing for the past month?"

"When you wouldn't see me later that day, I tried giving you space! You always want space when you're upset."

He laughs like I've lost my mind. "You really think that's what I wanted?"

Tucking my hair behind my ear, I focus on the design on the floor tiles, avoiding his eyes. "Yeah," I whisper.

Frustration spews out of him. "I didn't need space, Sophie. I needed YOU," he yells so loud his voice is all I hear over the sound of the party on the other side of the door.

Tears blur my vision, stinging my eyes like when I open them in a chlorine pool. "You never really lost me. My heart has always been yours." I reach for him, but he tilts his body backward over the counter to avoid me. I freeze. His fingers push into his eyes and inhales a deep breath. On the exhale he turns around to face the mirror, his palms pressed into the counter. When he looks up, I meet his gaze in the reflection.

"It's been four months since we broke up. Was I supposed to wait for you to come around when you made me believe you'd never truly come back?"

"Yes." I tangle my fingers through my hair and tug on it hard, my high ponytail loosening. He's supposed to know that I would. "You . . ."

"What? Finish your damn thought."

"You've always been it for me, Cooper. Of course we're supposed to end up together."

His stare burns through me so hot it could reliquify the Jello-O shots in the fridge. "How the fuck was I supposed to know that, Sophie?"

"I just . . . I think . . ." Frustrated, I stumble over my words, shrinking into the wall behind me. "I thought . . ." I attempt to breathe in confidence. "I've been trying to talk to you for the past month!"

"Well, you didn't try hard enough."

"So, you just got a girlfriend instead?" A silent tear slips down my cheek.

He sighs and turns to face me. "She's not my girl-friend. But we are dating."

"You mean you're having sex with her?" The question comes out even though I don't want the answer.

"Please don't do this, Sophie."

"Do what?"

"Put me in this position. Kylie is a good person. She doesn't deserve for the guy she's dating to be locked in a room with the girl he can't get over."

"Then you shouldn't be with her in the first place. It's been like three weeks. Just tell her," I beg.

"She wants to be with me, Soph. Without any bullshit. Or lies. Or kissing other guys."

"But . . ." My voice is small and lacking any confidence. I don't know what to do with this. I know it's not fair for me to be mad that he met someone else when I made him feel like he couldn't trust me. But it feels like he's being ripped away from me, and the vice grip around my heart is making it hard to breathe. "Cooper," I cry, desperate for him to hear me before it's too late.

"Look, Soph." His hands lock on either side of my face, and it takes all of my effort not to lean into him. "I appreciate the honesty. It's all I wanted from you from the beginning. It's what we promised each other. But I don't know." He sighs, and I study his pained eyes, the blue in them lighter than normal, like life has been drained from them. "Every day I see the image of you kissing JT when I thought you only wanted to kiss me. And you slept with him. You gave him the one thing you said you only wanted me to have. I can't unsee it, and I don't know how to get over it."

"Be with me. It'll go away. I'll show you, Coop." I lean closer, our faces inches apart. He doesn't retreat, but he doesn't lean in either.

The door beside us rattles when someone jiggles the knob. I keep my eyes locked on Cooper, but after holding my gaze for a second, he looks toward the sound. Turning back, he sighs. "I can't do this."

"Right now? Or ever?" My heart squeezes at the thought that he might already be gone.

He closes his eyes and takes a deep breath before he opens them again, dropping his hands from my face and stepping back. "I don't know. But I know that I don't want to fight with you. I hate it, and I can't be here right now. I came with Kylie, and I need to go find her. Don't make me a bad guy."

All I want to do is continue to talk this out, but I know it won't get me anywhere I want to be. "I'm sorry I pulled you away from her." I sigh in defeat. My heart feels like it's dissolving–like it has no reason to exist if it doesn't belong to Cooper. It feels like part of him still believes in *us*. But is that one kiss with JT enough to keep him away?

Twisting the knob to pull open the bathroom door, he holds his hand out for me to leave. Guilt rushes through me for forcing this conversation on Cooper. The need

I have for him over anything else is overwhelming. All I want to do is get out of this house and away from anything that reminds me how much love hurts and that Cooper might not stick around to make it feel differently again.

But leaving is the last thing I plan on.

28

COOPER

NOW

The bathroom felt half as small with Sophie and her confessions in it, suffocating me like being trapped with ten too many sprays of bad perfume. The second she's out of sight, I welcome a breath of new air before shutting the door.

What the hell just happened? I don't know where the fuck that came from, but Jesus Christ, that girl could not have worse timing if she tried. I can't tear my life apart based on one bathroom conversation with a drunk Sophie. Even if everything she said was true, I came here with Kylie, and I can't just leave with someone else. Sophie had weeks to be transparent, and I won't make a decision about us based on the one moment she decided to share the truth–conveniently the moment she saw me with another girl. I'm afraid to dig myself into a hole of false security. Maybe she'd make more promises and I'd believe her. But maybe she'd walk away again.

I splash cold water on my face and leave to take a walk around the block before I search for Kylie.

Thirty minutes later, I push open the front door of the house, closing it quickly to keep the outside chill where it belongs.

"Hey, baaaaby." A drunken Kylie stumbles into me. She's barefoot with her heels looped over her fingers.

"That was quick. I'm guessing you made a new friend?" I chuckle.

"Yup." She hiccups. "A few. I may have had one too many shots. Whoops."

I laugh as she stands on her toes to kiss me. Guilt hardly has time to take over because she nearly falls. I barely catch her with my hands around her waist and pull her to me. I can't be here anymore knowing Sophie is here too. I'm too distracted. I don't want to ditch Kylie. I don't want to mislead her, either. Fuck. Should I give Kylie a chance? A drama free relationship would be nice for a change. "Do you want to get out of here?" I yell over the Michael Jackson song someone just turned up.

She looks at me with a smile that in an alternate timeline I might think is beautiful and perfect. "Are you trying to take advantage of me, Cooper? It's only," she pulls my hand from her waist to look at my watch, "10 p.m.! It's practically the middle of the day!"

"I would never do such a thing." I pull her focus to another kiss, forcing myself into the distraction.

"I know." She giggles. "Look what I got." She wiggles a condom in front of my face.

"Yeah, we aren't using that." I laugh, pulling it from her fingers and shoving it in the pocket of my windbreaker in case she needs proof for her list.

"Suit yourself." She shrugs. "But yes, let's go home. I only have one more thing on my list." She scans the room. "OH PERFECT!" Kylie shrieks so loud it hurts my ears, and I squint like the sound is a blinding light. I follow her line of vision. "That girl I kissed earlier. Oh, and took like three shots with." She points to Sophie who is dancing on top of the kitchen counter. "Do you think a counter counts as a table?"

I wonder if Sophie is purposely making a scene or if she's actually trying to make progress on that list she has of her own. Of fucking course they both have an overlapping item on their lists. Girls and their damn lists. "A counter totally counts." The second half of this night, I'm just going to pretend the first half didn't happen. Tomorrow I'll decide what to do about all of this. "Go get up there. But if I can see under your tutu, you'll have a total of sixty seconds to dance before I drag you out of here."

"Promise?" She grins and hands me her heels, and I know no matter what I'm getting out of here as quickly as possible.

29
SOPHIE

THEN

Cooper, 19; Sophie, 16

Plopping another cheese cube in my mouth, I lean awkwardly against the Montgomery's marble kitchen counter. It feels so comfortable being here. Mom and I came over early this morning to help Melissa prep Thanksgiving dinner, and I made the most epic charcuterie board, moving around the kitchen for things I needed like I live here. At the same time, I felt uncomfortable, like I had shown up to someone's house unannounced and was waiting for them to arrive. Every sound made me flinch. Every shadow made me look up. I haven't seen Cooper yet today. He and Troy had already left on a motorcycle ride before I got here.

Even though he said we would still be friends, it's not the same as before. We hung out once more before my junior year started, for the season finale of *Beauty & the Beast* that aired the week after our breakup. It was awkward, us sitting on opposite ends of his couch instead of lying snuggled together in his bed. I haven't seen him in the two months since. I don't know how college is going for him. I've wanted to talk to him every day, but I decided to leave it up to him.

I still think I did the right thing. I just want what's best for him, and right now, that's not me. It doesn't mean this isn't hard. I've spent all my free time lost in paper worlds, mostly wondering why they make happy ever afters seem so easy–because they aren't real, that's why.

"Sophie." His voice hits me like a pillow being thrown in my face–startling but with so much potential to be comfortable. He's leaning against the archway between the hallway and the kitchen–damn he's hot in his black joggers and a slightly strained T-shirt–looking at me like he's surprised I'm here even though he had to know I'd be coming. Our families have celebrated Thanksgiving together every single year since Dean and Carter were born, before Cooper and I even existed.

"Hi, Coop. Umm. How are you?" Unsure of what else to say, I rip a grape off its stem on the charcuterie board and shove it in my mouth.

He takes a few steps to the fridge, opens the door and reaches for two Squirts. There's an entire row of regular, but the only Ruby Red is the one in his hand. "Fine," he says as he sets the cans on the counter next to me, reaching into the cupboard above me for glasses. "You?"

"I'm good . . ." My words trail off. "Umm. Do you think maybe we could," I pause, "be friends today? Just for today?" I beg in a desperate attempt for things to feel normal between us again.

He sighs, cracking the top on the Ruby Red Squirt and pouring it into the glass as he stands a foot from me. It takes everything in me not to reach for him. Instead, I reach for a handful of cheese cubes. "We are friends," he says, handing me the glass. Our fingers brush in the transfer and he pulls back quickly as if an innocent touch is a gateway drug to something more.

"It's just, you said things would be back to how they were and they aren't."

"I know. I'm sorry. I've been really busy with school, the fraternity, everything, just like you said."

"Okay."

"Okay. Well." He holds his gaze to mine for a few moments, but his attention leaves me when the front door swings open. With half a smile, he abandons me for the living room. I hear the sound of Troy and Cooper's secret handshake and fight back a laugh. They probably saw each other an hour ago before Troy stopped by Emily's.

Dinner flies by, and Cooper makes as much conversation with me as he does everyone else. Our brothers never really caught on to us dating all summer, too busy with their own lives and not thinking twice about us spending time together like we always have. Mom tried to ask me what happened a few times, but after my talk with Dad, I wanted to put it all behind me and told her we just felt we were better off as friends. Dad affirming my choice was enough, and I don't want anyone to contradict that. It's too justified in my head, and the way Cooper jokes around with Troy, filling everyone in on the joys of college life, only solidifies that. He catches my eyes a few times, and I swear there's gratitude in them for making the decision he never would have made on his own, but I could be imagining that to make myself feel better.

"Who's ready for dessert?" Mom asks the table as she walks in carrying an apple pie in one hand and a pumpkin pie in the other. All four boys shoot their hands up as if they weren't just groaning about being too full to move. "Cooper, honey, I only have two hands, but there's cupcakes for you on the counter."

"Thank you, Mrs. Porter," Cooper says with a smile that falls as he locks his eyes on me.

When Cooper returns with his treat, he's holding his phone in his other hand. "Heads Up?" he asks no one in particular. The parents have retreated to the living room with their wine, leaving the five of us to play. It's tradition–not Heads Up in particular, but games have always been part of our get-togethers.

"Let's do it," Carter says. "But if Cooper and Sophie are on a team, I get Troy *and* Dean." He didn't have to say it aloud. There's never a question of how the teams are divided. It's always been the same. Whenever there's an uneven number, Cooper and I always take the loss. It's like giving out a handicap like they do in golf to level the playing field.

I watch as Troy and Cooper have a conversation without words. Carter and Dean are oblivious to the awkwardness between Cooper and me, but I'm sure Troy knows every detail. "Deal," Cooper confirms as he concludes the silent exchange.

Troy, Carter and Dean take the first turn, Carter guessing five of the words the other two describe.

Passing the phone back to his brother, Cooper takes it. "Ready, Soph?" he asks with a glimmer in his eyes, and it feels like last year, like how we used to be.

Shifting my chair to face him more, I pull a leg under me and nod.

He presses *start* and holds the phone to his forehead. When the timer counts down from *3*, the name *Kristin Kreuk* appears on the screen. That's just dumb luck.

"Cat," is all I say.

"Oooh, umm. Kristin something. Kreuk," he says, slapping his hand on the table hard enough to rattle it when he remembers the name of the actress who plays the main character in our show.

"Yup," I confirm, and he tilts his phone down so it changes to the next word.

"Oooh. What we found under Carter's bed."

Carter attempts to interject, but Cooper swats his hand in his brother's direction as he says, "Socks." We both take a precious second to laugh at his expense, reminded of the time we were sneaking around Carter's room and Mike was forced to explain masturbation to us way earlier than we should have learned.

"You think this is a sport."

"Video games are a sport," he says matter-of-factly.

I roll my eyes and he tilts the screen down.

"I'll never get one of these."

"Tattoo."

Tilt. He doesn't need my confirmation to know he's right. He knows I don't believe anyone should get a tattoo unless they are confident they'll never change their mind about whatever it represents–and how unlikely I think that is.

"Your favorite food."

"Spaghetti."

Tilt.

"Troy's favorite food."

Cooper laughs. "Ice cream." Troy shrugs, not bothered by the idea that dessert shouldn't count as food.

"Damn, you're quick," Carter says with a shake of his head.

"I'm not proud of it." Cooper shoots me a wink.

With an eye roll and a prayer my brother didn't catch that, I force my focus back on the game. "You're afraid of these."

"Balloons are fucking terrifying," he groans.

Tilt.

I roll my eyes. Cooper chuckles right before he says, "Zac Efron."

"What the fuck," I hear Carter mutter under his breath, and catch the other two shaking their heads out of the corners of my eyes.

Tilt.

"Oh! Public sex." My cheeks heat a little at the word, and I catch the other boys raising an eyebrow. Cooper doesn't hesitate. "Playground."

I circle my hand indicating for him to guess again.

"Mmmm. Slide." Over the summer we caught strangers having sex in the tube slide at the park where we always skate.

"Uhhhh," Dean half chimes in, misunderstanding. Part of me wishes whatever he is thinking is true. The realization that I'll never get to experience that level of intimacy with Cooper has been a tough pill to swallow.

Cooper ignores him, flipping the screen down again with six seconds left on the clock. I freeze, my brain searching for another way to describe the word quickly enough. Four seconds. "Tablecloths at–"

"Cherries," Cooper spits out before I even finish my sentence and before he recalls what it reminds him.

The phone vibrates in his hand, making a dinging bell noise before it recalls our nine correct cards. I see the memory of our breakup resurfacing in Cooper's mind, but Carter's voice pulls him from it.

"Yeah, bullshit. This is why you two should never be allowed on a team." He laughs.

Cooper and I shrug.

Scanning the table, I soak in the moment. The boys are all smiling, joking and teasing. I glance at the parents in the living room, our Moms leaned into our Dads on the couch. All morning I was so worried. With how close our families are, it feels like there will always be this constant reminder that Cooper and I aren't together anymore, and there's no escaping it. But getting away from him would mean getting away from everyone else too. And that's something I could never do.

Cooper stands. "I'm getting another cupcake before the next round." He walks into the kitchen, and I slide off my chair to follow him, leaving our brothers to reach for a second slice of pie.

Taking a huge bite out of his cupcake, he holds the other half out for me. "Thanks," I say, accepting the gesture.

Even though he just gave it to me, he takes the cupcake from my hand and sets it on the counter. "Come here," he says softly, pulling me into a hug. "I'm sorry I've been too busy for us to be friends again," he whispers into my hair, "But we're going to be okay." I melt into his arms, counting to twenty in my head and reaching it three times over before he lets me go.

30
SOPHIE

THEN

My rarely worn blue jeans feel constricting as I jump into them–especially after all the food I ate on Thanksgiving yesterday. I pull the forest green Ducks crewneck from a hanger in the back of my closet as my dad yells from downstairs. "You almost ready, Sophie? Mike and Cooper are here." His name forces him into my thoughts as I tug my sweatshirt over my head. I get stuck in the wrong hole, suffocating in the cotton and panicking for a breath.

I figure out how to dress myself like a freaking adult, take a deep breath of *get ahold of yourself, Sophie* and walk down the stairs. "Why are Cooper and Mr. Montgomery here?" I sit on the floor to lace up my Chuck Taylors as I look at Dad, confused, when he walks into the entryway from the kitchen.

"What do you mean? We are going to the game with them."

"Oh. I didn't know that." Dad would forget everything if he didn't have Mom to remind him. I thought it was just us driving to Corvallis together for the Civil War football game.

"Ready?" he asks again as I stand from tying my shoes. It's like he's totally forgotten about our breakup three months ago. Cooper and I just now finding our friendship again doesn't seem to be on his radar at all. What better place than a game, though? Still, nerves rack through me as I open the front door. Our friendship finally feels like it's back on track, but I'm still unsure how different it'll look from the one we were on before.

As I slide onto the black leather in the back seat of Mr. Montgomery's G-Wagon, I let my eyes skim Cooper, completely dressed in black between his joggers and Duck hoodie. He looks up from his phone, a grin brightening his face at the sight of me. My heart fluttering steals my breath at the thought that he's genuinely happy to see me. "Decided to actually dress for the weather for once?" he teases.

I roll my eyes. "Don't act like you don't love my dresses."

Hunger flashes in his eyes. "I do love them." He drags his teeth across his bottom lip like he'd eat me up right there in the backseat of his dad's car if I let him. We might not be together, but I'd be lying if I said I don't love the effect I have on him. He shakes his head like he's trying to clear the thoughts running through it and focuses back on his phone.

The pregame chit chat on the radio takes a front seat to any conversation. Cooper is mostly on his phone, and I steal glances at him every few pages of my book. There's something different about him this weekend–even from Thanksgiving yesterday. Or maybe it's just that I haven't seen him in so long it feels that way.

We drive the hour to Reser Stadium and attempt to make our way through the chaos and crowds. The Civil War annual rivalry game is insane, and since we aren't on home turf, it can be a little rough winding your way through the sea of orange when you're wearing green. Dad and Mr. Montgomery were up ahead, but I lost them behind a pillar. My heart races as I spin around, looking for Cooper. He comes to a stop right behind me, the crowds pushing by around us. Relief hits me like a cold shower on a sunburn. "Why are you looking at me like that?" I question the stupid grin on his face.

"Nothing. Your ass looks good." He shrugs.

"That's why you're walking behind me? Cooper!" I swat at him.

"What?" He smirks. "It does. I'm taking advantage of the jeans."

What is with him being so horny today? What the heck happens at college that makes him so comfortable talking this way to me when he never has before? I give him a questioning look, his mood rubbing off on me. He takes a sip from his water bottle as he looks at the section numbers above us, his Adam's apple bobbing as he swallows. The way his lips taste on mine has already faded from my memory, and my chest pinches at the reminder.

His focus pulls to me. "Why are *you* looking at *me* like *that*?" He laughs, and I force my gaze to the cement between us, feeling the blush heat my face. I slowly shift my eyes to Cooper's in time to watch his tongue swipe across his lower lip. There's a reason I picture him as the guy in every book I read. He's so hot. And he's so *not mine* anymore, I remind myself.

"I'm not looking at you in any sort of way," I lie, knowing my face is betraying me.

"Uh-huh," he muses and joins the flow of the crowd, heading toward our section. I think I understand why guys need cold showers now–the thought of splashing ice water on my face feels like it's the only thing that would wash away the desires coursing through me.

"Cooper."

He hums at me over his shoulder in acknowledgment as we walk.

"I need to go to the bathroom first. Will you wait for me so I don't get lost?"

He scans the wall on the opposite side of the aisle until he spots a hallway with a bathroom sign at the entrance. Taking my hand, he weaves us through the people until we make it safely to the other side.

31
COOPER

THEN

I text my dad to let him know we will meet them at the seats and try to think about what snack I want. I run through all the options in my mind in an attempt to keep it off Sophie. She keeps looking at me like she doesn't know what's gotten into me.

It's sex.

I had sex for the first time last week, and now it's the only thing I can fucking think about. Waiting until Sophie was ready was something I was more than willing to do. But then she broke up with me, and it fucking sucked. I contemplated walking away from her altogether. I did. But I came back. I *had* to.

I know it's my fault we are drifting apart. She wasn't wrong. I've been so busy trying to keep up with everything and maintaining a relationship with her would have been a challenge. I could have made it work, though. I'd like to blame my busy schedule, but this has nothing to do with that. As much as I could understand Sophie's logic, I knew I needed a little time to break my habits with her. Not pulling her into my arms whenever she's near. Not kissing her sweet lips. Not texting her every morning and hearing her voice every night before I go to sleep. But I can't lose her forever, so I'm willing to give her whatever she needs, even if I don't like it.

I would do anything for her, but when I realized it was really over for us, I decided there was no reason to hold back from the full college experience I was embracing.

That's a lie.

That's my excuse.

What I was really doing was hoping the whole "get over someone by getting under someone else" motto would work. So, I hooked up with a sorority girl who keeps coming to my fraternity's parties. Would I have rather had that experience with Sophie? Fuck yes. But it is what it is. I'm not going to never have sex because it can't be with Sophie, and I thought it helped. That was, until I saw her yesterday.

My new problem is now that I know what to expect when it comes to sex, I can't get my mind off how it would be with Sophie. Someone I care about. Someone I love. Being around the girl I want to do it with most–but can't–is pure torture. Yesterday we were around our brothers all day, but despite the twenty thousand people around us, without so much of our family here, it feels like this is more intimate time together.

I don't want to jeopardize the progress we made yesterday. It felt good, like enough time has passed for us to transition back to how we were before we thought being *Sophie & Cooper* at this time in our life would work out.

Sophie exits the bathroom, and the way she scans the hallway for me in a panic like there's a chance she won't find me waiting makes my stomach flip. I can clearly get other girls in my bed, but still, the way I want the one who will never be under my sheets again leaves me a little frustrated. She visibly sighs in relief like she did a few minutes ago when she thought she lost me, and my brain battles between fantasy and reality. She doesn't want to be with me. Why does it feel like she might, though?

Her pink lips shimmer like she just put her sparkly lipgloss on, and I'm hit with a reminder of how they taste–like Sophie and cotton candy. Jesus Christ, Cooper. Keep it in your fucking pants. I need to rectify this mindset immediately.

"Hey, come with me," I say, reaching for her soft hands again.

She doesn't even question me. She just lets me pull her down the hallway. It's not until I push through an exit door that leads to a stairwell that her brows pull together.

The heavy metal door closes behind us, muffling almost all the chaos on the other side of it.

"What are we doing?"

There's a stairwell to my left, but there's no one in sight–only a few echoey voices from at least a few floors down. "It's too loud to talk out there."

"Oh, what did you want to talk about?" She sticks her hands in her back pockets and teeters on her heels.

"I wanted to apologize." I shove my hands into the pocket of my hoodie, feeling awkward, but holding her gaze anyway.

"For what?"

"What I said about your ass in your jeans."

Her face falls. "You didn't mean it?"

"I did. You know I'm attracted to you, Soph. More than anyone." She bites into her lip, reaching to tuck a strand of hair behind her ear. "But that wasn't appropriate given our situation."

"Oh, right. It's okay," she says, now running the ends of her hair repeatedly through her thumbs and pointer fingers.

"Not really. I don't want you to think I'm trying to win you back or something. You made your decision clear, and I want to respect that."

"So, you don't want to be with me anymore?" God, she's confusing. I swear she seems devastated by this as if I was breaking up with her.

"That's not what I said."

Her eyes flick back and forth over my face like I spoke a foreign language and she's trying to decipher my words. Instead of responding, she slams her lips against mine. The last thing I expected causes me to stumble back, breaking the kiss only slightly as she falls into me. Without a second thought, I grip either side of her neck, pulling her lips to mine again. Her lips part enough to let me deepen the kiss.

Cotton fucking candy. She tastes even better than I remember. The way our tongues tangle as they fall into an old routine is comforting. My dick twitches to life. Jesus Christ, I need to get it under control before there's no turning back. Call me crazy, but this right here might be better than sex. Well, unless that sex was with Sophie. I try to stay in the moment, but I can't help wondering what this means. I'm spiraling. I should stop her. I should ask what she's doing. I intend to break the kiss, but she grabs the strings of my hoodie, pulling me closer.

Without opening my eyes, I spin us and press her against the wall, my hands leaving her neck to run under her sweatshirt.

My fingers smoothing across her bare skin.

The way I feel her breath catch in our kiss at the contact.

How she loops her arms around my neck and runs her fingers through the hair at my neck.

Fuck. Did I make a mistake last week? If I could have another chance with Sophie, I'll regret being with someone else before her, and there's no way she'll feel good about it either. When my hands reach her bra, I slip them around to her stomach, my thumbs brushing against the skin beneath her breasts.

She adjusts herself so subtly I'm surprised I catch it, but it's enough to make my heart drop. It's enough to make me question if we are on the same page.

I break our kiss, leaving us both standing there breathless, her lips slightly swollen and the gloss on them gone.

"What was that?" I whisper as worry fills her eyes.

"Umm, I don't know. I'm sorry." Her hands have fallen back to my hoodie strings, and she twists them in her fingers. She pauses her words, dropping the thin black ropes like they burned her. "I shouldn't have done that."

"Why did you?" I ask, my hand still locked on her neck.

"I don't know . . . I just . . . missed you for a second, I guess."

"You still don't want to be together?" I hate that the words come out more like a plea.

She hesitates, and I can practically see the thoughts flashing through her mind before she shakes her head, slowly, her eyes welling with tears.

I sigh, defeated all over again. Instead of fighting her like I did the last time we had this conversation, I brush my thumb over her cheek before threading my fingers through her curls.

I look at Sophie's eyes, filled with the vulnerability I'm now shoving deep inside. "It's okay," I whisper, and she looks at me like she's unsure it really is. "Old habits are hard to break." I manage half of a smile and resist stealing one more kiss. Instead, I run my hand down her arm until my hand is linked with hers. "Let's just go watch the game," I say, tugging her back toward the door.

We enter the chaos of the stadium again. "Do you want a pretzel?" I ask over my shoulder as I drop her hand.

"Yes, please. With–"

I cut her off. "Extra cheese."

"Yeah." She grins, skipping an extra step to catch up to me.

32

SOPHIE

Now

Cooper, 21; Sophie, 18

The front door of the frat house clicks behind Kylie–with Cooper leading her out, his hand on her back and her heels in his other hand. Eyes narrowing, I grind my teeth before taking a big sip of whatever the heck this white drink is that I got from the tub on the counter. Huh. I prefer tequila, but this vodka is pretty good. Finishing my cup without a breath, I attempt to process my already fuzzy memories. I've had way too much to drink tonight but some things are impossible to forget.

A girl kissing me.

Finding out Cooper is dating that same girl.

Basically admitting to Cooper that he's the love of my life.

Him turning me down.

But I swear it felt like he wasn't actually turning me down. It seemed like he just didn't want to be a bad date or guy. Did I make that up in my head? Do I just hope that he ditches her after tonight and comes back to me or am I imagining this distorting reality? When I left the bathroom, I immediately found Kylie and befriended her, wanting to see if her story aligned with Cooper's. The only thing I got out of it was three more shots I didn't need and crossing the *dance on a table* item off my bucket list. But he just left *with* her. And the way he was touching her on the way out was not a "let's leave here so I can tell you we can't see each other anymore" kind of touch.

God, I'm so stupid. Stupid, stupid, Sophie. Why did I even come here? The room spins a little, the shots I took with Kylie kicking in. Closing my eyes, I brace myself against the counter.

"Are you okay?" I glance up to a semi-familiar face. I think his name is Logan? When I first got here and was waiting for Cooper to show up, he was flirting with me. I gave him my number when he asked because I wasn't sure how to say no without being rude.

"Umm. Yes." No. I'm far from okay. I want Cooper, and he just left with the wrong girl.

"Can I get you anything?" He can't make Cooper come back and leave with me. Maybe I should leave with someone else too.

Rubbing my lips together, I navigate the best I can through my alcohol distorted thoughts. "Do you want to get out of here?"

He grins. "Really?"

I nod. "Yeah. Let's go."

I guess dicks before chicks isn't a universal rule unless he doesn't recognize me. I don't care anyway. I need to focus on something besides the pain in my chest and the whirlwind of possibilities of what Cooper is doing with Kylie, so when Logan takes my hand, I let him lead the way.

Tossing and turning for the hundredth time, my eyes pop open, staring at the ceiling. I glance over at Logan, twisted in the sheets, the weight of his arm feeling heavier than it should over my stomach. No matter how many times I've readjusted myself, he doesn't stir. I guess some people sleep hard after they've been drinking. Not me.

Or maybe I just can't sleep for other reasons. My drunkenness wore off, but not until after Logan and I had already had sex. I was just crossing items off my list, which after hanging out with Kylie and her friends tonight–helping them with their own list– I realized it's a normal thing. Experiencing all that college life has to offer before settling down is exactly what I should be doing.

I close my eyes, recalling once again how stupid I am, knowing anything else is an excuse. I was so upset, blinded by my hurt, seeing Cooper leave with Kylie. I wanted to get back at him. But this didn't hurt him. It only hurt me.

How could I do this? To someone I love. When I love someone so much.

Every second of it felt wrong. His touch didn't send a rush of warmth through me. His kiss didn't evoke butterflies. Every second I wanted to stop.

But I didn't. Even though I know Logan would have stopped if I had asked. He's a nice guy. He's just not *the* guy.

An overwhelming urge to see Cooper hits me, stronger than it's ever been before. I reach to the nightstand, careful not to wake Logan, and check my phone. *2:37 a.m.* I gently slide his arm off my waist and slip out from under the sheet. Grabbing the pieces of my '80s outfit scattered around the room, I tip toe out of his room. I get dressed with only the bare minimum–my blue leggings and pink crop top I had with me in case I got cold. Bunching the rest of my costume in my hand, I twist the front door knob slowly, slipping between the smallest crack and into the apartment hallway.

Sighing once the door is secured between me and my bad decision, I lean against the wall and unlock my phone using Cooper's birthday as the code. Pulling up the map, I check the distance between here and his house. Four blocks. I skip calling an Uber, and decide to walk, letting the little blue line on my screen guide me like it's much more certain of the plan than I am.

When I'm two houses away, I swipe out of the map app and lock my phone. Darkness surrounds me outside of the evenly spaced street lamps outside every third house. No light comes from inside Cooper's house. He must be asleep. *Or he's in his room with Kylie.* My stomach flips, wanting to expel the alcohol and bad choices from the night. As I approach, I stare at his front door, wondering if he'll answer when I knock. Before I get the courage to cross his driveway, the front porch light kicks on.

Panicking, I squat down and hide behind the car parked on the street. I can barely see the entryway, and only because Troy's car is missing from the driveway. Kylie closes the door behind her and cuts through the front yard grass–alone. She stands on the curb for only a moment before headlights brighten my peripheral and a car comes to a stop in front of her. She slides into the back of what I'm assuming is an Uber, and the car drives off, taking her away.

Where is she going? What happened inside? Did Cooper kick her out? After sex? Did she just have somewhere to be? The possibilities swirl through my mind as I sit there, crouched on the side of the road, for at least twenty more minutes.

I have to know. I have to see him.

Walking to the front door, the motion activated porch light startles me when it brightens the entryway. With my heart thumping erratically in my chest, I reach my hand to knock against the white wood but change my mind before it makes contact. I twist in a circle, scanning the porch. I take two steps to the porch railing, bending to examine the wood. I run my fingers along the edge where the crossbar meets the column holding up the overhang. Finding the one inch slice of wood, I press on the spring loaded secret compartment, and it pops open. Pulling the spare key from it, I press the wood back into place.

Sliding the key into the lock, I twist the knob slowly, listening for any indication that Cooper is awake. It's completely dark inside besides the glow from the street light filtering through the kitchen window. It's completely quiet besides the hum of the refrigerator.

Still not having a plan, I walk through the kitchen to the living room. I set the clothes in my hand on the armrest of the couch, and scan the room. One of Cooper's black sweatshirts hangs over the back of the couch, and I pick it up. The crop top I'm wearing barely covers my boobs, and since I was wearing a spandex leotard earlier, I didn't need a bra. I slip my shirt over my head, replacing it with Cooper's hoodie that's at least two sizes too big for me. Scrunching the collar to my nose, I inhale the apple cider scent and sink onto the couch.

My eyes close, my head tipping against the back of the couch as I try to regroup. I shouldn't be here. I'm sober enough to know this is insane. But even just knowing I'm in the same place as Cooper makes me feel better. I still don't know what happened between him and Kylie, and I don't know how to wake him up and ask. Do I even deserve to know what happened after where I spent the last few hours? Probably not, but I'm selfish enough to need the answer.

"Sophie?" Cooper's groggy voice jolts me, my eyes shooting open and my hands flying to my chest. My heart pounds against my fingertips.

"You scared me," I whisper, more to myself than anything as I take him in through the kitchen window glow.

Standing there in only black basketball shorts, he rubs his hands up his face and wipes the sleepiness from his eyes and replaces it with confusion. "What are you doing here?"

Frozen on the other side of the living room, he doesn't make a move toward me as he waits for my answer. "I needed to be near you." *I need you to choose me.*

His face softens, and he crosses the room, sitting on the couch next to me. We stare at each other, neither of us saying a word. The sound of our breathing and the faded hum of the refrigerator holds the tension within them.

Reaching for me, he guides me onto his lap and I follow his lead until I'm straddling him. His hands run up my thighs, over my bright blue leggings, and settle at my waist under his sweatshirt. He wets his lips, his eyes flicking to mine before settling on my eyes.

I scoot closer, strengthening our connection, and his hardly audible groan vibrates through me. My hands are inside the sleeves of his sweatshirt as they fall to his neck, my fingers poking out enough to play with the short tips of his hair.

I love you is on the tip of my tongue. It almost rolls out, but I clamp my mouth shut, still unsure.

"What is it?" Cooper whispers.

"I . . . I'm sorry I just showed up."

He squeezes my hips then runs his thumbs across my bare skin. Having him touch me like this for the first time in months is almost too much to handle. "I want you here. I always want you, Sophie."

"You do?" Tears fill my waterline, and I beg them not to fall.

"Yes." He nods, watching me like he is waiting to see if the salty pools betray me too.

"But yesterday you said you can't do this."

"I didn't mean you and me." He chuckles. "I meant fight with you, especially in the bathroom of a fraternity house.

"Oh."

"I didn't want there to be anyone or anything between us. Kylie. Or alcohol."

"Yeah, that makes sense." My brain seems to forget that Cooper always has my best interest at heart, even if his translation doesn't land. God, I love him. "Coop . . ."

"Yeah?"

"I–"

His mouth presses into mine like he can't wait another second without fusing himself to me. My body melts into his in response, my arms wrapping around his neck and pulling us closer.

33
COOPER

NOW

I have no clue what words were coming out of Sophie's mouth, but my lips are on hers before she can finish her thought. The dark room blurs around us, and all I can think about is being closer to her. She was selfish with her timing earlier. She had no regard for the situation, for Kylie . . . for me–even if she was saying everything I wanted to hear. But now that she's here, and Kylie is out of the picture, I can't help but give in to her.

She presses her lips hard against mine, immediately parting them and allowing me to deepen the kiss. I groan at the comforting taste of her. She pulls back enough to speak, her words breathless. "Cooper, I need to feel you."

Fuck. I groan. The only other time we've had sex is the night I took her virginity, and I've been thinking about this moment ever since. My hands grip her thighs as I stand, and she links her ankles around my waist. She brings her lips back to mine in a frantic kiss like she thinks I might change my mind.

I back us through the living room and into the laundry room, wanting something more intense than my bed. She breaks our kiss to take in her surroundings as I set her on the dryer. Reaching behind her, I twist the timer knob and hit start. She gasps at the immediate vibration coursing through her and tries to kiss me again.

Instead, I bury my fingers in the underside of her hair, tugging her head backward, giving me access to her neck as I settle between her legs. I nip at her ear before kissing down her throat, warring between stripping her naked and loving the sight of her in my clothes again. Running a hand beneath the sweatshirt, I'm pleasantly surprised by the fact that she's not wearing a damn thing under it. I swipe my thumb over her nipple, noting its firmness and eliciting a groan from both of us as I kiss her.

My hands and lips abandon what they're doing as I drop to my knees. She holds my shoulders for balance as I loop my fingers under the band of both her leggings and thong, slowly sliding them down her legs.

Fuck, she's perfect. My fingers trail down her soft skin, my lips kissing down the same path as I tug the fabric away from her and toss it on the ground next to me.

I send my fingers and lips in reverse, working their way back up her legs until I'm close enough to wrap my hands around her ass and pull her to the edge of the dryer. Pushing my hoodie up her waist enough to give me better access to her, I drag my tongue across her wet center, my eyes rolling back. *Fuck, I missed her.*

Over the sounds of the dryer, I barely hear her breath catch as her fingers immediately fall to my hair. I eat at her. My tongue swiping inside. My mouth sucking her clit. My fingers digging into the skin on her hips. Her body vibrating in sync with the machine or her moans–I'm not sure which.

She stretches her legs over my shoulders, her toes barely reaching the corners of the washing machine behind me, spreading herself wider for me. She leans back on her palms, her feet pressing against the metal, her sweet pussy granting me more access with the tilt of her hips. I run my thumbs over the apex of her thighs and dive my tongue inside her again, flicking it over and over and feeling the vibrations pulsing through her body.

Running my hands up her stomach, I smooth them down her sides, over her thighs, reveling in having access to her body this way. Digging my fingers of one hand into the soft skin of her inner thigh to press her wider, my other hand finds her opening. I suck her clit hard as I drive my finger into her easily. "Oh my god, Cooper." With my tongue still firm against her and a second finger sliding in and out of her, I spare a glance up. Her eyelids are heavy as she watches me, biting into her lip, and it's the sexiest sight I've ever seen. I refocus my gaze on her sensitive skin in front of me, pulling out my fingers and dragging my tongue long and slow over her.

On an exaggerated catch of her breath, she tugs my hair hard enough to stop me. Hands still clinging to her thighs, I stand, pressing my hard length into her through the fabric of my shorts. Fuck. I picture condoms tucked away in the drawer of my dresser as she pulls me into a kiss. I don't want to let go of her. Not after so long of her being out of reach.

"Are you still on birth control?" I whisper against her lips.

She nods.

"Has anyone else ever felt you bare?" I ask, praying the answer is what I want to hear. I want something from her I know no one else has had. I've felt too out of control—like she's too far from me—and this could reconnect us.

"No one," she says with a heavy breath.

"Promise?" I pull far enough away to look at her eyes, to be sure.

"I don't trust anyone except you." The magic words bring me back to her. I push my shorts and briefs down, aligning perfectly. Before grabbing her hips, I take a second to finally pull the sweatshirt over her head. I readjust her to the edge of the machine then run my thumb over her to see how wet she is, still perfect from when my tongue was hot and firm against her. My other thumb joins in, spreading her wide enough for me to push into her.

"Fuck," I groan, stilling my movements for a moment, although the motion of the dryer continues some of the work for me. Her arms loop around my neck, her fingers tugging at the tips of my hair. I pull almost all the way out before driving into her. She moans, her head falling to my shoulder. I wrap my arm around her to hold her in place, to allow me deeper. "God, your pussy is so good." She bites into my skin as if my words sent her straight to the edge.

"I feel you everywhere, Coop," she manages.

I groan, feeling every part of my dick connecting us inside her, her arousal coating me and dissolving any friction as I push to the hilt. Fuck, she feels good–too good. I rub my thumb roughly against her clit, determined to make her come when I do.

Her toes fall from the edge of the washing machine behind me, as if she's losing her strength to hold on. Linking her ankles around my waist, she brings us closer. I drive into her harder, one hand gripping her hip, and the other threading through her hair, fingers tight on her neck as I kiss her. With each thrust bringing me as deep inside her as I could possibly be, my orgasm becomes imminent.

"Sophie, baby, I need you to come for me." Before all the rough words are out, waves of her orgasm pulse around me, pulling me to my own release. I keep up my rhythm as I spill into her and don't stop until her body has nothing left to give except for a few residual twitches.

Still inside her, I push her head off my shoulder with my hands locked on the nape of her neck. My lips brush hers between breaths as both of ours even out. I have the urge to punctuate each kiss with a verbal declaration of how much I fucking love this girl. But I don't give into it. Not yet.

Pressing my forehead to hers, I choose different words. "Everything is better with you."

A soft smile pairs with her freshly fucked glow, and I fall even more in love with her. Moving her hands from my chest to her face, she yawns behind them, and I can't help but chuckle. It must be at least 5 a.m., and I'm not sure if she's even been to sleep yet. "Let's go to bed."

I pull out of her slowly as she nods, reaching for a towel on the shelf behind her. Once we're cleaned up enough, I slide her off the dryer and she leans into my chest, wrapping her arm around my waist and refusing to let go the entire walk to my room.

She releases me long enough to pee and brush her teeth, and I tuck her into bed. As I'm about to crawl in next to her, her fingers brush my arm. "Can you get me a glass of water, please?"

"Of course." Locking my hand on the back of her head, I kiss her hair, letting my lips linger and taking in her faded floral scent I've missed so much. "Be right back."

The orange glow from the sunrise streaming through the kitchen window guides my way down the hall. With a glass in hand, I turn the sink on. As I wait for it to run cold, a phone lights up on the counter. It must be Sophie's. I set the glass down and pick it up without thinking twice. It's locked, but a preview of a text from a number she doesn't have saved has popped up on the screen: *Why'd you sneak out?*

34
COOPER

THEN

Cooper, 19; Sophie's 17th birthday

"Just need to make a quick stop first," I tell April as we drive away from the fraternity house. Troy and I live close enough to campus to walk to parties, but I showed up late after helping Dad with work.

"Okay," April says sweetly, scrolling through her phone as I get on the main road. I met her at one of the first parties our fraternity threw this year. She's in a sorority and shares my view on freshman year–the one I adopted after Sophie forced me into it anyway. We both try to take advantage of what college has to offer. That means we've hooked up a few times, but there is no level of commitment. It's nice. I enjoy her company.

I park in front of the midnight blue house that sits next to my parents' sage green one–not that you can tell with how dark it is. It may be nearing the end of Sophie's seventeenth birthday, but it's not over yet. Reaching in my back seat, I pull out the gift I've wrapped in a cut brown paper bag with a Nerds Rope tucked under the twine I wrapped around it in a haphazard bow. I hop out of the car, jog up to the Porter's front steps and leave the present on the welcome mat. I didn't write my name, but Sophie's is scribbled across the front. Once she opens it, she'll know who it's from anyway.

Opening the car door and sliding into the driver's seat, April gives me a pointed look. "What's up?" I ask as I put my car in drive and pull into the Porter's driveway to turn around.

"Was that a present for a girl? That you dropped off before taking me to your bed?" She knows our casual dating isn't serious, and that's reflected in her mostly teasing tone. But there's also a hint of envy or suspicion or . . . something.

"It's just a book," I tell her, and the sliver of worry fades as if it's a gift that automatically discredits the idea of romance. If only she knew Sophie, whose exact idea of romance *is* a book–not that I'm trying to romance her. Truth be told, I haven't tried to do much of anything with her since the football game last fall. I'm a sucker for traditions, that's all.

When we pull into my driveway, the front porch light kicks on. My eyes are immediately drawn to the plastic grocery bag knotted and sitting in the entryway. Apparently, Sophie is a sucker for tradition too.

"Cupcake?" I ask April as I pick up the bag, unlock the front door and lead her inside.

35
COOPER

THEN

Hopping out of my car, I walk through the grass that separates the two houses and leads straight to the back. I've been so busy, I haven't stopped by since I dropped off Sophie's birthday book three weeks ago. I always forget how nice it is to be home until I'm here.

On the Porter side of our joint backyard, Sophie's dad, Jack, already has the grill fired up and lined with burgers. On our side, Mom has an entire table laid out like a bar. One end has red Solo cups, a few bottles of Smirnoff and Malibu and an ice-filled bowl of red, white and blue Jell-O shots. The other end has fruit salad and trail mix. There are two coolers beneath the table filled with beer and pink and yellow lemonade.

Our parents don't mind if we have a little to drink as long as we don't drive after, but I rarely take them up on the offer. I might have a few vodka Red Bulls later, though, since it'll be a long night of Fourth of July games and fireworks. Soda works for now. I spot a can of regular and Ruby Red Squirt buried in the ice and reach for both.

Standing, I search the yard until I find who I'm look-ing for—the girl wearing a red sundress with her dirty blonde curls tied up in a blue bandana. Sophie and I have been in a good place since Thanksgiving and the football game. We haven't spent any time just the two of us since we kissed at the stadium and have only hung out at family get-togethers. It's not exactly how it used to be, but it's fine for now. I realized it's what I *need* to keep myself from staying hung up on her. When I reach her, her back is to me as she talks to her friend.

I wait until I catch Chastity's gaze. "Excuse me. Sorry to interrupt, but I think you have something in your eye." Sophie spins on her heel to face me and Chastity looks confused, wiping her thumb gently under her eye to avoid ruining her makeup. I grin. "Oh wait, it's just a sparkle."

Sophie deadpans, then slaps my arm. I swear I catch a hint of jealousy in her eyes, but I'm sure my ego is imagining that. "What?" I shrug.

Chastity giggles. "That was cute." I don't know her well, but I know she has four brothers and is comfortable with teasing. "If you don't want him, I'll take him," she says to Sophie, not even trying to whisper.

"He's not smooth at all," Sophie responds as if I can't hear them.

"Hey, I'm the funniest person I know," I interject. She has a popsicle in one hand but accepts the soda I offer her with the other.

"Uh-huh." Sophie rolls her eyes but can't fight a smile.

The three of us glance up when Dean yells from where he stands in the grass on the other side of the yard. "Hey, who's playing us?" He tosses a cornhole bag into the air and catches it. Marcus stands next to him.

"Dibs on Sophie," I yell right as "I call Cooper" bursts out of her. Marcus and Dean simultaneously groan. Sophie and I grin as we each take a side. The two of us are so unbeatable together it's rare anyone wants to play against us anymore. Dean must have had a lapse of judgment when he asked for competition.

Waiting for her first turn, Sophie sucks on her orange popsicle thirty feet from me. The memory of its taste triggers a slideshow of memories from every summer barbeque where the play between us was as innocent as the treat her perfect pink lips are wrapped around. *It's still that innocent*, I tell myself as I toss the beanbag toward my teammate.

An hour later, Sophie and I have won three games in a row. When no one wanted to play against us anymore, we gave up the board. It felt like a blast from the past. "Come on." I reach for Sophie's hand, wanting to extend this moment we're in. She looks around presumably for Chastity because when she sees her talking to someone by the grill, she links her fingers with mine, a warmth spreading through them I try to ignore.

She follows me to the edge of the yard and through the first two layers of trees to *our spot*. Standing in front of our pink and blue plastic tubing chairs, we take them in. They were cracked and faded before, but now they are covered in a layer of leaves and dust. It's been almost a year since we've been out here together, and based on the state of our chairs, I'm surprised to see the bird feeder full. I drop her hand to brush the earth off our seats before dramatically collapsing in mine. Sophie takes a seat next to me, her head leaning against the back. "I miss you, Coop." Sunshine chirps as if she agrees, and it gives me the impression that Sophie still comes out here on her own.

"I'm right here," I say as if her words are literal, pulling my eyes from the yellow finch to the way her red sundress clings to her body.

"I know. I just miss this. Us." She pauses. "Not relationship us. Just us," she says more shyly like she's afraid I'll misinterpret or be upset.

I reach for her hand again, my thumb rubbing over hers. "I know what you mean. I think maybe you were right, though, that this was best for us." She's still convinced letting me experience college the "right way" was the correct decision. I try to make the most of it even though I'm not convinced this life is better than how the past year could have been *with* her.

"So, you're happy?"

"As long as you're in my life in some capacity, I'm good," I lie.

36
SOPHIE

THEN

Relief rushes through me knowing Cooper is happy with my decision to break up. It feels weird to lie to him especially since we've never really kept secrets from each other, but I'm glad he can't tell I miss him as a boyfriend. I'm not sure that would do any good in keeping up this friendship-adjacent relationship we've been managing. It's challenging enough as it is. It's easy to fall back into our familiar comfort around each other, but it's hard to not want more. Being alone with him right now feels like a bad idea as it is.

"We should get back to the party," I say.

There's a hesitation I'm definitely misreading. "Yeah."

He stands, pulling me to my feet by my hands, but dropping them as soon as I'm up.

I'm not ready to miss him again. "Should we go see if everyone is ready for the egg toss?"

He finds his smile immediately. "Let's do it, partner."

"Where's Chastity?" Cooper comes into view, even though the only thing lighting the backyard is the sporadic fireworks exploding in the sky a few neighborhoods over.

"She left to hang out with her family. Why are you over here?" After we won the egg toss, I forced myself to go find Chastity and spend time with her instead. I haven't seen Cooper all evening. "Aren't you in charge of our fireworks?" The boys always light them off from the street in front of our houses. They would probably let me help, but I'd rather watch.

He grips the back of his neck like he's ashamed, but then a grin breaks over his face. "Yeah, they banned me. I almost blew my finger off. It's fine. I'll see how the other side lives tonight."

Chuckling, I bump my shoulder into his as I pass by, my arms full with two Mexican camping blankets. "You can join me if you want. But just a warning, once you sit with me, you'll never want to be anywhere else."

"I already know that. Lead the way."

Once we get to the back edge of the yard, I drop the blankets on the grass. I grab one and fling it open so it splays on the ground, tugging the corners until it lays flat. Sitting, I wait for Cooper to join me before adjusting the second one over us.

"I mean, I don't get the entertainment of you idiots lighting them off, but this is the best view."

"I'll be the judge of that," he says, getting comfortable on his back. There's space between us, but not much. The thought that I wish he was closer to me flickers through my mind, but I bury it.

"Trust me." I curl one arm under my head, remaining on my back but leaning slightly toward Cooper. He mirrors me.

"I do." His words feel more loaded than their face value. "So, how was junior year?"

"Hmm. Nothing really happened. You know me. OH. I decided what I want to do."

"Do about what?"

"My life, duh. Like what job I want."

His attention perks up. "You did?! That's not nothing. What do you want to do?"

"I want to be an architect."

There is no shock on Cooper's face when I reveal my life dream, only a knowing grin. "Tell me more."

I smile as the first of our families' fireworks explode above us–green arches bursting outward from their center. "I guess it should have been obvious, but it didn't really cross my mind until my art teacher pointed out the only things I ever sketch are houses and floor plans. I thought maybe it was just from seeing all the pictures your dad takes at the fancy houses he sells."

"But you don't think that's why?" I keep my eyes mostly on the sky as a succession of fireworks brighten it–sparkly red, blue, and gold trails overlapping each other.

"I don't think so. I looked up more specifics about what the work actually entails, and I love each aspect. I like that there are formulas for guaranteeing what you create will work, but that you get to be creative with it. It's like my books. They're designed for happy ever after, but the journey to get there is unique." *If only there was that kind of guarantee for success in every aspect of life*, I add to myself. He's taking in every word like he's truly interested, his eyes focused more on me than the string of fireworks that seem like they'll be duds until the tips of the trails explode in gold with a sizzle.

"OH, and the best part is," I glance sideways at him for a second, "is U of O has an architecture program. So, it makes sense to stay here."

"That's great, Soph." The excited words leave his lips as he simultaneously shifts more on his side, his hand landing on my stomach, right below where mine is resting.

I gasp at the unexpected contact and freeze my response in an attempt to decide how I feel about this. He held my hand earlier. It's not like this is much different. It's not a big deal. Except that every part of me wants him closer.

The first few months we were apart were hard, but the more time I spent away from him, the easier it became. But when he's close, the way he is now, it's torture that he's not closer. "Thanks, Coop. I'm really excited. I wish I could be in college now."

"Nah. Don't rush it," he says as I release a breath at the realization his hand seems comfortable where it is.

"You don't like college?" I ask as I adjust myself, scooting up the blanket, which in turn brings Cooper's hand closer to where I wish it was. I know I told him I only missed him as a friend earlier today, but I ache for him to cross that line–just for tonight, just for this moment.

"I love it," he says, slowly bunching the fabric of my sundress between his fingers. He's cautious, like he's feeling me out as the material pulls away from my legs. I don't move, hoping it encourages him. "But there are a lot of things I miss about high school."

"Like what?" Under the blanket, my hand finds his, my pinky hooking on his hand and giving a slight tug until I feel the scratchiness of the blanket against the skin at my hip.

Cooper's hands are soft in comparison as his finger draws small circles on my stomach. "Like . . . Having my friends all in the same place." What he's doing with his mouth feels completely disconnected from what he's doing with his hands. "I don't have classes with anyone I knew before."

"Good thing you're great at making friends." I tip my body ever so slightly toward him.

His finger trails along the edge of my lace thong, back and forth, slowly. "Mhmm. None of them do my laundry, though."

"Do you even need to do laundry more than once a month? You have like 37 pairs of joggers and just as many hoodies."

"Exactly." He smirks, and it takes everything in me to not press my lips to his.

Gold glitter explosions cover the sky above us–at least ten in a row. "Those are my favorite ones," I say, distracting myself.

"Mine too," Cooper agrees as his finger toys with the edge of the fabric. Luckily the crack of a firework hides the hitch of my breath in anticipation of having Cooper touch me.

"How's the fraternity?"

"It's good."

"But . . ."

"It's nice having brothers who always have your back. I was worried how things would be without football." His vulnerability isn't something I take for granted. I'm the one he'll admit defeat to after a bad game, when he's just angry around anyone else. I'm the one he came to when he was worried about getting into the fraternity in the first place. And when he didn't feel confident enough to ask his dad for responsibility helping his business. I know he is open with his mom and Troy but never in the way he is with me. At least that's how it used to be. Maybe it still is. "That part is great. It's just a full time job–all the events and parties."

"They aren't fun?"

"They are. It was just a lot to manage my first year. We hosted a big philanthropic event that took a lot of planning and a few smaller ones." I flashback to Ethan telling me to bring my yellow bikini to their annual car wash. A twinge of sadness for missing so much of Cooper's life hits my heart. "We go to every event the other fraternities and sororities organize. Plus our required community service each quarter. It would be fine, but it's a lot with how much I've been trying to work with Dad. I talked him into not hiring another agent and letting me help more instead."

"You did?! That's great! I'm proud of you." He gives me a half smile in the flicker of silver light above us. "I know it's hard for you to ask."

"Thanks, Soph. It was just easier to do all the things in high school, you know? And I was good at it naturally."

"I'm sure you're doing better than you think, Coop. Don't underestimate yourself." His mood has fallen a bit, and for some reason, I've always taken responsibility when it comes to making him feel better. "What do you love about college?"

"That I can sleep in and skip class without getting in trouble."

"Shut up. You do not do that." I laugh, realizing too late that it's bold to make an assumption about someone I can't claim to know anymore. But I'll always know Cooper. *Right?*

He chuckles, his touch unwavering as his fingers whisper across my skin along the line I'm not sure he'll cross. "I know. But it's nice that I *could*."

"What else?"

"That there's no one to tell Troy and me we can't eat spaghetti five nights a week or have ice cream for dinner."

"Your mom misses cooking for you." I can hardly keep my thoughts focused on what he's saying.

"Does she?" he asks, but I'm not convinced he's invested in the answer. His hand ascends, further from the part of me aching for him. His thumb brushes across my stomach, his fingers softly digging into my side.

"Yeah. It's okay, though. She has me. We go to the Saturday market together every week. On top of when I volunteer for story time at her library on Wednesdays. Sometimes I see her when I'm there to help the few middle schoolers I tutor. It's nice, especially since Mom and Dad work a lot."

His hand freezes. "You hang out with my mom every week?"

"Yeah." He didn't know that? "You know I work with her at the library, right?"

He shakes his head. "When we broke up, I asked her to stop talking about you for a while. I guess she never picked it back up."

"Oh. Well, is that okay?"

"What's mine is yours."

Without responding, I stare into the hazy night sky, the firework finale beginning, the boom of each successive burst vibrating through me.

Cooper resumes his movement, his finger now drawing small, soft circles on my skin. It's slow and lazy like it's second nature to touch me in a way he hasn't in a year, like he's comfortable. The thought of our automatic connection no matter how long we spend apart sparks a fire of doubt in me, wondering again if I made the wrong decision last year.

The sky is suddenly so bright it nearly takes me out of the escape I've been in with Cooper for the past fifteen minutes. He tugs on my hip and the instinct shooting through me says he's not going to give me what I want. He shouldn't–he knows better than me, anyway. Repositioning myself, I turn, giving in to his unspoken request and curling into his chest. He adjusts his arm around me, his fingers finding a new place in the strands of my ponytail.

"You're right," Cooper whispers. "This is the best view." Somewhere in between the explosions above us, he adds, "Too bad it always has to end."

37

SOPHIE

NOW

Cooper, 21; Sophie, 18

Sighing, I sink into Cooper's mattress, feeling like I'm floating on a cloud. Or maybe it's just because it's such a relief knowing Cooper and I are going to be together. That sex. Wow. I mean our first time–my first time–was good. Great even, now that I have more to compare it to. But this was better than with JT. It definitely exceeded my experience a few hours ago. Ugh. I wish I could take that back. But it's hard to even think about anything else right now because nothing comes close to sex with Cooper. It's like every part of my body sparks alive under his touch. I feel all of him in a consuming way that takes me to another world I could live in forever.

Cooper's door flings open, slamming against the wall with a thud that rattles me. What? I sit up, only mildly aware of the sheets falling from my body but all of a sudden thankful I put on one of Cooper's T-shirts. "What's wrong?"

Something flies through the air and lands on the bed next to me. My phone? He nods toward it with a scowl. What the . . . ? My heart thumps in my chest, anxiety dispersing through my veins.

"Open it," he demands.

I pick it up, my hand shaking as I punch in my lock code. A message thread with an unknown number is pulled up with a single text: *Why'd you sneak out?* Oh.

My eyes find Cooper's, and I'm sure I look guilty, but technically I didn't do anything wrong. Still, my stomach flips.

"Who is that?" He remains in the doorway.

"Ummm. Logan," I tell him with my eyes back on the sheets as I pull them over my chest as if they could create a shield for my racing heart.

"Who the fuck is Logan?" he yells as he crosses the floor until he's at the side of the bed looking down at me.

"A guy I met at the party tonight. Last night. Whatever." Maybe he would believe that Logan was just asking why I left the party. That sounds reasonable, right?

"And where exactly did you sneak out of?" I risk a glance at him in time to see his jaw clench.

I can't lie to him. It's okay, though. He slept with Kylie. It's fine. Although the way my stomach twists tells me it doesn't agree. "His apartment."

He laughs humorlessly. "You're joking, right? Tell me you did not fuck someone else, then came here to have sex with me."

I reach for him, but he steps back, my hand falling to the mattress. "Cooper. You slept with Kylie. I'm not mad about that. It was a mistake. I was upset."

"What are you talking about?" he snaps. "I didn't sleep with her. Not tonight."

"Yes. You did. I saw her leave here."

He grits his teeth, inhaling like he's trying to rid himself of the anger. "Yeah, she left because I told her I wasn't over my ex, and I couldn't give her the attention she deserves. Jesus Christ, Sophie. What do you think of me that I would sleep with you *right* after her?" When I don't reply he runs his hands up his face and through his hair, lacing them behind his neck. Leaning back to stare at the ceiling, he says nothing.

"Cooper?" I whisper. He drags his gaze to mine then sits on the edge of the bed, looking away, his hands folded in his lap. I scoot closer, cautiously, and brush my fingers against his arm. He still doesn't look.

Just when I think he's not going to respond, he speaks, eyes locked on his hands. "All I think about is you. Yes, I've slept with Kylie, but it was because after the JT shit, I thought you weren't coming back. I forced myself to try and move on. Maybe it was my fault for not being clear enough last night, but I was just trying to not be a dick and leave her alone, especially when she was drunk as fuck because *someone* encouraged her to get trashed." He glances at me during the accusation then returns his gaze to his fingers. "And you just . . . you slept with someone you don't even know. Like it means nothing to you. Like what you said in the bathroom was just words."

My heart sinks. He's too hurt, and now that I'm sober, I can see where he's coming from.

"What can I do to make this better?" I'm met with a silence that tears apart all the hope I had just a few minutes ago. "We're not getting back together, are we?"

He shakes his head, and I realize I said the last thought aloud.

After what feels like forever, he turns to me, linking our hands together. He studies my face, watching the silent tears slip down, and I know his decision is made. With a sigh, he finally speaks. "I'm exhausted, Soph. I'm sure you are too. But it's clear this isn't going to happen for us right now. I think . . ."

He's on the verge of his next words like he can't decide which ones are right.

"What?" My voice cracks, and he reaches to swipe the tear from under my eye.

"I meant what I said earlier. I hate fighting with you. I hate it. I lo–" He shakes his head. "I think we should focus on our friendship. That's what is most important to me."

"But–"

"We're not going to be together," he says firmly. "I want you in my life more than I need you as my girlfriend, and if I have to choose, considering I don't think we can make it in a relationship right now, I'm choosing friendship."

"We can work through this, though. Now that we both want to be together."

"That's the thing. I don't want that. Not right now. We can't have a relationship when we're hardly even friends."

I nod, conceding for now. "You're my person, Coop. I'll be whatever you need. And for what it's worth . . . I'm sorry. I'm really sorry."

"I know," he whispers, pulling me to his chest. He holds me there until my tears stop, until the sun is well into the sky, until I believe we might actually be capable of being just friends.

38
COOPER

NOW

Memories from last night and this morning play like a movie on the back of my eyelids. I open my eyes, hoping to blink away the visions, but she's in front of me. Sophie's head is inches from my face, her hair splayed over my pillowcase as she sleeps, and my hand is flat against the soft skin of her stomach under my T-shirt she's wearing. Rolling my eyes at myself, I take a breath and slip out of contact with the girl that drives me fucking mad in every sense of the word. Still, I couldn't bring myself to kick her out after finding out she slept with another guy before she came over. I wanted her here even though I'm frustrated as fuck. Hurt. Devastated. When I saw that text . . . I didn't want to believe it. Part of me hoped Sophie would deny it when I confronted her—whether it was true or not—but she didn't. The second guilt splashed across her face, her teeth sinking into her lip, her eyes shifting around the room, landing on everything but me, I was sick.

I don't know if I'm just in my own head about this, but I can't help from feeling like she keeps choosing someone else, anyone else besides me. The words she says aren't enough to prove otherwise. If there's any chance of us being in a relationship again, I need to figure out how the fuck to brush off the idea of her being with other guys, and we need to get to a place where I'll be confident her words and actions will align. The entire time between our breakup over the summer and when I met Kylie, no part of me even wanted another girl, thinking that Sophie could be mine again. Hell, I assumed it was inevitable that she would be until I saw her with JT. But even then, I didn't touch anyone else until my faith flew out the damn window I watched Sophie kiss JT through.

Staying just friends feels like the only solution for now, until we can clean up this mess we've made. And friends do not cuddle all fucking night. I need to get us both out of this bed. I gently pull back the covers and slide off the mattress to get dressed.

Crouching next to Sophie, I run my thumb across her cheek. Okay, fine. That's probably not a friendly motion, but I don't want to scare her awake. Her eyes flutter open, the sweetest sleepy smile appearing at the sight of me before it drops.

"Morning," I say quietly, forcing my hand from her. "Well, afternoon. It's almost two. Do you want to go to the diner?"

Her eyes flicker back and forth across my face, full of uncertainty. "As friends?"

"As friends." The words hurt coming out.

The smallest sigh leaves her lips, but she nods. "I don't have any clothes."

"I'll find you some." With that, I leave her bedside and shuffle through my dresser, pulling out the football sweatshirt from my freshman year of high school. It's the smallest one I have. I tell her I'll be right back and walk to the laundry room. The aftermath of our sex is blatant. Her leggings rolled inside themselves on the ground next to a hot pink thong. My hoodie has been thrown haphazardly, half hanging off the washing ma-chine. The end of cycle dryer light flashes at me.

Refusing to let myself replay the memory, I snatch her bottoms off the floor, turning them right side out as I return to her.

"Here." I lay her leggings on the bed next to my sweat-shirt. "You can wear these? Or we can swing by your house first. Whichever."

"These are fine. Thanks, Coop."

I stand there, feeling awkward, waiting for her to get out of bed.

"Uhh, Coop?"

"Yeah?"

"Can you leave so I can change? I don't have under-wear on."

"It's nothing I haven't . . . yeah. I'll be out in the kitchen when you're ready to go."

"Okay, thank you."

Two minutes later, Sophie joins me where I'm leaning against the kitchen counter, key fob in hand. "Ready?"

She nods and follows me to the driveway.

The entire drive to the diner is uncomfortable. So-phie sits with her fists curled into the sleeves of my sweatshirt and propped against the passenger door. She doesn't make a move to turn on our playlist like she usually would, but my thoughts are too loud to hear or process music anyway.

Holding the door open for her at the diner, she leads me inside, scanning the room for an empty booth. Her gaze stops on *our* booth in the corner, coincidentally the only one available. We each slide into either side of the cherry covered tablecloth table, both fidgeting in awkwardness–Sophie finger brushes the tips of her hair and I tug on the strings of my hoodie, bunching the fabric around my neck.

A wave of relief rushes through me at the sight of our waitress, Shirley.

"Hey, you two." She beams brightly, and we both manage a half-ass smile. "The usual?"

"Yeah–" I start to say, but Sophie cuts me off.

"Actually, we'll have chocolate, please. Thanks, Shirley."

When the poodle skirt and its wearer are out of sight, I scrunch my eyebrows at the girl sitting across from me. "What was that about?"

"Just trying to show you I heard you. That I know we are just friends."

"Friends don't compromise on milkshake flavors?" I quirk one brow at her, not tracking her logic.

"I just want you to have what you want, Coop. And you want chocolate." Her sad smile has no resentment or anger. Even if she's never said the words, I *know* that she loves me. It's just not enough right now.

I start to reach for her hand, but move them to my lap and keep them hostage under the table. "Thank you."

"Soooo," she says. "How's this quarter going?"

Ugh. I slump into the hard red plastic booth seat. "I decided to take this computer graphics class, thinking I could help Dad with more high tech real estate advertisements and marketing and whatnot."

"That sounds like a great idea." She smiles more genuinely, propping her chin on her fist as she leans forward.

"In theory. But turns out, it's not my strong suit. I'm barely passing and we're already almost four weeks into the ten week quarter."

"I can help you," she offers.

"Aren't you only taking gen ed classes your freshman year?"

"Yeah, but I have to take that class for my degree eventually. It doesn't matter when I learn the material. I don't mind."

"Thanks, Soph. That would be really helpful."

"You're welcome." Her eyes flash to Shirley and our shake as it's set down between us.

"French toast is on the way to soak up that hangover you have written on your faces." She chuckles as she walks away.

Sophie and I lean in for a sip from a thick red straw on either side of the glass milkshake cup out of habit. I pull back before we have some sort of romance movie moment and gently slide the shake closer to her. Jesus, this is awkward. But we're going to have to push through this part at some point, so it might as well be today. "So, how's your first year of college going?" I immediately wish I had asked a more specific question. Hopefully it's obvious I don't want to hear about any part of it that involves another guy.

"Umm, it's okay. Chastity and I have been working on our bucket list."

Oh great, I've seen that list. Half of it involves partying and guys.

She continues so quickly it's like she could see my stomach flip. "Mostly the non-crazy stuff. We've tried a lot of the local restaurants. Joined a few study groups and are doing well in school–despite all the partying she insists on."

"Do you like to party?"

"Umm. It's okay. I try to make the most of it when we do, although I feel like I don't make the best decisions when I drink. But I'd rather do that than be at home."

"Wait. What? Why?"

"Things with Dad have been . . . tense."

"Because of . . ."

"I don't know. You know how he is. He wants me to experience life, but he wants to control that experience. Mom has to remind him constantly that I'm old enough to make my own decisions, but he doesn't listen. And he keeps . . ."

"He keeps what?"

"Nothing."

"Tell me," I insist. "We're friends, Soph. You know you can tell me anything."

"It's not that. It's . . ."

"He's been inviting JT over." I don't ask. That's the only thing she could be hesitant to say.

She nods. "Luckily football season ended, so he hasn't had an excuse anymore," she adds, distracting herself by swiping her finger across the whipped cream on the shake and licking it off.

"You need to get out of there."

"I know. I wish I had moved into the dorms."

"I'd say you could move in with me and Troy, but . . ."

"Even I know that would be a terrible idea." She chuckles, lightening up for the first time today.

I finally crack a real smile. "We'll figure something else out."

"Yeah."

Shirley sets the red ceramic plate filled with cinnamon roll french toast on the table. Sophie and I reach for our forks, and as the first soft and sugary bite hits my taste buds, I wonder how long things can stay sweet.

39
SOPHIE

THEN

Cooper, 20; Sophie's 18th birthday

"I'm so jealous you get to live in the dorms," I whine as I sit on the edge of my bed. My parents didn't think it made sense for me since we only live ten minutes from campus.

The mattress sinks as Chastity joins me. "I mean, your parents did buy you a car as a consolation prize." She laughs.

"Yeah, you're right." I sigh. I love the new-to-me car they surprised me with yesterday, on my last day of high school, as a graduation and eighteenth birthday present. "I'm not trying to sound ungrateful. I'm just nervous for our first year of college, you know? It would be easier if we could do all the things together."

"We'll do all the things together, bestie. Don't worry."

Now that Cooper and I have drifted apart, Chastity is my only friend. I don't mind, but as much as being around people I don't know stresses me out, I know I'll feel so alone in college if I don't make some changes and get out of my comfort zone. It won't be easy to be together all the time like we were in high school.

I fling myself dramatically back on my bed. "You're right. I hope I can keep up with you! I just wish I was outgoing like you are. And brave. And confident. And fun."

"Sophie, you *are* those things." I glance at her, her wild black ringlets are as spunky as her personality. I think one of the reasons I love both her and Cooper is because they are extroverted, unreserved–the life of the party I sometimes wish I was. I just don't feel comfortable around many people to be myself. "I'm going to prove it to you," Chastity adds once she realizes I'm not going to agree. "Let's make a freshman year bucket list–things we both have to do to make sure we're making the most out of our college experience."

"Okay, I could probably manage that."

"Yes!" she cheers, rolling to her stomach and pulling her phone from the nightstand. "That was so much easier than I thought. This will be great for you, I promise."

"I know," I laugh nervously. "I want to get out there. I think this will help." I roll to my side, propping my head up with my hand.

"It will. I'll make sure of it." She opens the note section and types *Sophie and Chastity's College Bucket List*. "Okay, item number one is easy. Get drunk." She types the words before getting confirmation from me. We've already talked about this one. Neither of us has had even a sip of alcohol before, but we want to see what the hype is about.

"Okay, item number two," I add. "Have sex."

"Whoa. You're really going for it, huh?" She laughs.

I shrug. "Dad keeps telling me I need to get out there more–that this is the time in my life to experience everyone and everything before life takes away my options."

"I'm pretty sure by 'everyone and everything' he didn't mean guys and their beds. But yes. We are definitely losing our virginity this year." She adds it to the list. "You know what I want to do but have been totally afraid?"

"Hmm?"

"Take a pole dancing class. I heard it's so hard but so fun. Plus, it's sexy." Her eyes dance with mischief.

"That sounds like I'll hurt myself."

"Come on, Soph, it'll be fun. Remember that book we read where the girl pole dances for stress relief? Maybe you'll make a friend there too."

"Okay, okay. I saw an advertisement for a place by campus that does beginner classes on Saturdays."

"You're also totally getting those pink streaks in your hair that you've always wanted."

My eyes light at the idea. "If I have to." I giggle. "Add dance on a table."

"Seriously?" she asks, amused.

I sit, pulling the pillow into my lap and shrug. "Kat Stratford makes it look fun."

"Let's do it. Okay, I'm also adding skinny dipping, make the first move on a guy, join a club, and get a tattoo."

"I am *not* getting a tattoo."

"Yeah, you are," she says so matter-of-factly I almost believe her. But there's no way.

"Uh-uh. Not happening."

"Come on, Sophie. That's like the ultimate test of your willingness to make the most of college. You're always talking about how we have to experience life like the characters in our books. It's now or never, babe."

I groan. "Fine, but it's going to be small and hardly noticeable."

"Any tattoo counts in my book." She grins.

We spend the next half hour filling our list with over a hundred items–a few are as crazy as the first ones we came up with, but a lot are easy and simple like joining a study group and trying every restaurant near campus. We tried to choose things that either won't be possible or will be more difficult once we graduate college and are out in the "real world," with relationships and families and big kid jobs. When our list feels complete, we print two copies, doodling our name on our own list.

"I'm excited about this."

"Agreed."

"Are you sure you're going to be okay the rest of today? You can come to dinner with my family." Chastity takes my hands in hers and squeezes. Her parents are taking her out to celebrate graduating high school. I appreciate the gesture, but I'd rather do what I always do on my birthday.

"I'll be fine. I promise. I'm going to make cupcakes and read."

"Deal." She showed up first thing this morning with coffee and donuts, but her parents have an entire day of celebrating planned. "Maybe you should call Cooper to hang out," she says as I stand to walk her out. "You have to get your book from him anyway, right? It's been a while." Chastity has always been a major supporter of Cooper and me being together, regardless of how long we've been apart.

"Maybe. I'm not expecting him to get me a present. I haven't seen or talked to him much since Christmas," I say over my shoulder as I walk down the stairs.

"Sophie, this is Cooper we're talking about," she declares as if that says everything.

Rolling my eyes, I pull away. "We'll see. Go have fun. Seriously, don't worry about me. If Cooper didn't get me a new book I can go buy my own now that I have money from tutoring."

"Okay, bestie. Whatever you say. Happy birthday. Save me a cupcake before you give them all to Cooper." Retreating backward down my driveway with a knowing look, she waves above her head before sliding into her car.

Shutting the front door behind me, I hear Mom getting out the baking supplies.

An hour and a half later a few dozen red velvet cupcakes are frosted, and half of them are neatly lined up in a Tupperware. "I'm going to take these to Cooper," I tell Mom and she acknowledges me without a hint of questioning–even though I think it's a little weird I'm committed to this tradition despite the distance between us these days.

Grabbing the keys to my baby blue slug bug, I open the front door. I nearly trip over the brown paper bag wrapped gift on the welcome mat. A smile covers my face as I set the cupcakes on the porch and sit on the step, anxious to see what book Cooper bought this year. I rip open the wrapping and turn the book over in my hands, running my fingers across the cover. I love new books and that Cooper always gets me one from my wish list. Flipping through the pages, excitement builds inside me. I already can't wait to get back home and start this . . . 473 page journey . . . *Wait*. There's handwriting on the back of the very last page.

The year I realized I don't know you anymore.

That's Cooper's handwriting. Does he write in all my books? I would have noticed, wouldn't I?

Abandoning the cupcakes, I run back inside and up the stairs to the bookshelf in my room, my heart racing wildly. I tightly grip the outside of the book from my thirteenth birthday and seventeenth and pull them and all the ones in between down in one fell swoop. Setting them gently on my desk, I pick up the one from the year I became a teenager and flip to the back page.

The year I realized you're my best friend.

How did I not notice this? I reach for the book Cooper got me on my fourteenth birthday.

The year I noticed how beautiful you are.

He thought that even then? I pick up the book from my fifteenth birthday.

The year I first thought about kissing you.

I set book three on the stack I've already looked through.

The year I wished we were more than friends.

My sixteenth birthday. That was the week we decided to *be more than friends*. My heart leaps at the thought. I miss my person. Maybe more than I realized. I hesitate before checking last year's note, knowing it's the first one after we started drifting apart.

The year I missed you the most.

My stomach drops then fills with anxious butterflies wanting nothing more than to guide me back to Cooper.

I leave through our garage this time so I can grab my skateboard. After retrieving my cupcakes, I step inside the Montgomery's open garage to steal Coop's board too before driving straight to his house.

The chain unlatches shortly after I've knocked a few times. When the door opens, Cooper stands in front of me in gray sweatpants—and nothing else. Holy crap this man has gotten hot, his abs more defined, his body more mature. He has light facial hair now, and it looks . . . Wow, he's hot.

His eyebrows scrunch together and he scratches the back of his head like he's confused to see me. "Sophie, hey."

"Hi." I hold out his Tupperware of cupcakes awkwardly.

A smile slowly graces his face. "Happy birthday." I can't tell if he's happy to see me or excited about the cupcakes. "What are you doing here?" he asks, taking the treats from me.

"You mean besides bringing you birthday cupcakes?" I tease, anxious to get to my point while also not wanting to rush it. I'm scared. The guy who wrote any of those past notes might not exist anymore. He might not miss me in the way I've realized I miss him, especially now that he's in front of me. I have this overwhelming *need* for him like finding water after wandering for days in the desert.

He glances at the book I've been holding in my other hand before meeting my gaze. "Do you not like your book?"

"I hate that you don't know me anymore." The words tumble out of me.

"Oh." A mixture of recognition and worry flashes through his beautiful blue eyes. He hesitates. "You saw my note?"

Running my fingers over the tips of my curls, I hold his gaze. "I saw all of them."

He's confused. "You've never mentioned them before."

I nod. "I don't know how I missed them." I beat myself up on the entire ten-minute drive here. I'm not sure why or how it would have changed anything, but it feels like it matters.

"Wait." He sets the Tupperware on the ground of the entryway like he can't process my confession while holding it. He rights himself, leaning into the edge of the opened door, his hand supported by its grip on the inside door knob. "You didn't even notice them before?"

How embarrassing. He probably thought I was just ignoring his sweet gesture all these years. Shifting my gaze to the tight knots of the shoestring bows on my Chucks, I shake my head slowly. "I'm sorry."

His fingertips graze my forearm where it's holding my book to my chest, but he drops them immediately like he's unsure if he's allowed to touch me. His voice is soft when he says, "It's not a big deal. It kind of felt like a way to confess my secrets to you, I guess. That's so lame." He laughs and shakes his head at himself.

"Cooper?" I start, running my free hand over my pink sundress. His eyes follow the movement as he leans against the door he holds half open. My heart races as I frantically search his face, wondering if it's okay for me to be here, if the thoughts running through my head are anything like the ones running through his.

"Sophie?" He says my name slowly and as if I've let the silence go on long enough to question.

"Umm. Do you want to skate to the diner?"

I didn't realize the tension he was holding until his shoulders visibly relax. "Yes."

"Was it always this far?" I ask Cooper with a heavy breath, skidding my foot against the paved path by the river until I come to a stop.

He skates back toward me with a laugh. "Both my house and the diner moved. Didn't you hear?"

I roll my eyes, but it only makes his grin widen. "Come on." He holds his hand out until I take it, immediately feeling the warmth and comfort it sends through me. I couldn't have predicted this is exactly how I wanted to spend my birthday. "I'll get us an Uber for the way back."

"Thank goodness. I should not have to work this hard on my birthday," I joke, stepping both feet onto my board and letting him casually pull me along.

"Oh, I'm sorry, princess. How dare I accept an offer that was your idea and expect you to follow through without complaining." He chuckles.

"It's okay. You can make it up to me with a strawberry milkshake."

"Is that so?"

I smile, switching the grip on his hand to link our fingers together.

"You're making it hard to skate," he teases.

"You could let go."

"Nah, I'm good." He catches my gaze for a second before bringing his eyes back to the path.

When I'm away from him, things between us seem so complicated, but being around him makes being happy feel so easy.

Another ten minutes brings us to the entrance of the diner. Skateboard in one hand, Cooper opens the door with the other. He takes a step inside, but before pushing the door wide enough for me to get through, he pauses. He stares blankly at our table like there's a movie playing on a screen in front of him. I wonder if it's the memory that's rolling for me.

Guilt washes over me. My touch to his shoulder startles him, and he turns back to me. "We don't have to eat here, Coop," I whisper.

He looks inside the diner again then back at me. "I'm good. Let's make a new memory."

"Okay." I give him space to move forward on his own. I want this diner to be a good place in our lives again.

We slide onto the hard red seats of the booth where we always used to sit, stashing our skateboards under the table.

Shirley, the long-time waitress, doesn't skip a beat in greeting us, her pink poodle skirt fluttering as she stops in front of our table. "Cooper, Sophie!" she exclaims, her eyes focusing on me when she adds, "It's so nice to see you two here–and together." I don't look at Cooper for his reaction to her assumption. I don't correct her either.

"It's good to see you too, Shirley," Cooper's voice pulls me to look at him for a moment.

"What can I get for you? Cinnamon roll french toast and a vanilla shake?" There's a look of hopefulness in her eyes like she's cheering for our comeback and for everything to be normal between us. She's seen our friendship progress as much as anyone else. It hit me the second I saw him today that I want him back–I mean I've never not wanted him back. I just feel ready for it now that I'm older and will be in college and can give him what he deserves.

"Yes, please. Strawberry, though. No compromises for this girl's 18th birthday." Cooper shoots me a wink. Every second that passes today only confirms my decision more.

"Oh! Happy birthday! One strawberry shake with extra cherries coming right up!"

I grin at Cooper before directing my smile at our favorite waitress. "Thank you."

40
COOPER

NOW

Cooper, 21; Sophie, 18

"Hey, Professor Everett. Do you have a moment?"

"Mr. Montgomery. What can I help you with?" my computer graphics professor inquires from the other side of his teaching podium.

"It's not a secret I'm not doing great in this class." I tug at my hoodie strings, ashamed with how much I dropped the ball this quarter.

"It certainly is not." He chuckles. "Considering this course isn't required for your major, I'm surprised you registered in the first place."

"I know," I agree, shoving my hands into the pockets of my jeans to keep from fidgeting. "But it's important to me. I wanted you to know I found a tutor. Someone who can make it make sense for me."

"One of my students?"

"Not yet. But she will be soon." He's going to love Sophie just like I do. "Anyway, I just wanted to let you know I plan to turn my grade around before the end of the quarter and ask that you don't write me off yet." It's hard when a lot of my brothers don't prioritize school. Don't get me wrong, I can party with the best of them. But this is important to me too. For my dad. My career. I'm thankful as fuck Sophie is going to help me.

"I'm happy to hear that, Cooper. Reach out if you get stuck. I want to see you succeed, if you're willing to put in the work."

"I am."

"I hope time tells the same story."

"It will. Thank you."

Pushing through the green double doors, I exit the classroom. I hold one door open when I see footsteps approaching, and glance up just in time to see their owner.

"Oh. Hey, Marcus. What's up?"

"Hey, man. Not much. Professor Everett is helping me with the graphics for an app I'm working on."

"Oh, cool. What's this one?" Marcus designed his first app when he was nineteen. I think he ended up selling it, but I don't know any of the details.

"Nothing too exciting. It's for Jack, actually. He wanted his own program for his finance clients to stay organized. It'll allow him to see whatever they input too so he can better help them."

"Or better control them," I say under my breath, unable to stop myself.

He chuckles. "Aren't your parents friends with the Porters?"

"Yeah, they are. Just feeling defensive of Sophie."

"What's going on?"

"She's just having a rough time. Her relationship with them has been a little strained. Especially with Jack. He's having trouble finding the line between giving her the freedoms that come with being an adult and still wanting her to be his little girl."

"Huh. That's . . . interesting."

"Why?"

"Just took a different approach with Dean. It was his idea for him to go abroad. Something about how finding your potential is easier if you actually go looking for it."

I have no desire to dive into that psychology right now.

"Yeah, well Sophie probably wishes she could live in another country instead of her house these days. He's not a bad guy. She'll be nineteen in a few months, so it feels dramatic. You know how we were in our first year of college."

"Thank fuck our parents don't know." He smirks, adjusting his laptop bag over his shoulder.

A dozen blurry memories flash through my mind, and I question how we even survived the stupid shit we did when we got our first real taste of freedom. "Of course I want Sophie to be safe, but she should have the opportunity to craft her experience like we did, ya know?" *As long as it doesn't involve experiencing other men.*

"Agreed." His brows scrunch together, and his eyes dart to a thought. "I'm not sure if Diane and Jack will go for it, but Sophie could move in with me."

"Really?" I should have thought of that idea on my own. It's not only good, but it might actually work. The Porters trust Marcus–I mean Dean lived with him for years. Money might be an issue, but I'll help Sophie figure it out.

"Yeah. Dean's room is empty. And I could use a roommate who knows how to bake."

"You and me both." I laugh, all of a sudden craving red velvet.

"Well, talk to Sophie and one of you let me know?"

"Definitely. Thanks, Marcus."

41

SOPHIE

Now

"Do you really need all your books over here, Soph?" Cooper chuckles as he sets a box on the carpet of my new room, making it look way lighter than it is.

"Yes. They are my emotional support books." I grin, running my hand over the last dress I hung in my closet.

"All of them?" He quirks a brow.

I shrug. "Sometimes I just need to get lost in someone else's world, ya know?"

He crosses the room to where I'm standing and leans casually against the wall, feet crossed at the ankles, hands in the pockets of his joggers. His T-shirt hangs perfectly off the muscles he's maintained since he played football. This past spring quarter he joined an intramural dodgeball team with some of his fraternity brothers. Who knew throwing rubber balls at people could make you look like *that*—with his sleeves tight around his biceps, and the veins popping in his forearms as he carries my eight boxes of books in here with ease. Skating with me at least a few times each week has probably helped keep him in shape too.

Skating has once again become the perfect way for us to hang out as friends. There's no real risk of getting too close, of our skin accidentally touching for too long. It keeps us out of dark rooms full of bad choices waiting to be made. Flying down the concrete in crisp late-March air with the sun peeking through is all happy and light–just like our friendship has been these past two months since Cooper and I decided to be friends.

"Speaking of someone else's world. How are you feeling about this new phase?"

Right after Cooper and I agreed to be friends back in February he had a solution to ease the tension between my dad and I. His little girl growing up has been hard on him, and it's definitely stolen my joy from trying to make the most of my college experience. I finally convinced both of my parents to let me move into my brother's old room at Marcus' house during the break between winter and spring quarter.

If it were anyone else, they probably would have said no. But Marcus is practically family, and they trust him to look after me as much as they'd trust Dean. "I'm excited. Thank you for helping make this happen, Coop. This freedom already feels good."

Worry flashes at the mention of my freedom. We've successfully skirted around any topic of dating. We've been spending a lot of time together, but I don't know if he's been seeing anyone. I haven't even been on a date. It's not hard for me because I prefer keeping to myself. But even if it was, I'd still do what it takes to stay on track to our friendship turning back into a relationship. I just wish I knew when that was going to happen. I don't think he'd be happy if I were with someone else, but I get the impression he's still not ready for us to be together.

"Good. I'm glad," Cooper says, uncrossing his ankles to take a step toward me. "I'm proud of you, Soph."

"I didn't do anything." I close almost all the distance between us, my breath catching at his nearness. It's not like we haven't been close. We've partied a few times, and I've fallen asleep in his bed. The weight of his arm around my shoulder when he runs into me on campus and walks me to class is a constant phantom feeling whenever he's not around.

"Sure you did." He tucks a curl behind my ear, his finger whispering against my skin and sending a chill down my spine. I do my best not to seem affected as he retracts his hand back to his pockets. "You stuck to your guns, did research to prove to your dad this could be a good move for you, and you didn't give up until he agreed. You've never lived anywhere else. I know it's a big adjustment for you."

He's not wrong. As excited as I am, I'm equally terri-fied. I'm used to the house I've grown up in, the only place I've ever known and the routines I've perfected, ones I'm comforted by. I lean against the wall, my move-ment taking me centimeters from Cooper. "Yeah, you're right. I hope things are better here. Maybe I can have a better relationship with Dad with the distance too."

His tongue barely wets his lips and his eyes flash to my mouth. But then he blinks, like he just registered what I said. "Wait what?"

"My dad," I repeat, my pulse thumping a few beats faster. "I hope the distance is good for us. That he sees I can make my own choices."

"Oh. Yeah." He clears his throat and takes a step back. "Me too. I'm going to get the last few boxes. I'll be back."

"Alright," I whisper, my heart sinking as he leaves me standing there tugging on the end of a curl. Snapping myself out of the fantasy inside my head where Cooper kisses me and we finally find our way *back*, I sit on the floor in front of the boxes of my books.

My brother didn't leave much behind when he left for Costa Rica. I think he got rid of most of his things. But he's got two vertical stacks of books in the corner of the room that go halfway up the wall. The bookshelves that Cooper made me are bolted down and since this move is only until Dean returns in a year, I didn't think it was worth the hassle to move them. So, I unpack my books, lining them in stacks next to his. The third box has my favorite novels–including the ones from Cooper. I pull out the one from last year, flipping to the last page and running my fingers over the note: *The year I realized I don't know you anymore.*

We've done a good job re-learning everything there is to know about each other over the past few months, picking up where we left off over the summer after he left this note. I've learned how he likes his coffee now, the names of all his professors and his new ticks and tells when it comes to homework and when he doesn't understand something. I know his current favorite country artists. His drink of choice and where he wants to eat when he's hungover. Way more about the real estate industry than I ever planned to learn. I've noticed the ever so slight change in the way he dresses and how he styles his hair. But I don't know the one thing I want to–how he feels about *us* . . . the endgame, til death do us part, you're the only one for me version of us.

With three more months until my birthday, I wonder what this year's note will be, and I wonder what our relationship dynamic will be then. I glance up at the door softly scruffing against the carpet. Cooper walks in holding the last cardboard box with the word "bathroom" scribbled on the outside in Sharpie. He pauses barely inside the doorway, eyes falling to the book in my hand and my fingers pressed into the page below his handwriting. His eyes meet mine next, his tongue running over his bottom lip before he worries it between his teeth. It all happens in an instant and in the next one he continues on his path to the in-room bathroom.

Oh, God. That box. I hop up, then slow my roll so Cooper doesn't suspect anything. He hasn't just been helping me move. He's been helping me move *in*–meaning, unpacking my boxes with me. He can shove my underwear in a drawer all day, but he does not need to be digging around that box. It's not a conversation I'm ready to have with him–a conversation that crosses the line we are so carefully tightroping.

I'm thankful Mom and Dad were gone the day my vibrator showed up in the mail. The packaging wasn't discreet at all. When I was scrolling for new books to read a few weeks ago, an ad popped up for an app I'd never heard of. It not only reads sex scenes aloud like an audiobook but syncs with a vibrator. I'd never used even a regular one before, but I'm desperate. It's like I've gotten on a Merry-Go-Round. I'm spinning round and round holding on for dear life in an attempt to stay in the friend zone like Cooper asked. It's moving too fast to get off, and if I leap, I'll fall right into Cooper. I'm not sure he's ready to catch me yet.

The judgment I have for myself from actively trying to not want Cooper is driving me insane. He's not doing anything specifically to make me want him again. Nothing besides everything. Even the mindless tugging of his hoodie strings makes me want to claim him as mine, and I'm grasping at straws for coping mechanisms here, for holding true to my word. So instead, I've been dragging my foot, attempting to slow down my

Merry-Go-Round with distractions. Last month I read seventeen books. My new attempt is this app.

Nothing will compare to the way it feels when Cooper touches me. That level of ecstasy only exists with him. That being said, sometimes a girl needs to be taken care of–especially with this tension that's been progressively building over the past two months.

Before I'm all the way inside my bathroom, I know it's too late. He holds the light pink toy in his hand, no shame at all about the way he grips it in his palm, as he turns to me. His smirk looks like he's ready to tease me, but his eyes are on fire as if thinking about holding something that's been inside me is too much to handle.

"Cooper!" I snatch it from his hand, tossing it in the drawer next to the sink, my face heating more with every second that passes.

He chuckles. "Guess it's safe to say you've upgraded your tactics."

"Ugggghhh," I groan, my hands covering my face as I lean against the wall. "Can you not?"

With one hand braced against the counter, he uses the other to cage me in. Peeking through my fingers, I catch his tongue swiping over his lip before he bites into it. "Don't worry. Apparently now I have something new to add to my arsenal too." The thought of Cooper picturing me getting off as he takes care of himself feels like someone is shaking the tightrope we're on. I know I can't be the first one to leap, but I can't pull away either. My hands fall from my face, fingers twisting in the fabric of my sundress instead.

Our eyes are locked. His breath intensifies with every inhale, and I've been holding mine so long I might pass out soon.

A throat clearing snaps both of our attention to my room, where Marcus stands. "I made lunch," he says. "Not dessert, but it seems like you two might have that part covered." His chuckle echoes through my new room as he walks away, unfazed by our situationship. Cooper and I return to the previous moment, but it's not the same anymore. The tension has been replaced with awkwardness, Cooper tugging on the strings of his hoodie, and me twisting a curl around my finger as I spin out from between him and the wall to follow Marcus.

I don't want to talk about it. I already know what he'll say. Otherwise he would have stopped me. He would have kissed me.

42
COOPER

NOW

Cooper, 21; Sophie's 19th birthday

Leaning across the island in my kitchen, I tap the 0, 6, 1 and 3 on the screen, unlocking my phone. A little red "1" bubble appears next to my Snapchat icon, and I open the app. My stomach flips, despite already knowing it would be from Sophie. I've been trying to keep my distance since she moved. I mean, we still hang out all the time. But I've got a new two-foot rule I try to abide by at all times. I may not be able to prevent the vision of her little pink toy I found three months ago or that perfect face she makes when she *lets go* out of my head, but I've managed to keep my hands to myself.

I open her snap, a selfie of her showing the book I got for her nineteenth birthday to the camera as she sits on the couch in Marcus' living room, the sun streaming through the window behind her. The text across her picture reads: *Thanks for my book,* followed by a string of heart emojis. We have plans for tonight, but I wanted her to have something waiting for her–the brown paper wrapped gift that I like to think she looks forward to after six years. I dropped it off at Marcus' when I knew she'd be with her mom baking cupcakes.

Being friends with Sophie again has been . . . a roller coaster, to say the least. We haven't truly been *just* friends in three years, since the week of her sixteenth birthday and my high school graduation. Every time we are together, I wish we were *together*. But I still don't think we're ready. Despite the tension between us, I'm not sure the trust is fully back–at least not on my end. I'm scarred by the ease she seems to have in walking away, in falling into someone else's arms when she claims she wants me.

Grabbing one of the cupcakes next to me, I shove half of it in my mouth, balancing it there while I snap my own selfie as a reply. *Thanks for the cupcakes,* I add before hitting send. She must have dropped them off on her way back home from her mom's this morning. I was in the shower when my security notification came through, so I missed her stopping by, but I'll see her soon.

You're welcome, she replies in our snap text thread.

Happy birthday, Soph. I send back and lock my phone, shoving the second half of the cupcake in my mouth.

My phone lights up with a Snapchat notification, presumably Sophie thanking me.

It's a picture.

I open it.

My mouth falls open.

I pull my phone closer to my face.

Pull it away.

Pull it back in.

Like somehow it'll help me make sense of the fact that there is a nearly naked picture of Sophie on my phone. Her face isn't in it, but I'd know who it was even if the snap didn't come from her. I'd know her body anywhere, no matter how many years it's aged or how long it's been since I've seen her this way.

The picture cuts from her neck to right below her skimpy pink lace thong. Her dirty blonde hair has new highlights compared to when I saw her a few days ago. I only notice because her curls are perfectly positioned over one nipple. Her hand covers the other, but neither hides how fucking sexy she is. I haven't seen her this naked since January, five months ago, and the way my dick twitches is probably inappropriate considering we are just friends.

I shouldn't be turned on anyway. I should be mad because *what the fuck*. This isn't what we agreed upon. She shouldn't have sent a sexy picture that would take a lobotomy to get out of my head.

Against my poor judgment, I tap out of the picture to an unread message.

Sophie: *Please tell me you didn't open that yet.*

Me: *You can SEE that I did. What the fuck, Sophie.*

Sophie: *I swear I didn't mean to send it to you. It was for someone else.*

My blood boils at her message, at the thought of anyone else seeing her this way.

Jealousy.

Rage.

Attraction.

Everything I feel toward her is unmatched compared to everyone else.

I didn't get the impression she's been sleeping around, but it also makes me fucking sick to think about, so I try not to.

Me: *Why? Did you add sexting to your bucket list?*

Sophie: *What do you mean, why? I felt good today, and someone needed to see it.*

I'm probably angrier than I should be, but it already takes every ounce of willpower I have to not flick the worn and thinned rubber band every time I'm near her and revel in it snapping. And apparently she doesn't feel the same tension between us?

Me: *You shouldn't be sending pictures like that. You can't trust people that way.*

Sophie: *Don't tell me what to do. You don't even know the person I sent it to.*

Me: *Do you?*

Sophie: *So, I guess you didn't mean what you wrote in my book.*

Me: *What does that have to do with anything?*

These little notes have always been my stupid way of letting her know how I felt before we reached a more open and honest level of our friendship, but this birthday feels different, more complicated. This has been the hardest year for us, so I sat on what to write for an entire week, wanting to find the perfect thing that let her know how thankful I am that we've revived our friendship, how much happier I am when she's around–without making her think I'm ready for more. *The year I realized I never want to live life without you* is what I settled on.

Sophie: *You said you always want me in your life. So, don't push me away for stupid reasons.*

Jesus fucking Christ.

Me: *Of course I want that. But come the fuck on, Sophie. If you don't want me to tell you that you deserve better than sending naked snaps, don't accidentally send them to me. You shouldn't have expected anything else.*

Sophie: *You can't be a possessive ass and not want to be my boyfriend.*

She's right. It feels like we have this unspoken con-tract–one where we belong to each other, yet don't col-lect the benefits. It's not fair. Maybe it's not even logical.

I haven't touched another girl since I broke things off with Kylie the night of the 80s party, but I don't care because I don't want anyone else. Apparently I'm the only one of us on board with that contract, though.

Me: *Whatever. It's your life and your body. Do what you want.*

Sophie: *I will. Thanks.*

Possessed by sexual frustration and refusal to give into something else I'd probably regret later, I click on the image again, knowing the app will let me view it one more time. God, she's perfect. I hate everything about her being on the other side of this picture. I don't know what compels me to pinch the buttons on either side of my phone, but the screenshot flashes on my screen before minimizing and saving to my photos. Her message comes through almost immediately.

Sophie: *I can see that, stupid.*

Oh, fuck. I forgot you get a notification if someone screenshots a snap.

Sophie: *You better delete it.*

I don't.

I punch out the only good decision I'm capable of making right now.

Me: *Sure, Sophie.*

Sophie: *You're ridiculous. Forget our plans tonight.*

Me: *Already did.*

Instead of seeing if she responds, I lock my phone, shoving it across the counter and reaching for another cupcake.

43

SOPHIE

Now

"Come oooooon, bestie." Chastity tugs on my hand, dragging me into a bar we've never been in before. She was so excited when my birthday night freed up after what went down with Cooper. I groan internally. I was so stupid this morning. I don't know what I was thinking. The tension between us hasn't been nearly as high as it was the day I moved into Marcus', but there's always a glance or a brush of our skin or something. And then I read my birthday note, and I just . . . Well, I guess I read into it. I tried to reciprocate the move, but the second I sent it, a gut feeling told me it was *not* the right one. And Cooper's reaction only confirmed it. Despite it not being what he expected, the fact that he didn't say anything specifically about the picture has me craving a Mind Eraser shot.

I can't exactly claim it's my birthday since I'm only nineteen and my ID is fake, but for once I jumped at Chastity's offer to get extra dolled up to guarantee we pass as twenty-one and go dancing to distract myself.

The bar is darker than others around here. There's no windows. The only light comes from the neon blue bars lining the edges of the ceiling and hanging above the bar. I'm glad I dressed to match the vibe tonight even if it's not really *me*. I hope someone thinks I look good and replaces the confidence I lost earlier today.

The black cotton fabric of my dress clings to my body, hitting only a few inches below the black lace underwear Chastity insisted I buy when we went shopping a few weeks ago. She's in such a hurry to be as grown up as possible. If I could guarantee it meant life was more simple, I'd be in a hurry too. For now, I just follow her lead and let her make some decisions for me. Clearly, I'm not the best at making them for myself. I cringe again recalling the snapchat I sent Cooper. Catching a glimpse of myself in the full wall mirror behind the bar, I take in my loosely curled hair with the top half pinned up, and my makeup much darker than normal. I might not look like me, but I look sexy.

Leaning onto the bartop as we wait for the bartender, I take some of the pressure off my feet, my strappy black heels already rubbing against my skin.

"Your lips look lonely. Do they want to meet mine?" Oh, god, that was a terrible pick-up line. Sounds like something Cooper would say, although when he says cheesy things it's cute. I think it's the goofy grin he plasters on his face after. His stupid freaking adorable smile. And his natural charm of a Girl Scout during cookie season. *Ugh.* This isn't how it's supposed to be.

I turn to face the guy hitting on me. Men are so desperate. But it's fine. I am too. I'm desperate to forget about Cooper tonight. To be with someone and not think about him running his hand over me instead. To have them think I'm attractive and want to act on it. "They prefer tequila to warm them up at night," I flirt, leaning into the bar, my chin resting on my palm. The words taste funny, but I'm hoping it'll soon be replaced with alcohol.

"Well I can take care of that too," he says with a smirk, gesturing toward the bartender. When he finds his way to us, the guy orders four shots of tequila like he read my mind.

Cooper's happiness is important to me. I love him too much for it not to be. That doesn't make this any less hard. It doesn't make me immune to stupid decisions when I'm missing our relationship too much. But I'm trying. When we aren't together I've been focusing on experiencing new things and becoming a new Sophie–crossing off items on my list that I want to do, the ones that don't involve other men at least. But right now, I need to feel wanted, and the *dance with a hot guy you'll never see again* bullet printed on our list materializes in my head, complete with the little pink hearts Chastity colored around it.

I shoot the clear liquid back, skipping the lime and welcoming the burn. It's perfect in addition to the two Chastity and I took before we showed up.

"Better?"

"Much. You want to dance?"

"Lead the way." He holds out his hand, and I take it after tapping Chastity's shoulder and letting her know I'd be on the dance floor. Finding a gap in the black-light-lit room, I turn so my back is flush with his chest and grind against him. His hands immediately find my waist, running up and down my sides against the fabric of my dress. Even though I hate myself for it, I pretend it's Cooper's hands, warm and pulling me to him like he can't get enough, like he needs more of me.

A few songs blur by, the room loud and crowded and everything I hate. But this is what I need. Sitting at home lost in my books only leaves me lost in a world where Cooper is every guy and I'm every girl and it always works out for us in the end–but I'm starting to doubt it will work out for us in the end.

I spin into the stranger's arms, catching him off guard when my lips land on his. He recovers quickly, his hand smoothing along my lower back as he presses our bodies and mouths closer together. Immediately giving him access, his tongue dances with mine, the music and lights and liquor trying to trick me into thinking this moment is magical. It's all wrong, and nothing feels right, but I welcome the distraction anyway.

Thirty minutes later, I'm being pulled away from the dance for some fresh air and another drink. I don't know what I'm doing. Part of me thinks I actually need this experience. That I need to be with other guys to be able to know Cooper is the right one, that it's not nostalgia and comfort that's making me want him. And the other part of me wonders if I'm doing this to get his attention, to prove to myself that he still wants me and is just fighting it.

Everything in my gut tells me it's the second one because deep down I know my love for Cooper is more than just two hearts being connected for so long. And even though I know it's wrong, I go down that path anyway.

"Take a picture with me," I tug on the T-shirt of the guy whose name I still haven't learned. We are three shots deep–or maybe four.

The guy leans until he's pressed against me, fully in the shaking frame of my picture. I hit the round circle in selfie mode and my phone snaps a dark, slightly blurry but still distinguishable photo. Good enough. "I'm going to the bathroom. I'll be back in a minute," I say, turning on my heel without another word.

Once I've locked myself in a stall, I open my Snapchat app and upload the photo I took.

Since it's nearly midnight, I don't expect anyone to view my story, but still, I wait to see if Cooper does. I'm not sure what he replaced our drive-in movie plans with tonight, and I wonder if he's out at a bar too.

I *actually* go to the bathroom and wash my hands before opening the app again. Clicking to view my own story, I tap the eyeball with a "3" next to it. A girl from my biology class. Chastity–I should probably go find her. My stomach threatens to lodge itself in my throat when I see Cooper's name third.

I pray his jealousy overrides everything, that he asks where I'm at and comes to find me, to claim me as his. He's never liked the idea of me with anyone else. Maybe it's enough for him to snap out of it, for him to feel how I felt when I saw him with Kylie, for him to end this game we're playing.

But I stand there for five more minutes and he doesn't reply.

And by the time I crawl into bed two hours later, he still hasn't said a word.

44

COOPER

THEN

Cooper, 20; Sophie's 18th birthday
Today has been a blast from the past–and not just because we ate lunch at a '50s diner. The second we let our guards down, things between us are perfect. She's perfect–when she's not breaking my heart, that is. Today has been the complete opposite of the last time we were here. Instead of ripping apart, we're reconnecting. It's something I hoped for but never expected. Even if today only ends in us retrieving our friendship from where it's been sitting in a dark closet collecting dust, I'll be happy.

"You ready?" I ask Sophie, laying cash on top of the check and pulling up the Uber app on my phone.

"We can skate back if you want," she says with hesitancy.

"Nope." I pop the P as I choose our Uber.

"Thanks, Coop." The generic nickname always feels different coming from Sophie.

"Do you have plans for the rest of the day?" I slide out from the booth seat, grabbing both our skateboards from under the table and letting Sophie lead the way outside. As we stand on the curb waiting for our Uber, she picks at the fabric of her dress like she's nervous. I hate that some of her comfort around me has faded. "I don't have anything going on today, and Troy is staying at Emily's tonight. So, we can keep hanging out," I say, in case not having that information is part of her hesitancy. "Unless you want to go home. Don't feel obligated to stay with me."

She chews on her lip, looking at me through her eyelashes. This girl is so beautiful. "I want to. If that's okay?" she asks even though I've already invited her over. "I was thinking . . . maybe we could just hang out and get to know each other again."

We spent most of lunch talking, but it was about surface level things like her new car, job tutoring middle schoolers, how she's still been volunteering at the library. "Let's do it." Thinking about how I don't know her better than anyone anymore is a situation I want to remedy. I want to know every damn thing I've missed over the past two years that has molded Sophie into the girl standing next to me.

The Uber stops next to the curb, the driver confirming it's me before we slide into the back seat. I scoot her over with my hip until she's against the window, and I'm in the middle, allowing me to rest our boards against the seat next to me.

After confirming my address, the driver turns up the country radio station loud enough it would be hard to hold a conversation. Seeming to feel the same, Sophie doesn't speak. She leans her head against my shoulder like she isn't second guessing herself at all–a completely different vibe than she radiated a few moments ago. I pull my arm from between us to wrap it around her shoulder and she snuggles into me more. God, I missed this feeling, I missed her–thoughts that have been running on repeat through my mind all day.

Two minutes into the ten minute drive back to my house, Sophie pulls back, angling her body toward me. My hand grips the side of her neck, my thumb brushing her cheek without a second thought. Old habits. Her pretty brown eyes search mine as a stream of sunlight filters through the window behind her, making her silhouette glow. I swear this girl is the embodiment of my heart.

My face isn't more than a few inches from hers. If I leaned in, I could kiss her. I want to kiss her so damn bad, taste her again. Her tongue swipes across her lips. Does she want me to kiss her? I'm struggling to not misread her intentions today and which side of the line she wants to be on.

Without breaking eye contact, she runs her hand against my basketball shorts, picking at the fabric between her fingers. I may not know everything there is to know about Sophie anymore, but I do know what she wants at this moment.

Close enough to feel her breath on my lips and barely keep my eyes locked on hers, I say, "If you let me kiss you, don't make me stop." Residual fear and hope battle in my brain as I wait for her to respond.

"Kiss me, Cooper," she murmurs against my lips then presses into them without giving me a chance to oblige–like she missed me more than I missed her.

My stomach flips, an involuntary groan escapes and I'm fucking floating. God, I missed her so much. The thought runs through my mind yet again. I'd tell her if I could pry myself off her, but I can't. I tighten my grip on her neck, my fingers threading through her curls and pulling her closer to me as our tongues tangle together. The way we automatically find a heated rhythm you wouldn't believe it's been almost two years since we did this. My shirt balls in her fist, and she attempts to tug me closer.

The driver's not-so-subtle cough pulls me back to reality. Shit, I forgot where we were. Whenever I'm zoned in on Sophie, anything around me tends to blur. The car jerks slightly when we stop, both of us breaking our kiss.

"Thanks, man," I tell the driver loud enough he'll hear me over the Kenny Chesney song blaring through the car speakers. Setting our boards on my front lawn, I reach back for Sophie's hand, helping her out of the car. She closes the door behind her, and before she has time to make another move, I pull her into my arms. She's not getting away from me this time.

Her lips brush against mine softly, her hands pressing into my chest. I pull back before my lack of self-restraint overpowers the gentleman inside me and I toss her over my shoulder to take to my bed. "Come on." We each pick up a board to move them to the front porch.

When we get inside, I walk to the fridge. "Squirt?" I ask over my shoulder, louder than necessary considering Sophie is only a step behind me.

"You know I don't like–"

I cut her off by holding out a Ruby Red for her. She looks at me like I just offered her a flip phone or a Tamagotchi or something else random from our past. "Why do you have this?"

"Better to be prepared and avoid the Squirt debate." I wink as I crack the top of my original flavor Squirt. My small flicker of hope for Sophie and me reconnecting wasn't strong enough to purposely keep my fridge stocked for her, but I can't say pulling the last red can from the back didn't deliver a boost of serotonin. Still, I say, "Also, the shelf life of soda is like three years," out of self-preservation–an attempt to not give away that a day hasn't gone by where I don't think about her. This entire day feels like a mix of deja vu and a dream and like it's too good to be true, but I try to push any negative thoughts to the back of my mind.

"I missed your kisses," Sophie whispers against my lips as she sits with her legs draped over mine on the couch.

"You have no idea," I say before kissing her again, my arm wrapped around her squeezing her tightly. I definitely took advantage of the freedom Sophie wanted me to have, but damn did I miss her lips. No one else even comes close. I tangle my fingers in her hair as I deepen our kiss, reveling in her being here.

"Cooper?" I feel a quick pang of longing when she breaks our kiss, but my name coming off her lips sends a wave of bliss through me.

"What's up, Soph?" I ask, running my finger along the edge of her face and tucking a curl behind her ear.

"Do you . . . did you . . . you know . . . experience college the past couple years?" The nerves in her voice are what make me realize what she means.

The truth makes me feel guilty, although I'm not sure why. "Is that something you really want to talk about?"

She stares for a moment, then nods.

"I had fun," I say in an attempt to keep it vague. I know she can't handle details, and I don't want to give them to her.

"With a lot of girls?" She bites into her lip nervously as she waits for me to respond.

I can't help but chuckle. "I don't know what your definition of a lot is, but to answer the question you're not asking, I have had sex."

"Oh." She seems disappointed but recovers. "Okay, that's good. I wanted that for you." Her words didn't exactly come out right, but I know what she meant.

I'm not sure I want to know her answer to the same question, so I don't ask. "Are you excited for college?"

"Yeah, I am. I wish I was moving into the dorms, but it's still going to be fun."

"It's as much fun as you make it," I state the motto I try to live by.

"Chastity and I made a list."

"Oh yeah? What kind of list?"

She retrieves her phone out of her cross body bag on the coffee table. She unlocks it . . . *Wait.* Is her code my birthday intentionally? I retain the thought to come back to later when she taps a few times and flips the screen toward me.

Pulling my hand away from her leg, I take her phone and examine the list. "Wow, this is quite the list. You're going to do everything on here?

"Yup. I'm not outgoing like you are or have a fraternity to pull me out of my shell. So, I think this will help."

"Alright, well, I can totally help with some of this," I offer, hopeful I'm not overstepping or misreading what is happening between us.

"I was hoping you'd say that." Her smile reminds me I'd do anything this girl asked of me.

"So . . ." I trail off, my curiosity winning. "You haven't done *anything* on your list?"

She shakes her head. "No."

I'm not sure if she caught my drift, and I'm torn between doubling down on clarification or not. I start with the chicken-shit way. "Have you been seeing anyone?"

She lets her head fall to my chest, her arm wrapping around my middle. I lock my arms around her waist, pulling her closer. It feels like we picked up right where we left off, and nothing could make me happier. God, I missed this girl, and not just for the physical stuff.

"I tried dating a little." I can feel her words against my chest. "I didn't want to be the only girl without a date to prom and stuff, you know?"

I sigh thinking about her being alone surrounded by a sea of high schoolers. I never experienced that, and I know she doesn't mind being alone, but I still hate it for her. I rub my thumb across her hip. "I would have gone with you."

"I know. It was okay. I had a few fun dates."

"Just dates?"

She pulls back, confused about what I mean. Spit it out already, man. It's not going to kill you if she's had sex.

"When you say you haven't done anything on this list . . . you mean you haven't had sex yet?"

She shakes her head then leans against my chest again. "I never had the desire, I guess."

"There's nothing wrong with that. You shouldn't do it with just anyone."

"I know. I only want to do it with you." No words come out of my mouth as I try to process what she said. To my surprise, she elaborates. "I don't know how to describe it, Coop. I had the opportunity a few times, but it didn't feel right. The moment I saw you today, it's like that part of me unlocked."

I'm the one to pull back this time, and her head falling off my shoulder forces her to sit up. I take her hands in mine, my heart racing. "You're serious?" I don't know what else to say because while I always held out a small hope we'd find our way back to each other once she got to college, I tried not to count on it.

She nods. "I want it to be you. I always have. I promised you all my firsts, and I don't want to wait any longer. I'm ready."

All I can do is stare.

I should be ripping off her dress.

Or cutting her words off with my mouth.

Or running my hands over her body to relearn every inch of it.

"Cooper?" She laughs uneasily. "Are you okay? If that's not something you want, it's okay. You can tell me. I know you've probably been with a lot of girls who are more experienced."

"What? No. Sophie. Of course I want you. I want to pick up right where we left off."

"Really?"

"Really." I pause. "But not today, okay?" I don't know why I'm not leaping at the opportunity in front of me, but I do know today isn't the day. We've started building back what we had, but it's going to take more than one day for me to trust she won't leave again. Casual sex the past couple of years might have been easy for me, but sex with Sophie will be anything but casual. And I'm not sure how I'd handle her leaving again once we cross a line we can't come back from.

"Okay." There's a hint of disappointment in her tone, but it doesn't last long. She runs her fingers through the back of my hair, my head relaxing into her. "How's Carter?"

45
COOPER

THEN

"Hey, Mrs. Porter," I say when Diane opens the door.

"Cooper!" she exclaims with so much excitement I can't help but grin. "It's been too long since I've seen you over here." I'm not sure if she knows Sophie and I are dating again, but either way it makes me feel good she's happy to see me.

"Yeah, it has," I agree. "I was wondering if I could steal Sophie from you for the day?"

"Of course. She's in her room, I think. What do you two have planned?"

"It's a surprise." I use that as an excuse. I'm unsure how she'll feel about Sophie and I reconnecting, and I don't want to push my luck. "We probably won't be back until late, though. Do you mind if she stays at my house so we don't wake you? Plus, I kind of have plans for us for tomorrow too."

She hesitates, concern flashing across her face. "Sophie was devastated when you two broke up the first time."

She was? It didn't seem like it. I push the thought out of my head, not wanting to focus on the past, but I match her genuine distress. "I was too. Sophie and I are supposed to be together, though. We're working through it."

"You both are still so young, Cooper." What does that have to do with anything? "You have a lot more experience than her now that you've been in college for a couple of years." Ah. There it is.

I step inside the entryway, much more confident than the first time I had the *I'm dating your daughter* talk with her. "You know I would never intentionally hurt Sophie, and I would never make her do anything she's not ready for." Even if she claims she is. "We're just getting to know each other again. We're taking it slow. Really slow. I promise." Hopefully she catches my drift.

"Okay," she says hesitantly, but with more assurance adds, "I trust you to take care of my daughter." The familiar words put me at ease.

"Thank you."

Diane makes her way to the kitchen, and I take the stairs two at a time to get to Sophie's room.

I enter quietly, leaning against the door frame with my hands in the pockets of my joggers as I watch her. She's curled up facing away from me reading her book in sleep shorts and a tank top. I get a good three minutes of staring in before she notices me.

"Cooper." Her free hand flies to her chest. "How long have you been standing there?"

"Long enough to know you're completely lost in another universe." I laugh.

"Yeah. You always pick a good book for me." She smiles.

"Soph, you give me a list."

She shrugs. "Still."

I take the few steps to her bed–intentionally leaving the door open in case her mom comes to check–and crawl across the flowered comforter until I'm hovering over her. Her book is between us, a finger pinched between the pages to save her place. I pull it from her hand, reaching to slide in the bookmark from her nightstand before setting the book aside.

Instead of following my movements, her eyes stay locked on me. "What are you doing here?" she asks, knowing we didn't have set plans. It's been a few weeks since her birthday, and we both agreed to take things slow. Staying true to our word of getting to know each other again, we've spent most of these first few weeks of summer skating, talking, and kissing–I can only resist her so much.

"You're so beautiful, Sophie," I whisper, putting my weight on my forearm so I can slide my other hand through her uncurled hair. I love seeing her this way–no sundress, no makeup, no curls–the way no one else gets to see her.

"Stop." She blushes and throws her arms over her face.

I laugh and place a kiss on her arm. "Come on."

"Where?" She peeks out from behind her shield.

"Not telling. It's a surprise. Pack an overnight bag. Oh, and throw in those spandex shorts you wear under your dress when it's windy out. And a sports bra." Her brows crinkle. "Don't you trust me?"

"Yeah . . ."

"Then, get up. Do what I'm telling you!" I grin, hopping off the bed and reaching my hands for hers.

"Okay, okay." She slides off after me, her bare feet landing on her fuzzy white rug. "Why do I need an overnight bag? I should probably talk to Mom."

"Already did."

Her eyes go wide as they snap to me from where she's digging through her dresser. "She's okay with it?"

"I promised her no sex."

"Stop. You did not tell her that."

I chuckle. "Sure did." Sophie's shock is replaced by a pout. I invade her space, pulling the shorts from her hand and setting them back inside the open drawer, and wrap my arms around her. "I want you. So badly I have dreams about it."

"You do?" she whispers.

"Of course I do," I say like it should be obvious. "But we're not ready yet."

"It doesn't have to be perfect, Cooper. It just has to be you."

I fight the urge to carry her to the bed. "For starters, it will be perfect because it's you and me. But I've wanted this for a long time, and I think once we start, we won't be able to stop. I want our relationship to be about more than sex. You're the only girl it's ever felt like I can have both a physical and emotional connection with. I want to make sure it stays that way."

I know I've said the right thing when her eyes fill with adoration for me. I squeeze her tight to my chest, kissing her hair.

"I hate that you're making this decision for me," she says. "But I know you're right."

"Good," I say, pulling back. "Now, let's go!"

46
SOPHIE

THEN

I quickly pack my backpack with everything Cooper listed, plus some. Zipping it, he takes it from me and swings it over his shoulder.

Knowing I'd follow him anywhere, I let him lead me to his car without any more questions. Almost an hour later, he pulls off the road and onto a dirt path. "Where are we?" I'm having deja vu like maybe I've been here before, but I can't place the memory as we pull into a dirt parking area, my view blocked by a row of fir trees.

"At item number six on your list," Cooper grins as he pulls the key from the ignition.

Confused, I open the list on my phone, my eyes going wide. "Cooper, we're in public," I say, my eyes squinting, barely able to make out the swimming hole through gaps of branches.

He laughs. "If you're naked in private, it's called a shower, Sophie."

"Oh." I guess I didn't think this one through.

Cooper senses my hesitation. "Soph." His finger hooks on the side of my face and turns me to look at him. "It'll be fine. I'll make sure you're comfortable, okay?"

I sigh. "The whole point of this is to get uncomfortable." I glance back through the windshield. "Let's do it."

"That's my girl." He releases me with a grin, jogging around to my side of the car and helping me down. "Come on." When we push through the overgrown path, a shallow, crystal clear swimming hole lies in front of us. Moss covered rocks line the edges and there's a waterfall upstream. There aren't a ton of people, but still, it's *other people*. I've only ever been naked in front of Cooper.

Cooper scans the area before his eyes land on a massive boulder on the edge of the swimming hole. "This way." I let him take my hand and lead me across the rocks, careful not to slip on the wet moss.

When he's satisfied with our location, he drops my hand, replacing it with the T-shirt he's tugging over his head. I stare as the sun lights his abs as they flex with his movement. God, he's so hot. Oblivious to my gaping, he kicks off his joggers, folding them neatly on top of his shirt resting on a nearby rock.

His thumbs are hooked on the edge of his briefs when he notices I haven't made any effort to undress. He wets his lips and takes a step toward me. My heart races, flutters of arousal swarming my stomach. The way this man looks and the way he looks at me–I can't believe I get a second chance with him.

"Do you need help?" he whispers, close enough his breath brushes my lips. Still able to remember we aren't alone, I glance at my surroundings. I can't see anyone behind this rock, and I'm assuming that means no one can see us either.

I nod.

Cooper's thumbs brush across the bare skin on my shoulder. He places a soft kiss on my collarbone and continues trailing his lips up my neck as he slides the straps of my dress off my shoulders. It's warm enough for July, but the air connecting with my skin sends a chill through me. "This is surreal. Us being back together," I whisper, trickling water and a breeze through the trees the only other sound.

He drags the fabric over my breasts slowly as his lips reach my ear. "There is nothing more real than us."

I melt at his words. No matter how far we drift, he's always my constant, and we always come back.

He kisses me as slowly as he's teasing my dress down my body. It's torturous and perfect and every worry that someone might see us fades away. I break our kiss only long enough to step out of my dress, coming back to him to loop my arms around his neck and pull us closer. His warm skin against mine attempts to dissolve the chills running through me from the touch of his hands running up my back. Our tongues tangle together in the perfect harmony they've always had as he unhooks my strapless bra and pulls his chest back enough for it to fall between us.

His fingers press into the skin at my hips, sliding down until they catch on the layer of silk between us. He groans as he slips it off, immediately pressing back against me, his briefs the only thing separating my already sensitive skin and his hard-on.

Taking a step forward, he mirrors my movement, backing up until he's against the rock behind him. My hands trail down his chest until they reach the elastic band. Cooper helps me tug them off, and as soon as there's nothing between us, our kissing shifts from sweet to frantic, like we can't get enough.

It's been a few weeks since we've gotten back together. We agreed there was no reason to rush because in Cooper's words, *we have the rest of our lives*. I couldn't disagree more. I don't want to waste any more time than we already have, but I'm trying my best to be patient. I know he just wants to make sure I'm ready since it's such a big step.

I press into him harder, but he slips between the rock and me, his grip on my hip tugging me toward the water as he backs slowly into it. Trying to keep our lips locked, I stumble over the rocks in the shallow water, Cooper's smile evident in our kiss. His arms lock around my waist tightly as he slows down, backing us into the deeper pool of water. When we're deep enough I have trouble touching the rocky floor, I let my legs float up to wrap around his waist, the water swishing against his chest. We both groan as we connect in all the right places, and I can't help but grind against him as my head falls to his shoulder. "Fuck, Sophie. You feel so good."

He's not even inside me and my orgasm is on the verge of taking over. "Coop," I choke out, grinding against him as he backs against the rock underwater for leverage, pulling us completely out of any current from the water passing by. "Oh my god."

"I love when you come for me," he breathes against my ear.

"You always make me come better," I mumble, stuck in that in between before ecstasy kicks in.

He pulls back ever so slightly, forcing me to readjust the hold of my legs around him. "Better than who?"

What? Oh, he thinks I mean someone *else*. "Myself, silly." A visible sigh of relief deflates his chest. "Even when I think of you, it's never as good as the real thing." My orgasm is slipping away, but reassuring Cooper is more important.

His eyes flick to mine. "You think about me?"

"Every time," I admit.

On a groan he pulls me tighter, rocking my body against his. Within seconds, the friction against my clit pulls me right back to the edge, and I topple over it without warning. Breathless, I'm too overcome to move. Cooper grinds me against him, his head tipping against the rock with a groan. "Jesus Christ," he mutters. "You turn me on so much. I love that you're mine." His lips find mine again, and I'm just as desperate for the connection as I come down from my high right as his begins. His body convulses slightly as he increases the pressure between us. He slows to a still, and having regained some of my strength, I tighten my legs around him, leaving his hands free. They thread through the dry part of my curls by my face, the bottom wet and stuck to my skin. "I'm like a damn teenager when it comes to you." He chuckles.

Smiling, I point out, "I don't think that was the skinny dipping we meant when we added it to the list."

He shrugs, pulling my lips to his. "You're just an over-achiever," he says against them before kissing me.

We spent another hour in the cool water, holding each other, kissing, talking. The two times we might have been within sight of someone, Cooper shielded me like he was the Secret Service. Eventually I was ready to swap our waterbed for a real one, and we left.

"It's not even dinner time," I point out the obvious as Cooper pulls into his driveway. "I thought you told my mom we'd be out all night."

He shifts into park, pulling the key from the ignition as his gaze meets mine. He smirks. "I just wanted to sleep with you."

My eyes spark.

"Actual sleep, Soph." He chuckles. "You don't make my job easy, you know?"

"I know, that's the point," I sass. "My only goal in life is to become irresistible to you, really." I fight the grin on my face, but it's impossible.

Shaking his head, he reaches for the lever to open his door. "You succeeded at that a long time ago."

47

SOPHIE

Now

Cooper, 21; Sophie, 19

After retying the knot in the green Duck T-shirt of Cooper's, I tug on the hem of my jean shorts from where they gave me a wedgie. I'm thankful it's the end of June and not totally freezing out anymore even though I've worked up a sweat cleaning. I scan the kitchen. Almost done. I find the counter spray and paper towel under the sink and complete the final touches.

Standing to examine my work, Marcus' well-built frame shadows me. His deep brown hair is tied into a messy bun at the back of his head although he looks much more put together than when I go with that hairstyle. His tight black jeans and gray V-neck complete his signature look.

"Wow," he says. "It looks great in here. You didn't have to clean. Thank you."

"I wanted to help for your party tonight. It's the least I could do. I appreciate you letting me stay here, Marcus. In case I haven't made that clear." I've been here for three months now, and it's been better than I even imagined.

"It's too quiet here without Dean anyway." He pulls me into a hug, rare but comforting, the same way it would be from my brother.

Before I have a chance to respond, he pulls back, moving to the space behind me. "What's that?" He examines the carrot cake on the counter that's cooling, waiting to be frosted.

I grin. "That's for you. Dean said it's your favorite. There's walnuts too."

"Now this is my kind of rent payment." He picks a chunk off the side of the warm cake. I've been tutoring a few high schoolers. It's enough for gas and book money, but nothing substantial enough for rent. Marcus insisted he wouldn't take payment from me anyway, even though I know Dean used to contribute.

He shoves the bite into his mouth, turning back to me. "Thank you," he says after he swallows.

"You're welcome."

Marcus lists off everything he's going to do before the bonfire party he's hosting tonight while I frost his cake. Once I'm finished and it's in the fridge, I go to change.

I'm tempted to leave Cooper's T-shirt on in hopes he'll see it as a claim that I'm his. Although if he's mad, he might take it back, considering I think he forgot I have it. I definitely don't want that. Standing in front of my closet, the plastic hangers scratch against the rod as I slide each one to the right, inspecting every dress I own. I always wear sundresses. There's nothing special about them. And it's what Cooper always sees me in. He either gets that or the lazy side of me that's reserved only for a select few. Maybe that's part of the problem. Maybe it's that I stopped trying to impress him and now he's *not impressed*. The little black dress I wore on my birthday two weeks ago is tucked in the far left of my closet, and I slip the straps off the hooks on the hanger.

Cooper didn't say anything about the snapchat I sent him in my underwear. It was the first one I'd ever sent to anyone. Even though nerves sunk in the second he opened it, I thought he'd make me feel good like he always does. But he didn't say anything. So, after I posted the picture of me and that guy on Snapchat and he saw it but didn't reply, I went and found someone else to compliment me. It didn't work. I mean, plenty of guys checked me out. I ended up dancing with a couple of others and didn't buy my own shots the rest of the night. But none of it mattered. It's Cooper's reaction I wanted. It's his opinion that means something to me.

The only thing I can focus on is who I want to be with, wondering what he's doing without me, praying to a god I don't even believe in that we'll be together again because my life feels boring, mundane. And the only thing that makes me feel alive is him.

Shimmying into the thin black cotton, I run my hands over the fabric and smooth it out. Standing in front of the full length mirror I have propped against my wall, I yank the elastic from my hair, my messy bun falling into kinky waves. I run my fingers through it. Hmm. It looks good without effort for once. Sexy.

Sitting on the carpet, I darken my makeup until my reflection looks like something Cooper hasn't seen before outside of a dark and grainy Snap. I hope this works.

48
COOPER

NOW

The massive bonfire flame crackles as I round the side of Marcus' house. I spot a few of my old football friends, but I turn toward the house first. Not wanting to wait any longer to see Sophie, I let myself in through the porch sliding door. I'm losing my damn mind. Now that we're back to being friends, we haven't gone more than a few days without seeing each other until the radio silence I initiated on her birthday two weeks ago. I was sticking with the "If you don't have anything nice to say, don't say anything at all" rule–and I had nothing nice to say about seeing that Snapchat picture of Sophie with another guy. She turns to someone else whenever things aren't perfect between us, like she doubts we could be right if we aren't some golden couple. She said that to me once . . . that she wishes we were like my parents. Maybe the fact that things aren't easy between us anymore is part of what makes me so hesitant. I used to be able to read her mind, anticipate what she needed. It seems I've lost that touch, and maybe it's time to admit we aren't as meant to be as I once believed.

I've been simmering in the anger I refuse to accept I played a hand in, but now I'm having withdrawals. It has nothing to do with the fact that I need to know if she's with another guy, or that I can't get the image of her nearly naked out of my head. I don't look at that picture every day or anything either.

Lying to myself, I head down the hallway to Sophie's room.

Even without flicking on the bedroom light, I see her light pink comforter covering the mattress on the floor. The book she must be currently reading is on her pillow. A picture of Sophie on my shoulders in a pool is thumb-tacked to the wall next to her bed. We were playing chicken with Troy and Emily. It's from three summers ago, the first time we started dating. Time is strange. We've broken up, just like Troy and Emily did. But unlike them, we found our way back to each other. We always do. I *hope* we always do.

Realizing she's not in her room, I turn to leave, but Marcus' voice stops me in my tracks. "Is that what you had on earlier?"

"No. I felt like wearing something different." That sounded like . . . I step into the main living space. Sophie.

She spins on her heel, and I fall in love with her all over again. Jesus Christ, she's gorgeous. Usually I prefer the oversized shirt, sleep shorts and messy bun falling off her head version of Sophie she reserves for home. That was before I saw the little black dress version of Sophie. The cotton fabric is skin tight–thin straps and way too short. It hugs her body perfectly. Her usual curls cascade over her shoulders, but for some reason today they make her look older. Maybe it's the smokey eye thing she has going on. Or the fact that I'm not distracted by another guy and can fully take her in. Whatever it is–fuck. If I was a cartoon, my eyes would be popping out of my head right about now.

"Hey, man," Marcus greets me, oblivious to any tension between Sophie and I–whether it's angry or sexual I'm not sure.

I return the greeting to my friend, but my eyes stay locked on the girl in front of me. How the hell am I supposed to take them off her?

"What were you doing in my room?"

I roll my eyes at her insinuation that I don't belong in her space. Marcus catches onto our unstable relationship status and excuses himself from the room.

Grabbing her by the wrist, I pull her into her room and close the door behind us without bothering to turn on the lights. The glow from the moon and the bonfire through her window is enough to illuminate her body, arm folded across her chest as she glares.

I scan her body, and she stands there, letting me. My fist twitches at my side, a strong urge to bite into it and release some of the tension building.

"You can stop staring now," Sophie snaps a moment later, a hint of satisfaction in her voice.

"Why are you dressed like this?" I need to know who it's for.

She shrugs. "I can dress however I want." Her hands move to her hips like it'll help make a point.

I now have an unobstructed view of her chest. Her dress reveals the perfect amount of cleavage, like she's wearing a push-up bra, and the diamond sun necklace I finally gave her rests perfectly between her breasts. Fuck. If I stare much longer, I'm going to need to adjust myself. I force my eyes to stay on her face. "What are you doing, Sophie?"

"I'm trying something new since what I was doing before wasn't getting me what I want," she says confidently.

"So, what? You're trying to make me jealous again?"

"I'm trying to make you want me."

Jesus Christ, she's infuriating, and this is exactly why we can't be friends. Her being around other guys makes me jealous as fuck, but it also pisses me the hell off.

Her eyes flash to my fist clenched at my side. "Cooper," she whispers.

"What," I snap as my body reacts opposite by taking a step closer to her.

"Do you think I look good?"

I can't resist my hand gripping her hip, needing to validate her. The way her breath catches at the contact makes my dick twitch. Fuck. How could she not think she looks anything but amazing? "You're gorgeous." Her eyes search mine for sincerity, and I close the distance between us until her fingers latch onto my hoodie pocket and my breath is on her ear. My thumb brushes across her jaw before I bury my fingers into her hair. "Drop dead, can't think straight, do something stupid, kind of gorgeous."

"You didn't think so on my birthday." Her words are barely a breath against my lips but bring me back to reality like a bucket of water instantly turning red burning embers black.

I pull back, my hand falling away from her even though she still clings to me. "When you were taking pics with other guys." I deadpan, lust replaced by disgust. It makes me sick to think about her with someone else.

"I wanted to be with *you* on my birthday. But you practically forced me to cancel our plans."

She's not wrong, but that wasn't an invitation to meet another guy.

"Why are you mad I sent you that *private* snap? I thought you would like it, Coop. It was only for you."

Wait, what? Did she actually take that picture for *me*? "That's not what you told me."

"I know." She takes a step closer, and I don't move. "I panicked, okay? No one has ever seen a picture of me like that except you."

"That's not the kind of picture you send your *friend*." She doesn't understand. Apparently my body doesn't either, my fingers itching at my sides to reach for her.

"Then let's be more," she whisper-shouts.

In my split second debate, I immediately know I can't make this decision in the middle of a fight, while she's dressed this way, while it's affecting me like this. "No."

"But . . ." She can't find the words as she tugs on my sweatshirt when I pull away.

I stop as if her hold on my clothes is enough to keep me in place. "You need to figure out what's going on with you."

"What do you mean?"

My sweatshirt bunches as she grips it tighter in her fingers, but I keep my eyes locked on hers. "You really don't get it, do you?"

"Cooper, I . . ."

"You'll have to change more than your clothes to fix our problems." With a slight shake of my head, I brush past her and don't look back.

Despite it being a chilly night for June, Sophie's feet are barefoot in the grass. I take her in again, my eyes roaming her curves before locking on her face. After another minute without her gaze meeting mine like I expect them to, I tip back a shot of vodka from my now half empty Solo cup that's lacking its usual Red Bull. I suck my teeth, dissolving some of the burn in my mouth. She laughs at something the guy she's talking to says, her hand moving to rest on his bicep.

"You good, man?" Marcus' voice breaks through my thoughts. I must have been ignoring him because we were having a conversation. I couldn't tell you what it was about, though.

I'm about to tell him I'm fine, not wanting to get into it, but my jaw grinds hard enough to break teeth as I watch Sophie grab the hand of the guy she's talking to and pull him toward the house.

"I thought you were supposed to be looking after her now that Dean is gone?" I growl at Marcus although my eyes are still following Sophie as she guides the dude I don't know inside with a flirty smile. "How are you allowing this to happen in your house?!" I fling my hand toward the door, and Marcus doesn't even look behind him to see what I'm talking about.

"First, no one tells me what to do in my house." His voice deepens into a far more demanding tone than I've ever heard from him. It pulls my attention away from Sophie. "Second, it's her house too, and third, she's an adult. If you're so worried about what she's doing then you need to be the one to talk to her about it."

I take another sip of my drink, wishing the cool liquid could chill me out. The fire has simmered to embers now, and it feels like a symbol of my dying relationship with Sophie as I think about her fucking someone mere feet away with the intention of hurting me. It's one thing to *know* she spends time with other guys. It's another to practically *see* her fuck one of them. How can she not realize that instead of making me fight for her, this will ruin me?

I throw my cup into the coals, watching the remaining liquor ignite for a moment before it dies, the red plastic melting around it as it sizzles.

"Coop." Marcus' voice has softened but my glare is still hard.

"What," I spit.

"You need to sleep this off. Tomorrow you can figure out what to do. The couch is yours."

"You want me to sleep in the same house where the girl I love is fucking someone who isn't me?"

He looks at me, completely unsurprised by my confession. "Why isn't she your girl?"

"Because," I pause for a moment, every reason I could give him nowhere to be found.

He sighs. "Come on, I'll give you a ride home."

I don't even argue because I don't want to talk about this anymore, and I sure as hell can't be here anymore either.

49
COOPER

THEN

Cooper, 20; Sophie, 18

"You look great," I assure Sophie as she stands in front of the bathroom mirror tugging her black spandex shorts further up her stomach. The movement makes them look shorter, and she frowns in the mirror. I expected her to be nervous about skinny dipping yesterday, but I've noticed in the past few weeks that she has developed a few insecurities no matter what she's wearing. I'm not sure if it has to do with starting college soon or just growing up, but I'm doing my best to help her work through that. That's what today is for.

"Are you sure?" She twists her hands together in front of her, her arms blocking most of the bare skin between her shorts and light pink sports bra.

"I'm positive. There's nothing to be nervous about. Hardly anyone will see you, but anyone who does is damn lucky if you ask me." I kiss her forehead before tugging one of her hands until it untangles from the other and pull her toward the door.

With one hand, she fidgets with the hem of her shorts the entire drive. Her other arm is tightly hugging her waist, covering most of the bare skin on her stomach. As I pull into the parking space outside the small strip mall, I worry she might not go through with this.

Leaning forward to look through the windshield, Sophie shakes her head so dramatically I'm certain she might scramble her brain. "No way. Uh-huh."

"Look at me." I get her attention with my thumb brushing across her cheek. She glances quickly at me, but then returns her gaze to the sign outside the building in front of us. It's black with a neon pink picture of a girl dancing on a pole. "It's a beginner class. Everyone is new like you. They keep the lights low and the instructor is really encouraging and helpful." I researched a couple of the places in town to make sure I brought her to the one that would give her the best experience.

"I'm going to fall. I'm not in shape at all. I can still hardly skate to the diner without dying."

"Who cares if you fall, Soph? You know how many times I missed passes in football? Got tackled by people smaller than me? You remember that one time I tripped over . . . nothing? Literally nothing, Sophie." I laugh at myself, and it earns a half-hearted chuckle from her.

"I remember." She bites back a grin.

Fuck, I love this girl. I would do anything for her, especially if it means forcing her to do things she doesn't believe she can. I want to tell her, but the thought that she could leave again without warning scares me out of it. I'll focus on this obstacle for now. "You're going to kick ass. I can't wait to hear about it. I'll be back to get you in an hour, okay?"

She nods, her chest a little higher. My words shoot straight to her confidence sometimes, and it's one of my favorite things about us.

50
SOPHIE

THEN

When I push through the tinted glass door, Cooper's 4Runner is parked directly in front of me. He looks up from where he's leaned into the driver's side door. I run toward him, hardly giving him time to slip his phone in his pocket.

Feeding off my excitement, Cooper scoops me up and twirls me around before setting me on my feet. "Hey, Soph."

"Cooper, that was so much fun! I even climbed up part of the pole before I slipped off, but it didn't hurt." I don't have time to take a breath, so my words all rush out. "OH! And my core is way stronger than I thought. Maybe skateboarding is helping. I kind of sort of did this thing where I held my whole body up with my legs. I fell again, but it's fine. I'm not that far away from doing the splits either. I'm totally going to practice."

His grin continues to widen the more I ramble.

"What?"

"Nothing. I'm proud of you."

The encouragement activates the butterflies in my stomach. His praise has always meant more than anyone else's.

"Thanks, Coop." Maybe it's the compliment or the endorphins running through me, but before he can reply, I press him against his car door. He follows my lead without hesitation. His fingers thread through my sweaty ponytail, his lips press against mine, and his tongue easily finds its way to dance with mine. I savor every second of his kiss, pulling closer with a grip on the strings of his hoodie. He breaks our kiss, and I'm torn back to reality, having already forgotten we were in public.

"Okay, onto the next one," he declares.

"Already? We don't have to do the whole list in two days!"

He shrugs. "I know, but it's fun."

"Is there anything *you* want to do? Do you have a list?"

"Your list is my list. I like seeing you happy. Let's go."

"Okay, fine. Onto the next thing," I concede, reaching for the dial on his dash to turn up the music and keep my pole dancing high.

When we get back to his house, Cooper practically pushes me in the door and toward the shower, refusing to take one with me. Once I'm freshly clean and smelling like his apple cider scented body wash, I wrap a towel around my body and make my way toward the clattering noise in the kitchen.

I stop next to the fridge, taking in everything spread over his kitchen island and the chair next to it. "What's happening?" My eyes roam over the bleach, the bottle of pink hair dye, some cap thing, and a comb.

"I'm giving you highlights, duh."

"*You* are doing them?" I raise an eyebrow.

He shrugs, seemingly confident. "I watched a few YouTube videos. How hard can it be?"

My feet stay glued to the tile floor, the wooden kitchen chair trying to lure me to it.

"What's the matter? You don't trust me?" The magic words combined with his puppy dog eyes do the trick. Of course I trust him.

"Okay, let's do this." I sit on the chair and Cooper immediately picks up the comb to brush the tangles from my hair.

"What's the worst that can happen anyway? If I mess it up, we'll just dye all of it pink."

"Cooper!!" I turn around, slapping his stomach. He humors me with a fake *ooof*.

"I'm playing." I face forward again, taking a breath as he picks up the hair dryer, reminding myself he's never let me down before.

"Ouch!" I scream with a jump.

"I'm sorry." Cooper looks at me with wide, terrified eyes, nearly dropping my curling iron he picked up from my house while I was at my pole dancing class.

He still hasn't let me look at my hair, washing and drying it for me. It was the sweetest thing until he convinced me he could curl it too.

He cannot.

I laugh to assure him he didn't hurt me, take the wand from him and set it on the counter. "Just let me look at it," I tell him.

Nerves seep from his features, but he nods, following me to the bathroom.

Standing in front of the mirror, I flick on the light. I run my fingers through my dirty blonde hair, hot pink strands from the bottom layers peeking through. My shock must give the wrong impression because my boyfriend says, "You hate it, don't you? I'm sorry, we can go get it fixed by someone."

I turn into him, one hand pressing to his chest, and a finger pressing against his lips. "Cooper, I love it."

"You do?" His worry shifts to confusion.

"I can't believe you did this. It looks like a professional did it."

He chuckles. "Yeah, I'm never doing it again. That was the most stressful thing I've ever done in my life. But . . ." I wait for him to finish his thought. "You look hot."

I pull away to examine my reflection again. "I do, don't I?" The girl smiling back at me exudes happiness. This list really was the best idea.

51

COOPER

THEN

"Alright, I'm calling it. You two are too cute for me right now," Troy says with a sigh, the bonfire crackling next to him. I wouldn't want to be around us either if I found out my girlfriend of four years was cheating on me. Sophie and I have spent the better part of the past month and a half checking items off her bucket list ever since we went skinny dipping. The first few weeks Troy and Emily joined in on the fun until we showed up to her dorm to pick her up for a concert in Portland and Greg–the douche Troy claimed as a friend up until that very moment–answered the door with a very flustered and freshly fucked Emily.

"Hold this, please," Sophie whispers, handing me her just made S'more. She catches Troy before he walks away, looping her arms around his waist, clear she refuses to accept anything less than a twenty second hug. It only takes a few seconds for him to give in, wrapping his arms around her and his head falling to her shoulder.

She must tell him something because he nods against her, then says something in return as he pulls back, heartbreak clear in his gaze as it catches mine. I've agreed with Sophie since the beginning. Emily has never been good enough for Troy, but I also know how much love can distort your perception of reality and how easy it is to not hear anything anyone else tells you.

I give him a half smile and a goodnight before he turns on his heel and heads inside our house. Before he's even through the back door, Sophie is in my arms, sadness radiating off her.

"You okay?" I ask, carefully avoiding getting marshmallow in her hair as I pull her close.

Her head nods against my chest. "I'm sad. I don't like Emily, but I love Troy. I don't like seeing him like this."

"I know, me too." I squeeze her a little tighter.

She pulls away and reaches for her S'more. "He said he's happy we are back together."

"I think we can all agree on that." I grin, kissing her even though her mouth is full of graham cracker crumbles. She giggles against my lips, and it's the sweetest sound. I lick the chocolate remnants off my own lips while I contemplate my decision. "Soph?"

"Yeah?" She answers me, half distracted with the treat in her hand. When I don't reply immediately she shifts her attention to me. My fingers thread through her curls, my thumb brushing her jaw. Either she can read me exceptionally well, or I'm being as crystal clear as I intend without words. "Really?!" she screeches excitedly, nearly dropping her S'more.

"Yes, really." I smooth my thumb against her cheek as her eyes search mine for sincerity. Easily, I was ready to have sex with Sophie months ago–hell, years ago. But her being ready, *us* being ready to cross that line is a completely different story. There's no going back from this. This is all in because I know I'll never be able to let her go again after. Things feel different now, though.

I trust her not to leave. I'm confident we've found our way back to the friendship we had before.

She glances at her S'more like she's debating if she even wants to take the time to finish it. She's been asking me every week for the past two and a half months if this is the week.

"You can finish your treat." I laugh. "We have to put the fire out first."

"So we can start another one." She wiggles her eyebrows at me. I roll my eyes with a chuckle. I'm obsessed with this girl.

"Meet me inside. I'll be in soon."

She grins, shoving the last bite in her mouth before skipping across the backyard grass.

I chuckle, shaking my head and walking to the hose connected to the side of the house. The time it takes for every red coal to turn black feels longer than ever before. When the fire is finally out, I make my way to my room, kicking my shoes off at the back door.

"I turned the TV on. I didn't want to make Troy more sad." My lips twitch up at her consideration. Troy already texted to say he was going out.

"How loud do you plan on being?" I ask with a smirk as I close the door behind me, crawling across the bed to where she leans up against the headboard.

She shrugs with a mix of nerves and excitement. "I don't know. I don't know anything about this, Coop! I mean I would if you didn't make me wait so long!" she fake whines.

I straddle where her legs are kicked out across my navy comforter, bringing me close enough to inhale her mix of smoke and flowers. "I guess I should stop making you wait then, huh?"

"Finally!" She reaches for the hem of my shirt, but I stop her hands with mine. "What?!"

"Do you want to talk about it first? About what to expect. So you're ready."

"I *am* ready," she insists, tugging at my shirt again. "Come on, Coop. I read about it in my books all the time."

There's no way her books give all the details. "I'm not sure it's going to be exactly like your books, Soph. It might hurt."

Her eyes widen and she looks at me. "Really?"

"It's way different than my fingers." I brush my thumb across her jaw and weave my fingers into her hair.

She sighs. "I mean, I guess I knew that, but I didn't really think about it."

"I'm not trying to freak you out. I've just been making you wait, and I don't want you to be let down if it's not perfect."

"I won't be. I promise. If the first time is weird, we'll just have to do it again." She grins. "Oh. Don't we need a condom?"

I chuckle. I love this girl, always making sure we're prepared. "I have one." I open the drawer of my nightstand and pull one out, setting it on the bed next to us. I've never not used a condom during sex. I'm dying to know what it feels like. Someday I'll try it with Sophie. She's the only one I'd ever consider it with, but today isn't the day for that.

She glances at the foil packet, then meets my gaze again, a smile lighting her face. She starts to say something, but I cut it off with a kiss.

With my hands bracing her neck as I run my thumbs across her cheeks.

With my tongue tangling with hers, tasting remnants of S'more.

With sliding the straps of her sundress off her shoulders and letting them fall against her arms.

With running my hands down her body torturously slow as I kiss her, as her fingers play with the hair at the base of my neck like they always do when we're together.

When I reach her thighs, I slip my hands under the hem of her dress and smooth them up her skin until I reach lace. I've waited for this moment for so long. I want to rush into it while simultaneously putting it off longer so it won't end. My fingers slowly cross over the line from skin to lace until they rest gently on her hips.

Over the past couple of years, I've learned I like sex a little rougher, but with Sophie, it's different–at least this time. Sliding my hands over her stomach, I take the flowered fabric with me as I get on my knees. She lifts her arms for me to tug the dress over her head, leaving her sitting on my bed in pink lace underwear and a matching strapless bra. I let my eyes roam her body, taking in all the ways she's changed in the past two years. She was naked the day we went skinny dipping, but I wasn't able to fully take her in the way I get to now. "Fuck, Sophie. You're a dream. *My* dream. You know that, right?"

"Why, because my boobs are bigger now?" she teases, knowing very well that's not what I'm talking about. They have grown at least two cup sizes, though. I groan louder than intended at that thought.

"Come here," I say, tugging my shirt over my head then reaching for her and easing her onto her back. I move to hover over her, lowering myself enough for our skin to touch without giving her all my weight. When she looks into my eyes I'm surprised by the lack of nerves in them. She's just watching me take the lead like she completely trusts me. She always has, and it's something I don't take for granted. *I love you* is on the tip of my tongue. I know she feels the same about me, but something prevents me from saying it at this moment. Instead, I lean on one arm, my other hand running up her stomach, stopping when I get to her breast. My thumb traces the skin at the bottom edge of her bra, and she sucks in a breath.

My gaze meets hers again to find her still watching me intently. She's not making a move to speed us up, and I get the impression she wants to take in this moment like I do. I shift my weight to my knees so I can slide my hands under her back and unhook her bra. Tossing it to the side, I bring my attention to Sophie's almost naked body. She was beautiful before, but turning eighteen has transformed her. I palm both of her breasts, my thumbs rubbing roughly across her nipples that stiffen at my touch. A soft moan leaves her lips, and I need more. I lean to take a nipple in my mouth, nipping and sucking gently, pulling an even more sensual sound from her throat.

I grind my hips against her, already hard and wanting to make sure she's as ready for me as I am for her. I've had so many of her firsts already, and knowing I'm the one who gets to finish crossing them off arouses a primal desire to claim her in every way. Trailing kisses down her stomach, I stop when I reach the lace. I tug with my teeth before looping my fingers on the edge and pulling it off.

Sitting back on my heels, I take her in. I've seen Sophie naked a handful of times. I've touched almost every inch of her skin. I was always attracted to her, but the

Sophie in front of me now is new–more mature and exuding sex appeal–and I've never been more turned on. Her soft brown eyes glimmer with adoration as she watches me scan every inch of her body. When my need to taste her outweighs my desire to look at her, I lean forward again, kissing her hip. I trail kisses down her sensitive skin, placing a soft kiss on her center. "Open your legs for me, Sophie baby." I urge her by scooting down on the bed and wrapping my hands under her thighs. Giving myself better access by pushing her legs wider with my shoulders, I swipe my tongue across her, and she squirms a little.

"That's cold." She giggles, twisting her body away from me. I grin, tightening my grip on her legs and preventing her from moving out of reach.

I drag my tongue against her again, this time taking more. My eyes nearly roll to the back of my head getting to taste her after years of thinking I never would. A few more licks and any sign of chill has disappeared.

I suck on her clit, making her tense for a moment before she relaxes into the bed, opening her legs wider for me. "Good girl," I praise, running my thumbs against her soft skin as I continue to suck gently. My tongue teases her entrance. She squirms again at the contact, and I grin against her. I stiffen the tip of my tongue before diving in, flicking inside her and she writhes under my touch. A moan gets caught in her throat before she chokes it out. God, she's fucking sexy.

"Cooper," she rasps, and I know it's her way of begging for more.

"Just making sure you're ready for me," I breathe against her, releasing one hand from her thigh and sliding a finger inside her easily. I pull out and push back in slowly, my mouth keeping its focus on her clit. Adding a second finger, I feel her stretch around me as I curve them into her.

"This feels so good." Her words take me back to when I was eighteen, touching her for the first time.

"Jesus Christ, Sophie, you're going to make me come before I'm even inside you."

"Then get inside me," she demands. Damn, my favorite girl is only getting better with age.

I pull my fingers out, kissing her once more where she's most sensitive before pulling my shorts and briefs off. Sophie's eyes follow my movements, and mine never leave hers.

As I reach for the condom next to her.

As I tear open the foil with my teeth.

As I roll it over my fully erect cock that's begging for release from the girl under me.

I fall forward to kiss her, one arm propping me up, the other hand guiding our alignment. My heartbeat pulses in my dick as it twitches with anticipation. Without being able to wait for another second, I push into her.

The groan that leaves both of us as I fill her is more satisfying than any sexual experience I've had. She's tight, but her arousal allows me in as deep as I want to go—as I *need* to be. I'm so consumed by her, my brain fogs.

I hardly remember I'm in control, but I retrain my focus and pull out of her slowly before pushing back in. I sink in with less friction this time, but she's a little tense as she loops one hand around my neck, digging her fingers into my skin.

"You good?" I check in.

"Mostly," she whispers. I stop my movement, pulling back enough to see her clearly. She looks up at me, a soft smile on her pretty face, glowing from the moonlight coming through the window above us. "It just feels tight–like there's a lot of pressure. I'm good. Keep going."

"Are you sure?" I ask, running my thumb across her jaw.

"Never been more sure," she says before pressing our lips together as her fingers brush against my side.

I continue slowly despite her words. I'm torn between making sure she's okay and succumbing to the most intense pleasure I know lives on the other side of letting go. "I'm not hurting you?"

"You could never hurt me, Cooper."

Her trust is all the permission I need to bring us both to the edge. My hand runs down her thigh, encouraging her leg to wrap around my hip. I feel the moment when her discomfort turns to pleasure. She relaxes completely and paired with the new angle, I sink deeper inside her. Her moan aligns with my thoughts about how perfectly we fit together. Like she was made for me. Like I could have waited for her and not have regretted it.

Despite the condom, I feel closer to her than I ever have to anyone else. With every pump, I revel in every place our skin touches, in how we connect inside of her. I'm already close, feeling unable to control it. The way I have no control over how much I love this girl. Wanting her to come with me, I reach between us, rubbing her clit. The sound that gets stuck in her throat gets swallowed by my next kiss, and along with one more thrust, sends me over the edge. I continue rubbing circles against her as I pump in and out until she shatters beneath me, her eyelids fluttering closed and her grip on my neck tensing. I continue my movement, rocking into her until I'm certain we've both fully come down before gently collapsing on her and matching her stillness.

"How do you feel?" I whisper, searching her eyes as I comb my fingers through the hair by her face.

"Like . . . I'm both closer to you and still not close enough. I don't know if that makes sense."

"Like it's everything you ever wanted, but somehow you want more?"

She nods. "So, it was as good as–"

"No. Don't you dare finish that thought." I press my forehead against hers. "Nothing–no one–compares to you, Soph. Never has, never will." She gives me a shy smile I'll never be able to forget. "Trust me, some of my firsts were still left for you too."

52

SOPHIE

NOW

Cooper, 21; Sophie, 19

My finger hesitates over the call button. I haven't seen or talked to Cooper since the party at Marcus' house a month ago, but I don't have anyone else to call. All my new friends–really Chastity's friends–aren't good for much besides knowing where the best parties are, and I don't want Marcus to feel like he has to babysit me. I love living at his house and having new freedom I didn't have at home. I tap my finger to the screen and hold it to my ear.

It rings three times.

"Hello?" Cooper's voice on the other end automatically soothes me. My voice cracks on a quiet sob. "Sophie? Are you okay?" I can't tell if I'm imagining the concern in his voice.

I shake my head then realize he can't see me. "Can you come get me? I don't have my car."

The silence on the other end is deafening.

"Send me the address."

"Okay. Thanks, Coop."

I hear a sigh on the other end before he hangs up.

A few minutes later, a car drives past where I'm sitting on the curb, and my stomach flips. False alarm. It's not Cooper. I bat at the silent tears streaming down my cheeks, swiping my tongue over the salt on my lips. It's only another moment before a second engine purrs in the darkness then stops, idling on the street in front of me. My heart flutters as fear rushes through me. I don't know why I called him. I have no idea how mad he will be. I should have ordered an Uber instead of running to Cooper when he's not mine to run to anymore.

I stand as the unlock button clicks. Cautiously sliding into the passenger seat, I watch him watch me in the glow of the overhead light, the annoyance on his face softening slightly when he sees my drying tears. He doesn't say anything as I close the door and buckle my seatbelt or as he pulls back onto the street. It's still unclear if he's going to let any feelings for me override the distance between us, but it's me. He's always there for me. This is proof of that. I haven't seen him in a month and he's still here.

"Where did I pick you up from?" He doesn't look at me when he asks.

I tug on my fallen curls, eyes locked on my fingers.

"Another random guy?" I can't tell if it's jealousy or judgment in his voice, but it's probably the latter considering he doesn't want me anymore.

"Don't judge me, Cooper," I snap, then add in a whisper, "That's not fair."

"You make it hard not to when you fuck other people. Practically in front of me."

"I swear I didn't sleep with that guy at Marcus' party. I haven't slept with anyone since you. I promise. I was just trying to make you jealous." Every time I've pushed him away, I've been afraid it'll actually work. It finally did.

"Well," he says more softly, although his gaze is still hard on the road. "At least it wasn't JT." Why does he hate JT *so* much? I stay silent. It causes Cooper to glance at me before his eyes focus back on the street. The second must have been long enough to recognize the shame on my face, telling him that is exactly where I was. "Of fucking course. What did he do?" he growls, looking over his shoulder like he's about to make a U-turn in the middle of the street and go right back to JT's.

Touching his forearm redirects his attention. "No. Can you please just take me home?"

He scoffs. "Are you going to give me another piss poor excuse for why you're hanging around him again?" he asks like that is the real problem. In the past month, I've been clinging to anything familiar. Somehow JT fits in that category. I don't even hang out with him often, and it's not like we hook up or anything. When my plan to make Cooper jealous backfired, I kind of fell into a black hole. I wouldn't say I'm flirting my way through my sadness . . . but if I wasn't lying to myself I'd admit I'm looking for attention anywhere I can in an attempt to feel anything close to what Cooper makes me feel.

"What am I supposed to do? You know I don't have that many friends. And now that we aren't friends, I only have so many options. I'm not just going to be alone."

"We are friends." He looks like he's fighting the urge to add *stupid* at the end.

"We are?" I ask. "Because you haven't talked to me in a month."

He shoots me a pointed stare. "And regardless, the best 'friend' you think you could find is that asshole?"

"He's not as bad as you think, Cooper," I defend.

"Clearly. That's why you called me at 11 p.m. on a Monday night." Irritation rolls off him. "I'll be the judge."

"Umm." We hadn't hooked up since last year, but I felt like maybe I should give in a little or he wouldn't want to keep hanging out. "I was trying to be fun and easygoing and you know, do things . . ." I trail off.

He slams on his brakes aggressively, my chest jolting into the seatbelt. His car skids to a stop before he throws it into park in the middle of the back road to my house. Keeping his eyes forward, he clenches his fingers around the steering wheel. "Jesus Christ, Sophie," he mutters more to himself before facing me. His tone is much louder and more angry when he says, "Tell me you did *not* call me to talk about fucking someone else. We will *never* be that kind of friends."

"Well, you don't want to be together . . . I thought maybe . . ." If anything, he should be happy that I'd clearly rather be around him than do anything with someone else, right?

"If you think I want to hear about you fucking someone else, think again."

"I'm not talking about sex," I whisper. "He wanted a blow job. I said no, so he called me a tease." He tries to interject, but I cut him off by continuing. "He was so mean about it, Coop. But he's never been like that before."

"This topic is off-limits for us," he growls. "I don't ever want to hear about anyone else's dick in relation to what's mine." He realizes his misspoken words immediately. "What was mine. Never bring this up again. Do you understand?" He asks the question slowly like I'm a child who couldn't possibly comprehend. The street light infiltrates the car enough to see the war raging inside his bright blue eyes as he speaks. He's mad, but I also know he's picturing my lips wrapped around him.

I hold my stare for a moment before I nod.

His anger is replaced with worry. "Is that all he did? He didn't hurt you, did he?"

"He didn't hurt me," I confirm in a whisper with a subtle shake of my head. He acknowledges my response by shifting back into drive.

"He's still a piece of shit. You know that, right?" When I leave yet another question unanswered, not taking the bait in this one-sided debate, he adds, "You know I never had to ask for you to blow me." He smirks, and my eyes widen, mouth falling open. I can't believe he brought *us* into this. And the way he said it–I hate him for his crude thoughts aligning with mine. I didn't hesitate for a second with pleasing Cooper that way once sex was on the table for us. I loved the reaction I got from him so much I would have done it all the time if we hadn't broken up. So, why was it so hard for me to do the same with JT? With anyone else for that matter.

"You would never ask if you knew I wouldn't want to," I mutter in JT's defense like this is all a misunderstanding. "It's not his fault he can't read me like you can."

"Oh, so this is my fault? You're having problems with your new boyfriend because your ex is better than him?" He laughs.

"He's not my boyfriend!" I scream, conversation deja vu hitting me like a pesky fly that won't leave you alone.

"Do you realize how stupid you sound? Tell me, Sophie, what are you expecting to get out of this?" He pulls into my driveway, throwing the car into park but not pulling the key from the ignition.

"I don't know," I cry. "I won't see JT ever again. He doesn't mean anything to me." I pull my phone from my cross-body bag and unlock it, desperate to stop this fight. I open my text thread with JT. There's a new text from him saying he's sorry he pushed me and to come back so he can make it up to me.

Cooper covers my phone with his hand. I try to ignore the warmth that shoots through me at his touch and focus on his serious gaze boring into me. "I'm not your convenience choice, Sophie," he growls. "I'm not just the guy you can keep calling because I'd do anything for you."

He's anything *but* my convenience guy. I'm not trying to take advantage of him. I can't help when I need him. "Cooper, no. You mean way more to me than that. You're my person. And I'm yours." The moment the words leave my lips, they click into place as a certain truth. Screw what's been drilled into me, what I've been convinced about first relationships and their place in life. I know he's *it* for me.

He removes his hand covering my phone and my fingers, slamming his fist into the steering wheel. "I don't need you to be my person anymore, Sophie," he grits out.

Choking on my tears, I cry, "That's not true."

"You're delusional. If you cared about me, you wouldn't force me into situations I don't want to be in. I'm not here to swoop in like one of your book boyfriends saving the day. That's not my job anymore."

"Whose fault is that?" I snap. I know I'm *it* for him too, but he has to let me back in.

He glares, his grip tightening around the black leather. "I don't fucking know at this point. But I do know you're making it worse."

"I'm just a problem for you, aren't I?"

"Sophie, you're my problem, my solution, you're my entire fucking world. Don't you know that by now?" I'm frozen in place when he continues. "But each time I think about choosing you, about giving us another chance, you remind me why I shouldn't. I can't figure out how I'm going to give us another chance without blame or resentment or staying stuck in this toxic cycle. I can't handle it anymore. It's taking over my life. I revolve around you like you're the sun, Sophie, and I love the way you light up my life. But I need more than that to live. You're blinding me." He points toward the car door. "I'm choosing me. I'm done, Sophie. You need to understand that." A rush of relief leaves him with those words like he finally completed the final task of a challenging mission. My heart and lungs conspire against me, ceasing to work at the same time.

"No," I cry, wiping the backs of my hands across my eyes in an attempt to clear them, but all it does is make room for new tears as I wonder if getting back to what we had is even possible.

"Things are never going to be how they were between us," he says as if he's read my mind. "So stop trying."

"You came when I called, though . . ." I say under my breath.

"Don't take advantage of that." He stares straight ahead, waiting for me to get out of the car.

"Cooper. Come on. I miss you." I take a deep breath. "What if . . ." I hesitate, not knowing the effect my next words will have. I need him to snap, to remember how good it feels when we are *more*. "I miss the way you touch me, Coop. He doesn't touch me like you do. Or love me like you do. No one does." Cooper has never actually told me that he loves me, but I know he does. He *has* to.

He stares, the anger in his voice replaced by something else entirely. "What in the actual fuck is wrong with you?"

My eyes widen at his harsh words. That wasn't the reaction I was hoping for. I stay silent.

"I don't know where my Sophie is, but you're not her. Or maybe this is who you are now, and I need to accept it and move on." His fingers dig into his eyes like the motion will erase me.

"No," I whisper, more to myself than him.

The heat from the vents is the only thing breaking up the loaded air between us. Unable to handle us fighting for another second, I get out of his car, slamming the door behind me.

53
COOPER

NOW

Sophie storms toward her front door, but right before she reaches it, she turns on her heel and crosses half the distance back to my car.

"You know what?" she screams through the darkness.

Yanking my key from the ignition, I slam my car door, my Nikes audibly hitting the pavement as I approach her before I can stop myself. "Tell me, Sophie. What?" As if on cue, a crack of thunder booms behind the stormy, gray clouds I didn't notice in the midst of our bullshit. Of fucking course. We simultaneously tilt our heads. Water sprinkles through the air, misting my face and distracting me. As if that was enough warning, the sky opens up and rain pours from the sky. Water spots in Sophie's hair grow until she's sopping wet in front of me, frozen in place. She wipes her hands across her face, new tears mixed with the rain, but doesn't make a move.

I run my hand through my hair, water flinging off the ends. "What do you want?"

"I won't leave us like this, Cooper." I can barely hear her over the rain.

Laughing, I close some of the distance between us. "Since when do you care about how you leave me?"

"I do care!" she screams angrily like I've accused her of something terrible.

"That doesn't exactly track." I laugh humorlessly, with no idea why I'm still entertaining her, considering once again she's done exactly the thing that pisses me off the most. I have no clue why we are standing in the pouring rain. It's dramatic. Like everything else is between us.

Sandals slick against the concrete, she takes two careful steps closer, leaving only a small gap between us. Her wet dress clings to every curve. Fuck. Every time I see her she seems so much more grown-up than the last time. The outline of her lace thong is clear through the fabric. I stare a beat too long and she catches me, taking another step until she's close enough I could reach out and touch her. "Admit that you want me." She must have siphoned her declaration from the way I'm looking at her–a look that surely says all I can think about is ripping that dress off her wet skin and throwing her onto her bed.

There's no use in lying when she knows me as well as she does. "You were just with someone else. I'm not doing that shit again."

"No, I wasn't. I didn't touch him," she says at normal volume, but she's close enough I can hear her.

I search her eyes for truth, and can't tell if I find it, or if my need for her is deceiving me. "What do you want from me, Sophie?" The volume has left my voice, but the anger is still there.

She looks at her fingers where they are toying with the fabric of her dress suctioned to her waist. "You," she whispers, then jerks her gaze to me. "YOU," she says more definitively, like it's obvious, and I should know her better.

"Don't do this," I growl, my hands fighting their pull to her. I harness the same rage the rain has as it smacks against the cement. Maybe she didn't sleep with JT, but she was still with another guy. *Again.* Not to mention before that she was posting pics on her birthday with who the hell knows who.

"I can't help it." She presses her hands against my T-shirt covered chest, the contact feeling like the lightning that has yet to strike around us. Her touch, her words, they used to be the only thing that cooled me off. They don't have the same effect on fires started by her–at least not right now.

My fists clench at my sides. Do not fucking touch her, Cooper. She hasn't proven she can stay. She hasn't proven she's *only* yours. I take a small step back and her fingertips drag down my stomach. They catch on the edge of my shorts, heavy from how wet they are. I can't handle being here. I'm not capable of pushing her away much longer even though that's what I need to do.

My hands clamp down on her wrists, pulling them away from my skin. She doesn't flinch at how tight my hold is on her–she just keeps her eyes locked on mine. "I'm leaving," I say, but my body doesn't listen. *Tell me not to go.* I'm so mad, but her closeness is the only thing that always brings me back down.

Instead of retreating, she takes another step toward me as if she's reading my mind rather than hearing my words. The only solution I can think of is to replace any image of her being with someone else. "I swear to god, Sophie, if you take one more step, I will fuck you so hard you won't even remember what it was liked to be touched by him—by anyone."

"I only want to be touched by you," she says with a voice of confidence and seduction I've never heard before.

"You don't fucking get it," I growl. "You should never have been touched by anyone else in the first place."

"No one else will touch me again."

"Don't fucking play with me," I yell, determined to not let the feelings in my dick override my feelings about this. I don't believe her.

"Then play with me," she says so quickly I question if it's actually Sophie standing in front of me.

"Are you drunk?"

"No." The frustrated word lands hard like the rain on the pavement.

"High?" I doubt she is, but something *is* coursing through my veins, and I can't tell if it's love or hate.

"No." She closes the distance between us. My eyes follow her movement, and I hesitate. "You know you want me. And I only want you." I can't take back my next move, so I stare at her, waiting for my decision to be made either way.

I glare at her, grinding my teeth.

"What have you learned in all your practice for me, Cooper? Show me what I've been missing."

"Jesus Christ," I mutter. Where did this girl come from? I'm equal parts turned on and confused by the new person in front of me.

Still held captive by my hands on her wrists, she leans in just enough to kiss the spot below my ear that drives me fucking nuts before whispering, "I learned things too while we were apart." The shock of the statement makes me drop her hands and she uses the freedom to reach for my athletic shorts where I'm already hard, but I clasp my hand around her again.

"Do you really think that you being with someone else makes me want you more?"

"Don't act like you haven't been with other girls. You had plenty of experiences. And guess what, Coop? I'm willing to bet it taught you a few things that benefit me. Just like crossing things off my list benefits you."

She's not exactly wrong, and I give her credit for not backing down, but it only pisses me off more because she's missing the point. "You and this fucking list."

"You're supposed to be supportive of my list, not controlling of it."

"This isn't about the list, Sophie. It's about you always choosing someone else before you chose me. Stop using those damn bullet points as a scapegoat."

"I'm not," she screams. "I needed to do things for me. Why can't you understand that? Those guys were nothing more than a means to an end."

"I don't want to fucking talk about anyone else who has had what's mine." Possessiveness fills me as I disregard the reality of who Sophie belongs to, sick of this conversation.

"Then claim me already."

Heart thumping in my chest, any understanding around how we got here–to this place where she's anything but my safe space–blurs. I want to blame her, take it out on her. And right now that means fucking her until I regain the control she's taken from me. "This doesn't mean we're together," I concede. How am I supposed to stop myself?

She stares back, a challenge in her eyes, but she doesn't say anything–she just nods. With the confirmation, my hands fly to her neck, gripping her tightly as I pull her lips to mine. Our mouths crash together in line with another boom of thunder, leaving me instantly breathless. Between the taste of the girl I've been de-prived of and the rain, I'm drowning. Sophie's fingers dig into the skin on my back, her nails clawing at me like she needs this as much as I do.

54

SOPHIE

NOW

Slipping my hands under Cooper's wet T-shirt, I scratch my nails against his skin, using enough pressure to leave a mark. I need him to remember this tomorrow. I want him to think about me and the intensity we don't share with anyone else. Stepping toward the house without breaking our kiss, he follows my lead, backing up until we're stumbling through the front door.

He breaks our connection to slam the door and eagerly crashes his body back into mine where I'm standing in the kitchen. As his hands grip my waist, his lips find my ear. "I have fucking dreams about that Snapchat picture." He does? I know he took a screenshot, but still, he never said anything about it. "Not being able to touch you kills me," he confesses.

"That was a picture, Coop," I whisper back. "You can't do anything with a picture. But you can do whatever you want with me."

"Turn around," he growls.

"Why?" He's kind of scary, but it's also hot.

"Because I can't stand to look at you right now, Sophie," he bites.

"Why not?" I press, knowing full well he wants this as much as I do.

"If I look at you, I'll love you more than I hate you right now." *Did he just say he loves me?* "And that's not happening."

Oh. I flashback to the night I lost my virginity. Everything about that experience was a 180 from what it is now.

"So, you can let me fuck you over that counter or I can leave."

I don't want him to leave, so I guess my mind is made up. Even though I'm nervous Marcus could get home at any minute, I do as he says, taking the two steps toward the kitchen counter. Water drips off my dress as I hinge at the hips, leaning over the cold tile, my feet perfectly reaching the floor.

"Good choice," he praises, his voice dripping with satisfaction. I don't know if I love or hate it. JT tried to get me to do something different the first and only time we had sex, but I refused. He probably thought our sex was boring, but I wasn't comfortable with him enough to experiment. But Cooper, I trust him not to hurt me even when he's mad. I'm never embarrassed or insecure around him.

His hands smooth up my wet thighs, taking my dress with them. He pushes the fabric above my waist, sending a chill through me. His lips land on my lower back, warming the skin they touch. I want them everywhere. I *need* them everywhere. His kiss doesn't stay soft for long, the nip at the skin on my hips makes me suck in a breath. His fingertips dig into me hard enough to bruise, and I whine at the thought of him wanting to fuse himself to me in this way. He tugs the lace plastered to my skin from the rain, hooking a finger on each side as he slides the thin scrap of fabric down my legs, letting out a groan between each kiss he trails down my skin as he goes.

I step out of my underwear, and he falls to his knees, gripping my thighs and pushing them apart until I step wider for him. A satisfied moan leaves me when his tongue licks over my opening, creating a new layer of wetness.

He sucks on my clit, a rush of pleasure shooting through me. My entire body throbs with need for him, and I'm torn between begging for it and letting him take his time. I want whichever route helps him accept us being together is a *good* thing because our connection is so much stronger than with anyone else.

Spreading me with one hand, he slides in one finger of the other, eliciting a gasp from me. On the next pump, he adds a second, and the way he's stretching me feels too good. I bite into my lip, trying to refrain from screaming out. His tongue teasing me, his fingers inside me . . . the thought of his cock filling me, claiming me.

His lips land softly against my back again. "I want to hear how much you want this," he murmurs against me. His other hand smoothes up my side, the gentleness contradicting the way he's fucking me with his fingers.

"I need more, Coop," I beg, my fingers curled around the edge of the tile counter, unable to resist feeling closer to him, wanting us to be more intimate.

Without so much as a word, he removes his fingers. Before I register what he's doing, his shorts land heavily on the floor. "Jesus Christ, you're perfect," he mutters before slapping my ass. It stings in the best way, and I grip the counter to brace myself for whatever comes next. He spreads my legs wider with his grip on my thighs, his head aligning and toying with my entrance. The anticipation alone pulls me to the edge.

He presses into me, gentle only on the first thrust. A groan vibrates through him as he grabs my hips for stability, and he slams into me the second time. Feeling him fully inside me is so satisfying, I moan, barely hearing his under the breath curse as he continues to drive into me, heat and pressure building in my core.

His hand slides from my hip to my front, massaging my clit in rough circles. "Fuck, Sophie. I'm not going to last long." His movements become jagged like he's losing control. "Get there with me."

It's his words "with me" that hit harder than him driving into me. I unravel, pulsing around him as he comes. My toes curl into the floor, every cell in my body feeling energized.

When we both come down, he pulls out of me. For as alive as I feel, I can't bring myself to push off the counter yet. Twisting me by my hips to face him, he pins me between him and the counter. He pulls his wet T-shirt over his head. His faded spiced apple cider scent consumes me–somehow not washed away by the rain–drawing me closer to him. As his mouth finally connects with mine, the cool fabric of his shirt hits my inner thighs. He wipes at me gently, clearing away the evidence of our sex.

Once he's satisfied, he drops the shirt on the floor, and I feel him pulling away from our kiss. I grab fistfuls of the wet fabric of my dress clinging to my waist and tug it over my head before he has time to call it quits. I reach behind me and unhook my navy lace bra, letting the straps fall off my shoulders before tossing it onto the floor.

Cooper watches my movements like he's torn between making me stop and waiting for whatever happens next. I don't give him the opportunity to decide. I grab his hands, forcing his palms to my breasts, driven by confidence only because if there's any chance he's going to walk away after this, I'm going to make sure it's something he never forgets. "Cooper." His heady eyes drift from my chest to my face. "You know that picture was for you, right? *Only you. Specifically for you.*"

His face hardens at my words. "I don't believe you."

"I'll swear on whatever you want me to swear on, Coop." I lock onto his gaze and whisper, "The only thing I was wearing in that picture was the same underwear I wore the night I gave you my virginity. I don't share my memories of you with anyone."

He pins me against the counter with his hips, groaning as his thumbs swipe over my nipples which immediately stiffen under his touch. I use his distraction to my advantage, running my fingers through his hair at the base of his neck and kissing the spot below his ear that drives him crazy. I drag my tongue along his skin, tasting a mix of salt and rain, and nip at his ear lobe. He groans, and he's close enough I feel him already getting hard again. I suck gently, tightening my grip on his neck.

"You better be up for round two if you're going to tease me," he huffs.

55
COOPER

NOW

Sophie places her hand over mine, pushing my cupped hand from her breast and dragging it down her body. "You tell me if I'm up for it," she whispers into my ear before nipping at it again. Fuck that feels good. She's using a combo of moves she knows I love and new ones I haven't experienced. I try not to worry about who she's learned anything else from.

I swipe my finger over her, turned on even more by how ready she is for me again. "Fuck, you're wet," I curse under my breath and her hand still on top of mine puts pressure against me until my finger slips barely inside. I overpower her, pulling my hand away. She whines at the loss of contact but stops when she realizes I'm not done with her yet. I lift her by her hips and set her on the counter, reminding myself again that we shouldn't be together. But I can't bring myself to not take advantage of the girl in front of me, to not act on the image of her naked in that picture and the one of her coming undone for me on the dryer that's been seared into the back of my brain for months.

At this point, I'm fueled by both love *and* hate–you couldn't pay me enough to shut this down.

I kneel on the hardwood floor in front of her, pushing her legs over my shoulders and grabbing her ass to slide her to the edge of the tile counter. My tongue swipes from her entrance to her swollen clit, tasting our combined release. She lets out the sweetest sound I've ever heard. Her back arches with her moan, and I glance up as she bites into her lip, her head tipping back. God, I love the control I have over her.

I suck her clit and her hands fly to my hair, gripping the strands, begging for more. It's nearly impossible for me to not give this girl anything she wants. I drag my tongue the length of her again and circle her clit with the tip. The way she squirms and her legs locking around my neck only makes me want her more. I tease her entrance with flicking licks, her sweet moans music to my ears.

I spread her with my thumbs before twisting my tongue inside her. Fuck. I can't help but groan against her, the vibrations eliciting a rare curse from my sweet girl's lips. God, I love her.

"Cooper," she chokes out my name, making my dick twitch. She murmurs her next words to herself and I can't make out whether she says, "I love *you*," or, "*this*."

I have a short lived battle in my brain–debating whether to try and likely fail in a relationship or push her away in self-preservation. I choose neither option for now, plunging my finger deep inside her as I suck her sensitive skin.

Sophie shakes around me, her grip on my hair tight enough to pull me closer. I glance up as pure ecstasy takes over her features. I alternate short licks near her opening and sucking on her clit as I fuck her with my fingers, working them inside her as she pulses around me. The way she lets me consume her, I would eat her every morning for fucking breakfast if she was mine.

When she's come down enough, I stand, careful with her as I lay her back against the tile and climb onto the counter, needing release from the girl under me. It feels like I'm suffocating and she's my only source of air. It's intoxicating in a way I equally love and hate.

She loops her arms around my neck, pulling my lips to hers, greedy for a kiss. "You're so good at that," she murmurs against my lips.

"There's a lot of things I'm good at." I can't help but grin as I push inside of her again. She bites my lip hard, inviting me to play rough.

I thread one hand through her wet hair, bracing myself with my elbow on the counter. With the other, I roll her nipple between two fingers before palming her whole breast roughly. Goddamn, she's hot.

"Are you this wet for everyone, Sophie?" I breathe into her ear, and she shakes her head against me. "Answer me with words."

"Only you make me like this," she chokes out in a whisper, nearly paralyzed as I pound into her.

"You will be the fucking death of me, Sophie Porter." I groan. Even though I just came, I'm not going to last much longer. I'm like a teenager when it comes to her.

"You feel so good inside me, Cooper," she says, still in a post-orgasm semi-sedated state. "You're so deep." Her eyes lock on mine as I drive into her. "Come for me."

Fuck.

I slam into her harder, and faster, her hands moving to grip the edges of the counter to counteract my movement. "Come for me, Cooper," she chokes out again, and it does me in. A wave of relief shoots through me as I come–like six months' worth of tension has been released. Tingles prickle my skin and my thoughts blur. I can't do this. Holy fuck, how am I going to let her go again? I need to get out of her and out of here. I ruin the enjoyment of the tail end of my orgasm by pulling out and hopping off the counter like it's on fire. My abruptness startles Sophie, and she sits, confused and immediately closes her legs.

Tears well in her eyes, and I force myself to look away. Once they slide down her face, it'll be that much harder for me to walk away. As I bend to pick up my shirt, I catch her arms folding over her middle. As I find my shorts, she slips off the counter and struggles tugging her dress over her head.

"What just happened?"

I yank my shorts on, unsure what I'll say.

"Cooper." Her voice is full of worry. I don't make eye contact. "Cooper, look at me," she yells.

"What?" I reluctantly bring my eyes to hers, attempting to remain as neutral as possible.

"Don't do this," she cries.

"Do what?" I feign oblivion.

"Pull away from me. You can't deny that," she flings her hand wildly at the kitchen counter, "meant something. You can't tell me there isn't something special between us."

"Don't give me that bullshit. I'm not dumb enough to think this changes anything."

"But you said–"

"Anything I said while I was inside of you doesn't mean shit. After all this time, you're still playing me. It's time to tie a knot in our yo-yo string. I'm done. We're done."

"Fuck you, Cooper."

I'm shocked by the words that come out of her pretty pink lips, but bite back a smile, smirking instead. "You just did."

I can't think clearly with her half-naked in front of me, but I know I shouldn't be here, that neither of us is stable enough to be together. She stares at me, her eyes asking if I'm being for real right now. "I'm serious, Soph. I'm not doing this back-and-forth shit with you anymore. I told you this wouldn't mean anything."

"You're a liar."

"Fine. I'm a liar, Sophie. Either way it doesn't matter. We're not starting a relationship based on you trying to make me jealous with someone else. You have no regard for how that shit affects me."

"I'm just trying to make you see that you want me, that you're happier with me! It's exactly what time and experience has shown us. And you're still going to walk away?"

"Yes," I force out, attempting to push her further from me. As much as I love this crazy woman, if I let her back in, she's going to break me again–I can feel it. I can't let that happen. The damage of losing her again would be irreparable.

"Seriously? Just like that?" She searches my face.

I pause long enough I worry she'll see through me. "Just like that."

She must not know me as well as I thought because she bends to snatch her panties and bra off the ground. "I can't believe you're doing this." She shimmies her underwear on and yanks her dress back in place.

"Can't you see that we don't work together?"

"CAN'T YOU SEE THAT I LOVE YOU?"

My heart races, pounding against my chest with an intensity that rivals a mosh pit at a concert; I can hardly focus on sorting through my own thoughts. She's never said those words before, and she shouldn't be saying them now, not like this. I scrub my hands down my face wishing it would ease the turmoil I feel.

I don't realize I haven't said anything until she speaks again, and I pull my hands from where my fingers are pressed into my eyes. "Cooper. Did you hear me? I said that I love you." Her voice is far away like an echo from the other end of a slide. My head spins. Knowing that we've been in some sort of fucked up love is one thing. Finally hearing her say it out loud is another, and I can't deal with it. Everything is wrong. She should be whispering it back with a smile on her lips after I've told her first. When she's in my arms and when everything feels *right*. But it's all wrong, and I hate myself a little for it happening this way.

Still, I need to focus on everything I hate about us, or she'll destroy me again. So I don't say it back, and without another word and without turning back to look at her, I walk out the door.

56
COOPER

NOW

Sophie's bedroom light flicks off only ten minutes after I leave. My car is still parked in Marcus' driveway as I stare at Sophie's window replaying her voice screaming *I love you* over and over in my mind. My hands tug on the short strands of my hair, my eyes closed, head tipped back against my seat. Why am I not in her room right now? Why do I keep pushing her away when she tries to get close again instead of telling her how much I love her too?

Because she keeps leaving. Yeah, she comes back, but it's always so manipulative.

Because I'm always there for her but what about when I need her? I'm the only one she calls but I'm not the only one in her bed.

Because maybe there's something to this "first love" thing—it's called that because there's more after it. Maybe we're just the ones we learn from to prepare for the real one. Maybe stories like Mom and Dad *are* the exception to relationships. *Maybe the idea that you should search through your options has been right all along.*

The passenger window rattling with three knocks startles me out of my daze.

Marcus peers through the glass, opening the door and sliding into the seat as soon as I hit the unlock switch.

We sit in silence for a moment.

"Did you just get home?"

It occurs to me I'm in nothing but my basketball shorts, having tossed my wet shirt in the backseat.

He nods toward the windshield and I glance to the top of a garage where a little light glows on a camera. "Got a security notification on my way home. Wasn't expecting to see foreplay going down in the driveway, but if that was any indication of what was going on inside, I wasn't about to join you."

I shake my head, too mad to feel any guilt.

"It smells like sex in here."

With a half-hearted chuckle, I turn to him. "Yeah, you might want to wait another minute before you go inside."

"I don't even want to know."

"Are we turning you off from love yet?" I sigh.

Marcus laughs, his voice deep with a touch of sadness. "Just taught me to communicate better than you idiots."

I roll my eyes. "You're welcome."

"Dean is miserable in Costa Rica."

My brows push together, confused by the direction shift.

"He never found the courage to tell Maci how he felt."

"Sophie knows how I feel."

"She knows that you've loved her since you were a kid?"

"Not in those words. It's not enough."

"You don't think the way you love her is enough?"

Tapping my fist against the steering wheel, I give myself more time, delaying the inevitable admission. "No. It's not unconditional. I can't even see her with someone else without losing my mind. I'm mad at her all the time."

"But you still love her despite that. Isn't that what unconditional means?"

I don't know how to answer that. It feels toxic—all of it. Neither Sophie or I deserve it.

"What if she's miserable without you and just sucks at dealing with it? What if her unconditional love for you keeps her stuck?"

"Some days it seems like she has moved on."

"Or maybe her acting out is her way of coping with the fact that she doesn't think she's supposed to love you."

"Our friendship was going just fine how it was."

"Uh-huh. So, eventually you would have found some-one else to be in a relationship with?" He turns my words around on me.

My mouth opens but nothing comes out. I can't imag-ine feeling about anyone as strongly as I do Sophie. And it kills me thinking she'd ever feel more for someone than she does me.

"Say there *is* someone better for both of you. You'd still rather her not be in your life at all?"

I stay silent, visions of my life without Sophie in any capacity flashing through my mind. My chest tightens more with each thought as I picture her dissolving out of every scene in my future. Graduation. Running my business with my dad. Marriage. Kids. Ten other things in between.

"You know as well as anyone how important family is—how crucial it is to surround yourself with the right people who are always there for you."

I nod, thinking back to the morning I opened the front door to see ten year old Troy standing there, needing a family. "What's your point?"

"You don't let go of those people just because you're mad at them or because they slip up or because things get hard." He chuckles, shaking his head as if he was recalling and discarding a memory. "Maybe you and Sophie never find your way back to each other romantically. But you two are important to each other. You always have been. Are you willing to give that up?"

My head falls back against the seat. "No." I take a breath. "But how the fuck can I be friends with her when I'll always compare anyone else to her? How can I watch her be with someone else? *Marry* someone else?" I open up in a way I never have with Marcus—considering we aren't *that* close. Christ, this isn't even a conversation I've had with Troy or Mom. But this isn't a real estate deal with steps to walk me through the process. And I'm at a total loss.

"That I don't know. But don't you think it's worth trying to figure out?"

"I wish I could figure out where it all went wrong in the first place."

57

SOPHIE

THEN

Cooper, 20; Sophie, 18

Dad hands me a pair of chopsticks when the server places my bowl of ramen on the table in front of me. "How was your architect major meetup today?" I'm excited I have already declared my major, although I think it's been inevitable since I was seven and refused to use anything as a coloring sheet besides copies of floor plans that Mr. Montgomery would bring home from work.

"It was good," I say, breaking my chopsticks apart and adjusting them in my hand. "A bunch of freshman design majors were there too." I dip my chopsticks into my broth, coming up with a scoop of noodles. It's nice they have this get together the week before school so I can get comfortable before classes start.

"That's great, honey," Mom chimes in. "I'm glad you're . . ." Her eyes shift to the space behind Dad and me, her words trapped in her wide open mouth.

Dad and I turn simultaneously. A lady stands behind us, but I have no idea who she is. The judgment hits me that she looks kind of homely–her fake blonde hair is a little greasy and stringy. Her clothes look like they're designer and might have been an expensive, latest-trend at one point, but years of wear have destroyed them.

She's close enough I can smell the cigarette smoke that's fused into the fabric.

"Mary," Dad spits.

Wait, Mary? That's the name of his ex-wife, the lady who he married right out of high school. She developed a gambling addiction and stole all of his money.

"Hey, Jack," she seems unbothered by his venom. "It's nice to see you. It's been a while."

"Not long enough," Dad mutters under his breath.

"You must be Diane." Mary addresses my mom as I sit there bewildered, taking in the scene. Her gaze shifts to me. "Which must make you Sophie."

Please never let me be so crazy that I stalk my ex's family–I send out the silent prayer, although I doubt Cooper will ever be my ex again and I already know everything about his family. I nod out of instinct and politeness.

"You have no right to talk to my daughter. See yourself out, Mary."

Her eyes go wide at his attack as my mom scolds him with his name.

Dad ignores his wife, shooting daggers at his ex until she backs away toward the door.

"Jack, that was a little harsh don't you think?" Mom berates him.

"No. Harsh is her ruining my life." Dad has only ever talked about his ex-wife as a tale of caution. Every time Dean went to a school dance or had a date, he'd stop him on the way out the door and remind him to be careful. I always thought it was a tad dramatic. The way he speaks is like a teenager whose life has been "ruined" by a trivial thing.

"Your life looks pretty great from where I'm sitting," Mom replies calmly.

"You know what I meant." He turns to me. "That witch right there is exactly why you don't rush anything, Sophie. It's why you take your time to separate love from infatuation so you end up with what and who you truly want." It's been a while since he's shared this insight, and this time it has more bite than it ever has.

"Don't scare her, Jack."

"It's okay, Mom. I think after eighteen years of knowing Cooper I'd know if my feelings are real, Dad."

"Years aren't the only factor. Age and experience matter too, Sophie. Some things you can't know until you've had real world experience. I don't want you to end up like me."

"With an awesome kid?" I grin, brushing off his concern. Cooper is definitely not anything like that. Mom and I both scoop another bite of ramen up with our chopsticks and Dad catches on to the fact that we won't be entertaining him.

58

SOPHIE

THEN

Cooper: *Just got to Mom and Dad's. Be over in a sec. Can't wait to see you.*

My heart flutters at the text. It's been two days since Cooper and I had sex for the first time, and he's been so busy at work with his dad, I haven't seen him since. It's been impossible to stop thinking about what happened, about us–how close I feel to him and how much closer I constantly want to be.

Me: *Wait there. Meet me in your room.*

He doesn't reply, but three minutes later I open his bedroom door slowly to find him sitting on the edge of his bed.

"Hey, Soph." He grins as he stands, meeting me in the middle of the room and pulling me into his arms.

"Hi," I manage between kisses.

"I missed you," he breathes against my lips, one hand against my lower back pulling me closer and the other threading through my curls.

A giggle escapes me. "You just saw me."

"Mm-mm. It's been too long." He pulls back from the kiss but doesn't loosen his hold on me.

"I guess we better make up for lost time then." I grin.

His eyes darken as I watch him recall our recent memories, and it turns me on just as much. He attempts to shake it away. "Someone will come looking for us. I promised Mom I'd help her get ready for the party."

"We'll be quick."

He shakes his head. "If you think I want anything less than taking my time with you, you're crazy." His teeth sink into my lip when he leans into a kiss.

With a grip on his neck, my fingers twisting into the short strands of his hair, I step backward. He follows my movement, letting me lead him to the bathroom connected to his room. "I'll be quick with you then," I murmur against his lips.

His eyebrows scrunch as I tug him into the bathroom and close the door behind us.

"Sophie," he says somewhere between a statement and a question.

I press him against the closed door. "Mhmm?" I grin through my words and into a kiss, letting my hands wander under his T-shirt. The feel of our skin touching calms me to my core–not that I've needed calming lately. Everything in my life is so great, everything is perfect since Cooper and I found our way back to each other. I hope he knows that. I want to *show* him that.

His hands brush slowly up my arms, leaving a chill in their wake as my fingers find the button of his shorts. "What are you doing?"

"Making you feel as good as you make me feel," I whisper, tugging the zipper down as I lock my eyes on his.

He groans and the sound only makes me more excited. I've never done this before, but I've read about it in my books. I can do it. I want to. And Cooper will help me if I need it. "What are you thinking?" He catches my hesitation as I flash through a few scenes I've read to hype my confidence.

"Just thinking about how great you are." I slip my hands under the band of his shorts and briefs, shimmying them down.

"Oh yeah?"

I adjust my dress so it doesn't catch on my knees and lower to the tile floor, taking Cooper's already hard length in my hand as I do.

His finger hooks under my chin, redirecting his gaze back to him. "You don't have to do this, Soph." There's a war in his body, torn between not wanting me to stop and making sure I'm comfortable, but I know he means what he says. He would never make me do anything I don't want to. That only makes me want to do it more.

"I know." I smile, biting into my lip to contain my excitement. I'm not sure if it's weird I'm excited to give my first blow job, but I don't think it's so much about that as it is about wanting Cooper to know how I feel about him, to want him to feel as good as he made me feel the other day, as good as he makes me feel every day–whether he's touching me or not. "I want to."

Another groan escapes him, his head falling against the wall as my lips touch the tip. Sliding my hand down his length, I slowly follow with my mouth, wetting him with my tongue as I go. I sneak a glance to make sure I haven't done anything wrong yet, and the sedation that's washed over my boyfriend gives me the last bit of confidence boost I need. He's biting into his lower lip as he watches me. When he catches my gaze, he combs his fingers through my curls with a gentle touch. He's patient–no demand or control or urgency.

I return my focus to the task in my hand–and mouth–it's bigger than I expected it to feel but sliding as deep as I can go doesn't make me gag. He hits the back of my throat, and I grip his hip for stability. With my other hand, I squeeze his balls and the groan that gets stuck in his throat on the way out makes me smile against him and I slide my head back. "Fuck, Sophie," he chokes out, his voice rough and low.

Moving my head back and forth, I find a pace that feels maintainable. I suck a little harder and increase the pressure on his balls–that seems to be something he likes.

"Jesus Christ." I vaguely register the sound of his head falling back against the wall again. "Sophie." If sex had a voice, my name rolling out of his mouth is what it would sound like. He taps my head before lightly tugging on my hair. "I'm going to come. You don't have to–"

I cut him off with a slight shake of my head, already deciding I would fully commit before we started. The only other warning I get is my name choked out one more time. His fingers freeze where they're tangled in my hair. I hadn't choked up until this point but nearly do when the warm liquid fills my mouth in short spurts. His orgasm pumps through him against my tongue, and I try my best to continue my movements until he relaxes. I don't back away until I'm sure he's done, pulling his fingers from my hair.

Standing, I spit in the sink. I could probably make myself swallow it, but the feeling of his cum in my mouth is strange—like when they pull the fluoride tray out of your mouth at the dentist. Turning to him, I make a face, scrunching my nose and sticking my tongue out. "It's not the taste. It's the texture. It's weird."

He chuckles. "Come here."

My "I'm sorry" is muffled against his chest when he pulls me to him.

"Yeah, you have nothing to be sorry for. That was mind-blowing, Soph." He kisses the top of my head. Pulling back just enough to transfer his kiss to my lips, he lets his hands wander beneath my dress. In one smooth movement he presses me against the bathroom counter lifting me until I'm sitting. His hands smooth along my legs as he pushes my dress above my hips. "My turn," he mumbles with his lips pressed against the inside of my thigh.

59
COOPER

THEN

"Cooper." Sophie's dad, Jack, gets my attention as I walk by where he's manning the grill at our family's annual end of summer barbeque.

"Hey, Mr. Porter." I abandon my mission to get another drink.

"I wanted to talk to you about something." His usual laid back demeanor is nowhere to be found, replaced by a seriousness I've never experienced from him in my almost twenty-one years of life. My heart thuds in my chest. I always imagined the day I ask for his permission to marry Sophie, I'd feel as calm as I would be asking my own dad for something important. But an indescribable fear washes over me as I wait for his next words.

"What's up?" I try to keep my cool.

He glances around as if he's making sure no one else is close enough to eavesdrop before closing the lid to the grill, blocking the heat that was warm against my face. Setting the spatula on the side table, he locks his eyes on me. My stomach bottoms out. "It's about Sophie."

I figured. "Is she okay?" I ask with urgency, as if I wouldn't be just as likely to know anything about Sophie as Jack would. I scan the party for her, finding her right where I left her a moment ago, smiling in conversation with Chastity, to get her a Squirt and a plate of cheese and grapes.

"That's what I wanted to talk with you about. You need to break up with her."

"Excuse me, what?" I chuckle. He must be joking. Our families have been team Sophie and Cooper since we were old enough to show any sort of favoritism to another person. Even when we broke up before there's always been conversations about us finding our way back to each other. Now that I'm thinking about it, though, maybe it was just *my* family.

He shakes his head slightly, as if recalling a memory. "You have to remember how young you both are. There's no rush to be together and Sophie is about to start college. This is the time for her to figure out who she is, what she wants, and have experiences that won't come later on in life."

I take a breath in an attempt to eradicate any anger from my voice. "You're saying she can't do that if she's with me?"

"I'm telling you that from experience I know how crucial this age is for anyone–not just Sophie, for you too, Cooper. I'm sure it'll be hard now, but you'll thank me for this one day, when you realize how important it is to discover who you are without someone else first, to make sure you end up with the person who truly compliments you."

"I don't understand." Frustration builds in the fists clenched at my sides. "You don't think Sophie and I are good together? We're meant for each other," I argue. "I can tell you that right now." The only thing keeping my voice low is not wanting to draw Sophie or anyone else's attention to this argument.

"I know you think that now, but I was naive at your age too."

It clicks what is happening here. "It's bullshit for you to project the ramifications of your decisions onto my life, onto Sophie's." I've respected this man my entire life, but that respect is fading with every word that comes out of his mouth.

"Think about Sophie. This is why you two broke up the first time, isn't it? Because she believed you should experience college on your own, your own way. Don't you think she'll want the same for herself?"

"No. Why would she want to do things alone when I can help her?"

"She'll be distracted by you, blinded to potential opportunities she should experience."

"Opportunities or people?" I spit.

"I'm not implying what you're thinking, but whatever comes her way, I want her to be able to make the most of this time.

"No. I don't hold her back. If anything, I encourage her. She can still do whatever she wants and be with me. I'm not breaking up with her."

"I'm not asking you. I'm telling you."

"You're telling me to break your daughter's heart? Some fucking dad you are." My filter is nowhere to be found, the million thoughts zipping through my head taking up all my brain power.

His hand lands firmly on my shoulder, and it takes everything in me not to pull away, to save a sliver of respect from the man who practically helped raise me. "If you care about my daughter, you'll do what's best for her. She'll ultimately realize this is what's best for her too."

Shrugging his grip off my shoulder, I glare at him. "Don't make me do this."

"I can't make you do anything, but I know you'll make the right decision." He ends the conversation by lifting the lid of the grill and grabbing the spatula, turning away from me. I'm aware he's trying to distort my thoughts, yet his conviction has me genuinely considering that he could be right. I am young, and Sophie is even younger. How can we be so sure we are each other's endgame? Am I being selfish not wanting to give her up when it might be what she needs?

No. What she needs is me. I spin to see my girl no longer where I left her. Assuming she went to get her own plate of food since I didn't come back, I storm toward my parents' kitchen. As I step into the house, soft voices from around the corner in the living room stop me in my tracks.

It's Chastity. "Sophie, this wasn't the point of the list. The point was to have new experiences, with *new people.*" Tempted to crash their conversation and add my own two cents, I take a step. I freeze again when Sophie cuts in.

"I have Cooper. He's all I need." My heart skips at the words. God, I love her.

"I'm not saying Cooper shouldn't be your friend, but he shouldn't be your whole world, Soph. It'll keep you from experiencing college. You agreed to this list. Half of the things on here were your idea–things that weren't meant to be done with Cooper or with a boyfriend at all."

"We made that list before we got back together . . ." Sophie's voice trails off like she's wondering if that matters.

"Part of you wants to do all those things, though. You need to go do them."

Silence is Sophie's only response.

"And what are you going to do when he has his fraternity stuff? What about when he graduates two years before you and has to work all the time? You'll be stuck at school alone."

Again, Sophie doesn't speak. She doesn't argue or answer. Fuck. Am I the only one who can't see this all makes no sense. Am I being naive? "Do you really think so?" Insecurity laces her soft voice as she questions her friend like the concern is valid, and betrayal boils my blood. She doesn't believe in us the way I do. She didn't two years ago, and she still doesn't.

Not waiting to hear the rest of the conversation, I veer toward the stairs. Not bothering to glance in the direction of their voices, I take the steps two at a time until I get to the top and immediately slip into my old room, closing the door behind me.

Sitting on the edge of my bed, my mind whirls trying to decipher what all this means–everything Jack said paired with Sophie's lack of saying much at all. I ignore the text that comes through from Troy asking if I want to play a game of basketball in the driveway.

I ignore the one from my mom asking if I can bring a bag of ice outside.

I ignore all three from Sophie asking where I am.

I'm sitting at my desk, elbows digging into my knees, fingers digging into my hair as the fourth one comes through.

Sophie: *I'm starting to worry, Coop. Are you okay?*

What if everyone is right? What if I'll just be a distraction from everything she should experience in college? Even Sophie thought I needed to be apart from her when I started college. How is this any different? If she believed it for me, she must believe it for her too. I hate not knowing what I should do. I always know what I want.

Me: *No.*

Sophie: *What?! Tell me where you are.*

The panic in her voice can be heard perfectly in my mind through her text. I don't know what choice needs to be made, but maybe when I see her, I'll know.

My head jerks toward my door flying open a few moments later, panic emanating from the beautiful girl in front of me.

"Hey." She rushes to me, her hands gripping either side of my head. "What's wrong?"

My gaze bores through her, as if I can see the wall behind her. Fuck. How can our relationship be wrong when her existence alone makes everything feel right?

"Coop."

I glance up to meet her gaze, shaking my head. "Nothing. It's nothing."

Pressing my head to her stomach, I wrap my arms around her, pulling her toward me. She grips my head, her fingers massaging through the strands at my neck. "Are you sure? You can talk to me." Her voice is soft and sweet and full of worry.

Instead of answering, I breathe in the vanilla and jasmine on her skin, letting the calmness she brings me win this battle, wondering if this feeling alone is enough to win the war.

60

SOPHIE

NOW

Cooper, 21; Sophie, 19

The stream of light shimmering through the crack in the curtain wakes me. Rolling over with squinty eyes and a pounding headache, I reach for my phone on the floor next to my mattress. *8:36* reads in white letters overtop a picture of Chastity and I floating on tubes at the lake last summer. I fling my arm to the other side of the bed, hoping it will land on Cooper but knowing it won't. Instead, I'm met with a rush of memories from last night. Going to JT's house. Fighting with him. Calling Cooper. Fighting with *him*. The rain. The sex. Him leaving.

All our words come flooding back, and I run through them again with a clearer mind. I still meant what I said–that I love him, that I don't want anyone except him. But the harsh reality is that he didn't say it back.

No one seems to understand. It's evident by the fact that nothing has changed since last summer. He's not willing to communicate, to see my side. I might not be perfect, but he doesn't trust me and we're never going to be together if that's the case.

I slip from under the pink covers and pull a light green sundress from a hanger in my closet. I smooth my hands over my hair, tangled from the rain and Cooper's fingers last night, and slide on my Chucks, not bothering to untie them.

Ten minutes later, I'm pulling into my parents' driveway, next to my mom's Crossover, thankful Dad has left for work. Approaching the midnight blue house I know so well, I let myself in with the keycode on the front door.

"Mom?" I yell once I've clicked the door shut behind me.

"Sophie, honey?" Her voice gets louder as she steps into the entryway from the kitchen.

A burst of tears flood out of me, and I choke on my words. "I don't know what to do, Mom."

In the next instant, she's in my space, pulling me into a hug. "Talk to me. What's going on?" She releases me, guiding us toward the couch in the living room.

I curl into the soft gray cushion, tucking my legs under me before looking at my mom. "Do you think I'm old enough to be in love with someone?"

"Absolutely." She smiles sadly, tucking a strand of hair behind my ear. "Are you talking about Cooper?"

I nod.

"I know that you love him."

"You do?"

She smiles more genuinely this time. "I remember when you were three and Cooper started kindergarten. You were so upset you couldn't spend the entire day with him anymore. You'd cry all morning and run outside, trying to chase Melissa's van down the street."

"I did?"

She nods. "I'd swoop you up and carry you inside and you'd cry his name all morning, completely inconsolable. You were honestly a brat for weeks." She laughs. "As soon as Cooper came home from school every day, he'd run across his backyard to get to ours, his little hand knocking on the sliding door with that goofy grin of his." She gives me a sad smile. "One day after the first few weeks of the same routine, Melissa was over for lunch. You tugged on her sweater, looked up at her with those pretty brown eyes of yours and said, 'Can I live with you now? I think it will make Cooper happy. I will be happy too.'"

I laugh through my tears, wiping at my eyes again. "What did she say?"

She said, "I'm going to remind you that you said that when you're married and he's the reason you have never-ending laundry." She laughs again. "You had no idea what she was talking about. But Melissa was convinced even then there was something special between the two of you."

"Do you think he's *the one*? How do you know? Did you think your first husband was *the one*?"

A mix between a laugh and a sigh leaves my mom. "I was so young when I met Jimmy."

"You were my age weren't you?" I interrupt.

"Yeah, I was, but you can't compare us."

I scrunch my eyebrows.

"Is that what you've been doing, honey? Thinking things with Cooper will end up like they did with Jimmy?"

"Maybe. And Mary," I admit. "Things don't work out when you're that young and you haven't experienced enough life or . . . I don't know. I've been working on a bucket list. You know, checking things off so I can get whatever experiences I'm supposed to have before I can know what I want or don't have a chance to do them anymore."

"Oh, honey. That's not how it works. There's not a set path, and every situation is different. I won't even touch the topic of Mary and your father, but Jimmy and I were so much different than you and Cooper are. We didn't know each other the way you two do. We thought love could conquer everything and didn't factor in everything else that is important too."

"Like what?"

"Well, for starters, it mattered that he wanted to travel the country in a remodeled van, and I didn't. It mattered that he didn't want kids, and I did. Honey, I'm not sure there's a way to guarantee you know if someone is *the one*. Sometimes you just have to take a leap of faith, you have to see what happens."

"Do you think . . . if I do think he's the one . . . can that be true if I want to do something for me first?"

"I think sometimes you have to love yourself, but that doesn't mean you love someone else less. It's not something you can run out of."

"I'm just not happy, Mom. I love Cooper, but things aren't working between us. I know part of it's my fault, just as much as it is his. And I definitely blame Dad a little bit. I think the only way to figure this out is to take some real space, to get an unclouded idea of what's working and what isn't. To figure out how to be who I need for me, and who I need to be for him."

"Okaaay," she draws out the word. "I can get behind that. What are you thinking?"

"That maybe I could go stay with Dean for a couple of weeks before school starts?"

She smooths her thumb across my cheek. "I think that's a great idea." Her eyes spark like a lightbulb above her head, as if it was her own idea. "He's been doing well in Costa Rica, coming to terms with his own decisions and figuring out what's next for him."

Decisions? I make a mental note to figure out what she means. "It's settled then. Will Dad be okay with it?"

"You let me worry about your father. You just focus on clearing your head, planning your future, and deciding if that is in alignment with Cooper."

"Okay." I don't know what else to say. I want things to be fixed right now, but I know I'm going to have to put in the work and stop avoiding it like I have been for years.

"Everything is going to be okay, honey."

"What if I make things worse, Mom?" I watch my finger tug on a strand of hair, embarrassed that I've spent years letting stupid thoughts get in my way. "What if it's too late to get him back?" I whisper.

"That boy has fought your father for you. He's been a few words short of trying to convince us that he loves you more than we do." The corner of her lips turn up. "It won't be too late."

61

COOPER

NOW

Not even binge watching all four seasons of *Beauty & the Beast*–save for the last episode–can get the memory of Sophie screaming that she loves me out of my head. Except for the vision it alternates with, of her under me on the kitchen counter.

Her words play over and over like a song permanently stuck on the repeat setting.

You can't do anything with a picture. But you can do whatever you want with me.

You feel so good inside me.

Come for me, Cooper.

Sulking in my room about our inevitable downfall for the past week probably isn't the best decision. But what the fuck else am I supposed to do? I know I need to take Marcus' advice. That I need to fix things with her so we can figure out how to be friends. But I don't know where to start. I at least prepared for the first quarter of my senior year. I also started the training course for my real estate test. I've turned down anyone asking me to go out outside of mandatory back-to-school fraternity events.

But tonight, I knew it was time to get out of my house and out of my head.

Ethan and I walk into Jameson's like we own the place. We probably could have bought it by now with all the money we spend here.

"Hey, Jess," Ethan flirts, and I chuckle. He won't leave her alone. Luckily, she's a good sport.

"Hey, boys," she says as she turns from the beer taps to face us, unfazed by his charm. She pours us two vodka Red Bulls without asking for our order and slides them across the wooden bar, taking my cash in return.

"Thanks," we say in unison.

"What are you getting into tonight?"

"Trouble," Ethan says, clinking his glass to mine. "Making Coop forget about Sophie for a night."

Confusion etches into Jess' face as I elbow him. Hard. Her eyes shift to the other end of the bar before coming back to us, pity now in her expression. "Let me know when you need a refill. I'll check on you in a bit."

"Pool?" Ethan asks.

"Yeah, let's do it." We make our way to the billiards room off to the side of the bar, one of the orange felt lined tables available. I rack the balls as Ethan retrieves cues from the stand on the wall. He still hasn't come back by the time I'm finished, so I look up, freezing in place. Even through the dim red lighting, the disgust on his face is clear. Following his line of vision, I'm met with a view I'd be happy to never see again.

JT leans against one of the pool tables, feet crossed at the ankles, chalking the end of his cue. Does Ethan even know who he is? I cross the room, gaining Ethan's attention only when I'm in front of him. "What's up?" I ask, ignoring the rage I feel inside me toward JT for a reason I'm unaware of yet–besides the obvious. I don't know why I hate this guy *so* much more than any of the others. More than the guy Sophie posted a selfie with.

More than the one she hooked up with the night of the 80s party. Maybe because I feel like he started it. He was the first one to take her away from me when all I wanted was for her to come back.

"This fuckhead is talking shit about Sophie," he growls quietly, not ready to draw attention to us.

I'd question how he knows he's talking about *my* Sophie, but what are the chances it's a different one? "What did he say?" My blood is already boiling at the possibilities.

He keeps his glare on JT as he talks to me in a hushed tone. "Something about her being a little slut. How long she'd been a tease, but he finally managed to get her wrapped around his . . . let's just say he didn't say finger." He cringes at the implication.

My mind whirls questioning the timeline. Is he referring to the past or did something happen between Sophie and JT *after* I picked her up from his house? Regardless, I can't let him fuck up her reputation that way. I take a breath, running through my options in my head, trying to stay calm.

JT doesn't give a fuck who hears him as he says, "Sophie is like a puppy, coming whenever I call." He chuckles. "Or every time I fuck her. Those young ones are good for the ego."

Jesus fucking Christ. "What did you just say?" I shove his shoulder until he twists to face me.

"I'm pretty sure I wasn't talking to you."

"I don't give a fuck who you're talking to. Keep her name out of your mouth."

He smirks. "That's not the only part of her I've had in my mouth."

"If you don't punch him, I will." Ethan's hands flex into fists at his side.

"I got it." JT is too drunk to register my words before my fist flies into his cheek with a crack. He curses as he stumbles back, abandoning his pool cue that falls to the floor to steady himself against the edge of the table. Fuck that hurt. I shake my hand.

He makes himself upright to swing at me. I lean backward, avoiding contact easily with his slowed reaction time from all the beer. I probably shouldn't take advantage. In my split second hesitation, Ethan steps between us, shoving JT against the wall. The crash of his body against the wood vibrates the paintings above him. Ethan smashes him near his eye. His ring must have cut him because bright red blood dripping down his cheek comes into view as Ethan moves out of the way, like he knows it's my turn.

I take a step, the smell of sour beer mixing with iron in the air, and without wasting another second, my fist slams into JT's jaw, blood spewing from his lip. That one didn't even hurt. Adrenaline courses through me, already ready for the next hit.

JT's hands fly in front of his face to protect himself, his friends not coming to his defense. A crowd has formed a circle around us, though. I should probably get the hell out of here, but I'm not finished.

"Don't ever fucking talk about her like that again," I demand.

JT coughs, his hand reaching for the edge of the pool table for support. "Who the fuck are you?" He laughs maniacally, spitting blood from his cracked lip onto the carpet. "You're more than welcome to my leftovers. Just remember to thank me for making her nice and loose for you." The wicked glimmer in his eyes forces me to punch him in the gut.

He curls over with a groan as Ethan's hands land on my shoulders and pull me back. "Okay, man. It's time to go," he says hurriedly right as Jess appears in the room.

62
SOPHIE

Now

It took less convincing than my mom and I expected to get my dad to agree to me going to Costa Rica on my own, but I have a feeling she didn't tell him my reasons. Four days after Cooper left me standing in Marcus' kitchen, I was on a flight to Central America. It's been a week since I arrived in Costa Rica, and my return flight isn't for another six days. I expected the change in scenery to help, but I can't shake the unsettledness I feel about my life.

Dean's studio beach hut isn't big. When you walk in there's a small kitchenette and brown wooden table straight ahead, a floor-to-ceiling window to the right, with a perfect view of the ocean. To the left is a double bed with a dresser doubling as a nightstand next to it. The air mattress Dean has been sleeping on leans against the wall connected to the small bathroom. It's a tight fit for the two of us, but it's easy to stay out of each other's way. My brother works during the day so I have the whole place to myself. When he's home he gives me space too. I know he's there if I need him. The problem is, I don't know what I need, and I think he can sense that. He hasn't asked me why I'm here or pushed me to talk. He makes us dinner and we just hang out on the beach, chatting about books or other things without personal emotional attachment. The old spark my brother used to have seems to have faded a bit. It's the opposite of what I would have expected based on what Mom said about him coming to terms with his decisions and own breakup, but for some reason, I think my being here is helping to liven him up. I hope we can open up to each other before I leave.

Scribbling my pen on the blueprint draft paper as I sit at the table leaves nothing but an imprint. And now a scratch on the paint as I throw it across the room and it hits the wall hard before falling to the worn wood floor. Maybe I should be enjoying it more, but I'm too stressed. I constantly let my mind wander to what Cooper is doing and how much I miss him, but I still have no inclination of what needs to change for us to make our relationship work.

Needing a new pen to work on the sketch in my architecture book, I pull on Dean's top dresser drawer handle–it's the only storage in his tiny place. Clothes. I shut it, repeating the process with the two below it and finding the same. The bottom drawer sticks a little. I yank on it so hard it comes off the track, and I stumble to the floor next to it. Not clothes. Curiosity gets the best of me as I shuffle through the contents now in disarray. It appears to be more like a junk drawer than anything. There's a phone charger. A tub of surfboard wax. A pen. Yes! I pull it from under Dean's passport, the movement sliding his travel ID to the side. *Wait. What's this?* Replacing the pen in my hand with a photograph printed onto paper, I pull the dark image closer. The view out my bedroom at Marcus' flashes through my mind, noting this picture was taken in his backyard down by the bonfire pit.

Looking again, I make out Marcus on the left of the picture. He's talking to a girl in the middle of the photo. Dean doesn't seem to be engaged in the conversation, but his arm is around the girl's waist. That must be Maci? I think that's her name. The photo was taken from the other side of the fire, the flame lighting streaks between the shadows over their faces. Even with the terrible quality, I can tell he's looking at her in a way I've never seen him look at anyone—like he's in love with her. I wonder if that's how Cooper looks at me. *Looked*, I guess. I'm not convinced he still feels the same.

I gently put the photo back as if it's a prized possession that needs to be handled with care. Something tells me it's important to my brother.

There's not much else in the drawer besides the *Guide to Central America* book. As I pick up the drawer and lock it back in its tracks, the book shifts, the corner of a sheet of lined notebook paper under the book catches my eye. I pull it from its place, immediately recognizing my brother's handwriting in black ink covering the entire page. I shouldn't be nosy. I should put it back and respect his privacy, but how can I *not* read it?

Maci,

The first time I was going to tell you was the morning you found my Guide to Central America *book on the kitchen counter. I couldn't bring myself to do it because we had just had sex for the first time. It was so much different than it's ever been for me-with anyone. I needed to test the theory because I thought it had to be a fluke. It wasn't. I noticed you running your fingers across the cover later that day before I took you home. I almost said something then too, but I didn't want you to think it was my way to get rid of you, that that night had meant anything less to me than what it did.*

My first instinct is to stop reading, to be grossed out hearing about my brother's sex life, but it's almost sweet. I lean against the bed, settling in.

The second time I almost told you was when you pressed me on the girlfriend title, after the football game. I'd never had the urge to be anyone's boyfriend before. I wanted to give you that title so badly, but I knew I couldn't. I was too selfish, too afraid to lose time with you, that I didn't tell you why.

Was that the football game where Dean told Cooper that JT was my boyfriend? Anger flames inside me, mad at my brother even though I have no right to be. I would have misunderstood too, and it's not like I've ever really been open with him.

When I got back from Honduras with my family, you were the first person I wanted to see. I remember you sitting on the bench outside of the library waiting for me, and I thought to myself Maybe if I just tell her the truth, she'll wait for me. *You were so excited to hear about my trip, and you were the only person I wanted to talk about it with. But I knew I couldn't tell you without* telling you, *without lying. So, I said nothing.*

The first party you came to at my house was hours after I had booked my flight and committed to leaving. I ignored you the entire time, wanting to prove to myself I would be okay when we weren't together anymore. I felt so unsettled all night until I was with you. I wanted you to ask me to stay, but I couldn't even bring myself to tell you I was leaving. You told me you liked me. It was the first time it occurred to me that I might love you.

As soon as I saw you on New Year's Eve, I knew it was time to tell you. I was going to tell you. But then you had so much doubt that I wanted you there I couldn't stand it. I pulled you to me, and I didn't want to tell you I was leaving anymore. I wanted to beg you to come with me.

When I made you leave school on the day I told you . . . God, Maci, I've never felt more connected to anyone than I did with you on that day, in every moment I've spent with you since I saw you in that gold dress on Halloween. When you went to the bathroom after the last time we had sex, I almost canceled my flight. You came back and crawled into my arms wearing my T-shirt and you looked so happy. I didn't want to break your heart, but I knew if I didn't, I would break it later, and it would be even worse.

I know all these reasons don't make it better that I didn't tell you, but I needed you to know anyway. This has never been about me lying to you or trying to lead you on. This was about me being selfish and trying to hold onto you as long as I could. I had to leave because you deserve more than that, more than I can give you.

I hope someday I can be the man you need, the man you deserve. If I can't, all I want is for you to be happy, Maci.

scribbled out line

Dean

With the edges of the paper pinched between my fingers, I reread the letter. Thoughts of Cooper fade from my mind, replaced by a rush of emotion hitting me as if this belonged to a love story I was invested in. By the time I get to the end again, I'm crying, my tears falling in big splotches on the paper, causing the ink to bleed. I'm not a hundred percent sure what this is, but the love I feel coming from it is not something I ever expected from my brother. It's a side of him I've never seen. I have to know more.

Putting the letter and drawer back in their places, I change into my yellow bikini, sliding my shorts over top and making the five minute walk on the sun-warmed sand.

When I reach the paddle and surf board shack where Dean works, he's closing the door behind him. He turns when my shadow crosses the sand next to him. "Oh, hey, Soph. I was just coming home. Did you want to surf?" I know I haven't made the most of my time here so far, but Dean has dragged me out onto the water a few times, and I've managed to catch a few waves.

"Umm. Actually, I was hoping we could talk. But we can do it out there." I point to the calm water with a perfect cotton candy sky backdrop.

"Yeah, sure." He pulls two boards from the rack, handing me one.

When we've paddled out past where the waves break, I sit on my surfboard, letting a foot dangle on either side in the clear ocean water. The soothing sounds of the ocean calm me as my brother mimics my position. His hair has grown and lightened since I last saw him a year ago, but his dark eyes are familiar as they catch my gaze.

"Do you want to talk about why you're here?" he asks. There isn't any judgment in his voice. Dean and I have always gotten along, but we've never had the kind of siblingship where we truly open up about things. I think it's because we're over three years apart, so it's hard to relate when you're younger. Last year when he was a college senior and I was a freshman was the first time we really hung out as friends and that was only for a quarter since he graduated early. I think he wanted to keep an eye on me, but he had no idea the kind of things that I got into. I didn't want to bother him with it or worry him. I definitely didn't want concern for me to keep him home from Costa Rica. I know he would have stayed back if he felt I needed babysitting.

"I don't know where to start," I admit. There's too much I've kept from him, from everyone, but now that we're both older, I think we might be able to relate more than I've thought in the past. I don't know what's been going on with him either, and maybe it's time to change that.

"We've got nowhere to be, so start at the beginning."

I take a breath. "Okay. Can I ask you something first?"

"Yes."

"Do you believe in soulmates?"

"Yes," he says with confidence, and it surprises me since it seems he's given up hope on Maci.

"Do you think yours is Maci?" I ask quietly, hoping not to upset him.

An emotion not quite but similar to pain washes over him. "Yeah, I do."

"I read your letter," I admit.

His eyes snap to mine, filled with anger. But the emotion washes away with the next subtle flow of the water. "You shouldn't have read that." He sighs.

"Has *she* read it?"

"No."

"Why not?"

"It doesn't matter."

"I think it does."

Lost in his head, he doesn't respond.

"Dean."

He lifts his foot slightly above the water line before kicking it down, sending a splash of drops across the surface. "I fucked things up with her, okay?"

"What happened?"

Again, he doesn't reply.

"What does the scribbled out part say?" I press.

His chest heaves with a deep, audible breath. "I love you."

"I love you too. Now tell me."

"No." He chuckles. "That's what it says."

"Oh. Why did you scratch it out?"

"Because it would have been selfish to tell her that way."

"She didn't know that's how you felt?"

"No."

"This letter could have changed that."

"Well, it's too late. She's with someone else now." My heart sinks at his words, imagining what it would be like for him to open up social media and see her with another guy when he's four thousand miles away. I'm not sure if that's better or worse than when I saw Cooper kiss Kylie from four feet away.

"I'm sorry, Dean. That sucks."

"Thanks."

"But . . ." My brows pinch together as I try to piece my thoughts together. "Why did you break up with her?"

He sighs, leaning back on his palms against his board. "I didn't want her to miss out on her life while she was waiting for me to get mine together."

"You don't think she could have had a good life and been there for you at the same time?"

"No. I messed up a few things. I'm not sure if we could come back from it, but I'm sure it's too late now anyway."

The worry that it's too late for Cooper and me flashes through my mind again. "But if you're soulmates, won't you always find your way back to each other?"

"Maybe, but I wasn't the person she deserved." He's open with his vulnerability in a way he's never been before–at least not with me. "I didn't know what the hell I was doing with my life. She was the only thing that kept me grounded and made me feel like I was doing something right. But that's too much to ask from someone. I don't know if I deserve another chance."

"You're a better guy than you believe, Dean." He gives me a half-hearted smile. "I think I messed up too."

He stays quiet, still leaning back on his palms and waiting for an explanation.

I tug on a strand of hair, my eyes trained on my board. "I think maybe Cooper is my soulmate." I glance up to gauge his reaction.

"I could see that." He smirks, but then it fades. "What happened?"

"I thought . . ." I'm embarrassed to admit the logic I thought was so sound at first. I take a breath. "This whole idea that you need to experience life before you settle down. I thought there was no way my first boyfriend could be *the one*. Deep down, I don't think I believe that, but I'm not sure my actions aligned."

"Maci has been my only girlfriend."

"Yeah, but you still dated other people, didn't you?" I mean *slept with*, but that feels like a weird thing to ask my brother.

He nods. "Yeah. Why do you think your first can't be your last?"

Shrugging, I say, "Mom and Dad. I think."

"Really?"

"Did you know Dad told Cooper to break up with me?"

His eyes widen. "Seriously?"

I nod. "Yeah, last summer. Something about how if he really loved me he'd let me experience life before settling down." I laugh. "Sound familiar?"

His under the breath laugh and shake of his head tell me a thought was clicking into place. Maybe he sees he's been influenced by our parents' relationships more than he thought. "Dad told Cooper that based on his own experience. But just because he's an adult doesn't mean he always knows better, Soph. Just because we share the same blood doesn't mean we have to share the same story. Mom and Dad drew the shit end of the stick which thankfully for them and us turned out to be a blessing in disguise. I found the love of my life without having to go through the mud first. I'm lucky as hell I found her when some people never find theirs. Somehow you're lucky enough to have found yours too. It's probably too late for me. I don't think it's too late for you, but don't play a game with time and risk waiting until it is. You don't have the luxury of checking out your other options to make sure you're picking the right one."

His last thought hits me so hard I'm surprised I don't fall off my board. Have I just been assuming I *do* have the time because Cooper has always been there? But . . . "Mom and Dad both didn't get lucky with their first try. What are the chances I did? What are the chances that *both* of us found our soulmates on the first try?"

He chuckles. "What are the chances Mom decided to go on the specific singles cruise that Dad also won on a radio contest? Life is weird, but the way they relate to each other makes their relationship stronger, I think. You and Cooper connect on other things. Instead of understanding similar experiences, you went through a lot of them together. That's something not a lot of people can say."

"I think that's why it felt too good to be true. For a while I thought you have to have all kinds of experiences, you know, before you figure out what you like and don't like–to make sure you're not settling with the first option."

"You think you'd be settling with Cooper?"

"I thought maybe once I went through the things that gave me experience and taught me lessons or whatever that we could be together after–if we are meant to be. You know, like how if you and Maci are meant to be then you'll find her when you go home." After reading that letter, I'm rooting for them. I wish I could meet her.

"That's not how it works, Sophie. I stuck to the story I had in my head so hard that I hurt Maci more than I needed to. What she deserved was for me to always tell her the truth. To be upfront about my own thoughts so she could make decisions with all the facts instead of left to her own assumptions–instead of me choosing her life path for her. What she deserved was for me to not make her doubt how I feel about her." He pauses. "Have you hurt Cooper?"

"I mean, it's not like I've cheated on him or anything. I mean we've hardly even been officially together."

Dean chews on the edge of his lip like he can't decide on his next words.

"What?"

"It's just . . . Thanksgiving last year."

"What about it?" That was right after Cooper found out about JT. My stomach flips at the thought of having sex with that dickwad.

"Yeah. That. Whatever it is you just thought about is what I'm referring to." He chuckles.

"I . . . Cooper isn't the only guy I've been with, but we weren't together," I justify. "We were broken up."

"Because of Dad." He shoots me a pointed look, furrowing his brows.

"Cooper knew I needed some time. I had to figure out what I wanted my life to look like. And I did. I made a list of all the things I was supposed to experience, especially in college. I went through the motions to get there. I did my homework. I volunteered at the library. I drew sketches of a hundred houses. I read so many books that I caved and got a Kindle. Yeah, I partied too. And hung out with some other guys. So what? That's part of it all."

"Why couldn't you do those things with Cooper?"

"He thinks he knows what I need. How could he when I don't even know?"

"Okay, I see what you're trying to say . . . but do you see how maybe to him, it just felt like he wasn't good enough for you?"

"No. I told him it wasn't about him. Plus, he's the one who kept turning me down. Saying we should just be friends."

"So, you think he meant you should date other guys?" Why won't he drop this?

"It's not like I was in a relationship with them. He didn't want to be with me."

"Do you really believe that?"

So many thoughts flash through my head it's like white noise, fuzz I can't sort through. "Umm."

"That's an excuse for someone who doesn't want to commit."

"Says the guy who wouldn't make Maci his girlfriend."

"I haven't been with another girl since her."

"Come on, Dean." I pull my legs into a criss-cross on top of my board. "You're telling me you didn't find *anyone* else when you found out she had a new boyfriend?"

"Yes."

Oh. I run through my decision, through every other guy I've let in who wasn't Cooper. Ian on prom night. We just kissed, though. That wasn't a big deal. And Cooper and I weren't even really friends then. JT. Okay, that one got a little out of hand. I didn't plan on him inserting himself into my life . . . and me. Logan . . . He can't hold that against me. I thought he was taking Kylie home. I probably should have gotten confirmation on that first, though . . . it was right after I told him he's it for me. But it didn't look good. The guy on my birthday was just . . . it's Cooper's fault. He rejected me after I sent him that picture. And JT again . . . okay, there's not an excuse for him.

"Trying to justify your decisions?" my brother asks. I want to bite back, but there's no judgment in his tone. Only understanding. I nod. "Are they good enough? Are they worth making Cooper doubt how much you care about him?"

"No." The word falls out of my mouth without so much as a second thought. I did this to us. Tears spring to my eyes, the pink and orange streaks of the sunset looking more like watercolor through my blurry vision.

"I'm not trying to make you feel bad, Soph. Just giving you a new perspective. And did you ever consider that maybe him trying to control your situation is more him feeling like he has no power over your commitment to him?"

I did not consider that.

"I'm not saying all your logic is wrong. I just hope you can figure things out between you two before it's too late."

"If Cooper is the right one, he'll be there for me no matter what, right?"

"I don't know. I think it depends on what you do. At some point he'll accept that you can't fully commit and settle for someone who isn't the one for him."

"I just . . . I don't know, Dean. Am I ready to be in a relationship for the rest of my life? How do I know if I'll be able to give him what he needs? I've let him down so many times."

"I'm willing to bet he probably just needs you."

My stare is full of doubt.

"You two have loved each other for your entire lives already, despite everything. And that's never changed, has it?"

I shake my head.

"And all your favorite memories, do they have Cooper in them?"

All the best parts of my life include him. I nod.

"Do you wish you could change anything about them?"

"No. Of course not."

"So, why would you want to make the best memories with someone else when you could make them with your best friend instead?"

I stare blankly at my brother.

"Maci has no fucking clue how much I love her. She's with someone else now, and I can't even be mad about it. I can think we should be together all I want but it doesn't matter if she doesn't know I feel that way, if she doesn't *feel* I feel that way–or if enough time has passed that she's given up on us. Now, I'll never get to find out what forever with her could be like. Don't you think it's worth the risk of finding out you're *not* meant to be if it could mean realizing you *are*?"

"Yeah, Cooper is worth the risk. He's worth every-thing."

"I think that's your answer right there."

"What if he doesn't believe I'm serious? That this time will be different?"

"Then you do something different. Prove things will be different."

I lay back on my board, kicking my feet out–unsure what to say, what kind of plan to come up with. My mind is whirling, cursing myself for not talking to my brother sooner, having a feeling he might be what I needed all along.

"So, what are you going to do? Lie here and hope things magically work out like they did for Mom and Dad? Be an idiot like your brother who is too chicken shit to tell the girl he loves that she's his whole damn world. Or go fight for Cooper?"

"Fight for him," I say confidently, flipping to my stomach, ready to paddle to shore.

"I didn't mean right now, dummy," he jokes. "You're still stuck here for six more days."

63
COOPER

Now

"Proud of you, kid," Dad says, raising his beer to clink it against my vodka Red Bull.

"Thanks, Dad. I'm ready to get to work and pull my weight." Today I did a mock presentation of a contract perfectly. I've been going over all the ins and outs of them, trying to get my mind off Sophie and on my future.

"I know you are. I'm anxious to see what we can do with this company together, especially once you pass your tests."

"Crazy to think you built this all on your own."

"Not on my own."

"It's your company. Don't downplay it."

"It wouldn't exist on my own, though. At the very least it wouldn't matter."

"Well, luckily for me, you've helped set me up for success. I just have to put in the work now, and I'm the only one I need for that."

Dad's eyes narrow as he takes a sip of his beer like he's contemplating his next words. "Is this about Sophie?"

The melting ice cubes in my drink swirl in the liquid as I shake my glass before bringing it to my lips, avoiding eye contact or confirmation.

"Did you know your mom and I almost got a divorce?"

My eyes shoot to his. "I remember you guys fighting when I was younger, but I don't recall it lasting long or being that bad."

"It was *Mom packed a bag for me and told me to leave* bad."

My eyes widen. I thought everything was generally great between my parents. They've always been that role model couple that makes you think *when it's right, it should be easy*. "Did you leave?"

"No. I refused. It snapped me out of my depression after losing my job. It gave me the fire to create my life–*this* life. But I knew I wanted her by my side to do it."

"So, she just forgave you?"

"It took time. I needed to prove I could be there for her in ways I hadn't been recently."

"How did things even get so far out of control?"

"One day at a time, until they all added up to be too much."

"Yeah, it's like . . . I see where Sophie and I started, and I look at where we are at now and I don't under-stand how we got here. The breaking point happened overnight, yet it's been happening forever."

"When you've been together so long, it's easy to zoom in too far. It's like when you were working on agility for football. You'd get so frustrated not seeing day to day progress, right?"

I chuckle. "Yeah," I confirm, not sure where he's taking this.

"Unfortunately relationships work like that some-times but in a negative way. You keep doing little things that don't seem like they matter. But when you look back, you realize how far you've fallen from where you used to be. You're blinded by your focus on the day over the entire experience. Let me ask you something. Do you treat Sophie as well as you did when you two first started dating?" There's no judgment in his tone.

Exhaling a breath and a sigh, I admit, "Honestly, no. I get so frustrated with her sometimes. I don't want to, though."

"The end goal isn't to make sure you both are always better than the day before. It's not possible. The goal is to stay the course, to show up every day and to know you will have off days. You have to focus on the bigger picture and the end goal. You have to focus on what will bring you growth rather than dwell on the small things that make it easy to tear you apart."

I lean against the back of the bar chair. "Sometimes I feel like she's self-sabotaging. She says she wants us to be together, but her actions don't always align. Somehow she feels further away every time she takes a step closer. That doesn't make sense." I shake my head. "How did Mom believe you were going to fix everything? I'm worried I'm always going to resent her for the times she didn't show up for me how I needed her. And if I can't let that go, how can I be there for her?"

"If you're both committed to making it work, you'll figure it out."

"You and Mom make it look easy. It's like you can read each other's minds. I feel like I used to be able to read Sophie so well, but somewhere along the line that ability went away."

He chuckles. "That's just practice and time."

"I've known her for almost two decades. How much time does it take?"

"It's not the same. It's different when you live with someone, when you have to make major life decisions with them that involve being on the same page–when being in sync directly affects whether you sink or swim."

"How will I know if we can do this without drowning?"

"You'll know, son." He reaches across the small high top table to squeeze my shoulder. I hope he's right.

64

COOPER

THEN

Cooper, 20; Sophie, 18

The string lights draped over the patio at Sweet Cheeks Winery enhance the magic for everyone celebrating love tonight at Mom and Dad's 25th wedding anniversary party. I was able to convince Sophie that everything was fine at the barbeque two days ago, but I have successfully avoided her since, thus evading my dilemma. She found me as soon as she got here, but my parents needed me, and I've somehow made it through cocktail hour without running into her.

Grabbing a beer at the open bar, I scan the white linen covered tables for my girlfriend. The crackle of the microphone draws my attention from where I stand in the back corner.

"Hi, everyone," my mom says, a patio full of people giving her their full attention. "Thank you all so much for coming to celebrate Mike and me. Our lives are fuller because of each one of you. But this guy right here," she leans into Dad and he wraps his arm around her, "I wouldn't have all of you if I didn't have him first. As many of you know, when Mike and I met, we went to rival colleges, neither of us owned a car or a cell phone, and yet, here we are. What most of you don't know is that we almost ended before we truly began. When I ran into him for the second time–"

My dad tugs on her hand bringing the microphone toward him. "When you stalked me like a crazy person until you found me." Everyone laughs and my dad releases the speaking power back to his wife.

"As I was saying, when I magically ran into him by the forces of the Universe, I had an entire group of friends try to talk me out of it. Maybe they were tired of driving to Eugene every weekend–we all know the parties are better at Oregon State." Half the crowd boos while the other half cheers. "Eventually, I started taking the bus."

"Until you made me buy a car," Dad chimes in.

"Without that car we wouldn't have Carter." She's not embarrassed by the implication at all. Everyone looks to where my brother is leaning against a high top table, his champagne glass raised to the air, taking in the attention like it's a compliment to him.

"My point is, life will always try to get in the way. But having your person is like a guarantee you'll always be able to get through any obstacle you face."

Dad takes the microphone. "When you know, you know. Even at eighteen, I knew the moment I left you at that concert that if I found you again, I'd never let you go. I just wasn't smart enough to figure out how to find you."

"To me," Mom says, looking at my dad like she'll never fall out of love with him, "and my stalking abilities."

"To Mike and Melissa," someone in the crowd yells and everyone raises their glass.

A shadow crosses the table I'm standing next to. I look up as I pull my beer to my lips.

"Quite lucky, your parents," Jack says.

"It has nothing to do with luck," I retort, avoiding eye contact and letting my eyes scan the patio again in search of Sophie.

"They're the exception, son. Life doesn't just magically hand you the right person when you're too young to do the right things with them."

My scan is halted when I spot Sophie, leaning against a table on the opposite side of the patio. She's talking to a guy I vaguely recognize–a son of one of my mom's friends. Jack follows my gaze. "Ian. He took Sophie to prom."

I glance sideways before hesitantly finding Sophie again. She looks comfortable, her finger tracing the rim of her glass as she gives the guy her full attention–not at all searching her surroundings for me.

"She needs other experiences, Cooper. She can't know what she wants unless she also discovers what she doesn't."

I take a breath to steady my anger. "It's a bit cynical to think no one could be as lucky as my parents, don't you think?"

"Not cynical. Realistic. Look at her."

I haven't stopped staring at the way she's leaning on her palm. Her finger still tracing the rim of the glass. Her pretty pink dress hitting right above her knees. Her curls perfect. Her skin soft.

"She looks happy," Jack notes.

"She is happy."

"You're not next to her. Can't you see other things besides you make her happy? Don't you want that for her?"

"Of course I do. But that's not mutually exclusive to being single." I fight back, but my confidence in what I'm saying slips with every thought Jack adds.

Sophie reaches out, her hand landing on the forearm of the guy she's talking to. My gut tells me this is all innocent. He's just a friend. She told me herself she hardly wanted to go to prom–she felt like she had to. I know she never had sex with this guy, with anyone besides me. But she has kissed them. She probably kissed this guy. It would be naive to think she'd never be questioning about experiencing things with someone different–to know what it's like, to satisfy the curiosity I already have. I can't give her *everything*.

With a double slap of his hand against my shoulder–as if he can sense my crumbling beliefs–Jack leaves me to my thoughts.

Leaving my half-empty beer on the table, I weave my way through the high tops, glowing under the strings of lights.

"Sophie." Her name falls from my lips as my hand lands on her lower back.

She startles, pulling her hand away from the guy in front of her like she's been caught doing something wrong. "Coop! Hi." She immediately turns toward me but looks back. "It was nice catching up, Ian. I'll see you later?"

"Yeah. Later, Sophie."

"I missed you," Sophie says with a soft smile. She leans into me, but I step back–enough to evade her touch but not enough that she falls. Her brows scrunch together, her smile falling. "What is it?"

"Who was that?"

She chuckles. "Ian? A friend. We went to prom together."

"So, you've kissed him?" I'm torn between possessiveness and understanding the point her dad has been trying to convey.

"For like a second." She laughs again, brushing me off.

I contemplate my decision.

"You're not really concerned about him, are you?"

I stare back.

She tugs my hand until I reluctantly follow her. We slip around the side of the building and when she stops, I sink against the wood paneling. The only light is a soft glow from the party.

"Cooper. What's up with you? Don't you trust me?"

"Yes." A vision of her kissing Ian after prom flashes through my mind, but I know she'd never cheat on me.

"Then what's the problem?" She steps closer to me, her hand finding a familiar place on my neck.

Without reaching for her, my words come out emotionless. "I think we should break up."

"Wait, what?" Her thumb rubbing across my jaw freezes.

"I'm sorry," I mumble, not able to make eye contact.

"Look at me," she demands. "What is happening?"

I refuse to obey her command but answer her question. "You know this is how it has to be, Soph. It's exactly like last time–just the reverse. It's your turn to experience college the way you let me."

"But I'm going to be there *with* you." Her other hand reaches for me and her grip on my face forces me to look at her. Shades of shadow cover her, faint lights only coming from a window toward the front of the winery to my right and the twinkle lights around the corner on the left. "You're being insane. This makes no sense."

My eyes are glazed over, unable to focus on her. If I do, I can't do this. I can't watch her heart break even if we both know this is what's for the best. "Cooper!" She waves her hand in front of my face, but it might as well be invisible.

My silence is interrupted by Sophie's lips crashing into mine. She's forceful-enough for me to let her in. I taste salt and for a moment I wonder if they are my tears. Gripping her shoulders I press her away, breaking our connection. Wet lines streak her face, fresh tears following the paths carved out for them.

"We aren't breaking up." She's practically begging me.

"Yes." I pause. "We are." The bitterness of the words I was told to say just a couple days ago by her father completely overtake the sweet taste of her on my lips. This isn't just Jack speaking, though. His request was practically endorsed by both Chastity and Sophie-Sophie's lack of response and actions a few days ago being a tipping point. It's been bothering me ever since. Even if I could look past it, I love her enough that if she could find happiness elsewhere, I'm willing to give her that.

"No, we aren't," she says with a mix of anger and panic in her voice.

"Christ, Sophie, don't make this harder than it has to be." I turn out of her grasp. "You made the choice for me, and it was the right one. I'm doing the same for you."

She storms in front of me. "So, this is revenge for me breaking up with you *two years ago*?" The hostility in her voice has removed every other emotion from it.

"No, of course it's not." My eyes shift across her face. She's standing in front of me like she's torn if she should take a step closer or back away. "I've known you forever. Don't you think I know you well enough to know what you want by now?"

"You really believe this is what I want?"

"You might not see it now, but deep down, yes. You know how hard this decision is. Please don't make it harder," I beg. Even if this is what needs to be done, it still fucking sucks.

"Cooper," she cries, reaching for me. It takes every bit of strength I have to step away from her grasp. "Why are you doing this? Is it Ian? I promise there's nothing between us. I've never seen him as more than a friend."

"This isn't about him. It's about you. You need to experience college the way it's meant to."

"Cooper!" she raises her voice. "We are literally at a party celebrating a love that started IN COLLEGE."

"It doesn't matter. The exception isn't a rule."

"We had sex less than a week ago!" Her volume makes my eyes flash toward the party, hoping no one heard her. The sounds of the event enter my awareness, but I don't see a single person. "You made me wait forever, claiming it was something special. Now you're going to act like it's not a big deal?!" Her words barely make it out through her sobs.

I focus back on her beautiful, broken face, the pressure on my chest making it hard to breathe. "I'm sorry." The reasoning that has been burrowing its way in now feels set in stone, the rocks in my lungs unmoveable.

"We just had sex," she cries again like I didn't hear her the first time. Fuck, it hurts–thinking about her being with anyone else, about how getting that part of Sophie was everything I had been waiting for and now it might never happen again. I would have never slept with her if I knew this is where we'd end up. But I'm better off making the break now than suffering through it later.

"Why delay the inevitable?" She needs to understand this is how it's supposed to be. "I won't be the only person you sleep with, Sophie. Just like you aren't the only girl I've fucked."

Fuck. My words nearly knock the wind out of me as they thump against my chest, but the blow they serve to Sophie is harder. More tears immediately spring to her eyes. She opens her mouth to say something but clamps it shut, choking on a sob instead. I try to take the words back, but she spins out of reach so quickly, running to the back of the building, leaving me standing there.

My fist slams into the wood, screaming in pain as a sliver of wood lodges into my skin–just like I deserve.

65
COOPER

THEN

Staring at the dust collecting on my popcorn ceiling, I wonder who the fuck was dumb enough to invent something so stupid. How the fuck would I even clean that? Not that I would. God, I hate everything right now. I dipped out of the party the second I loaded the last box of decorations into Dad's car. I kept myself busy, avoiding everyone, but I didn't miss Jack's sly smirk as he led a crying Sophie to the car. Every moment since, I've been at war with myself about whether this is the wrong choice. Once I got home, I *knew* it was and tried to take back the words I said to Sophie.

I've called her a dozen times. Texted her ten times that amount. I rip my phone off the nightstand, opening our text thread, pages of blue bubbles staring back at me. I can't fucking do this. I can feel that she's not here, that she's slipping away, that she's not mine. It's killing me. I didn't even give her a chance. I let Chastity manipulate her thoughts the way Jack did mine. And then I broke her with my own words. "I'm going to fix this," I mumble to myself. I can't be without her, and once I apologize, I know she'll feel the same.

It's nearly midnight by the time I pull into the Porter's driveway after I spent twenty minutes circling the block. I know I shouldn't be here, that I should wait until morning or until I have a clear head or not care what Jack thinks at all. But I can't do any of those things because I can't go another second with Sophie believing she's not *the one* for me, that I don't need her more than anything else–despite anything else. That I made a mistake and that I can give her every experience she wants and needs.

The motion activated light kicks on as I approach the porch. My fist slams against the front door repeatedly, and I know he can see my face on his security camera. I don't stop knocking until the door swings open, Jack standing there in plaid pajama bottoms and a T-shirt. Diane stands at the bottom of the stairs taking in the scene.

"It's the middle of the night, Cooper. Is everything okay? Where's Sophie? I thought she was upstairs." Panic rushes through his voice as he looks behind me. He thinks there's been an emergency.

There has.

"No, she's not alright. She's not with me. How dare you manipulate me into this." I shove past him until I'm inside, slamming the door behind me, the walls of the entryway shaking with the force. I'm mad I let him do it in the first place, but I won't let anyone stand between us–not even her father.

"Look, Cooper, I know you care about her–"

I cut him off. "CARE ABOUT HER?" I laugh humorlessly. "You think I *just* care about her? I'm so fucking in love with her that I can't sleep. Or eat. Or do anything else for that matter without knowing she's mine. I don't care what you say anymore. You can tell me over and over we shouldn't be together, but I refuse to live without her." I can feel moisture forming in my eyes and dig my fingers into them in a frustrated attempt to keep from getting more emotional than I already am.

His hands land on either shoulder, and I glance up to see both shock and empathy on his face. "You need to understand I'm just looking out for my daughter."

"No, you need to understand this isn't whatever happened in your first marriage." I regret the words as soon as they come out and try to backtrack. "I'm sorry. What I mean is you're afraid what happened to you would happen to Sophie. I get it, but you need to let it go. Someday I'm going to marry her, and I hope you'll support that, but I won't abandon her now, or ever. I won't hurt her or take anything from her. I won't put her in a shitty spot where she ever doubts how much I love her or think anything else is more important than she is. I want to give her everything. Some people *do* know this young. She's it for me. Maybe it's crazy I know that so young. Hell, maybe it's some Montgomery magic that lets us find our soulmates so young. But I love your daughter. I hope that's enough for you because this entire family is important to me, and I don't want to lose any of you because of this."

66
SOPHIE

THEN

Yelling in my dream blurs into yelling in real life. I rub my eyes, swollen from crying myself to sleep, and flip my phone over. It's after midnight. Pulling back my comforter, I step onto my fuzzy white carpet. Sliding on my slippers, my hand reaches for the cold metal knob on my bedroom door, ready to investigate. Another scream from downstairs stops me in my tracks. It sounds like . . . Cooper? Why is he here in the middle of the night? And why is he yelling at my parents? I try to piece together the muffled conversation.

I slowly open the door to avoid the creak and step into the hallway at the top of the stairs.

". . . I love your daughter. I hope that's enough for you because this entire family is important to me, and I don't want to lose any of you because of this."

Did Cooper just tell my parents he loves me? He's never even directly told me that. My heart beats so loudly in my chest, I can't hear a response. The urge to understand what's happening wins over my need to stay hidden. I work my way down the staircase, my mom's voice freezing me in my tracks again halfway down.

"Cooper is not Mary, Jack."

"I never said he was," Dad barks.

"I know you're projecting. But based on that scene, I feel like you're going to push our daughter away. She's old enough and smart enough to make her own decisions."

My brain tries to puzzle together what happened, but I don't have enough pieces.

I jump down the last few steps, and both my parents shift their glances from each other to me.

"Sophie, honey," my mom rushes to me, wrapping me in a hug. I return the embrace but quickly pull away.

"What's going on? Where's Cooper?"

"He left out the back door, so I'm guessing he went next door."

I doubt it.

I rush past my mom, not taking the time to look at my dad because I have a feeling I should be mad at him. The sliding door is still unlocked from Cooper's exit, and I don't bother closing it once I've passed through.

I take off through the grass until I reach the trees lining the edge of our property.

The moonlight is strong enough to reveal Cooper sitting in his chair leaned up against a tree. He startles when I appear in front of him, like he was too distracted to hear me hurtling toward him.

"Sophie," he mumbles in surprise, springing to his feet and reaching for me.

I take a step backward, and his hands fall between us.

"I'm sorry about everything. I'm sorry for breaking up with you. It's never what I wanted."

My head is spinning in an attempt to make sense of everything. "What's going on?" I ask cautiously.

"Your dad . . ." Cooper starts, "he made me break up with you."

"He what?!" I fume but feel pulled to redirect my anger. "And you listened to him?"

"What?" Confusion is evident on his face even with only the glow of the moon shimmering through the trees. It's like he thought that reasoning alone would be enough to let him off the hook.

"You listened to him? When you claim you love me. Which for the record cannot possibly be true if you haven't even told *me*."

"You know I love–"

I cut him off. "No. Stop right there. This is exactly what I was fucking talking about with the miscommunication thing. You should have told me what my dad said. We should have been able to talk this through–"

"I heard your conversation with Chastity too," he interrupts, his voice desperate. "It echoed everything your dad was saying. You not fighting for us felt like confirmation that everything they were saying was true."

"Oh, and you breaking up with me is your way of fighting for us? Makes a whole lot of sense, Cooper."

He tries to take another step toward me, and I back away again.

"Sophie, I'm sorry. I fucked up." He yanks on the strings of his hoodie so hard it scrunches the hood. "But I want to make it up to you. I need us to be together." His hands twist until they are tangled in the strings.

"Do you even hear yourself, Coop? If you *needed* me so badly you wouldn't have left in the first place."

He groans in frustration. "That's not fair. You're not taking the other factors into account." He reaches for me faster than I can pull away this time, his hands gripping my waist and tugging me to him. I don't back away, but stand there emotionless, my hands between us, pressed to his chest, debating if I should lean in or push him away.

"Don't think I forgot about what you said to me."

He cringes. "I shouldn't have said that. I'm sorry, Soph. I've been trying to call you, text you–anything–to tell you that."

"You can't just take words back, Cooper. You hurt me. You took something precious to me–hell, it meant more to *you* than it did to me–and then you used it against me, like it doesn't matter. How can I even trust you after that?"

"I didn't mean it. I don't know what I was thinking. I had just talked to your dad–"

"Stop blaming my dad. You're a grown up, Cooper. He's not responsible for your choices."

"But–"

"No. You said those words to me. Not him. You. You intentionally hurt me, more than just with a breakup."

"I'm sorry. I know it's my fault. I take responsibility for it. Let me make it up to you. Please," he begs desperately.

"I need time to think about this."

"Think about what? It's been three hours. We can just go back," he pleads.

"No, Coop, we can't." This is harder than the time I tried to teach myself to crochet. Harder than learning how to ollie on my skateboard. Harder than the first time I walked away from him. Way harder.

"Why is it always so easy for you to let me go?"

"That's not fair. Even if I can pretend you didn't use sex against me, you broke my heart. And how can I believe you won't do it again when you can't even talk to me, can't even think through your decisions?" Pain is clear in his eyes, tears sit on his waterline, threatening to fall. Cooper never cries. Not even when he tore his ACL junior year of high school. I shake my head, expelling the empathy clouding my decision.

"It was stupid. And impulsive. But we can get through this. We get through everything, but we can't do that if you run away again. It's always been us against the world."

"It feels like it's us against each other." My own words deepen the cracks in my fragile heart, and they seem to do the same to him. I realize this wasn't as easy for him as I thought, but I continue anyway. "My dad was just trying to protect me. You're supposed to be the one who protects me now. How can you do that if we aren't together? And if I can't even trust the things you say?" My voice cracks. I try to take a deep breath but only manage a shallow one, choking on a sob.

"I thought I was protecting you, Soph. I thought I was giving you what you wanted."

"All I ever need is you," I cry. "But you chose to let me be in pain, to cause it. That's not love. It doesn't matter the reason. And even worse, it could have all been prevented if you just talked to me first. But you didn't, and right now I can't forgive you for that."

One of his hands shifts from its grip on my hip to its familiar hold on my neck. "But you will, right?"

"I hope so."

"Sophie, promise me. Please. I'm sorry. I hate myself for hurting you. Please let me make it up to you. I'll spend the rest of my li–"

I press my fingers against his lips to cut him off. He silences immediately, but I can tell it's hard for him. "Cooper, stop. You're scaring me. This is too much. I was trying to figure out how to let you go, and now you're telling me you never want to leave."

"I'm sorr–"

"Cooper." He's not hearing me. "I need time."

"How much?"

"I don't know. Maybe everyone is right. I mean, working on my bucket list has been fun. If that's what this time of my life is for, maybe I should do it."

"I want to help you, experience it with you. I've been doing that this entire time."

"This is all too much for me. I think I need to focus solely on experiencing college right now, and not have a relationship in the mix."

"That doesn't even make sense Sophie. I can make your experience easier, better."

"I'm sorry, but . . . I don't trust you right now."

He drops his hold on me like I physically assaulted him with my words. He's always been the person I trusted more than anyone, and I know this hurts him. But he really hurt me. I've been so broken, so alone. Chastity was right. He isn't just *my person*, he's *everything*. That's too big of a risk, too much responsibility to put on one person.

"I'll give you whatever you need." He closes the distance between us again. I freeze, waiting to see what happens next. His hand softly cups the back of my head, pulling me toward him into a crushing hug. After a moment, I try to pull back. His head shakes against the top of my hair, and he squeezes me. "Twenty seconds," he whispers. I relax into his hold but refuse to let it pull me under. At least another thirty go by before I try again. This time he lets me.

He touches his lips softly to mine, holding them there for a moment before pulling back enough to press his forehead to mine. "I want us to get through this, okay?

I want us to be all-in, endgame. Not one foot out the door. I'm not going anywhere."

"Okay." My voice isn't much louder than the darkness surrounding us as I disconnect. "Well, I guess I'll see you later." He doesn't say anything, so I walk away from him.

When I hit the grass of my backyard, I look back in time to see his blue chair fly into the tree, breaking alongside my heart.

67

COOPER

NOW

Cooper, 21; Sophie, 19

"Fuck," I curse, slamming my palms against the steering wheel, my head falling against my seat. How the hell am I supposed to tell Dad I failed the National Real Estate Broker's Test? Especially after I talked him into letting me take it a year before I graduated, claiming I was ready to start selling on my own. I passed the Oregon State one, but fuck, the national portion . . . I don't even remember learning about half of what was on there. I shouldn't be surprised considering I could hardly focus on any of the ninety hours of training I put in–ninety hours I now have to find the time to put in again, on top of all my schoolwork, so I don't fail again.

The first week that went by without hearing from Sophie, I was able to distract myself. I know I walked away in the middle of a fight–right after sex–but she always comes back. When the end of the second week rolled around, I started wondering if this time would be the one that was different and couldn't focus on a damn thing. Not that it's directly her fault, but I still blame her and our situationship as the reason I failed this damn test.

I sigh, pulling my phone from where I put it in the center console and tap it against my palm, debating my next move. I'm losing my damn mind. Ever since I punched that douchebag last week, Sophie is all I can think about–not like that wasn't the case before. But this is different. I can't seem to work through it in my head or get her out of it. The way she's under my skin but is off giving herself to other guys drives me insane. Especially since the other guys are men like JT. She's always been such a light for me, but it feels like it dims each time she gives away a piece of herself to another man. I'm afraid if I don't fix this, she'll burn out–we'll burn out.

Fuck Marcus' idea to be friends with her so she can be part of my life again. All I want is to be near her, to hold her, breathe in her flowery scent. I just want one kiss, one that I know will leave me on a high for far longer than makes sense, that will make me feel like everything is okay. I need her, in every way.

Me: *What are you doing?*

I go to toss my phone back in the center console and drive home from the testing center, but it vibrates.

Sophie: *Picking up my books for the new quarter. Why?*

Me: *Oh, okay. Nevermind.*

Sophie: *Do you need something?*

Me: *Idk*

Sophie: *Is everything okay?*

Me: *Just a shitty day. It's not a big deal.*

Sophie: *What do you need?*

Me: *You.*

Sophie: *Where are you?*

Me: *On my way home.*

Sophie: *Okay, I'll see you soon.*

Closing the front door, I leave it unlocked. If Sophie left after her text, she should be here any minute. I make my way to my room, tossing myself backward on the navy comforter, not bothering to turn the lights on. Lying in silence, I hear the front door as Sophie twists it and lets herself in. "Cooper?" her sweet voice calls to me, full of worry.

I don't reply. She'll find me soon enough.

Her head pokes through my doorway, the natural light from the living room behind her helping me see. My eyes quickly shift over her dirty blonde curls to her . . . jeans? Why is she wearing jeans? I keep my question to myself as Sophie makes her way to me. The mattress sinks a little with her weight as she sits on the edge of the bed, and the second her hand lands on my shin, instant relief flushes through me. All the stress I have around work and school dissolve away. "What happened?"

I sigh, sitting. I worry my movement will make her pull away, but her hand never leaves my leg. "I failed."

"What do you mean? Failed what?"

"My real estate test."

"What? I thought you weren't going to take that until you graduated?"

"I wasn't. But I needed the distraction. I needed something to focus on. Something other than . . ."

She waits a moment to see if I'll finish my sentence.

"Something other than what?" she asks cautiously.

"You." I pause, feeling vulnerable and hating it. But what we're doing isn't working for my life. "And all the other guys who have touched you, looked at you, doing who knows what else." Distress fills me as the thoughts invade my mind for the hundredth time. "I want us to be friends, Soph. But it's too hard to be your friend when I know what it's like to be more."

"I'm sorry that I told you that stuff. I know that was crossing a line and really messed up. I should have kept it to myself." I note she's not saying she shouldn't have been around them. Still, I say what I need to.

"I want us to be honest with each other, to be able to tell each other everything." She tries to interject–probably to note that I just said there are things I don't want to know. My eyes stay locked on where her thumb brushes against the skin on my leg, afraid to see her reaction as I continue, not letting her get a word in. "Sophie, I lied the last time I saw you. You *are* my person. You've been my person since I was old enough to realize my favorite person didn't have to be my brother." She laughs softly, and I force my gaze to hers. Her eyes are focused on me, listening to my words without giving away how she feels about them. "I can't stand when we fight. It's fucking hard when we're apart. God, Soph, even when I hate you, I want to be near you. Even you in this room right now makes everything seem better. I miss you. I miss us." I hold my breath, waiting for her to respond.

She pulls her hand from me, and my stomach drops.

I'm about to beg her not to go when I realize she's taking off her shoes.

She crawls across the bed to me, sitting criss-cross, her thigh resting against my outstretched leg. "I'm so relieved to hear you say that. I miss you so much. But, you're not a failure, Coop," she whispers as she presses her hand to my chest. The way she dropped what she was doing, to be here for me now . . . Maybe things *can* be different. "You'll do better next time." All I can think about is if *we* can do better next time.

My original intention was for us to find our friendship again like Marcus encouraged before asking for more. But being here with her now—none of that shit from the past matters. All I want is for us to be together. "Sophie?"

"Yeah?"

My eyes flicker across her face as she stares back patiently. "I love you."

Her chest stops rising with breath.

Her hand grips the fabric of my shirt.

Her eyes water, and a silent tear slips out. I catch it with my thumb, pressing my palm to her face. "What is it?"

"I didn't think I'd ever hear you say it."

"I'm sorry I didn't say it when you did. I'm sorry I never told you a hundred times before that day. I'm sorry you felt the need to say it as a way to manage my anger. You deserve more than that." My thumb rubs against her soft skin and she leans into my palm.

"We've both said a lot of things we don't mean." My stomach flips, wondering if she doesn't believe the ones I'm saying now.

"Do you not think–"

She cuts me off by placing her hand over mine. "I love you, Cooper."

I shake my head with a laugh, my hand sliding to her neck and my fingers threading through her curls.

"What?"

"Do you remember when you were sixteen and you came over for that slip 'n slide party?"

She nods, her eyebrows pushing together. "Yeah?"

"You were teasing me in the bathroom." She grins, recalling the memory. "That was the first time you told me you loved me. You didn't mean it the same way you do now. I remember thinking 'I can't wait until she gets there.'"

"You already were?"

"I've loved you for as long as I can remember, Soph." I watch another tear slip down her pretty face and brush it off her soft skin with my thumb before it falls off her chin. "I've been doing some version of living the past three and a half years, mostly without you. The world kept on spinning somehow. But it's so much brighter with you in it, Sophie."

Scanning her face, I try my best to burn the look of adoration she has for me right now into my memory.

"Come here," I say, tugging her to the bed. "Wait. Are you even comfortable in those? Why are you wearing them?" My fingertips run along the thigh of her jeans.

"Oh, umm. Just trying a new style." Insecurity laces her voice.

I sit back up, but she remains where she is lying on the bed. "Let's try that again. You hate jeans."

"I know. Umm." She twists a strand of hair around her finger, her eyes locked on it. "JT said . . ." Of fucking course this has to do with JT the jerk. "He said that I should wear clothes that show off my body more. That my sundresses make me look like a child."

Closing my eyes, I take a breath and tell myself not to ruin this moment getting angry over something JT did that doesn't matter anymore. A flood of satisfaction rushes through me knowing that he got exactly what he deserved on the other end of my fist. The lack of confidence he's instilled in my girl over the past year makes me more mad than anything. It's my fault for letting her go in the first place.

"Sophie." I try to win her focus. When it's clear she won't look at me, I run my thumb along the small sliver of soft skin showing between her jeans and short sleeve crop top. She hesitantly looks at me. Even in the darkness of my room, I can see insecurity seeping out of her. "For starters, you are breathtaking no matter what you wear. You could be wearing a garbage bag and you'd still be the most beautiful girl I know." She bites into her lip, unsure how to take the compliment. "If you don't want to wear your dresses anymore because *you* don't want to, then okay. But don't let anyone make you feel like you should give up something that makes you *you*."

"I hate these jeans," she whispers.

"I know you do. So, take them off, and come lay with me."

"Are you trying to get me naked?" Her eyes are filled with vulnerability like she doubts my intentions.

"No. I'm trying to get you comfortable. Because you're going to come over here and let me hold you. And once you're tangled up with me, that's where you're staying."

She moves from the bed and shimmies her jeans down, revealing her toned, smooth legs. I didn't have much of a chance to notice the other night, but she must be skating on her own. I drink her in, eager to run my hands across her soft skin. The tiny triangle of fabric covering her attracts my attention, and I resist the urge to bite my fist, seeing her half naked in my room again. "Do you want shorts?"

She shakes her head, lying on my bed and scooting closer to me. She cuddles into me, her leg flinging over my waist and her arm wrapping around my stomach. Her head snuggles into my chest. My hand smooths against her thigh sprawled over me, the other cradling her head as I kiss her hair. God, I've missed her being close. When she releases a deep breath, she melts into me, bringing us even closer somehow. "This is exactly what I needed," I tell her.

"You're all I need, Cooper." She snuggles in tight, but I hook my finger under her chin, tilting her face. I can't go another second without my lips being on hers.

The kiss is soft, her lips warm against mine. It's everything I've been missing. Our lips linger, not moving, just pressed together, and I feel more at peace than I have in a long fucking time.

68

COOPER

Now

The orange glow of the sunset seeps into my room via the living room when I wake up from our nap. I'm hot and a little sweaty, confused for the split second before my heart thumps in my chest. Did I imagine Sophie was here? I close my eyes on a breath, my fingers pressing into my eyes hard enough to erase the dream.

The soft twang of Darius Rucker's voice sings from the kitchen and instant relief rushes through me. I slide off my bed, slowly making my way down the hall. Leaning against the fridge, I take in the scene in front of me.

Sophie sits on the kitchen island, watching a pot of water boiling on the stove. She's barefoot, in nothing but one of my sweatshirts, her feet dangling beneath her as she sways to the song, singing along quietly.

She slips off the counter, stirring whatever is in the pot. The silence between songs reveals my breath and she spins slowly, a smile lighting her face at the sight of me.

I don't waste any more time with space between us, taking a few steps until I'm in front of her and pulling the wooden spoon from her hand to set it on the counter beside us. Her hands immediately loop around my neck, her fingers running through the back of my hair, the smile in her eyes matching the one on her face.

Slipping under the sweatshirt she's wearing, my hands smooth slowly from her thighs to her hips, skimming over the lace in between. I tug her closer, locking my arms around her at the same moment my lips touch hers. Even though we kissed a few hours ago, the softness of her mouth against mine, the smile I feel as she pulls me closer too, makes it feel like a first kiss—full of the promise that comes with new beginnings.

"I missed you," I whisper against her lips.

"Me too. I went to Costa Rica."

My brows scrunch. "You did? When?"

"The past two weeks. I got back a couple of days ago."

"How was it?"

"It was good . . ."

"Why do you sound unsure?"

"I just . . . I realized how unhappy I was."

"With me?" My heart rate triples, worried we aren't on the same page right now.

"No." She squeezes me tighter, reassuring me as she finds her words and breathes in deep. "After we broke up the summer before I started college, I tried to escape everything happening in my own head by trying new things, completing my bucket list. I thought my dad was right. That finding the things I love would only come from experiencing what's *not* meant for me too."

"That tracks." My laugh comes out heavier than I intend. I feel like I missed too much of her, *of us*, because of her dad and his stupid logic and both of us listening to it.

"I was so unhappy forcing myself to do things I didn't *really* want to, at least not all the time. Like drinking, partying . . . other guys," she adds in a whisper. "And you know what I realized?"

I rub my thumb across the bare skin on her back under my sweatshirt, letting her know she's safe to continue.

"When you're sad, even the things you love are tainted. When you're miserable, everything seems worse. Things you enjoy aren't enjoyable because you're consumed by being so out of alignment. It's confusing. I told myself I couldn't possibly know what I truly love yet because my dad said so. I loved you, Coop. But I didn't always treat you like it. I made poor choices that made me unhappy then spiraled into a version of myself that was hardly capable of soaking in the moments I actually wanted to be present for. I kept doubting myself, that I could know that it was true without contingencies–only once I was a certain age. Once I experienced a certain number of things–or people. That wasn't fair to you, and I'm so sorry." She pauses, searching my face.

"You said loved."

"Huh?"

"You said you *loved* me."

She twists my hair at the nape of my neck through her fingers, smiling. "I was just stating that *I did*. In case there were doubts, ones that would have been justified. I did love you. I do love you. I'll always love you. You're it for me, Coop. My heart has always known that even if my brain wasn't always on board."

I breathe out a sigh of relief. "So, we're on the same page now? We're doing this?"

She nods. "But I want us to be different this time."

"What do you need from me?" If she's committed to making some changes, I am too.

"I need you to trust me."

"I–"

She pulls a hand from my neck and presses a finger to my lips. "I need you to believe that I'm always going to try my best when it comes to you. And I need you to come to me if you're doubting me at all and give me a chance to course correct before you get upset. I take full responsibility for not always being good to you, Coop. I did a lot of stupid things thinking jealousy would bring you back. But I also genuinely thought some of my choices *would* bring you back. If I get off course, I want you to help me. I want to learn together. I want all of this together."

"Deep down, I think I knew you were never trying to intentionally hurt me. I just felt like I knew what was best for you and got frustrated when you didn't seem to agree. All I ever wanted was for you to be happy, Soph. I want to be the guy–the only guy–who knows what you need before you do so I can give it to you." Even with the new information I have about my parents almost getting divorced when I was a kid, it's so clear how in tune they are with each other. My dad always knows how to cheer up Mom and how to solve her problems. I want to be that for Sophie.

"I know, and I love you for that. Part of it is my fault because I've always counted on you to remain my safe place even after I try to burn it down. But we need to grow together. And that means sometimes I need to learn how to do things on my own before you step in. My happiness is too much to be responsible for on your own."

"I'll always be your safe place."

"And I'll do my part to keep it that way too. I'm sure we'll always find something to disagree on or argue about. I know you'll always be on my team. But it makes a difference if I show up with a match or a cupcake. I want to be your safe place too, Coop. And to do that, I know I need to find my own peace again–to be happy in my own space so I can bring it into *our* space. You deserve the best version of me–a happy version of me. Not the one who is off making stupid decisions because she is listening to someone else's words instead of her own heart. So, I'm making a plan to fall in love with the things that bring me the most joy again."

"Like what?"

"Honestly, what I was doing before. Trying new things made me so much more thankful for hobbies I took for granted. Reading, drawing sketches, skateboarding. I might keep pole dancing, though." She smiles so wide it's contagious.

"Oh yeah?"

"Yeah. But most of all, I want to fall in love with you all over again."

I squeeze her to me by my grip on her lower back, her eyes full of the adoration for me that maybe I've been taking for granted. "I'm sorry I was part of the force trying to control your life and decisions. It kills me to think I could have taken this away from you."

She kisses me once on the lips then lets me continue.

"I was so scared of losing you as my person that I made decisions that undermined our potential to be more. I hope you'll forgive me for that."

She nods.

"We can do this."

"Yes, we–oh shoot." Sophie tugs away from my grip and reaches for the wooden spoon on the counter, stirring the water and catching the pot from overflowing just in time.

I chuckle. There's a downside to not seeing anything but her when she's around. "What are you making?" I ask even though I can see the spaghetti noodles swirling in the bubbles.

"Something I made up." She grins and I raise an eyebrow.

"Sophie, baby, I love you," the words flow effortlessly, "But you don't cook."

"Hey, that's rude! It's going to be good. I promise." She pinches the noodle she spooned out of the water between her fingers, blowing on it. I intercept it on its way to her mouth, biting it away from her.

"Double rude," she teases, spooning out another noodle to test. "Go away, I'm busy, and you're bothering me."

I chuckle, hopping to sit on the island counter to watch her work. She rolls her eyes as she grabs either side of the pot with hot pads and dumps it into the strainer in the sink. She returns the noodles to the pot and makes her way around the kitchen like it's her own.

Assuming she's just making spaghetti, I expect a jar of sauce to come out of the pantry cupboard. Instead, she opens the fridge, pulling out a carton of eggs. I keep my questions to myself as I observe her cracking four eggs right into the pot of spaghetti. She mixes them in before she sprinkles salt and pepper, a handful of shredded cheese in along with small chunks of cream cheese she apparently pre-cut. Jesus Christ, what is she doing? I chuckle and she ignores me, stirring her creation until she's satisfied.

She spoons the mixture into two bowls and tops it off with crumbled bacon. She must have made that while I was sleeping too. Handing me a bowl, she reaches into the drawer beneath me for a fork and sticks it into the noodles. "You're welcome." She's never cooked for me before and the way pride splashes across her face with her smile makes me hope this isn't the last time, even if whatever this is tastes like shit.

"What exactly am I thanking you for?" I laugh, twisting a chunk of stuck together pasta with my fork.

"It's breakfast spaghetti. Duh, Cooper."

"I thought you made this up?"

"I did."

"Then how was I supposed to know what it was?" I chuckle before shoving the bite in my mouth.

Sophie shrugs, her look encouraging me to eat. I chew a few times then stare into the eggy cheesy noodles in my bowl.

Before I've even revealed a sliver of emotion, a grin breaks out on her face. "It's so good, huh? I can tell you love it. I created it with you in mind."

I consider teasing her, but I don't have it in me to break the smile I've been missing so much even for a second. "It's great, Soph. Thank you." Even better than dinner is knowing how much I'm ingrained into her thoughts and actions even when we're apart.

69

SOPHIE

NOW

"Soph, I don't think we have time to take two days of vacation right now." Cooper looks up at me from where he sits on his couch, the soft yellow glow from the sunrise shimmering through the window behind him. I let myself in the front door after waking him up with a phone call and bouncing into his living room more than excited about my idea.

"Sure we do. School doesn't start for four more days. I already talked to Troy. He said he knows for a fact you don't have any fraternity things in the next 48 hours, and he checked with his uncle. The cabin is all ours. I planned everything for us so you have nothing to worry about."

"Did you forget I failed my test last week? I need to study before school starts and I hardly have time."

Reaching for his hands, he takes mine and stands. My arms link around his neck and he pulls me closer by the waist. God, I missed this so much. I missed him so much. "I'm so happy we're back together, Coop. I just want to take a few days alone before we have a million things to do. You can even bring your books, and I'll quiz you if you want."

His brow quirks. "And you'll reward me for each answer I get correct?"

I roll my eyes but can't fight a smile. "Go pack your bag. We have a full day planned!"

"Yes, ma'am," he teases, kissing me on the lips before obeying my command.

Twenty minutes later, Cooper is in the driver's seat, hand on the back of my headrest as he backs out of the driveway. I open our shared playlist and scroll through to set up a queue instead of a random shuffle. There are at least ten more songs on here than the last time I added some.

"What's that smile for?" Cooper asks, flashing his eyes back to me when I look up before they are locked on the road again.

"Nothing. I just love you."

He reaches over the center console, sliding his hand between my thighs. "I love you." He squeezes my leg, a jolt of happiness rushing through me.

Cooper makes the two and a half hour drive to Sunriver, Oregon in just over two hours, despite my insistence to slow down. He said it's my fault because he can't wait to see what I have planned. It occurred to me this is our first vacation alone. We've been on a few family vacations, we've even been to the cabin before, but never just the two of us.

We drop our bags in the entryway of the A-frame log cabin. The first level is an open floor plan with a kitchen on the right and a movie room past it. On the left is the massive A-shaped full wall window shining light onto the entertaining room. There's a fireplace on the left with a curved row of sitting chairs and a dining room table on the wall opposite.

"I love it here." I sigh, already thinking about curling up in one of the oversized leather armchairs with a book later.

Cooper's arms link around my waist from behind, his chin resting on my shoulder. "I love *you*."

I twist in his grasp, my hands falling to his chest. "You've said that at least seven times since we left the house this morning," I tease.

"Are you tired of hearing it?" He tucks a curl behind my ear before sliding his hand in to grip the back of my neck.

"Never."

"Good." He kisses me in a way I know I'll never tire of, but I pull away anyway.

"Okay, go get your swimsuit on!"

He grins before grabbing both our bags and taking them upstairs. I follow closely behind, unzipping my pink duffel when it's on the bed and pull my hot pink bikini from it. Cooper slips his solid black shorts on so quickly I hardly get a good look as I'm stepping out of my dress. It's so strange having this level of comfort with someone, but Cooper knows every part of me. He's the only one I never have to hide from. Even though we haven't had sex since we officially got back together a few days ago, I don't even think twice about stripping in front of him to change, and no part of me cringes or wants to retreat as he shamelessly takes in the view. I'm both anxious and patient when it comes to us being intimate again. It will happen when it's right.

We make it out of the cabin surprisingly quickly and hand in hand make the fifteen minute walk to the marina. It's peak season and even though it's only eleven in the morning, it's almost 80° out and the boat lined dock is packed. There's way too many people around for my liking, but once we're on the water, it'll just be Cooper and me, and I can't wait.

Check-in is a breeze since I thought ahead and re-served a kayak. We walk down the tan floating dock that splits like a plus sign, and Cooper guides me to the quadrant in the back right, where a marbled orange boat awaits us. I shimmy out of my white jean shorts and toss them into the front compartment along with Cooper's T-shirt and our bag of snacks. He grips the side of the two person kayak with both hands to balance as I slide into the front seat. Looking up at him I say, "You know what Dad told me once?"

"What's that?"

"That before I date any guy, I should kayak with him first. It takes enough communication to know if you'll be able to make the relationship work."

Cooper chuckles, but there's not as much lightness in his voice as I had hoped for. I hope someday Dad can believe in us the way we do. "Of course he said that. He must not have known that we are more than capable of making it six miles downriver."

"Guess we'll find out right now," I joke. Whenever we come with everyone else, we get canoes or paddle boards, so Cooper and I have never kayaked together.

He unties the rope and tosses it inside the boat before hopping in the back, making it sway a little in the dark water. It's shallow enough here I see a few fish swimming through the seaweed below, sunlight reflecting off their scales. Pushing off the dock, Cooper guides us into the open river. Once we're in the middle of the open water, I scan the scene, my blue paddle resting across my lap. "It's so peaceful here." The tree lined banks on either side of us are at least a hundred feet apart, and away from shore the water is much more clear than it is by the dock. The sun glitters across the surface, my shoulders already warm from the rays.

Up the bank a few hundred feet is the Mexican and Peruvian place we'll eat dinner at later. All the seats along the windows have a perfect view of the river. The thought of one sip of their killer margaritas through a salted rim already has my mouth watering.

"This is my favorite place," Cooper adds. The edge of his paddle dips into the water to my right as he makes a gentle stroke on that side before switching to the other, guiding us toward the walking bridge that crosses the river up ahead. I grasp my paddle, dipping the white blade into the water on my right, just in front of my body. It goes a little deeper than I expected, and I struggle to get it through the water. The pressure sends our boat to the left a little, and I attempt to balance it by dipping my oar deep on the left. The second it's back in the air again it clashes with Cooper's paddle–hard.

"Sophie, the person in the back is supposed to steer." He laughs as he says it, but it annoys me. I'm just trying to help. "And we have to be in sync."

"I can't see you! How am I supposed to stay in sync when I can't see you?"

"You could just let me do it."

"No. I want to do it too. Let's switch."

He chuckles. "There's no way we could switch without falling in."

Laying my paddle back across my lap, I pick at the hem of my bikini bottoms. "I don't want my dad to be right." The words slip from my mouth too quickly to take back.

There's a tap of the paddle against the plastic of the boat. A barely audible sigh leaves Cooper as his hand lands on my shoulder, his thumb brushing across my skin. "He's not. I know I get frustrated when we're not in sync, but I know it's not possible every time. I'm working on it."

"Okay," I murmur.

His thumb brushes across my shoulder again. "Look at me," he says softly. When I twist in my seat, his hand slides down my arm until it's resting on my wrist. "Soph, nothing–no one–is perfect on their first try. Sometimes we mess up, sometimes we overcorrect. We just have to find our groove."

I nod slightly, my eyes searching his.

"Maybe your dad thinks the tell of a good relationship is how well they can kayak together–do anything together. But I think he has this false idea that it should always be easy. I thought that too once. But I think it's really about people who are patient and care enough to figure it out even when it's not easy. We're doing all of this together, remember?"

"Yeah, you're right. It's hard not to let him get in my head. He's my dad, you know?" I hate that somehow his logic holds more weight to me, even when I know it's not always right.

"I know. It's hard when it's family. But you and I are family too. We always have been. Plus, we're older now and we've made it so far. We're capable of sorting through the nonsense at this point, okay?"

"Okay," I agree, a little more confident. Desperate to change the mood, I break through the silence with a splash of water from my hand, straight to Cooper's face. I turn to see his reaction, catching his grin under his hands as he wipes the droplets from his skin. "You're such a brat," he says.

"Your brat." I stick my tongue out before turning forward again.

"Promise?"

I nod.

A few miles downstream, we've fallen into a semi-consistent rhythm, our paddles only clashing a few more times. I stop when I notice Cooper taking a break, resting my paddle across my lap and reaching into the front compartment for a couple of bottles of water.

I hand one to Cooper, looking over my shoulder as a family with three small kids paddle by in a canoe. The mom is trying to pass out juice boxes, but the two boys and a girl–definitely all under the age of five–are too busy playing around, tipping the boat from side to side.

"Do you want kids?" Cooper's voice invades the scene unfolding in front of me.

"What?" I shift my attention to him, twisting in my seat.

"Do you want kids?" he repeats. "I don't mean like right this second, but like . . . later?"

"Oh, umm." I guess this is an important conversation to have if we plan on being together forever this time, but it wasn't on my radar that it would happen anytime soon. I debate between my honest answer and the one I think Cooper wants to hear–but I can't for the life of me figure out what he *wants* to hear. I mean, he's a young guy. Surely kids aren't on his agenda anytime in the near future. Especially since he's trying to build an empire with his dad. But on the flip side, family has always been important to him, and his parents had Carter really young.

"Have you never thought about it?" he pries.

Of course I have. I like being prepared for things in my life, having a vision for what direction I want to go for major milestones so I can do my research and make educated decisions. "I don't want you to think I'm crazy."

"You're a little crazy." He holds his hand in front of his face, scrunching his nose as he brings his thumb and pointer finger close together. "Seriously, though," he says, dropping his hand to the paddle in his lap, his skin glowing in the sun.

I take a deep breath. "There's this kid who comes to the library where I volunteer for story time. Max. He's so sweet. He came for a few weeks consistently. Then I didn't see him for six months. I was worried that something bad happened to him, but we don't have contact information for the kids. Their parents are always with them." He can't see where I'm going yet, so I just continue. "He came back a few weeks ago, but this time there was a different adult with him. Turns out, he was in foster care. The first family was forced to give him up when his bio mom came back in the picture. When she was out of the picture again, he got assigned a new foster home. I guess he kept talking about reading time until the new mom figured out what he meant and was able to bring him back. She's working on adopting him now."

"I'm not quite following, Soph."

"I think . . . I don't think I want my *own* kids. I think I'd rather try to adopt one or maybe like three. I think it would be special to take in children who have been shown the darker side of life and bring light into their world, and to show them the potential they have when someone believes in them. I know I could do that with biological kids too, but I don't know . . . does that sound crazy?"

Cooper eyes me for a long moment, chewing on his lip, and I don't notice it was to fight back a grin until he speaks. "Not crazy. I wouldn't mind having a kid of our own. But to be honest . . . ever since Troy became part of our family, I've had similar thoughts. It's not just about what we did for him, but what he did for us. I loved my family before but it just feels complete with him in it, you know?"

Nodding, I agree. "I can't imagine your family without Troy."

He grins.

"Coop?"

"What's up?

"You said 'our.'"

He laughs. "If you think I'd raise what would surely be a wild child with anyone but you, then you *are* crazy."

"Even if that means they have a Grandpa Jack?" I whisper.

He leans forward, kissing my shoulder, his lips cooling my already sunburnt shoulder. "We aren't our parents, Soph. It'll be up to us who we let into their life and in what capacity, okay?"

I'm still unsure. I want my dad to want this for me.

"He'll come around."

I nod as he presses his forehead to mine. "Thank you."

"For what?"

"Never giving up on us."

"Never."

70

COOPER

NOW

"Wow. I forgot how beautiful it is out here," Sophie says from where she's tucked under my arm as we walk back from dinner. Her head is tilted back, trusting me to guide us, as she looks up at the stars sprinkled across the dark sky. After kayaking all day, we sat on the deck at the Mexican Peruvian fusion restaurant along the river, eating ceviche and sipping margaritas until they closed.

"We're here." I squeeze her shoulder softly, encouraging her to watch the step in front of us that leads to the wrap-around cabin porch. "We can stay out here if you want? I'll grab a blanket and we can lie under the stars."

"Yes, please. Perfect ending to the perfect day."

I kiss her temple, releasing her and digging the cabin key from my boardshorts pocket to run inside. Sorting through the entryway closet, I pull out an old comforter and meet Sophie back outside. She's standing on the worn wooden porch, in front of the A-frame window, in nothing but her white shorts and pink bikini top. Her tangled hair from a day of adventure flows down her back as she stares into the night. My heart thumps in my chest, thankful beyond words this girl is mine again–forever this time. It's easier to be patient knowing we have the rest of our lives, but it's been nearly impossible to keep my hands off her all day. Tonight is the first night since we got back together that we're actually staying *together* overnight. It's not that we haven't wanted to. We just want to appreciate each other's company and revel in happily being in the other's presence.

Sophie doesn't startle when I come up behind her but joins me on the blanket after I flap it gently in the air before letting it settle flat on the porch. Her head finds my chest the moment I'm lying on my back, and I wrap my arm around her shoulder, the other folding under my head as a pillow.

We lay there silent, the heat from each other keeping us warm enough as the light chill of night takes over from the heat of the day. Random thoughts flicker through my mind, a train going down a wild track that leads to a burning question. "What happens in the last episode of *Beauty & the Beast*?"

She squeezes her arm around my waist. "I don't know."

I glance down at her and her gaze shifts from the sky to me. "What do you mean?"

"I never saw it. I couldn't watch the ending without you."

The series finale aired the week after we broke up. I brush my thumb across her shoulder. "Me either."

She presses up, leaning on her elbow, her hand moving to my chest. "I can't believe you watched that whole show with me."

"Of course." I rub my hand across the skin on her back, tugging on the ends of her hair. "It's our thing."

"I had to bribe you with cupcakes to watch the first episode."

I grin. "I totally would have watched without the cup-cakes."

She playfully slaps my chest, but then a seriousness stills her. "That's when I first realized I had real feelings for you."

My brows scrunch together. "When I tricked you into making me cupcakes?"

"No. The second week of the show. You had your first game of the season that Thursday, remember? You won, and someone was throwing a house party to celebrate."

"I remember . . ." I'm still not quite following.

"Troy and Dean were both going. You didn't know I was behind you, but I overheard your friends begging you to go. I was about to leave and text you that we could watch the rerun another day, but you didn't even hesitate. You didn't even make a vague excuse. You told them that you already had plans with me and I was who you wanted to celebrate with."

I recall the memory. It was the start of junior year and the first full game I played in high school. I felt damn good. Mom and Dad were so proud. They never encouraged me to drink, but I knew they'd let me go to the party and pick me up if I asked. But I hadn't even needed to think about it. I loved my team, but outside of game time, Thursdays were reserved for Sophie. No matter what. The revelation hits me like a wave that smooths the sand rather than disturbs it. "I've always been yours, Soph."

"I was so convinced it would be one-sided. When you told me you had the same feelings that day out in the woods, I could hardly wrap my head around what I thought would always be just a fantasy."

Instead of replying with words, I turn on my side, gently rolling Sophie onto her back, my hand smoothing over her stomach as I press my lips to hers. She hums in satisfaction, her hand running up my arm. I bring my hand to her jaw, thumb holding her chin, locking her into a slow kiss. She opens her mouth just enough to grant me access, our tongues tangling without rush.

I can feel the strain in my swimsuit already, Sophie's confession and nearness more than enough to turn me all the way on. My fingers leave her jaw, dragging down her neck. Across the soft skin between her breasts. Past the thin string of her bikini. Lightly over her stomach until I reach the hem of her shorts and feather my fingers along the edge.

She deepens our kiss, threading her fingers through the back of my hair, and it's the permission I need for us to cross this line again. Her shorts are undone with an easy snap, and I slide the zipper down. I break our kiss to trail soft ones following the same path my fingers took. Kneeling beside her, I tug both her shorts and bikini bottoms as she lifts her hips, leaving her nearly naked beneath me and glowing in the moonlight.

When I shift my gaze up, I'm met with Sophie watching me take her in. I lay back down, putting my weight onto one side as I lean into her, my hand finding her waist. "That day in the woods . . . the moment right before I told you I wanted to kiss you . . . our whole lives flashed before my eyes. Everything we *might* have if you wanted to kiss me too. I was fucking terrified that you might not. But I was more scared of missing out on the vision in my head if I didn't take the chance."

"Thank you for taking that chance for us."

I grin before pressing my lips to hers again, untying the strings of my shorts with one hand. I manage to tug them off and kick them to the side as I kiss her. As I hover over her. As I settle between her legs.

I reach between us, but rather than play with her, I just align us. I press into her slowly, feeling she's just as into this moment as I am. Inch by inch I sink into her, her arousal increasing as I do. As I fill her, I feel every place we connect and the way she stretches around me in a perfect fit.

Once I'm inside, I pull my hips back at the same torturously slow pace before rocking back in, taking every inch the same as I did the first time. "You feel so good," I breathe against her neck, before kissing toward her jaw.

Her fingers still tangled in my hair, she kisses the skin before my ear, sending a pulse straight through my cock. Fuck, I love it when she does that. "Can you stay slow, just like this?" she whispers.

I answer her request by maintaining a speed that gives me time to feel everything between us. The smooth push and pull of my dick inside her with every slow thrust. My skin rubbing against her clit when I'm to the hilt. The cool breeze on my back. The hard porch beneath us. The smell of fresh air mixed with the faded flowers and sunscreen on Sophie's skin.

I push my knee against her thigh, opening her wider for me as she wraps her other leg around my back. This time when I press into her, I hit even deeper and the connection sends a chill through her, a wave of goosebumps covering her skin. I soothe the ones on her neck as my fingers thread through her hair, thumb locking onto her jaw.

I kiss her long and hard before pressing my forehead to hers as my hips do the work. Her breathing picks up, soft moans escape her lips, and her hand flits from my neck to my lats, skimming to my waist and up my arms–as if she wants to touch all of me at once–as if she's reaching for control. I feel her tighten slightly, squeezing my cock enough to let me know she's close.

"Fall over the edge, Sophie," I whisper, pulling almost all the way out of her.

She shakes her head ever so slightly, her breath catching as I push back in. "I don't want it to end."

"We're never going to end," I assure her as I retract just barely. When I thrust into her again, she tumbles, shattering over the edge. Fingers of one hand tighten their grip on my hair. Her others dig into my side. Her heel locks onto my back.

"Oh my god," she manages in one breath, her stomach clenching against mine as her orgasm explodes through her. Her pussy tightens around me with the next wave, and it sends me over the edge with her, nearly knocking the breath from me with the way a flood of tingles shoot through my body. I manage to stay steady with my hips, pulsing with each pump, her body seeming to pull me in as we come together.

On the next breath, I wet my lips before pressing them against Sophie's. Even with just the moonlight, I can see her flushed cheeks and her fully sated smile as I still inside her. "Whoa," she says, the stars reflecting in her eyes.

"Good?" I chuckle.

She hums as I brush my thumb softly along her hairline. "So good. I'm so happy we found our way back to *us*. You're everything to me, Coop. I want that to be clear in everything I do from now on so you never have to question us again."

"We made our mistakes and did our time. It's all in the past, and all I want to do is focus on our future." I pull out of her slowly, taking my weight off her.

"I think our future is bright," she whispers, glancing back up to the sky. "Like these stars."

"Like you." I roll to my back, pulling her to my chest.

71

SOPHIE

NOW

I dragged myself away from Cooper even though it was the last thing I wanted to do. But I had already made plans with Chastity to celebrate surviving the first week of Sophomore year, and I didn't want to bail on her.

Dressed in a basic green sundress and my hair tied back in a loose ponytail, I link my arm with my best friend's as we walk into Jameson's. "Ugggghhh." My head tips back dramatically when I spot JT leaned against the bar. Chastity scans the room until she sees him too.

"He's such a tool," she says, tugging me toward the other end of the bar.

The bartender, Jess, has barely taken our drink orders when JT slides onto the stool next to us, his feet still planted on the ground and his ass half on the seat so he can lean toward me.

"Hey there, Sophie. Miss me already?"

"No." I glare at him without fully glancing his way.

"I see you didn't take my advice. Still dressing like a child."

I do my best to ignore him.

"At least it makes for easy access." I can hear the sly smile in his voice without looking his way.

"Shut the fuck up, JT," Chastity snaps. "You're just mad she has a boyfriend a thousand times better than you. A real man."

"Ha. I doubt that."

Chastity snags my phone from my hands, tapping the screen so it lights up with a picture of Cooper and me kayaking in Sunriver.

JT grabs it from her before I can take it back, pulling it to his face. "This fuckface is your boyfriend?"

"Yeah, what's it to you?" my best friend taunts. I tug on her arm, wanting out of this conversation and away from JT.

He laughs. "Yeah, he's a real man all right."

My head snaps to look at him. The way he said it made it sound like he knows Cooper. "What?"

"Oh, your little boy toy didn't tell you?"

"Tell me what?"

"He tried to punch me when I wasn't looking."

"He did not." JT is so full of it.

Jess sets our drinks in front of us. "I remember that fight but not like that. You got your ass kicked, dude. And had it coming. Don't let him fool you. Cooper almost knocked him out." She smirks before turning to help another customer.

I can't wait to hear this story from Cooper, knowing whatever JT says will be a lie. I shrug. "I'm sure you deserved it."

He scoffs. "I didn't do shit. He couldn't handle that he got stuck with my leftovers."

"Actually–" Chastity starts, but I cut her off by slapping my hand against her shoulder.

"He's not worth it," I tell her and turn back to JT. "Get lost."

"You'll come crawling back, just like you did before. I'll see you then, Squirrel." He adds a wink before pushing off the bar and returning to his friends.

Gross. What did I ever see in him?

My best friend must be wondering the same because she scrunches her nose as he walks off.

"I need a drink," I tell her and wave Jess over.

"You have one."

"More than this. I can't believe Cooper punched him."

"You're not mad at him, are you?"

I tap my phone screen, lighting the lock picture again to look at the man I wish was here. "No. Well, maybe only because I didn't get to punch him myself."

"I kind of thought you'd be angry."

"Me too." I black out my home screen, deciding to talk with Cooper later and give Jess my attention when she's back in front of us. "Two shots of tequila, please." She nods and turns to the line of liquor bottles behind her. "But ever since what went down with Dad, I think I got caught up in the idea that Cooper shouldn't ever make any decision for me or without me. But most of the time, he really does have my best interest at heart, and I believe he'd think twice before doing something that needs to be talked through with me." I chuckle. "I think everyone can agree on punching JT without debate."

"Definitely." She licks the space between her thumb and pointer finger before shaking salt on it as Jess sets shots in front of us. "Alright then. To my bestie knowing what she deserves." We clink our tiny glasses together before tapping them on the table and shooting them back.

72
COOPER

Opening the glass door to Jameson's bar, I pull my phone from the pocket of my joggers to see if Ethan is on his way. We were going somewhere else, but Sophie texted a while ago and invited us to join them. Crashing into someone on their way out, I jolt a step back. Shit. I look up.

"Oh. Hey, Chastity. Sorry about that. How are you?" I glance behind her, checking for Sophie.

With both hands on my chest, she shoves me back through the door and into the cool night air. "Where have you been? I've been trying to call you."

I unlock my phone and click the call log. There's three missed calls. "Whoops, sorry. What's up?" All of a sudden it hits me that something might be wrong. "Is Sophie okay?"

"Yeah, I just accidentally got her really drunk."

I quirk a brow. "Accidentally?"

"I was proud of her for telling off JT–nice job punching him by the way. I'm sad I missed that. And one shot turned into like five." She's talking very fast, all her sentences slurred together, making it hard to follow. "She doesn't drink as often as I do, and I'm not sure she had much to eat today."

"She had five shots?" My eyes widen as I process. She texted me when she got here only an hour ago. "Where is she?"

"Oh fuck," Chastity mutters under her breath.

I follow her gaze right as Jack speaks. "Chastity. Where's Sophie?"

"Oh uuuh. Hey, Mr. Porter. I thought Diane was coming to get her."

Ignoring her remark, Jack fixes his stare on me. "Cooper. Of course you're here. I'll deal with you later."

"What the hell does that mean?" His problem with me seems more personal than him just wanting to protect his daughter. I don't fucking get it, but that's a problem for another day. "What's going on Chastity?"

"Nothing. Everything is fine. I'm just too drunk to drive, and I didn't want to send her in an Uber alone."

Jack chuckles. "See, I'm not the only one who doesn't think you two should be together. This shit is what happens when you hold onto your past."

"With all due respect, Mr. Porter," Chastity snaps, "Pull your head out of your ass. I called Cooper first. Then Diane. Not you. You're way more of a problem than he is."

Jack scoffs, and I try to push past Chastity while he tries to push past me.

She pins her hand to the door frame, preventing either of us through without force but locks her eyes on me. "You'll get her home safe?"

"Of course I will. Let me through. Please."

She sighs. "Good luck." She lets me duck under her arm then kicks her foot out to keep Sophie's dad away. Thank fuck for that.

I spot Sophie immediately. She's walking toward the bar from the bathroom hallway. The strap of her green sundress is falling off her shoulder and her curls are tied back into a sloppy ponytail. I don't notice JT until his arm snakes around her waist, pulling her close to him.

The whole scene makes my stomach flip like an undercooked pancake. I bolt toward them, but before I can get close enough to punch him again, Sophie shoves him away. "Don't touch me again," she snaps so clearly I wonder if she's actually that drunk. But then she haphazardly tries to adjust her dress strap, only for it to slide right off her shoulder, and she doesn't even notice. My chuckle brings both of their attention to me.

"Cooper!" She leaps into my arms. I barely have time to react but catch her as her arms loop around my neck. She leans backward, hanging all her weight on me, and I can't help but smile as I keep us stable. There's a drunk, but dreamy look in her eyes, when she says, "My hero. But don't be fooled. If you hadn't already punched him, I totally could have taken him."

I brush my fingers against her lower back, pulling her to me. "You totally could. You ready to go?"

Her eyes lock on mine as if she's seeing me for the first time tonight. "Hi. You're here."

"I am." I chuckle. "You're really drunk, huh?"

She sighs. "Yeah, Chastity and I did a lot of celebrating about me standing up to JT. Fuck him, ya know? How could I ever want him when you exist? How could I want anyone when you exist? You know what I'm saying?"

"I know exactly what you're saying." Finally she understands. We stand for at least a minute in the middle of the bar, me just holding her and relishing in the warmth of her body, her with her eyes on me, seemingly oblivious to how much time passes. "Are you ready to go home?"

"Yes, please." Her arm wraps around my waist, her head leaning on my shoulder as I walk us toward the exit. She pulls an arm away to stick her middle finger in the air, turning her head back for a moment–presumably to see if JT caught the bird she's flipping him.

My precious girl. I've only ever heard her curse a couple of times in my life, and here she is giving no fucks.

Sophie glances up at me. "I want to go home with you," she slurs against my chest. The cool night air hits us as I push open the glass door, and a shiver runs through her. "Oh, wait. I forgot I'm hanging out with Chastity," she says, spotting her best friend where she's still holding Jack captive outside.

Ethan reaches the entrance right in time for round two of the chaos. His eyes skirt across the scene as I catch his attention. "Hey, man. I'm going to take Sophie home. I'm sorry I'm bailing." I know he'll understand. I turn to Chastity. "Do you need a ride?"

"Actually, I kind of wanted to stay." She glances at Ethan. They aren't really friends, but they've partied together a few times. "I'm not Cooper, but you can keep me company if you'd like."

"Let's do it." He doesn't hesitate or ask questions about what's going on or add to the drama. He's the kind of brother who makes me thankful I joined my fraternity, despite my reservations. He always just goes with the flow and has my back.

Sophie hugs Chastity, eying her dad with curiosity over her shoulder. Chastity thanks me for coming as she releases Sophie and links her arm with Ethan's, tugging him inside.

"I'll take Sophie from here," Jack demands, reaching for his daughter.

Sophie pulls away, her head following her eyes as she looks between us. "Who thought it was a good choice to call Dad?" she whines.

"I am the right choice," he says. "You're coming home with me."

Sophie raises a very drunk and over dramatic eyebrow at him. I have to bite back a laugh. "No. I'm not. I pick Cooper. Just like I should have the first time. None of this would have happened if I hadn't let you get to me before."

A rush of relief flows through me, and I reach for her again. She smiles up at me. "Also I'm choosing you because your bed is more comfy. Oh! And you have that pillow you got for me. And because you have pizza at home."

"Okay, Soph. I'll make you pizza rolls." Jack tries to object, but I cut him off. "I'm taking her home. I haven't had anything to drink, and I'll take care of her. Whether you like it or not, I love her, and you know I would never let something bad happen to her."

"I don't think that's a good idea." He glares. "She's vulnerable right now."

"Actually, she's been standing up for herself all night. She doesn't *need* me. She definitely doesn't need you."

"I sure do want you, though," Sophie chimes in, her adorable drunkenness lightening the situation.

Jack's stern gaze shifts between the two of us. "No." He reaches for his daughter again.

I step toward the man who unfortunately will be my father-in-law someday, blocking him from Sophie as she clings to my arm. "Yes," I say firmly. I turn toward my girl, bending slightly to level with her. "Let's go home," I whisper.

"This isn't over," Jack snarks behind me.

It's frustrating as fuck things have to be this way with him. Why can't he let this go and accept we're right together? "Actually, it is," I snap back. "We're done letting your opinions sway us into something that has only hurt us. You are the one creating the pain you're trying to prevent. If you can't see that then I don't know what to tell you, but you're the one who needs to grow up." Pulling Sophie close to me, she wraps her arm around my waist as I lead her down the street to my car, ignoring the words Jack yells after us. She's rambling about how angry she is the entire way, but it's not clear what she's saying. Wanting to forget about her dad, I don't ask her to repeat herself as I open the door to my 4Runner, the overhead lights casting a glow over her body as I slide her into the passenger seat. When she's sitting, I buckle her in. As it clicks into place, her hand falls to my bicep.

"Someday, he'll remember how much he loves you, Coop." She says the words like I'm worried. It would be nice if Jack could see the light, but I don't give a fuck what he thinks anymore. For Sophie's sake, I do hope he comes around eventually.

"Either way, you always have me."

"Thanks, Coop. After you feed me pizza, let's just talk, okay? God, you smell good."

My teeth sink into my lip, biting back a grin. She's so fucking pretty. The elastic has somehow disappeared and her blonde curls have almost completely fallen. She's got a light pink gloss on her lips like she somehow thought to reapply even though she's trashed. I bet it tastes like cotton candy. Her lashes are dark and wispy, making her eyes stand out against her lightly freckled skin. For some reason, our first date flashes through my mind.

"Sounds perfect, Soph." I shut the door before walking around the front of my car and sliding onto the driver's seat. By the time we make it home, Sophie is sleeping, leaning against the car window. I sit and watch her for a few minutes, so thankful her choosing me this time feels like she means it.

I scoop her up in my arms, and she stirs, although she doesn't open her eyes. Her arms ring around my neck and she nuzzles her head into my chest, her body temperature way hotter than normal. I manage to unlock my front door using the hand from the arm wrapped around Sophie's back then softly close it with my foot once we're through. I walk her down the hallway to my room and she grumbles as I put her on her feet, and immediately leans into me for support. Trying to keep her upright, I awkwardly pull her toothbrush from the drawer, help her brush her teeth, and force her to drink a glass of water.

Back in my room, I pull down the comforter and she crawls under it, laying her on her side on the navy sheets. She immediately folds her hands under her head, her eyes closed. I pull the comforter over her shoulder and kneel on the ground next to her. In a sundress she's had forever, and nearly asleep with her fallen curls draped across the pillow make her a vision I recognize easily–like watching a movie scene you've seen a hundred times. I tuck the stray strands of hair on her face behind her ear. "Get some sleep, Sophie." I make a move to join her on my side of the bed.

"Wait," her soft voice brings me back to her level.

"What's up? Do you want more water?"

"No." I'm close enough that I can smell the tequila that's somehow still on her breath as she sighs. It mixes with the same sweet flowery body spray she's always worn, and I'm pulled closer to her like she has a magnetic field. I can't believe I ever let her get away. Her eyes remained closed, but I can tell she's about to continue her thought. "Cooper?"

"Yes?"

"I thought we were going to talk."

I try not to laugh. "We can talk tomorrow."

"I want to talk now." Her voice stomps out the words like a child throwing a temper tantrum in the grocery store.

She seems to have sobered up enough to *maybe* have a conversation, although there's no guarantee she'll remember it. "Okay, hold on." I take my shoes, shirt and joggers off, sliding into bed next to her. She turns to face me but keeps her hands curled under her face like a pillow.

"You punched JT," she whispers.

"That guy is like a cockroach that needs to be sprayed with Raid. He deserved it." I rest my hand on her waist, rubbing my thumb softly against her hip to counteract the hostility of my words.

"He really did." A few tears travel the short distance from the side of her eye to her pillow.

"Why are you crying?" I swipe a tear off her cheek, leaving my hand locked on her neck. "I'm sorry I didn't tell you. I know you hate the miscommunication thing and that we've disagreed in the past on whether or not what I do is protecting you. But I couldn't *not* punch him. I'm glad you didn't hear the shit he was saying."

She sighs. "I'm not mad. If I knew how to punch, I probably would have done the same tonight." A quiet laugh bursts from her lips. "Jess said you totally took him down. I wish I could have seen it."

"Ethan helped. I got a couple of good swings in, though. The best part was none of his friends came to his defense."

"I'm glad you're in my corner."

"Always."

"Okay." She smiles, biting into her lip. "Is it time for you to hold me now?"

"Come here." I chuckle, reaching my arm out. She rolls into me, her head nuzzling into my chest.

When she's perfectly in place, her hand falls to my chest, drawing soft circles against my skin. "Can we keep talking?"

"Sure. What do you want to talk about?"

"I don't know. Ask me something."

I hum against her hair before kissing the top of her head. "What do you want our life to look like?"

"That's a big question."

I can't be sure but the circles she's drawing on my skin seem to have shifted to hearts. I scratch my fingers gently over her shoulder. "No thinking twice. No questioning what someone else would think, including me. Or worrying about if you'd ever change your mind. What would you *love*? Right now. As the Sophie capable of knowing how to fight for her happiness."

"I just want you." Her arm wraps around my middle and she squeezes me tight. It's the best fucking feeling.

"You have me. What else?" I'm not sure why it hit me all of a sudden that maybe it's okay if I can't read Sophie's mind and anticipate *everything* she needs. Maybe asking her and being willing to give it is enough.

"Ummm. To design houses that you sell."

"We'd make a pretty good team."

"I think so," she says wistfully, her drunkenness seeming to be replaced with sleepiness.

"What do you want right now?"

She hesitates. "To move in with you."

"Done." I don't even pause.

"How come you never got a new roommate after Troy moved to California anyway?"

It would feel wrong to give up Troy's room. I've been hoping he'll move back to Oregon after the sabbatical he's taking to get away from Emily–to get over her–but as much as I love him, I'd still kick him out in a heartbeat for Sophie. "There's only one other person I'd want in my space."

I feel her smile against my chest. "So I can really move in with you?"

"Yes." I chuckle. "As long as you don't hate me when you realize how much I hate doing laundry."

She tilts her head, looking up at me with a grin. "But I only want to live here until we can buy a place together."

"Or build our place?" I'm not sure why the idea never occurred to me before. "You could design our house someday. Only if you want to, of course."

She springs up, slapping her hands onto my chest like the idea electrifies every cell in her body. "Really?"

"Yes, really." I chuckle.

"Can we have a library?"

I nod, pushing myself up until I'm sitting and facing her.

"Can we have a giant windowless exterior wall so we can project a movie onto it like at the drive-in?"

"Sounds perfect." I grin, sitting on the bed and tugging on her thighs until she swings one leg over, straddling me.

"Caaaaan we have a pole in the living room? So I can practice my dancing without falling on my face in front of other people?"

"We can absolutely have that, but in the bedroom." I smooth my hands up her thighs until I reach lace.

"Can we kidnap Sunshine and move her to our new house?"

Now she's just testing me. "Sophie?"

"Uh-huh?"

"Can you just assume I'll give you whatever you want and let me kiss you now?"

"There's only one thing I really want anyway."

I press my lips to hers, stealing a soft and quick kiss. "Ask for it."

"Can we just be happy now?"

Holding her tight to me, I flip her on her back in one smooth motion and hover over her. I press my lips to hers before murmuring against them, "I thought you'd never ask."

73
COOPER

3 YEARS LATER

Cooper, 24; Sophie's 22nd birthday

"Cupcakes are ready!" Sophie yells from the kitchen.

Closing the door behind me, I make my way down the hallway, brown paper package in hand. It's been a busy week between Sophie's finals, her graduation ceremony, and the two houses I just closed on. But we're never too busy for tradition–or my favorite girl's birthday.

"Happy birthday," I tell her for the third time today, with a firm grip around her back to pull her to me. Her arms link around my neck as her mouth connects with mine, her usual cotton candy lip gloss taste replaced with the sweetness of homemade cream cheese frosting. I hum against her lips. "You taste good. Just like you did this morning."

She pulls back to swat at me playfully. "Cooper!"

"What?" I shrug, swiping my finger into the last of the remaining frosting in the Kitchen Aid bowl. "My tongue knows what it likes." I lick the frosting off my finger with a smirk. "And what *you* like." My pretty girl rolls her eyes, and I can't help but chuckle. Fuck, I love her.

Grabbing the freshly frosted cupcake she holds out for me, I kiss her lips again before taking a bite. She stares at me, expectantly, but it's not for praise on the treat.

I chuckle, finally holding out my gift wrapped in brown paper–like always.

"Is this what you want?" I grin, waving it in the air then moving it behind my back and demanding another kiss before handing it over.

She rips open the wrapping, not even bothering to check out the cover before flipping to the back page to read the words I've written. A photo slips from between the pages and onto the tile floor, but she ignores it.

The year we lived out our dream.

Her eyes scan over my writing a few more times before she bends to pick up the picture. It's a picture of an open field, surrounded by trees. Our pink and blue plastic tubing chairs sit in the corner of the frame.

"What is this?"

"A piece of land."

She stares flatly, her expression saying *no shit* without needing words. "Whose land?"

"Ours." Her eyes widen. "But only if you love it. I didn't sign the contract yet. It's contingent on you wanting it too."

She nods, tears welling in her eyes. "Thank you, Cooper."

"You're welcome. We can go see it tomorrow."

"I bet it's perfect." She reaches for my hand, transferring her excitement to me as she squeezes it. "This is definitely going to be the best year yet."

"I couldn't agree more." I kiss her as an excuse to step closer. "Now, what do you want to do before your graduation party tonight?"

"Actually, I have something to do. The last item on my bucket list. How mad would you be if I just left you and my parents to set up the party? I already helped Mom make all the food yesterday."

"I thought you quit the list?"

"I did. Well, I crossed out all the things I didn't feel like aligned with who I want to be. But there were a few I still wanted to try. And there's only one left."

"Which one?" It's been so long since I've seen it, I don't remember what's on it anymore.

"You'll see soon. I'll be back in like five hours."

"Five hours?!" I chuckle. "Alright."

"I'll meet you at Mom's?"

"Sounds good." I press a greedy kiss to her lips, pulling her into me until her arms link around my neck. I don't stop until she tugs from my grasp, insisting she needs to go.

SOPHIE

Me: *Meet me at our spot?*

I text Cooper as soon as I pull into my parents' driveway, thirty minutes before the party is supposed to start. Knowing he'll meet me there, I opt to walk through the side yard between our houses and cut straight to the back to avoid any detours talking to whoever is already here.

Our pink and blue chairs sit in the same place they always have–Cooper must have only moved them for the picture in their new home. *Our home.* I stay standing, trying to avoid my white Chuck Taylors getting dirty from the dead leaves covering the ground. And also because our chairs are definitely on their last leg. I'm not very confident in their ability to hold us much longer. Sunshine's chirp draws my attention to where she's perched on the faded red bird feeder. Despite the aging of my favorite things, it feels like just yesterday Cooper was sitting across from me, confessing he'd been thinking about what it might be like if we were more than friends.

"Hey, Soph." His voice infiltrates the memory playing in my head and the scene morphs back to reality.

"Hi." I grin.

He closes the distance between us, his lips pressing to mine as his hand slides into my curls and grips my neck. As he deepens our kiss, he runs his fingers along my neck, tracing the back strap of my dress on the way to my waist. His hand freezes. My hair brushes across my back as he gathers it in his hand, pulling it to one side. He pulls slightly out of my grip, enough to look where his fingers grazed.

"What is this?"

I hold my hair out of the way, twisting so he has better access to my back. "The last thing on my list. You can look." My heart pounds in my chest, simultaneously confident and nervous.

He gently pulls on the gauze taped to me. The final corner of the tape pinches off my skin, and I fight the urge to look back at Cooper's reaction. His thumb brushes over my shoulder, slightly above my new tattoo.

Without facing him, I can feel him silently taking it in. The yellow finch, sitting on a branch, surrounded by delicate lavender purple Harebell flowers that run the length of the straps of my dresses.

He chuckles, bringing my attention to him. "Has Sunshine seen her portrait?"

I twist my back toward the bird feeder, and as if she actually knows what's happening, she chirps. "What do you think?"

"I can't believe you got a tattoo. You've always said it's crazy to think someone could be so certain about something to know they'd love it forever."

"That's what Harebell flower means: constancy and everlasting love. Cooper." I take a breath. "Thank you for being my constant. No matter where we stand, no matter what has happened between us, no matter how far apart we *feel*, you're always there. And you're always going to be the reason I want more for myself, for my life. That's forever."

"It's perfect for you. You're perfect for me." His lips are soft against my forehead.

I peer up at him through my lashes. "Endgame," I whisper before pulling him into me.

More from Tisa Matthews

If you loved this story, check out the **Finding Home** series on Kindle Unlimited.

And Then There's You is book one, following Maci's love triangle with Mack and Dean.

I Love You, So What? is book two, following Lexy and Troy's story.

Can We Just Be Happy Now? is book three, following the story of Dean's sister Sophie, and Troy's best friend Cooper.

Tied Up In Riches is book four, following the story of Brooke and Marcus.

While books three and four can be read as stand-alones, books one and two of the series should be read in order for the best experience.

Home is an extended epilogue featuring a POV chapter from each main character in the series! It's meant to be read after you've finished the series!

Unhitched is a standalone, modern day romance jam packed with 2000s nostalgia and swirled around with the turning 30 identity crisis. It's written by a millennial for millennials.

Acknowledgements

What a roller coaster this book has been–both Sophie and Cooper's story and my journey writing it has been a ride full of ups and downs. It *gave me a thrill* and *made me sick*. Writing ANY book isn't for the faint of heart, but writing a dual timeline book is seriously no joke. This was out of my comfort zone and skill set as a writer so far–there was so much I needed to learn and work through. I'm so thankful I did, but there are a few people I really couldn't have completed this story without.

Brooke, as always, *thank you for being my person*. There's people I go to for help with different aspects of my story, and then there's you (see what I did there haha) . . . the person I go to for all of it. Thank you for reading another first raw draft. For being there for me through every vulnerability hangover and every melt-down. For writing me sex jokes. For defending my characters as if they're your friends, for always making time for me and for having my back no matter what. You are so much more than *just* the best damn assistant.

Heidi, thank you for making sure all the real estate chapters were on point and helping me paint a picture of Sunriver. Somehow, I think so many of the details in this book were inspired by you. It's not a surprise considering we've been friends for 25 years, which is really what I want to thank you for–Thank you for always being there for me in every phase of my life . . . but most importantly sticking through my own Sophie phase. It's a long gone part of my life, but you're still here, and there isn't anyone else I would have wanted around all this time.

Alexa, thank you for always hyping me up, for reminding me how impressive my writing can be, and how proud I should be of my books. Thank you for telling everyone you know about my babies. For reading parts of scenes in screenshots a million times. And of course, for making up a secret language with me. Our experience behind the scenes of these stories has been one of the best parts.

Krissi, thank you for reading so many scenes out of order and context. For helping me research the most obscure questions (I had to pause typing to laugh out loud) to help with book accuracy. For always sending me songs that remind you of my babes. For understanding Sophie on the level that I do. We may have met because of Taylor Swift, and bonded over books, but it's become so much more.

Katie . . . you have just been such an unexpected light in my life. Or more like little gold rays of sunlight filled with sparkling pink gems. Thank you for being you, for sliding into this project and into my life and of course, for loving Cooper the way I do.

Heather Garvin and Dani Keen, thank you so much for helping me figure out the plot development and sticking through rearranging and rewriting until I hit the plotline that made the most sense. So much of my growth as a writer is because of you. *Check out their books on Amazon!*

Cindy, thank you for bringing my vision for this cover to life. It's so beautiful and makes me so happy every time I see it. The colors, the vibes, the details—it's perfect.

Jason, thank you for helping me work through feedback and ideas and always playing devil's advocate with me no matter how many times I tell you it'll be the last time I need to play. You did more for this book and my sanity than you'll ever know.

Kristen, thank you for being my enneagram checker and helping me make sure Cooper and Sophie felt in alignment with their personality no matter what choices they were making. This was something new I did, and I really loved letting that guide the story!

Katelyn . . . as if I didn't love my favorite author, Kandi Steiner, enough, she brought me you. I'm so thankful that after wandering around a bookstore to find that meet and greet line, I ended up next to you. It was such a serendipitous moment that created our friendship, and I'm so thankful for it and all the help you've given me with this story.

Michaela, I'm so excited about our new author friendship. Thank you for making one of the final read-throughs of this book a priority, and I'm psyched to continue working with you . . . especially on both of our fake dating stories in 2024!

Sam, thank you for being such an unexpected friend and final beta reader who I stumbled across on Critique Match at the last minute. Thank you for flying through my book and giving so much insight to help strengthen so many scenes.

Alexis, Elizabeth, Shylie, Aarika and everyone else who read my words early, answered polls in my Instagram stories, debated concepts and ideas with me behind the scenes, cheered me on, shared my posts, hyped me up . . . I could not have written and published and marketed this book alone. I know so much time and energy was put into this story by so many other people besides me, and I'm forever grateful for every ounce of it.

Oh, and of course, the biggest thank you goes to my husband for helping me with research, especially in making sure the washing machine scene tracked. ;)

PLAYLIST

Afterglow - Taylor Swift
How Are You - Emma Lynn
24 Hours - New Rules
What If I Don't - Shaylen
How Do We Go - Alexandra Kay
Friends Don't - Maddie & Tae
Grew Apart - Logan Mize & Alexandra Kay
Twice - Canaan Cox & Shaylen
Never Say Never - Cole Swindell & Lainey Wilson
Maybe Next Time - Jamie Miller
I'm Only Me When I'm With You - Taylor Swift
One Percent - Canaan Cox
History In The Making - Darius Rucker
Take It Slow - Connor Smith
Stayed a Summer - Erin Kinsey
Happy and I Hate It - Mitchell Tenpenny
Red Flags - Josh Ross
Back To You - Selena Gomez

About the Author

Tisa Matthews is an open-door romance author, constantly on the lookout for inspiration from everyone she encounters. As a psychology graduate from the University of Oregon (just like Sophie and Cooper!), she loves creating depth in her characters and worlds while exploring development typically consistent with age. Her current dream is to return to Oregon, the source of so much inspiration for her first series and the place where she first truly realized her dream of writing a novel.

CONNECT ONLINE:
@tisa.matthews.books